WE SHALL BE

MONSTERS

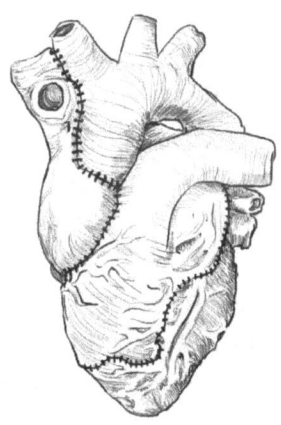

EDITED BY DEREK NEWMAN-STILLE

Renaissance.
Diverse.Canadian Voices

WE SHALL BE MONSTERS Edited by Derek Newman-Stille.
ASHES TO ASHES © Day Al-Mohamed; LOVE TRANSCENDENT © Lena Ng; CHIMERA © Andrew Wilmot; EXCERPTS FROM THE PERSONAL JOURNAL OF DR. V. FRANKENSTEIN, M.D. © Alex Acks; THE PATCHWORK GIRL © Evelyn Deshane; RAGDOLL IN RAGTIME © D. Simon Turner; ENOUGH © Jennifer Lee Rossman; SINS OF THE FATHER © Randall G. Arnold; I, IGOR © Liam Hogan; WANTING © KC Grifant; THE HILLTOP GATHERING © Cait Gordon; MONSTER © Halli Lilburn; THE PERFECT HUSBAND © JF Garrard; MUSCLE MEMORY © Kev Harrison; THE SOLUTION © Corey Redekop; FRANKENSTEIN, INC. © Max D. Stanton; F.-A POST-MODERN PROMETHEUS © Eric Choi and Joseph McGinty; THE LAST CONFESSION OF DOTTORE GEPPETTO © Joshua Bartolome; FAMOUS MONSTERS © Arianna Verbree; UNFASHIONED CREATURES © Priya Sridhar; TERRA COTTA CHILDREN © Lisa Carreiro; MORE © Kaitlin Tremblay; MOTHER MONSTER © Victoria K. Martin; WOLLSTONECRAFT © Ashley Caranto Morford

Cover art, design, typesetting, and interior design by Nathan Caro Fréchette. Edited by Derek Newman-Stille. Copy edits by Myryam Ladouceur.
Legal deposit, Library and Archives Canada, December 2018.
Paperback ISBN: 978-1-987963-41-0
Ebook ISBN: 978-1-987963-44-1

Renaissance Press
http://renaissancebookpress.com
info@renaissancebookpress.com

Dedicated to my creator: my mother.

Thank you, Wendy Newman-Stille, for bringing this creature (me)

to LIFE

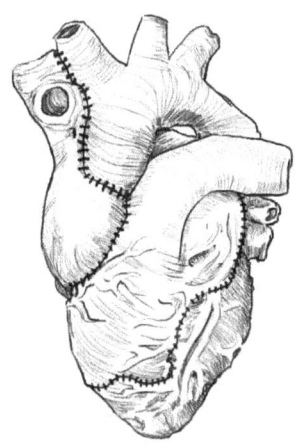

CONTENTS

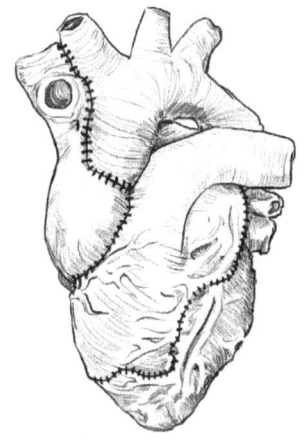

INTRODUCTION: BACK FROM THE DEAD

DEREK NEWMAN-STILLE

What is it that keeps dragging Frankenstein's monster back from the dead? What makes it keep returning again and again, a pale shadow of humanity to remind us of our inner monstrosity?

We create our monsters to tell us something, to speak back to us. We create them to tell us what makes us different from them, what defines us as human. But that boundary is thin and monsters frequently break through it to remind us that they are our creations... that they come from us and that they are us.

200 years ago, Mary Wollstonecraft Shelley created a monster after a night of storytelling with Lord Byron, Dr. John Polidori, and Percy Shelley. She created a creature that spoke to the issues of her age - the uncertainty of

medical science, the power of obsession, the fear of death. These are themes that still echo in our imagination, that occupy our anxieties. She examined ideas of abandonment, notions of family, ostracism, bodily change.... aspects of the human experience.... and she stitched these fears together into a monster, an assemblage not only of flesh, but also of ideas, fears, speculations, and possibilities.

As a disabled person, Mary Shelley's creation speaks to me. It speaks of a body modified by science. It speaks of medical control. It speaks of ostracism and isolation. But it also speaks of resistance.

I wanted to assemble stories together that reflected some of Mary Shelley's passions, fears, anxieties, and ideas, but also reflected this current cultural moment. I wanted stories that invited questions about what has changed over the course of 200 years. I wanted to play the part of Victor Frankenstein and resurrect something quintessential in these tales, to bring together a group of stories that honoured Mary Shelley's legacy while also opening up new possibilities, charging Shelley's tale with the lightning strike of inspiration.

The authors who contributed to this collection imagined new possibilities, gave voice to the things that dwelled on the fringes, at the margins, and told stories that needed to be told because they are too frequently silenced. They pulled threads from the cultural imagination and wove them through the flesh of Shelley's tale, infusing it with new speculation and possibilities.

These stories raise critical questions in their sublime, dark beauty, asking us to reflect on our relationship to our bodies, to reflect on who has power over whose bodies, to think about what makes us human... and what makes us inhuman, to see beyond simple binaries of us/them, self/other, hero/villain, human/monster. These are stories that COMPLICATE and that embrace the beautiful possibilities of complication.

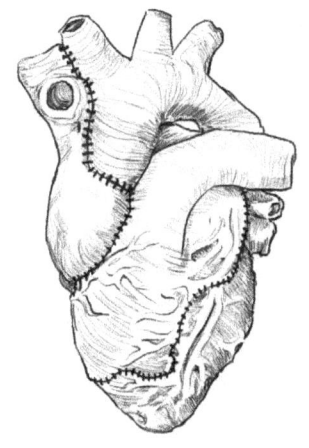

ASHES TO ASHES

DAY AL-MOHAMED

23 August 1888

Day 1 - Post Mortem

It is with an unsteady hand that I write these words. What has become of me can only be described as a singular occurrence of the most unusual nature.

This morning, I awoke as usual - early, but with a peculiar lethargy. At first, I could not discern the change and so went about my usual business - doing some correspondence and preparing my lecture for the evening. However, I could not escape it - the silence. It was as if there were a pause between one moment and the next, but instead, the silence just continued on. Like the space between heartbeats. Silent, unmoving, dead. It was then that I realized that something was very wrong, not with the world, but with me.

I put my hand to my chest. There was no gentle rise and fall. Grabbing up my stethoscope, I checked again. Nothing. No comforting thump-thump as the chambers contract and relax. Perturbed, I exited my lab and went up the stairs towards the boudoir seeking my shaving glass. Holding it with numb hands in front of my face, there was no tell-tale fogging.

I seem to have died.

24 August 1888

Day 2 - Personal Oddity

This morning, I again woke to find myself in this strange state of being - dead and yet not dead. I can only be grateful that yesterday I had the presence of mind to dismiss Mrs. Adkins, my housekeeper, for the evening, and prevail upon a dear friend to present my lecture. Rigor mortis starts in the thin facial muscles, and I could feel my jaw and facial muscles responding less and less. Over the day it extended throughout my whole body. In hours, I found myself immobile.

Thankfully, the rigor has abated, although I have pronounced lividity along the right side of my body from how I spent the night. I had forgotten that without a heart to pump it, blood merely pools.

As a surgeon of the Royal College of Physicians, I am in a unique position to assess my own case. I must document my symptoms - I have already begun my medical notes as well as this more personal journal of my thoughts. My scientific training seeks an answer. Pasteur's experiments,

Koch's postulates from his work at the Imperial Department of Health, Sir Lister's germ theory of disease; I have pulled book after book and read page after page. Is this a unique reanimation? Why did this occur? How?

Although my heart no longer pumps, should I eat? I opened the heavy drapes this morning to view myself in the mirror: eyes sunken; skin the pallor of a fresh corpse. It is critical that I acquire the equipment necessary to investigate my condition.

Due to my absence last night, my colleague at the Royal College, William, stopped by this evening to inquire about my health. I put him off. He cannot learn of this ailment. We have shared many secrets, but I fear that this would strain our relationship beyond even his capacity. I have seen those poor souls imprisoned in Bedlam and have no wish to become a subject of medical experimentation.

25 August 1888

Day 3 - Perpetuity of Science

I find myself anxiously checking for signs of putrefaction. With the buildup of gases and bacteria within my body, it is only a matter of time. Already, Mrs. Adkins has expressed concern over my lack of care over my appearance and urges me to better explore the benefits of London's West side; perhaps spend an evening at the theatre. Her attentive ways, while beneficial for a bachelor's life, now only serve as a risk for exposure.

People have wondered what happens after death. But I am denied an answer. As this body continues to decline, I must consider what happens to me. I am a man of science. I cannot say that I have given overmuch thought to matters of the soul, should such a thing exist. Now, I find myself fervently hoping for some sort of resolution. My unbeating heart trembles at the thought of an eternal existence in this decaying shell. Soon, there will be nothing left but my intellect, tied to rotting meat and bone with no semblance of humanity remaining.

Well past dusk, I visited William for the ingredients I needed - arsenic, creosote, mercury, turpentine, and various forms of alcohol. Even in the dim gaslight he noted the pallor of my skin. I dismissed his concern, avoided his gentle touch, and wished him well, wondering if we would meet again.

Long-term preservation requires a number of different techniques. Regardless of how embalming is performed, the body will eventually decompose. My experiments have not yielded answers to this gruesome malady. I must be more aggressive in my treatment.

26 August 1888

Day 4 - Persistence of Thought and Clarity

So here I exist between the ticks of a clock; the beats of a silent heart. I now have to actively drive away the flies. My appearance is more that of a corpse than a man. My stomach is distended and solid to the touch; the greenish discolouration spreads out and tints my body. The stench from my flesh can no longer be masked through camphor or liniments or flowers, nor can I risk leaving my residence in all but the darkest of nights.

The heat of high London summer is an added complication that will ensure I succumb to this strange disorder even more quickly. I have ordered ice to be delivered, but it will only slow the decomposition of my body. If a God existed, how could He condone such a punishment? What sin could I have committed to deserve this? I fear that as the decay continues I will lose not only my clinical objectivity, but my very mind... that which makes me human. That is what I fear most - losing myself.

It is with some trepidation that I attempt my next experiment. An old treatise by Luigi Galvani on the use of electrical induction and bodily tissues and a novel, *The Modern Prometheus*, I discovered, all but forgotten, amongst my professional works has led me to some profound conclusions. However, to test my theories requires a subject. I cannot inquire as to any residents of Newgate or Bedlam so I must find them from the streets. Tonight, I shall venture to Whitechapel district. There I will find the hungry, the desperate, the hopeless - who are more than willing.

27 August 1888

Day 5 - Prevalence of Philosophy

I found my first maggot. Several. I expected it, but it does not make the event any kinder. I watch them do what I have done for so many years as a part of my profession. We are not so very different - dismantling the machinery that is Man. So many, I've forgotten their names - criminals, foreigners, the insane, and unbaptized. All in the name of Knowledge. No, that is a lie, I never knew their names.

As I watch the writhing maggots, I wonder to what end they toil beyond the satisfaction of their own hunger. And how dare I presume that my purpose was ever any loftier than theirs. It was with some difficulty that I shook the dark humour that had overcome me to return to the streets.

There is so much poverty in the poor alleys and byways, but tonight I could feel the fear. Bobby Peel and his Metropolitan Police have been very active but I have been cautious. Amidst the coal-fired stoves and the foul and heavy air, I can find my subjects. And there, down by Buck's Row, I went about my grisly work with knife and bone-saw.

Mrs. Adkins's services have been terminated. I could not risk discovery. William visited again, and once again I refused to see him. He is so angry with me. In my mind, I still see his long legs, his strong shoulders in a tapered jacket, and full lips. It is those I miss the most. I am truly sorry that I could not attend his prestigious Lumleian lecture, but such a visible public venue is too dangerous. However, he did bring the additional ingredients I requested: wax, resin, cinnabar, balsamic herbs and talcum powder. Camphorated oil and wine, balsamic herbs and these other ingredients will fill my putrefying bodily cavities. But I am running out of time to find a curative.

28 August 1888

Day 6 – Pressing Matters

I read over my previous entry and recognize the loneliness and isolation caused by my affliction. I wish I could speak with William; to share this burden. Has fear outgrown my love? Or is it just vanity? My hair is almost completely gone now. The elasticity of my skin can no longer hold it. My nails and teeth are in similar disarray. It seems an odd thing to weep over hair, particularly considering my current circumstances, and yet it feels like a very visible piece of my humanity is stripped away. I must be particularly cautious now as this loose skin indicates that my muscle tissues are failing. Already my legs have begun to refuse to obey my will.

The Vigilance Committee was patrolling the streets last night, but I cannot stop. I am not dissimilar to the diseased oak tree. I may be able to graft on new additions and changes, but as the core rots, the evil spreads. More often, I find myself contemplating an eternity that I can smell, and see and feel and taste, and yet be denied life.

I struggle to return my focus to what is necessary: the grafting of bone, muscle and sinew. The hacksaw, the scalpel, blood and bone - the physician's friends. Then why does my soul hesitate where my hands do not?

29 August 1888

Day 7 - Purgatorial Existence

My experiments grow more grotesque and desperate with every hour's passing. The hacksaw is traded for an axe; the stitches are, by necessity, large and awkward. My hands have lost their surgeon's dexterity and skill. But of course, they aren't my hands anymore. These hands have long, slender fingers, a woman's hands. Flyblown, flesh barely clinging to bone, my hands - my original hands -, float in a jar of arsenic-water on the shelf behind me. Even now, I cannot bear to give them up.

I am Pygmalion, but rather than create a lover of stone, I sculpt a new form for myself. A terrifying amalgam of body parts cobbled together and brought to life through Tesla's currents - Frankenstein's monster, a wretch, with horror in my heart and blood on unfamiliar hands. And with each additional death, I buy time. Time to find - if not a cure - some measure that does not condemn me to this purgatorial existence. Even now, I know the new flesh will slowly blacken and blister.

There is just not enough time; not to think, not to philosophize, not even to consider either the source or impact of what I do. All that matters is the next part, the next desperately needed piece to replace the decomposing whole.

30 August 1888

Day 8 - Penitence

Sweet William. Why did you not listen? Why did you come to my home? To my lab? Even now, your body laid out on one table, and your head on another, all I see is you and I together in my bedchamber, our bodies twisted in the sheets, skin shiny with sweat. You have given me everything and yet, I still want from you one more kiss.

There just wasn't enough time. But with your death and one last exchange I can preserve this unlife. Our connection isn't science or medicine, electricity or alchemy, but passion.

This will save me.

You will save me.

Forgive me, my love.

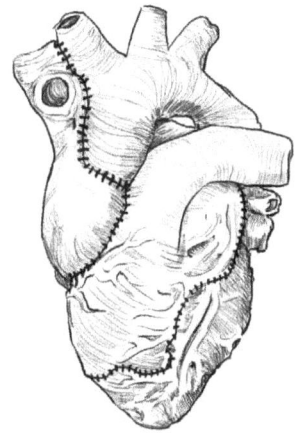

LOVE TRANSCENDENT

LENA NG

There she lay, all luxurious Titian hair flowing from the wooden table, the pale skin of her face coloured with only the faintest hint of English rose; translucent skin masking eyes likely an unadulterated blue; lush mouth about to impart a secret; a string of virginal pearls hung from her long, delicate neck; the curve of her breast proud and innocent despite the roomful of men surrounding her with their penetrating gaze.

This slumbering beauty. This sleeping Venus.

There seemed something inherently wrong with dissecting her.

"Closer, students, closer," the bearded, bespectacled professor called and waved a beckoning hand. "Although this may be your first time to see Woman in all Her glory, it certainly won't be the last."

The students took a step closer to the silent, cold goddess, sharp, steel implements in hand.

"Who will do the honour of the first cut?" the professor asked. No one moved. "Come along," he coaxed the reluctant students, "We cannot in good conscience practice surgery on living patients."

James swallowed and his Adam's apple seemed to catch on the knot of his cravat. He loosened the silken noose. Maybe there was something wrong with the air — it was too thick, too hot, not enough was getting into his chest and his face flushed a deep red.

The professor nudged James forward. "Go on then, young man," he said, "She's waiting."

James rolled up the cuffs of his shirt. He moved the shaky tip of the scalpel to the base of the girl's throat. She can't hurt anymore, he thought. The knife parted skin in a bloodless line. He slowly cut through layers of dermis, fat, and muscle, uncovering the mystery of woman though the mystery of the heart still lay trapped within. When he felt he could cut no more, the professor took over.

With gloved hands, the professor made a cross-cut slice through a mass of spongey tissue. "Observe the black cavities in the lungs — this woman died of consumption."

The professor spent the hour dissecting, lecturing, illuminating young minds to the female enigma, Latin terms echoing in the dissecting room. The room's atmosphere was hushed except for the faint scratch of pen on paper. Finally, at the end of the discourse, after all was revealed, the professor asked, "Any questions?"

"Where is the soul?" a voice from the back called out.

The professor stroked his beard and chuckled. "That is a question for the clergy, not the doctors."

"It was awful," James told Olivia, his educated, pale blonde fiancée of two years, over Darjeeling tea and scones with clotted cream, in the dark-green wallpapered room of her parlour. "Awful, yet fascinating. Her lovely face, her beautiful skin, her fine figure attributed to her disease. Consumption. But beneath the fair skin were muscles, nerves, fat, and blood. Soon she will be a skeleton. Death and disease. With all our innovations—the railways, the steamships, the electromagnet, and engines —when will we learn to conquer them? Everything she knew, everything she felt — gone."

Olivia shuddered. "Let us hope to never die then." She refreshed their teacups and placed another watercress sandwich on James's plate.

James took a cautious sip of the steaming tea. "We know so much, yet there is still so much to learn. The nature of life and what lies beyond." Thoughtfully, he ate his sandwich. Olivia smiled and gave him another.

From there, they turned from the morbid and macabre and touched upon the details of their upcoming nuptials. Time quickened as it always does when with loved ones and soon it was sunset. They parted after all was settled.

Little did James know that would be the last he would see of Olivia. That night, the chimney in her bed chamber had blocked and the coal-burning fireplace consumed all the air in her room, suffocating her in her sleep. At her funeral, clothed in white lace, she looked as though she were still sleeping.

"You are a man of science," the old woman said, after James had placed five shillings in her hand, "yet you are here." A scarf covered her iron-grey hair, and rings of silver hung from her ears and around her wrists.

"Science doesn't give me answers," James replied, as he stared into her cloudy eyes. Cataracts. "Perhaps you will."

The woman's mouth made a sly movement. "But there you are wrong. Science *does* give you the answers. Answers, however, you do not wish to heed."

"In medical school, there is no cure for death."

"Do you believe there is?"

"I believe in a life beyond death."

"And you have a love from beyond the grave."

The colour drained from James's face, leaving a ghostly mask. "Yes." He rubbed heavy, red-lined eyes. "Can I speak to her?"

The old woman reached her clawed hands across the velvet-covered table. He put his hands into their grasp. She took a deep breath and closed her milky eyes; the cataracts did not stop her from seeing into the ether, into the afterlife. The air turned eerie, uncanny, and a horrid chill passed over James's frame. The crystal ball on the table gave a menacing glow and it seemed to fill with the fog of London. Flashes of lightning bolted within.

The old woman snapped open her eyes. The white haze had disappeared; her eyes were clear, they were blue, and they seemed to belong to another. They shone. "James?" Her voice had changed from that of an old woman into a familiar one, a beloved one. "Where are you, James? I can't find you." Tears spilled from the old woman's shining eyes. "The earth is damp and I'm cold."

The chair clattered to the ground as James leapt from his seat. "I'll bring you home, Olivia. I'll bring you home."

He fled from the fortune-teller's parlour into the night.

14

The school's library was empty at this late hour. Science does give you the answers, the old woman had said. And there was a case of resurrection, he recalled — aside from the ones depicted in the Bible — a procedure developed by a Genevese doctor, a Prometheus who created a monster by resurrecting a corpse. Feverishly, James pulled out the old manuscripts. Books with yellowing pages covered in anatomical ink illustrations piled upon the library tables, upon the floor. Words inscribed in ancient Greek or Latin — words for medical terminology. *Metatheria. Myringotomy. Myxoma.* Science, not spells.

Finally, when James was about to despair, he came across a dusty diary. Signed across the parchment cover page were the words "The Diary of Victor Frankenstein." He flipped through the pages, marked with an elegant copperplate. Within, the details of harnessing lightning, capturing the spark of creation, and creating life itself were outlined before his devouring eyes. The warnings were clear as well: what Frankenstein had created was a creature, a monster, a crime against nature.

But his fiancée was not a monster.

The earth was damp and she was cold.

The tip of the shovel dug into the loosely packed earth, a metallic scrape with each push of the blade. It smelled of worms, of evening after the rain. Shovelful after shovelful of dirt grew into a pile around the new grave. Black beetles took wing and small worms,

15

displaced from their homes, burrowed into the ground, escaping the nocturnal light. James's shoulders ached in his lonely exertion, the dankness of the night at its witching hour raising gooseflesh on his skin. The moonlight, cold and bright, revealed the rows of crumbling headstones, mouldering mausoleums, placid stone angels with down-cast eyes.

Olivia, I'm here for you. I'll save you, my love, from the grave. From death. We will conquer it together.

There was a cracking sound as the edge of the crowbar was hammered into the casket, separating it from the lid held down by coffin nails. The stench of decay filled James's nostrils. The smell of the grave, a familiar smell from the dissection room, but not an odour he could get used to.

"What d'ya think you're doing?" a sullen voice said in a thick, rough accent. James clenched the handle of his shovel. He halted his digging and slowly turned around. A burly man crossed the cemetery with his own shovel in hand, a sheen from the top of his bald head visible even in the darkness of the hour. "Bugger off. This is my territory."

"What does the medical school pay for bodies?" James said through gritted teeth as he stood waist-deep in the grave. "I'll double it."

"What have you got there?" the man said in lewd appreciation, catching a glimpse of pale blonde hair. "Pretty thing. I can see why you can't leave her in peace."

"How much do you want?"

"Maybe I don't want anything. Maybe I want a turn."

The stark look on James's face could frighten the devil himself. He raised his shovel.

The burly man's shoulders squared at first and his chin jutted. Moments passed as he sized up James's implied threat. Then he laughed, a cynical sound. "Not into cold bodies when I've got a warm wife at home. Give me a couple of guineas and she's yours." James reached into his pocket and the coins clinked into the other man's hand. The burly man's tone changed back to a sullen menace. "I'd better not see you here again."

James turned back to his grim task. "You won't." The burly man departed under the down-cast eyes of the stone angels.

When the last of the coffin nails were loosened, James pried away the wooden lid. There Olivia lay, her blonde hair splayed against the ivory silk coffin lining; fair, pale skin of her cheeks once soft, now shiny with a creeping brittleness; tender, graceful hands crossed over her breast; the clean, white lace of her funeral attire untouched by the embrace of the grave; lips which looked as though she could be awakened with a kiss.

James covered her cold body with a wool blanket, as though it could warm her icy skin. "Olivia, you were taken too soon." He gathered her into his arms. "But soon you will return to me."

By the co-operation of God or the devil, foreboding storm clouds blackened the sky. The howl of the punishing wind rattled the leaded windows, the draft pushing its way through the house— through the towering spires, through walnut-panelled rooms, through empty bedrooms.

James wrapped wires around greying arms and ankles, at the base of a pulseless neck. Wires which travelled through the tin-plated ceiling and to the roof, attached to a lightning rod.

A bright flash split the dark sky. The rumble of thunder. The sizzle and spasm as electric current travelled down metal and met flesh.

From the body on the table, a deep, gasping breath, as one emerges from drowning. Together the muscles tensed. *My God, her heart! Is it beating?* James's own heart thundered in his ears.

Finally, the dear body relaxed. The pale eyelids opened and eyes of grey-blue, the colour of fog over the ocean's waves, met his. James wrapped his arms around her, the heat from his body gradually warming hers, and after a moment, she embraced him back.

"James," she said into his ear, "I heard you calling my name. Over the surging rivers which pour into the sea, over the empty mountaintops, across the ceaseless sky, I heard my name. You called me back."

"Yes," he said over his silent tears, through lips which kissed her eyes, her cheeks, her chin, "yes. I wasn't ready to let you go."

"I was an angel."

"You are an angel."

"I lost my wings and fell to earth."

A vise seized his heart and guilt weighed down James's tears. He had wielded the knife that cut off her wings. He tightened his embrace. "I caught you. You're now home."

Over the next few days, James rubbed his eyes and pinched himself but he wasn't dreaming. Olivia had returned, more or less, and he took her strangeness for the trauma of rebirth. He asked her many questions and sometimes she answered, though he couldn't quite understand her words.

"You never eat," James said at the dinner table. Olivia's cheeks were gaunt and her skin had grown paler and parchment-like. Soon she would become a wraith.

"Maybe I only need water," she replied. Olivia glanced out the window, the pale sunshine glinting off her pale hair. "So, this is life after death. I thought I'd return as a butterfly. Something flying free."

18

With a quick, graceful movement, she rose from the table to the window sill. The iron handle creaked as she turned it and pushed open the glass pane. James could see a fuzzy shape wiggling on the sill.

Olivia reached out and took the caterpillar into her palm, the long fingers of her hand gently hiding its orange-haired body. When she opened her hand, James saw orange stained-glass wings which slowly opened and closed. "Fly away," she said, and her lips brushed where wing joined plump, black body. Her voice held yearning, as though she wished she too could drift upwards into the sky. She blew on the small creature. It lifted off from her palm and fluttered from the window with the lilting breeze. She watched it until it vanished.

The scalpel dangled above her throat.

"Stop," James whispered. The light glinted from the blade. "Stop," he said again. The knife's tip touched skin. "Stop!" James leapt from his seat and screamed.

Startled, the student surgeon looked up from the specimen. James stood panting amid a room full of alarmed looks, and a wild light blazed from his eyes. The professor hurried to him. "Students," he called out, "you are dismissed for today. Review chapters eight through ten and tomorrow we will discuss."

James's shoulders were still shaking as his fellow students filed out from the room. He avoided their pitying glances. At home, Olivia grew thinner and thinner; no morsel of food would pass between her lips. The bones of her shoulders and hips grew sharp. Her body was animated, yet it was not alive, not in the sense that she needed sustenance. The joy of her return was overshadowed by the fear of losing her again. James felt the professor's hand on his shoulder. "You need time to grieve," the professor said, his tone compassionate. "Not enough time has passed for professional detachment."

James stared at the body lying on the table. Young and cheated of all that life could give. "If you take her apart, how will you put her together again?"

Behind his spectacles, the professor's concerned expression mixed with sympathetic understanding. "My son, all that is left is the body. She doesn't hurt anymore. The soul is already free."

James twisted the professor's sleeve. "But what if there was a way to bring her back? To steal her away from death's grasp?"

The professor's gaze changed from sympathetic to assessing, clinical. "You speak of madness."

"I speak the truth."

The professor saw the fervid belief in James's expression. He weighed the logic of arguing with a madman. "What if I believe you? That there is a way to resurrect the dead? Have you not considered the morality of your actions? God has already claimed her. Could you live with the knowledge that you have pulled a soul from Heaven back to the suffering of earth?"

That night, as Olivia drifted into sleep, James examined the white edge of her cheek bone, visible through eroding skin. Her sleeping expression seemed to say "Love keeps me here. But love will also set me free. Do you love me enough to let me go?" No matter what he did, beneath the fair skin were muscles, nerves, fat, and blood. Where was her soul? It was trapped in a mortal shell; death had already claimed her body. He put his hand over her slowly-beating heart.

"My love, I release you." He fell asleep curled up her arms.

The next morning, James was not surprised that Olivia had vanished. In her place was a room full of butterflies.

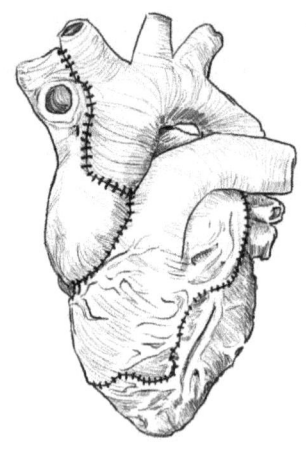

CHIMERA

ANDREW WILMOT

"The cyborg is a condensed image of both imagination and material reality, the two joined centres structuring any possibility of historical transformation . . . [It] appears in myth precisely where the boundary between human and animal is transgressed."
— Donna Haraway, "A Manifesto for Cyborgs"

I

He sits surrounded by demons. They whisper vivisection, critical analysis. Their words hover, overwriting the mouths of passersby like bad voiceover, incongruous with the movement of their lips. They follow him, disembodied, when he goes into his room each night and builds a barricade of cushions, pillows, and bed sheets against the door.

Behind him, stacked in a corner between the end of his bed and the closet, are fifteen canvases — self-portraits in acrylic at various stages of completion, their progress interrupted by slashes straight through the material; by blooming scorch marks made with a can of hairspray and a lighter; by dirt and mud and blood smeared across their surfaces in childish rage. And when he hasn't the blood for them, he does three hundred jumping jacks, two hundred bicycle kicks, and one hundred crunches, and wrings his clothes out over a small mason jar and watercolours with his sweat, using brushes restored with hair woven from his own head, thinning in patches, a poorly kept lawn. The canvases are pungent, like the den of an alleyway surgeon; he hangs a new, fresh pine scented car air-freshener from his ceiling every week.

In his lap, a handful of bloody tissues used to wipe the stain from his lips. To his left, splayed across another tissue, blotted blue, are numerous shards of broken plastic scattered overtop the ink reservoir of what was once a ballpoint pen. To his right, nestled in unwashed shag speckled with paint, a small sandwich bag of yellow arrowhead-shaped tablets.

He removes one of the tablets, stares at it in the palm of his hand. They say it's dangerous to take on an empty stomach, he thinks as he fetches with his other hand a half-inch piece from the pile of broken plastic. He places the shard between his lips and swallows. Feels as it descends his esophagus, already cut and scarred, its walls rungs of a ladder. It gets lodged partway and he starts coughing, hacking globules of blood and small chunks of flesh into the tissue in his lap.

"A_____, are you okay?"

Holly's voice comes through the floor as if smothered by a heavy blanket. He scratches out loose, abstracted consonants in response. Places a hand against his upper body, to try and force the words, but they won't come; they've fallen between the jaundiced, visible ridges of his chest.

Not wanting to waste another moment, he pops the arrowhead and, with difficulty, swallows.

The tablet lands in his stomach with the weight of an apple dropped into an empty barrel. Almost immediately, he begins to disseminate: his fingers stretch like taffy until the skin between each bone snaps and becomes a bubble; his arms separate at the joints; his legs; his torso; his neck; his head pulling free — effortless dismemberment as the individual pieces of him lift off from one another to settle into individual orbits.

His head, weightless and untethered, bobs downward; sees the pieces of himself floating farther apart, his body the surface of a lake rippled by a stone's throw.

Her voice again, closer: "A_____, can you hear me? Is everything okay?" She pounds on the door; her strikes like sheet metal, battered and bruised. He attempts to raise his head but can't control the direction in which his newly planetoid-like appendage moves. The world is made lighter; as the bubbled pieces of himself begin to glow—yellow at first, then deeper into gold — he loses sight of the finer details of his existence: the whole into which the separate parts combine; how long it's been since he's eaten; how long before he can eat again.

"A____!" In his periphery, like a sliver through the veil, he sees his mountain of cushions and pillows being pushed aside and the door opening; hears cursing; feels hands on his shoulders shaking him as his bubbles pop and reform. Weight flooding back into him, a river pressurized.

"What have you done?" she screams, face emerging from the gold.

Her hands on his wretched, narrow shoulders, he lurches forward and vomits blood and plastic all over her.

II

He smells the hospital room before seeing it — a crude cocktail of antiseptic and Pepto-Bismol. He keeps his eyes shut, listening to the gentle, rhythmic beeping overhead. He counts the sounds reflexively: six, twelve, eighteen—

"I know you're awake."

He opens his eyes. Holly sits in a chair next to the bed, elbow propped on the armrest. Her frazzled black hair is pulled in a lopsided bun; strands of grey normally hidden by her mesh of curls twist and reach out like weeds.

"Your breathing changes," she says, exhausted. "You think I don't see but I do."

"... ow ... ong?" The effort scrapes his wounded throat.

"How long? Thirty hours. I waited the first few, then went home and got you a change of clothes. Had to — you'd pissed yourself. Once you'd finished vomiting on me, that is. There was blood in it — in the vomit. My shirt looked like someone had swaddled a dead raccoon. So, you know, thanks."

He's about to apologize when she produces the sandwich bag of arrowheads. "Found these while waiting for the ambulance. On the carpet, alongside blood and pieces of Bic pen. Couple of aneurytics as well — flushed the rest." She paused. "You're lucky I don't call the cops."

"I'm..."

"Sorry?" She approaches his bedside. "Is that what you're trying to say?" Shakes her head. "I knew you were struggling, but I... How long have you been doing this to yourself?"

He puts a hand to his throat as if for strength. "It was... my first—"

"No —" she grabs his right arm, turns it over "— this."

The underside of his forearm, so thin she can wrap her fingers all the way around like a leather-wrapped bone bundled by five plump, brown twigs, is as jaundiced as the rest of him, with one notable difference: a fly strip of red, exposed tissue two inches in length, where his skin's been removed.

"They found the missing patch when they pumped the contents of your stomach, along with the rest of the pen and fucking little else."

He looks away.

"What is this? You need to talk to me, A_____." When he doesn't answer, she adds, "Talk, or I call your mother."

"It's all I can stomach." He enunciates as if through television static.

"What do you mean?"

He swallows; she glimpses his agony. "Everything else makes me feel sick."

"But the plastic—"

He frowns. "I thought I wouldn't want to... that it'd be easier if..."

"If it hurt." Holly lets go of his wrist. "They're holding you for a psych eval."

He nods. "I understand."

"No, you don't. They'll keep you here if they think you're a threat to yourself. You know that, right?"

"I'll convince them," he says. She looks at him skeptically. "I'll do it. I will."

"Yeah, but... should you?" Her words strike with a force neither anticipates. She stares at the floor, leaves when the doctor enters alongside his colleague, a therapist whose name A_____ forgets five seconds after being introduced. The therapist, a woman in her mid-forties, immediately starts asking questions: Have you ever been diagnosed with an eating disorder? Pica, Bulimia, Anorexia Nervosa... She rattles them off like a grocery list. A_____ says no, emphatically, telling her that he got overwhelmed by school; he wasn't taking care of himself, not properly, but he will now. He gives her his word. The therapist observes his legs — like jointed metal rods with sheets draped across — and draws a mental comparison between their width and that of his arms; the distended belly

26

void of muscle lining, and pictures she's seen of starving children in unnamed third world nations.

He reiterates: he slipped up. He'll do better. She won't see him again because everything's under control.

He recites the same promise to Holly on the drive home.

His voice is still serrated. "I feel like shit for putting you through this," he says as they pull into the driveway of the peacock-blue, two-storey row house they rented together at the start of second year. It'd been her idea. She'd talked about wanting to move out of her parents' house since they were seniors in high school, sitting across from one another in art class as they had since eighth grade. She told A_____ her plan, enlisted him when they both got into Emily Carr, said if they each got jobs they could save up and get a place together in the Downtown Eastside by the start of the school year.

But A_____ never did anything without running the variables, coming up with some sort of plan. It didn't take him long to be convinced, though. It was only after he'd moved in with her that Holly saw how that planning bled into all facets of A_____'s life, right down to the meals he would eat — the same ones, every day, carefully portioned out at specific times. Gradually she noticed his portions dwindle, the timing between each meal, usually so exact, stretch wider and wider.

She exits the car. "Did you hear me?" he shouts, scrambling out after her. "I said did you —"

"Yeah, I heard you." She faces him and he sees in her the recesses of her exhaustion.

"I mean it. I feel awful."

She places her palms on the hood of her orange hatchback. "Are you telling me this because you want to, or because you want me to accept your apology?"

"Both, I guess."

She hesitates. "I want you to speak to someone about this."

"Like a therapist? Didn't I just do that?"

She turns and stalks off toward the house.

"Hol? Holly?" He follows her inside, catching the front door before it drifts shut. He grunts and pushes it open, its density seeming to have increased in an afternoon. He feels its weight all the way through to his legs, tired after such little exertion. He finds her in the kitchen draping her coat over the end of one of the two chairs pressed up against the folding plastic dinner table.

She rummages around inside the fridge. "If you won't talk to someone about this, then I'm taking control of the kitchen." She turns, points to the other chair. "Sit." She observes the way his hand subtly moves across the surface of his stomach.

He exhales as he sits, the day's events perched atop his shoulders. As Holly pulls a pan out from the drawer beneath the stove, A_____'s eyes drift to the centre of the table and a small, scattered pile of Holly's books and notes. He flips through the first book on the pile as she continues talking, not really listening.

The text is a compendium of contemporary art history, from the Dadaists of the early twentieth century to modern times. He flips mindlessly, stopping when a single image catches his attention:

A man, naked, suspended several feet in the air in a cross-legged position. Metal fishhooks penetrate his skin at various spots, long cables looped through the ends of each hook, the flesh stretched and tented at every insertion point.

A_____ inspects the caption at the bottom of the page. The artist's name is Stelarc.

A dishtowel slaps A_____ in the face. He looks up, sees Holly holding a carton of eggs.

"I asked what you thought," she says.

"About what?"

"Breakfast for dinner."

He touches his stomach again. "I'm... actually not that hungry."

"Bullshit." She slaps the eggs down on the counter.

"And my throat," he says, gently massaging his neck. "It still hurts."

"Right," she sighs. "Your throat." She exits the kitchen then, slamming the front door a moment later. She soon returns carrying a cardboard box beneath one arm, the edge of which digs into her stomach. She sets it down on the kitchen table atop the messy pile of art books.

A_____ reads the label stamped to the side of the box: ASSURE HIGH-PROTEIN MEAL REPLACEMENT.

She tears open the side of the box and pulls out a small plastic carton. "I picked this up while you were talking to the therapist. It's supposed to help you get back where you need to be." She hands the carton to A_____, who admires it suspiciously.

"Go on," she says. "Try some."

Reluctantly, he pulls the tab on the carton and, without smelling, takes a sip. "Gah!" He holds it at a distance. "It tastes like strawberry sand, only somehow worse." He places it on the table, pushes it away.

She nudges it closer. "More. All of it."

"Seriously?"

"This or eggs. Your pick."

It takes him fifteen minutes to nurse every drop from the carton. She keeps her eyes on him the entire time, watching as one hand routinely moves to his stomach, as if he expects it to expand with each consecutive ounce.

Finished, he makes his way upstairs. Neither says a word.

He vomits in the night, into the trashcan by his bed. Silently, so as not to wake Holly down the hall. He'll wait until she leaves in the morning before heading to the restroom to dump out the contents: one carton of Assure and several more flecks of throat tissue.

Awake, unable to sleep, he tugs at the bandage covering his forearm. He lied about his wound to the therapist, claiming he'd eaten himself while high; that he hadn't known what he'd done. He works his fingers beneath the bandage, enough to touch one of the loose edges of skin, and thinks again of Stelarc and the way his body and flesh seemed to separate — effortlessly, weightlessly — and he starts to tear off another strip.

III

He sleeps until noon but doesn't rise for another two hours, when sunlight enters through the gap in his curtains. He swings his legs off the edge of the bed, on which he makes almost no indentation, and reaches for an oversized sweater, paint crusted on its sleeves.

He goes downstairs as Holly is returning from school to change and get something to eat before she heads out again for her late shift at the café down the street.

She drops her backpack on the kitchen table and goes to the fridge, turning when she hears A_____ enter behind her. She glances at the sweater. "Aren't you a little hot?"

"It's cold," he says.

"It's May."

He sits at the table. She notes how he favours his right side, as if the fabric of the sweater were more abrasive in spots.

"Can I get you anything?"

"I'm fine."

She takes another carton of Assure and puts it in front of him.

"I said I'm fine."

"I know," she says, returning to the fridge.

He waits for her to say something more, but the admonishment never comes. He nudges the carton aside. Directly ahead, poking out from the top of Holly's backpack, he spies the text from the day prior. He starts to reach for it when she storms over to the table, picks up the carton of Assure, and presses it against his chest. He sucks in a pained breath — hard, a bullet in reverse.

She stands back. "I did not touch you that — Lift up your shirt."

"What?"

"Lift up your shirt. I want to see where it hurts."

He hugs his sides. She lunges for the hem of his sweater and starts to wrestle it up past his arms, which he locks into place.

"Stop!" he cries, but Holly perseveres, using the sweater to force his arms up. That's when she sees it: a fresh strip of red along his right side, three-quarters of an inch wide, the top of which sticks to the fabric via a thousand infinitesimal life lines.

Holly continues to lift the fabric from the wound, slowly, as if removing a bandage a hair at a time. Beneath the open gore, the contours of his ribs are pronounced. She lingers on the startling visual until, having had enough, A_____ grips the hem of his sweater and tugs it from her hands.

"That's enough," he says.

"What are you doing to yourself?"

"It's fine," he says again.

"This? You think this is fine? You're eating yourself."

"No, I'm —"

She pokes the tender area and he jerks inward. She goes to do it again and he slaps her hand away.

He holds up his bandaged forearm. "This is all I can eat. Do you get that? This is all that stays down. Everything else …"

31

Holly's demeanour softens. "A_____, please, I'm asking you, as a favour: I want you to talk to someone about this."

"No way. I'm not interested in hearing about all the ways I'm fucked up when I know I'm not."

"But—"

"I'm fine."

She punches the table. "You're not!" She stares and he makes a point of looking away. She waits several seconds, feeling like she's trapped in a one-way staring contest, then returns to the fridge, opening a drawer to the right. She removes a black-handled paring knife from inside, holds it to her soft forearm, and before she can talk herself out of it, makes a rectangular incision along the side, careful to avoid any arteries as she slices free a wafer-thin layer of flesh.

Only when she starts to cry at the first corner of the incision does he look to see what she's doing. He gets up, grabs the dishtowel looped over the faucet, and presses it against her wound to staunch the flow of blood.

"Hol, I don't—"

Knife still in hand, she lifts free the swatch of skin and presses it into his outstretched palm. He meets her eyes. Small beads of sweat cover her forehead, travel down the sides of her nose.

"You... don't have... any more... to lose."

He closes his fist around her skin.

"Please," she says as he guides her to the table, "let me take you to... a group, maybe. Not a therapist, people like you."

He nods reluctantly. "Okay," he says, the skin in his hand growing heavier each second.

IV

At night, A_____ dreams of the past: going to class; going to work, a late shift in the sporting goods department of a Canadian Tire. He can't remember when he stopped attending class; he only remembers falling asleep more and more during studio crits. It soon became too much work to get out of bed in the morning, especially after working the night before. The mornings grew longer and he started missing his afternoon shifts, and then his evening ones. And then he simply stopped.

Holly was furious when she discovered he'd been fired.

"I told them I wasn't feeling well," he said.

"Did you tell them anything else?"

That night he tried Firefly for the first time, while scoring the insides of his throat. He thinks back to it regularly, sketching himself bubbled in individual packages, the whole disconnected, isolated into clearer parts; he sees the pieces of himself for how they really are.

Downstairs the next morning, he opens the fridge. Inside he finds, tucked between cartons of Assure, a small, plastic-wrapped plate containing three narrow strips of skin. Atop the wrapping, a piece of paper on which the word "Please" has been hastily, shakily, written.

He takes the plate and, turning, spots Holly's art history text left open on the table, copious notes protruding from it as if the book were literally bursting at the seams with content. He sits and flips through it until he finds Stelarc again in a chapter on body amplification and the cyborg. Holding a strip of Holly's flesh pinched between two fingers, he reads about the *Third Hand*, a mechanical apparatus the artist attached to his right arm, the *Extra Ear*, an internet-enabled antenna on his left forearm, and the *Stomach Sculpture*, a camera swallowed to record the functioning of the digestive system.

A_____ turns the page and drops the piece of Holly's skin. He stares, dumbfounded. The image, taking up the entire page, shows Stelarc nestled at the heart of a six-legged pneumatic contraption. Titled *Exoskeleton*, the piece is a true extension of the human body. Additional images show the machine in motion, responding to the artist's gestures as if conducting a silent orchestra.

A_____ glances to the left, to the plate of Holly's skin, and an idea takes hold. He gently replaces the plastic wrapping.

That night, upon returning from work, Holly takes A_____ to his first support group meeting.

"You don't need to drive me," he says. "I'm perfectly capable of getting around on my own."

"And if I trusted you this wouldn't be an issue," she says, adding, "Thank you."

"For what?"

"For taking what I left for you. I won't pretend to understand, but... I'm glad you're starting to take better care."

His stomach gurgles then, and he hopes she doesn't hear it over the sound of the car.

She pulls up to the False Creek Community Centre and shuts off the engine. She puts a hand on his protruding knee. Side by side his two legs together are the width of one of hers. "I'll be here to pick you up at the end, okay?"

He nods and gets out of the car, sketchbook in hand. He waits for her to start the engine and drive away, but she doesn't — she watches instead as he climbs the steps and disappears inside.

The interior of the Granville Island structure is bright, with exposed wood beams everywhere. He follows paper signs taped to walls guiding him to a small boardroom, the inside of which is lined with tables hosting coffee and tea in two large urns, alongside a selection of stale supermarket pastries on one tray, and diced veggies and dips on another. In the centre of the room, twenty plastic chairs are arranged in a loose circle, half occupied.

He takes a seat as a blonde woman with a nametag reading "Lara" stands and welcomes everyone to the meeting. She points to her nametag, laughing nervously as she repeats her name. Her awkwardness radiates as she assures all present that no one needs to speak if they don't want to. She steps back then, opening up the floor.

There's silence at first, coughing, light shuffling of chairs, and then a young woman with long, dark hair thinning in spots stands and addresses the room. Her face is gaunt — her cheekbones appear as if drawn in place with eyeliner. She says her name is Jia, that she's only twenty-one, and that she hasn't eaten a meal without purging afterwards in two years. She trembles as she speaks, and A_____ can't help but picture her body separated into pieces for further analysis. He sees her arms and legs and torso as if they are beneath the lens of a microscope; sees her as a work in progress.

After Jia is Alice, then Steve, then it's time for a break. People rise from their seats and amble over to the coffee and tea; a few peruse the vegetable platter. Two look longingly at the pastry display, keeping several feet of distance as if fearing that sugar is communicable.

A_____ spots a young woman off to one side, leaning up against the doorjamb as if deciding whether to make a break for it. Her brown hair is tied so tight it's as if she's attempting to slim her face by pulling the skin taut against her skull. In one hand, she holds a small bundle of napkins; with the other she gently kneads her stomach.

As A_____ approaches, she tears a napkin in half and stuffs one of the pieces in her mouth. She chews, extensively, and swallows.

He points to the remaining piece. "That looks a little bland."

"Don't care about the taste," she says softly, ensuring her voice is low enough for just the two of them. "I just want to not be hungry."

He raises his bandaged forearm. "I know what you mean."

Her eyes widen. "You mean you—"

"It's not so bad," he says, shrugging. "It's calorie free."

She raises an eyebrow, unconvinced. "How do you figure?"

"Well, it's all me. Just… re-distributed. It's a wash."

"I… I suppose." She touches her stomach again. There's a gentle bulge to it. She catches him staring and moves her hand away. When he meets her eye again, she's blushing. He smiles and tells her he's sorry — he didn't mean anything by it.

"It's just, I do that too."

"You do?"

He nods. "I know what it's like, to see the places that need the most work; to want things to be clearer." He glances quickly over his shoulder. "I think I can help."

"How?"

"You ever tried Firefly?"

V

Holly picks A_____ up two hours later. She notices he clutches his sketchbook with both hands, as if afraid someone might come up and steal it. She asks how it went. "Fine," he says. "Can we just get out of here?"

"Yeah… sure." And she pulls away from the curb, stopping when she spots a young woman stumble out of the Community Centre clutching her midsection in pain. Holly is about to pull over again when another woman and man exit the Centre and offer their assistance.

Arriving home, A_____ heads upstairs and shuts the door to his room. His back to the wood, he waits, listening for Holly to disappear inside her own room. He hears the soft click of the door twenty feet away and exhales, releasing a weight of tension as he opens his sketchbook and flips to the middle, where three bookmark-shaped patches of skin are pressed between blood-soaked napkins. He takes them out of the sketchbook and goes over to the nightstand, beneath which sits a mini-fridge. He opens it and shoves aside several bottles of water and energy drinks, pulling a rectangular Tupperware container out from behind. He pops the lid and lays the lengths of skin inside, atop the pieces Holly had left for him.

He comes downstairs the following morning early enough to catch Holly still in the kitchen, washing a frying pan in the sink.

"This is a surprise," she says. She places the pan on the cool stovetop and retrieves a carton of Assure from the fridge.

He waves it away. "No, please... I can't."

She sighs. Reaches again for the paring knife on the counter by the sink. She goes to cut her right forearm, forgetting that it's already bandaged from the previous day.

He observes as she lifts up the right side of her shirt to just below her breast and proceeds to slice a crescent wedge from her side, starting an inch or two above her hip, which spills over the top of her jeans. She shrieks and he sees sweat pouring down her face in tiny rivers.

She lets the knife clatter to the floor and, hands shaking, pulls free the portion of skin with just the tips of her fingers, like removing an errant eyelash with a pair of tweezers. She holds it out for him — "I... shouldn't be enabling..." — and slumps into his arms. Her weight pulls both of them to the ground.

"Hol?" His voice is muffled by her shoulder covering his mouth. He starts to push, manages with some difficulty to roll her off him. He tries again to rouse her, but to no avail; runs to the washroom and grabs gauze and a roll of surgical tape from the first aid kit Holly purchased when they moved in. He sops up the excess blood and patches her new wound. When finished, he hooks his arms through hers and, thighs trembling, heaves her into one of the kitchen chairs. He props her limp, lolling head against the wall for support.

When he's sure she won't tumble over in her sleep, he scoops the crescent wedge of skin off the floor and takes it upstairs; puts it with the others. Then he grabs his sketchbook off the nightstand and flips to a blood-speckled page near the centre, to an illustrated schematic amidst printouts of human and animal anatomy.

The design is of an exoskeleton, the upper body similar to his own, only wider and more developed; its legs, however, were a cheetah's, their inner workings a series of pistons that could — if properly implanted — propel a human being great distances and with tremendous speed. He makes a mental note of the design before returning downstairs.

Holly stirs in her seat, rolling her head against the wall as if attempting to gain momentum. She opens her eyes when he takes his coat off the back of the other chair. "What're you doing?" she asks almost drunkenly, as if emerging from anaesthetic.

"Heading out," he says, avoiding direct eye contact. "I, uh, I need to get some supplies." He pauses. "I'm producing again."

She smiles and nods, or maybe her head simply bobs atop her neck. Either way, he watches until her smile fades and her eyes close before making his escape.

VI

A_____ spends four hours combing through a junkyard a kilometre from the house, stuffing pieces of scrap metal and random assemblages into a large pillowcase deep enough for a body. Gradually the pillowcase takes on a threatening polygonal shape, rods and spires jutting out at random. Several times he's stabbed by its contents, though he barely notices.

It takes him forty-five minutes to haul the materials home again. He sees that Holly is still sleeping, though at some point she moved herself to the couch in the living room. He creeps past, careful not to make too much noise as he drags the pillowcase up to his bedroom. When he comes down again, Holly is awake and upright.

"Thought I heard you come in," she says, groggily. "Where'd you go?"

"Out. Getting supplies. I didn't mean to wake you."

"It's okay." She straightens up. "You've got a new idea?"

He nods. "Still in the early stages, but yeah, I'm working on something."

She grins then like a proud mother on her child's first day of school. "I knew you'd find yourself again. You just needed some time."

His hand moves to his stomach, but for only a second. He clears his throat. "I need to go back out."

"More supplies?"

"Group, actually. There's another meeting tonight. I thought maybe I should —"

"Right! Okay, just give me... give me a sec to..." She tries to stand but fails, gripping her side as she falls back into the couch.

He goes to her, pulling a patterned blanket folded over one arm of the couch and draping it across in a single motion. "It's all right," he says. "I can get myself there. You rest, okay?"

She mumbles in agreement and is almost immediately unconscious again. He notes the pallid look of her cheeks, the hard lines around her eyes, before leaving.

He catches the bus to Granville Island and walks the rest of the way to the Community Centre. Inside the same small boardroom, he spots several returning faces, and only two new. Among those returning, he eyes the woman from the previous night. She wears a chunky black sweater that looks like it's swallowing her as she hugs herself, watching the front of the room.

She looks up when he enters. Her eyes narrow and she offers a near-imperceptible nod, which A_____ returns.

For the next hour, he alternates between watching her and the clock on the wall, occasionally shifting his gaze to whoever is speaking, so that it at least appears he's paying attention.

She comes up behind him at the start of the break, as he stands holding his sketchbook in front of the coffee urn. She takes him by the arm and pulls him into a broom closet down the hall.

She presses him up against the wall. "Have you got any more?" she breathes. He pulls a Firefly from his back pocket and gives it to her. She swallows without hesitation. "I was reading about it last night," she says, waiting for it to take effect. "They were trying to make an apocalypse pill. It's true — it was meant for population control. They wanted to break people's bodies down over time, to die off in record numbers. They planned to distribute it to small towns, take out whole populations in places where they could blame the water supply, or some rare disease, and no one would care enough to look into what really happened."

She sighs. He pays careful attention as she extends her hands in front of her, and though he can't see it, he knows she's coming apart at the seams.

"Oh god." She grabs her left thigh, cups it with both hands. "This. All this."

He pulls the paring knife from inside his sketchbook, taps the blade's edge against her left thigh. "You're sure?"

She yanks her jeans down on one side, exposing her smooth thigh. Nods. "I never knew... never saw it right before."

She holds her breath as he cuts from her two long strips: one narrow, like two fingers side by side; and one twice as wide. He gives her the smaller of the two strips and watches as she devours a piece of herself. His stomach rumbles as he places the wider piece in the pages of his sketchbook, alongside the bloodied paring knife. He thinks briefly of cutting free a piece of himself but decides against it at the final moment — he didn't know where to carve.

He leaves her to collect herself. On the way out of the Community Centre, he passes another group in session in a different room. The bodies inside are all large, closer in shape to Holly's; their skin rolls beneath their shirts, spills over the waistbands of their pants and skirts. He imagines their pliability, envious. He documents their excesses and thinks: I can *help*.

VII

Holly wakes still on the couch. It's morning, though she isn't sure what day. She rolls over, cries out when her bicep and shoulder rub against the fabric. She discovers her arm is bandaged in three new places, with blood blotched like a fresh rash. On the ground next to the couch, she spots the first aid kit from the bathroom, open, emptied of its contents — including a topical anaesthetic used to numb skin. Among the mess of items, she identifies the paring knife, recently bloodied, atop used and discarded paper towels drenched — no doubt — with her blood.

She hears sounds of construction from above: hammering, vibration from a power drill, metal clanking to the floor.

"A_____?" she shouts, though her voice doesn't carry.

More noise: clanking, large objects shifting about, scraping, tearing the fuck out of the carpet.

She forces herself off the couch and heads upstairs, feeling the newness of her injuries with every step. At the top, she stops in front of the closed door to A_____'s bedroom and knocks twice; waits; pounds with her fist.

She turns the knob. The door opens a crack — it's blocked at the base by more cushions and even clothing piled up against it like a snowdrift. Through the narrow opening, she detects mechanical debris littering the floor as if a car had been driven upstairs and dismantled. She's about to give it another push when a skeletal arm darts into view — a thin wire of muscle visibly separated from the bone, with only a sickly covering of skin stitching them together. The door slams shut.

Holly tries the knob again but it's being held from the other side. "A_____?"

Inside the room, A_____ leans his entire body against the door, digging his heels into the destroyed carpet for support. He's shirtless, in a pair of shorts that balloon out over matchstick legs, crosshatched with sores and shadowed depressions. Sweat rolls down his chest, his torso, yet he shivers.

Through the door: "Can I come in?"

"Not right now. I'm... exercising."

There's a long pause, and then: "What happened to my arm?"

"I, uh, got hungry. I didn't want to wake you."

"So... you thought it would be okay to..."

He puts his ear flush with the door. He hears the hitch in her throat.

"I wish..."

"Yeah?"

"I just wish you would've asked."

"I'm sorry," he says after a pause, all his strength still pressed up against the wood. Were she to throw her full weight into it, he knows he would not be able to keep her out.

She doesn't respond. He presses harder against the wood. "Holly?"

"You sound..."

"What?"

"Hollow."

He waits for her to say more, but more never comes. When, a moment later, he opens the door, she's gone.

Retreating back inside, A_____ re-stacks his makeshift barricade. In the middle of the room, atop an egg crate amid junkyard debris scattered like an overturned bucket of Lego, sits a mechanical limb — a leg, specifically, though not human. Its shape and make is that of a cheetah's, with a powerful upper thigh and long, slender, bone-like apparatuses optimized for speed and impact.

Covering the mechanism's joints are many strips of moistened skin layered across one another, stitched together with fishing twine like a quilt of different fabric swatches. The strips cover only a portion of the whole, its inhumanness evident as A_____ picks up the artificial left leg and slips his own inside its exoskeletal structure. He fumbles around the interior until finding and attaching Velcro strips looped through the structure's internal systems, wrapping them around his leg. Finished, he takes a deep breath and stands.

The sensation of strength is immediate, unparalleled. He bends his new appendage, noting how the accumulated skin appears to bulge under the pistoned orchestration, as if real muscles were being flexed. He takes a few steps around the room, paying careful attention to his newly redistributed balance.

Nestled inside the new leg, A_____ feels lighter and more capable than ever before. He looks down then and catches an errant strip of skin flapping free from the appendage, its stitching having come undone. He quickly tucks it back down, smoothing it in place with his spit, noting the spot for later when he returns to his sewing.

VIII

A_____ stands in the Community Centre's broom closet a week later with a woman he thinks is named Sarah. They met earlier that night, at Overeaters Anonymous. Alone together, in the confined space of the broom closet, he's confronted with her every curve, her startling lack of angles or hard edges as inches of her blossom out from beneath her clothing.

He touches her soft bicep. "This is what I'm talking about," he says, pinching her flesh. "Do you see?"

"Do I see what?"

"Where you can do better."

Her expression flattens. "You mean you don't — I thought you wanted to —" She sighs. "Never mind," she says, and angles her way to the door.

"Wait." He touches her arm again, and with his other hand produces a Firefly tablet. The sketchbook with the knife bookmarking its pages rests on the ground at their feet. "I can show you what I mean."

She pulls free and swats the tablet away. It drops to the darkened floor. "Get that shit away from me."

A_____ drops to his knees, starts searching for the tablet. Sarah pauses at the door, hearing a soft, mechanical whir come from A_____'s surprisingly abundant hips and legs. She leaves just as he finds what he's looking for.

He stands again to see Sarah walking away. She turns a corner, and in her place he beholds a young man he'd previously seen at the back of the room,

44

listening to other people's stories as he plied the fat on his stomach, the insides of his thighs. A_____ smiles to himself.

He returns home that night carrying, along with his sketchbook, a plastic shopping bag bulging with the shavings of others. The bag smacks against his new legs, barely contained by a loose-fitting pair of sweatpants. He walks the entire way, faster than he'd ever moved, feeling as light as air — as if he could break into a sprint at any moment and not be winded.

Holly steps out of the kitchen as he shuts the front door. She's about to speak when she notices, for the first time, his new legs practically bursting out of his sweats.

"A_____, Christ.... Are you okay?"

"Never better!" He angles the shopping bag of skins behind his legs.

"Because you look —"

"Like I'm taking care of myself," he supplies. "That's because I am, finally. Hol, I've never felt so good."

She notices the bag. "I went grocery shopping earlier. Got stuff to cook for dinner tonight."

He shakes his head. "Thanks, but no thanks. I'm not hungry. I already ate," he adds quickly, pointing to his thicker, inhuman legs. "See? Things are changing — I'm getting better."

"But your chest..."

"What of it?"

"It's like wet clothes over a sewer grate. You just look... frail."

The hair on his neck bristles. "Well fuck you very much."

"Come on, I didn't mean —"

"No, I get it." He stalks upstairs without another word.

"A____!" She hurries back into the kitchen, grabs the first thing she can find: an apple peeler. She runs the blade down a mostly healed patch of forearm, cutting deeper than she means to. Tears streak her face as she removes the bloody, ragged strip of skin. She hurries back to the foot of the stairs, flesh pinched between her thumb and index finger as if a damp tissue, but he's already closed his door before she can call up to him, leaving Holly stuck holding a piece of herself and not having the first clue what to do with it.

IX

The pounding and drilling goes all through the night. Holly hears everything; between bouts of changing her gauze, she asks herself what exactly he's building, and how they have arrived at such a point in the first place.

She rises early the next morning, soon after A____ stops working. She tries not to make a sound as she tiptoes downstairs, shoes in hand, and heads out the front door.

She'd only seen his family's home once. Not long after they moved in together, one night after their respective shifts, he requested she pull off Oak. They wound their way through a maze-like subdivision until arriving at a craftsman-style home. She pulled up to the curb and waited as he ran inside to pick up something he'd neglected to take with him when he moved out. He didn't invite her in. She'd not met any of his family and knew very little about them, save his mother's name from when he begrudgingly listed her as his emergency contact on the rental agreement form.

She retraces the route they'd taken what felt now like a lifetime ago. The house appears the same as she remembers, though perhaps more dilapidated in places; the lawn an overgrown mess of weeds where every neighbourhood cat and dog regularly comes to shit.

Holly approaches the front door and knocks. There's no answer. She backs away from the house, observes the face of it. The drapes have been pulled across every window, and there are no lights on inside. She knocks again, louder this time, and catches quick rustling of the drapes in the window to her right — so slight it could be a gust of wind or the exhalation of a heating duct.

"Hello? Is anybody there?" Holly cups her hands over her face and peers through the window. Everything inside is filtered as if through a fog: misshapen piles on chairs that could be people, or merely stacks of unwashed clothes; dishes towered high on the kitchen table easily mistaken for hoarded newspapers from decades past. No movement, though — not so much as a breath.

"It's about your son. It's about A_____," she calls through the glass. Still, no response.

Holly turns to leave. She makes it to the end of the walkway when she hears the door open. She turns and sees a woman in her late fifties in the open doorway, clutching a forest green shawl that casts most of her face in shadow. Black, grey-streaked hair erupts from beneath the edges of the shawl. She stands with a slight hunch.

Holly approaches cautiously. The closer she gets, the more visible the woman's trauma: shadows fade, and swatches of discoloured skin emerge, pieced together by still-healing scar tissue like rivers on a map. What remains of her face more closely resembles that of a mannequin's, its skin healed tight against the skull and plied with enough makeup to give the illusion of reality. What little of her hands and neck could be seen sport the same markings of violence from which she's only partially recovered.

Observing the woman in full, Holly feels the wounds along her arm and torso start to burn, as if in resonance. "D____?" she says. "You're A____'s mother?"

The woman nods.

"My name's Holly. Your son's been living with me. He... he's not well."

D____ nods again but remains silent.

Holly regards her inquisitively. "You... understand what I'm saying, right? A____ is sick. He needs help."

"And?"

Holly is shocked. The sound from the woman's mouth is hard, metallic, like a knife scraped against a whetstone. "And... I want to help."

D____'s eyes move to the bandages visible beneath the cuffs of Holly's shirt — bits of white not entirely soaked through. She glances up at her again. "I don't know what you expect me to do."

"Just talk to him!"

The woman shakes her head. "I don't have anything more to say." She pulls back her shawl and Holly sees the extent to which her skin has been peeled away and replaced, slowly, over years, the surface a gleaming mess of keloid veins bisecting her face with distressed fault lines. "And I don't have anything more to give."

She returns inside then, leaving Holly alone on the path outside the house.

Arriving home again, Holly finds the front door ajar. "A____?" she says, stepping over books and papers and bits of drywall strewn throughout the living room as if a herd of animals had paraded through. At the base of the stairs, entire chunks have been taken from the wall — torn clear as if in a furor.

"A____?" she calls again as she ascends, avoiding the spots on each stair where it looks as if something has punched straight through. At the top of the stairs, she finds the door to his room on its side, cleaved in two.

In his stead she discovers papers strewn similarly to the chaos of the rest of the house. She picks some of them up, shaking off bits of drywall, discarded car air-fresheners, lifting them out from under bolts and pieces of metal plating. She finds illustrations and diagrams, printouts of various animals' anatomies, pencil sketches of what appears to be an enlarged human suit with the legs of a cheetah and the arms of a gorilla. And beneath it all, she finds her art history textbook, stolen from her backpack, open to a page on the Australian performance artist Stelarc.

She goes to leave, stops when she feels something give beneath her foot. Lifting it up, she sees a single strip of human skin, a tone that didn't come from either of them.

There's crashing downstairs. She drops the pages and runs to the top of the stairs in time to see A____ wedging himself through the doorway at an angle, grinding flakes of paint and plaster as he forces his startlingly oversized body through the entryway.

No, not just oversized; his body is an exquisite corpse of trichotomous beings: its arms and legs are foreign, animalistic, and its over-muscled torso belongs to a man twice A____'s natural size.

She gasps. "What have you done?"

He forces his way through the door, and she's able to discern the mechanical joints where they bulge through his clothing; she hears them whine and grind as he moves forward, each step striking with considerable force. Up his arms and around his neck, the exoskeleton is layered in a papier-mâché-like construction of skin; his head, almost comically small, sits like a mismatched toy piece atop the whole.

"Hol," he says, "you've no idea how great I feel! The things I can do now —
how fast and strong I've become. It's like nothing I..." He sighs. "I've never
felt so... light."

She stands mouth agape, her mind working to pair the creature in front
of her with the A_____ that she knows.

"What do you think?" he asks.

"I think... you're a monster. You look nothing like you used to."

His face twists in anger. "What the fuck do you know?" He spits the words
like sunflower seeds, forcing her up against a wall. "I feel fantastic."

As he approaches, she sees more readily the skin blanketing the
exoskeleton: a patchwork of a thousand different voices.

"I don't believe you," she says, putting her hand to her nose to stifle the
stench of flesh and blood and oil.

He smashes a hole through the wall to his right. "How dare you!" he
shouts.

Holly listens as his voice echoes deep inside the exoskeleton, all that
empty space hollow.

"This is what I want." He's just inches away. "This is what I'm supposed to
be."

She stares into his elevated chest as he speaks. Beneath his left arm, she
spies a loose flap of skin not stitched together as tightly as the others.

"Don't you see?" he says. "Don't you get it?"

She raises her head, stares him straight in the eye. "I do."

She grabs the loose flap of skin and pulls as hard as she can. Where it
comes free it tears a hole large enough for her to insert one hand. She rips it
wider and with both hands pushes through the opening, all the way up to her
elbows — pulling and tearing at everything she can get her hands on. Skin
getting torn to shit, scraped raw as she collides with and works around the
exoskeleton, she keeps tearing.

"No!" he shouts, trying to throw her off as he backs away. But Holly doesn't let go; she's lifted off the ground as he flails. Her hands wet with both their blood as her fingers crack and break.

He swings her around, eventually shedding her like a tick. Soaring clear of the exoskeleton, she maintains her grip around another flap of skin and pulls, the force of her being flung unravelling a long, connected string of tissue, exposing the piecemeal construct beneath — a skeleton-like structure. Along its rungs are hung dozens of air-fresheners to protect him from the stench of his own rotting creation.

A_____ staggers back another step, two, before the combination of loosened joints and tearing skin sends him toppling. His torso spins off its connecting axis, its own weight wrenching it asunder, and the entire creation crumbles to the ground like a card tower detonating.

Across the room, Holly lies in a heap, a strip of skin still clutched in her fist. She lifts her head and stares toward the rubble of A_____ several feet away. She doesn't see his head, not right away. She crawls to the debris field, and amid destroyed limbs of salvaged metal and flesh from countless others, lie small, gangly limbs like those of a child grown too tall overnight. They don't move, but she sees clearly the muscle separation of a body starved.

She reaches into the mess still smelling of pine and rancid flesh, searching for what parts of it are real. Wraps her fingers around what she assumes is an arm, but is actually a hip bone so clearly outlined in all its curvature it's barely recognizable. She grips the fiercely modelled bone and inch by painful inch pulls A_____'s semi-conscious body from the miasma of his failed work. Around him, the remains of his superstructure crumble.

Free of his creation, A_____ shudders, his whole body convulsing in the early summer air. The heat from outside doesn't touch his skin, nor warm his frigid bones.

Holly witnesses, clearly, the extent of his transformation: a naked figure reminiscent of death, body that of a boy, gaunt face not much more than an adult's silhouette. A____'s belly is small and distended, and she can count every vertebra in his spine without having to search for one.

He continues to shiver, dazed, and she crawls over and atop him. Feeling the chill of his too-small frame, seeking to replace it with her own warmth.

X

A____ wakes the next day unsure of the time, or even how he got upstairs and into bed. He has only vague memories of being pulled from beneath the threads of a nightmare.

He swings his legs over the side of the bed and stands. Curses as something sharp digs into the sole of his foot. He looks to the ground and sees the scattered remains of his exoskeleton: nuts, bolts, wire stripped bare.

From the bottom drawer of his nightstand, he takes — from a hidden location, taped to the inside of the drawer — the last of his Firefly tablets and throws them in the wastebasket at the foot of his bed. The container already overflowing with the crumpled sketches and printouts he'd used in the construction of his creation. He stares at the discarded shreds of his work, still unsure what to feel about any of it. He leaves his room.

At the base of the stairs he spots ready drywall and gallon canisters of latex paint stacked up against the wall. On the other side of the room, piled by the door, are five large trash bags stuffed to capacity with all that remains of his other body.

He smells food but can't tell what's cooking — can't recall which smells belong with what. He wants to retch but chokes back his bile and walks into the kitchen anyway.

Holly stands at the stove with her back to him. She's dressed in a robe that looks like something his mother would wear, her hair looped in a messy, insomniac's half-knot.

She turns at his approach and they stare at one another. For the first time he sees on her face the scars for which he's responsible — those made with and without a knife. Her arms and hands are bandaged up, but when he stares at them she just shakes her head, pulls his eyes back to hers as if to tell him no, don't even.

He swallows and it hurts, and he doesn't know if it's because his throat is still healing, or if the prospect of food — of real food — reads to his body like an attack for which he no longer has the defences.

"It smells good," he croaks. His voice like a mouse inside a cathedral. For a moment he thinks someone else has spoken.

"There's plenty," she says, "... if you'd like some."

His hand moves toward his stomach, and then he stops. Palm hovering in mid-air.

The hand is still a thing he's reclaiming — like the rest of him. The detour into Stelarc's world was an escape from himself, another body overlaid atop his. It was a barrier against the world, though just as empty as his own. The other could only ever be hollow. But he can learn to fill *this* one.

"I would."

She serves them and they sit down together. She watches as, slowly, wincing, he eats every bite. Without saying it, she knows that behind each morsel that passes his lips exists an entire conversation — a bargain made with himself alone. But now she understands the framework of the calculations going on beneath his surface.

She's learning.

They're learning.

They'll get there.

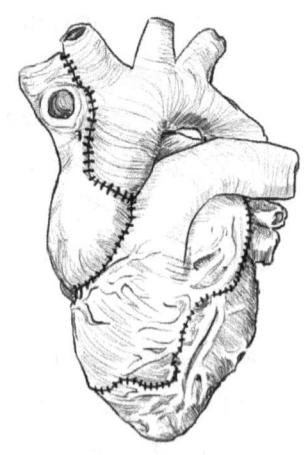

EXCERPTS FROM THE PERSONAL JOURNAL OF DR. V. FRANKENSTEIN, MD,

DEPARTMENT OF PATHOLOGY, OUR LADY OF MERCY HOSPITAL

ALEX ACKS

February 1, 1962

Aha! I have at last become capable of bestowing animation upon lifeless matter. Or rather, once-living matter now consigned to blue bin bags and queued up for the incinerator. The key has turned out to be fetal tissue — more potent stem cells, I suspect. Why everyone still insists on mucking about with bone marrow and cancers instead is beyond me, when Haeckel and Weismann already took a few blind steps in the right direction over half a century ago.

On the other hand, it might have something to do with how few women are willing to allow postmortems on their miscarriages or stillbirths. Burial or cremation rules the day, such waste! And they look at me as if I'm the monster for asking.

Success amounted to but a few cells today, fluttering back to life and then dividing in Nutrient Preparation 361A after — see laboratory notebook 7, pages 21-23. But the longest journey begins with a single step. The important part is that, according to the notation on the waste receptacle, the cells had been dead for at least twenty-four hours! This is the breakthrough I've been looking for! They're alive!

Calendar item: yet another conference with human resources tomorrow. Ho hum.

February 8, 1962

Even more encouraging news. See notebook 7, pages 45-49 for details. Cells are alive and dividing beautifully, the real question is how to integrate them. Chimerical process a must. But it's working. It's working!

NIH grant, here I come.

March 9, 1962

Nothing from the NIH yet.

Autoclave broke down today. Have borrowed the pathology department's unit for the evening, but it's certain to be missed if I leave it in the subbasement lab. The old beast shall simply have to be repaired. Time to start doing the rounds with the banks again. One of them must be willing to do another loan off the "good name."

March 21, 1962

Cease and desist letter from NIH. Mentioned "pranks." Disappointing.

However, as if the world has been reading over my shoulder and taken my monetary despair into consideration, received far more interesting mail today. Envelope with no return address, unsigned letter requesting a clandestine meeting with me at midnight in the hospital parking garage. Intrigued.

March 22, 1962

Oh, how the tables turn. This is delicious.

I arrived at the parking garage at the appointed evening hour with a - thankfully unnecessary - derringer in one pocket of my lab coat. Though he'd taken care to swath himself in a long black coat and conceal his face by means of a scarf and hat, the identity of my attempted mystery man was plain. He reeked of that special pipe tobacco he's always smoking, and I recognized the nasal whine that I've had to listen to drone on and on every week for grand rounds since I was a mere resident. It was Dr. Pembroke. Chief of the stodgy, sneering hierophants that have made it their mission to quash even my most mild research proposals.

While the temptation to call him out by name was fierce, I decided I would play along with the ruse. I'm quite glad that I did.

"I've heard about your experiments," he said to me, his voice only slightly muffled by the scarf.

"What experiments would those be?" I answered.

"To bring life to the unliving."

"What of them?"

This was where it became even more interesting. "Could you create a child?"

"I should think so." Hadn't he actually read any of my proposals before rejecting them?

"What would it cost?"

"For me to create a living human child?"

"For you to create a living human child for myself and my wife."

And suddenly, all became clear. I considered the amount of funds I might actually require and added to that the numbers listed on the various credit card and loan statements I had stacked in my desk drawer. Then I multiplied it by two, for a bit of safe padding... and because Pembroke has mocked me one too many times.

He made a gratifying choking sound at the number, but then said "All right."

"All right?" No, I should not have spoken that as a question. "Of course, all right. I shall expect regular payment."

"And I shall expect regular progress reports."

"I will also need —"

"No," he interrupted me. "I will not give you anything but money."

Ha! His cowardly effort to leave me holding the bag should any local graves be discovered plundered was obvious. But fine, I'd rather not have him wasting my time with inferior efforts anyway. We shook on the deal.

I suppose there are other questions I ought to have asked, such as why he and his wife have not sought to adopt a child, or sought fertility treatments, or any of the rest. Or what he proposes to do with a child that has no legal standing or birth certificate, because it would not be born in the most conventional sense. But such mundane details do not concern me in the slightest; they are his problem and not mine.

My concerns begin and end with whether the cashier's cheque he handed to me - which had better be the first of many - clears.

March 23, 1962

The cheque has cleared. Celebratory cigarette and nip of brandy in the lab before returning to work.

April 30, 1962

Reanimated cells growing well, but integration a problem. Ended up with a tray of nothing but kidneys. But very nice-looking kidneys.

May 22, 1962

I do wish Pembroke would stop bothering me with little notes and phone calls in which he comically attempts to disguise his voice.

I said I would deliver.

I did not say when.

Has he failed to notice that regular human children require a good nine months of building time? Why does he think I deserve less than that in my own creative process?

Though in all fairness, I am much more brilliant than a mere biological process (and one that is often faulty at that).

June 15, 1962

Another setback. Don't wish to discuss. Tired.

August 6, 1962

I know that I can make this work. I just haven't found the right combinations of molecules and doses... but the principle is sound. I have never been one inclined to melancholy or despair - not like Mother - but I feel those demons scratching at the back of my mind like relentless rats.

Back to the lab. Obstetrics reported multiple miscarriages in the ward today, and I'm not about to let all that excellent raw material go to waste even if the patients are being irrational and uncooperative. Sleep is an inconvenience I can do without.

October 16, 1962

I've done it! After feverish — quite literally since I seem to have taken ill — weeks of work, I have done it! It is all a haze now, a fog of medications lifted from the curiously unstaffed pharmacy while a storm threatened to tear the world outside asunder.

The lights within the hospital flickered as each lightning strike sent a surge through the power grid and each gust of wind threatened my efforts with darkness, but I was not deterred. I arranged my newest samples in the nutrient bath I had prepared and applied chemical treatment and electrical stimulation as I had done so many times before. But on this occasion, I watched as the disparate bits of flesh and hints of bone that I had been treating, knit together into a whole that wiggled variegated fingers and blinked milky eyes before grunting out its unhappiness at the ambient temperature of my lab. A triumph of biology. A first, giant leap that shall lead to our eventual triumph over death itself, and I alone shepherded it into the world.

Celebratory cigarette and brandy. The cigarette made my creation cough. The brandy made me vomit up a bit of blood. I may wish to have that looked at.

October. 19, 1962

Met Pembroke in the parking garage again to hand over my creation, as promised, in exchange for the final cheque. He looked down at the creature as I offered it to him, swaddled in a green infant blanket I had stolen from the supply closet, and said, "That baby is very ugly."

I looked over my creation again - at the multicoloured patchwork skin, the slightly odd joints. It wiggled its fingers at me, all ten of them as was proper, and gurgled as I have often heard human infants do, though perhaps a bit more gutturally. There was nothing wrong that I could apprehend.

"All babies are ugly," I said. "You simply don't have the hormones washing through your brain to force you to believe it isn't."

"So ugly, it's cute," Pembroke murmured through the scarf that still obscured his face. "My wife likes ugly dogs."

"There you go then." I deposited the creature in his hands. It kicked one foot free of the blanket and started thumping him on the chest. "I think it might be hungry."

I might have liked to say more but was beginning to feel quite dizzy and ill. I'd be damned if I vomited or passed out in front of the man. He'd probably try to take the cheque back.

He was still staring silently at the creature as I walked away.

October 24, 1962

I have nearly recovered from a ghastly round of what I can only surmise was food poisoning and influenza combined. About time. My lab has been without me for far too long.

Nothing from Pembroke but didn't expect anything. At the least, I surmise my creation is still alive since Pembroke hasn't complained.

October 25, 1962

Useless! Useless! All of the lab notes I took during that fateful night are useless! They are incoherent babble in handwriting that's markedly terrible even for me. I can't make heads nor tails of them.

I'm going to have to recreate the entire process from scratch!

But my creation.... I realized that perhaps if I am able to study it, I shall gain some insight into what exactly I did that night. I stormed into Pembroke's office, slamming the door shut behind me.

Pembroke took his pipe from between his lips. "What do you want, Frankenstein?" he asked, coldly.

"I want to see it," I said.

He turned a particularly greyish shade of pale. "I don't know what you're talking about," he sputtered.

"Let us not continue this ridiculous charade. I knew it was you from the moment you first spoke in the parking garage. And a few days ago, I handed a creature that I had created in my lab to you. I want to examine it."

If anything, he went paler. I wondered idly if he might faint. "You have no proof!" he said.

Which was true enough. Things were always safer with deniability. However: "I don't need proof," I countered. "I can simply spread the truth about like manure and see what grows from it."

"No one would believe you. You're a well-known quack."

There was the sneering Pembroke I had so long grown to despise.

"All it takes is one person," I said. "Are you willing to wager your entire career on my disrepute?"

He slammed his pipe down on his desk hard enough to crack the stem. "What do you actually want?" he hissed.

Oh, did he think I was going to demand more money? Clinically, I considered that for a moment, but money was no longer the issue. My ruined notes were, and greed was not a worthy distraction from the pursuit of such important science. "To examine my creation," I said, then quickly added: "Regularly."

"Impossible."

"You can bring it here, to my lab in the basement, or I suppose I could take myself to that ostentatious mansion you call a house."

He inflated like a bullfrog. "I'll call the police on you!"

"Good. I'd rather we use my lab anyway."

"I'm not going to—"

"Think of them as baby health checkups," I cut him off. "You wouldn't want anything to go wrong, would you?"

Come to think of it, regular checkups were a good idea, and I somehow doubted he'd want to explain the situation to a pediatrician.

"Fine," he said, "I'll bring it tomorrow. Now get out of my office."

Oh, but I could feel the loathing just rolling off of him as he glared at me. But of course he loathed me - I'd been right and he'd been forced to humble himself to ask for my help. And now I was right again, if unintentionally. Really, I was very good at this.

October 26, 1962

First checkup went well, though I have no further insights into how I actually created the creature. Frustrating. But it is gaining weight well, and, according to Pembroke, has been suckling vigorously when presented with bottles.

Pembroke did deliver one complaint at the start of the interview, quite red in the face: "And we can't tell if it's a boy or a girl!"

I shrugged as the creature grabbed at the front of my lab coat with one variegated hand. "It's composed of both male and female material in unknown proportions. I really couldn't say either way."

The horrified look he gave me is something I shall treasure until my dying day, even if I'm still not certain what was behind it. I carefully disengaged the creature's pudgy fingers from my stethoscope. I do recall that babies always loved grabbing that during my residential pediatrics rotation.

"Wait until it's old enough and I'm sure it'll tell you itself," I added.

Pembroke did not seem to find this helpful.

April 15, 1963

Creature and I are in vigorous disagreement as to how my name ought to be said. I have repeated the pronunciation multiple times. It insists my name is "Pranky." Then it giggles. I am pleased with this remarkable progress of neurodevelopment — very early compared to human infants produced the old-fashioned way!

I am also fairly certain it is mispronouncing on purpose.

December 17, 1963

Creature brought in today by Pembroke. It had a cast on its arm. Curious for something infant-sized to have injured itself in such a way. Focussed on checking bone density, did biopsy to make certain everything is as it should be.

Pembroke had no further information on the source of the broken bone; claimed it happened while he was at work, and he saw to the setting of the bone himself.

Promised I would drop off lab results by his office in a few days.

December. 20, 1963

Lab results normal, bone looks quite beautiful under the microscope, actually. Osteons are perfect, lacunae well-spaced, short-term growth evident. I do excellent work.

If only I'd written it down coherently.

November. 12, 1964

Creature informed me today that its name is Kelly, interesting because Pembroke had never bothered to do as much. It also attempted to hug me upon arrival for appointment. Well, actually, it succeeded in hugging me. Quite strong for its size. Pembroke seemed very displeased by this.

Shall have to ask him to wait outside from now on, as his presence is making cognitive testing difficult to impossible. Today's result would have been disappointing if I believed it for one moment, but Kelly kept looking at Pembroke instead of paying attention to me. Not atypical for a child, just annoying.

Which is also, on consideration, not atypical for a child.

May 2, 1965

I was right, examinations go much more smoothly without Pembroke glowering in the corner. Had a conversation with Kelly today, which I believe shows my creation to be quite brilliant and extremely cognitively developed to go with the apparent accelerated physical growth.

As I might expect.

Kelly: You're my doctor?

Me: I created you, as a matter of fact.

Kelly: Mummy says God created me.

Me: Your mummy is lying. God doesn't exist.

Kelly: Do you lie?

Me: Everyone does.

Kelly: That can't be true.

At this point, I noticed a nasty bruise on Kelly's back.

Me: What caused this?

Kelly: I fell.

Me: I see. Now tell me, have you ever lied?

Kelly: Yes.

Me: As I said. Everyone does.

Kelly then inquired about the anatomy chart I had hung on the wall quite some time ago and had never bothered to take down. I explained the various terms and systems and found my creation to be a quick and curious student. We'd moved on to cell growth when Pembroke burst in, red in the face, and shouted that he was a busy man and hadn't come here to have his time wasted while we played.

September 2, 1966

Pembroke informs me that Kelly has begun school with normal human children, as it is of an appropriate size and mental capacity if not age. Kelly informs me that its classmates are quite cruel.

"Of course they are," I told it. "That is the nature of all people, to be cruel to anyone who is different. Particularly to those who are brilliant, and you most definitely are. Children are merely less subtle."

"Why did you make me different?" Kelly asked.

"It was not my intention to do so," I admitted. "I wished simply to prove that I could make you at all."

Kelly fell silent, swinging its tiny feet from the edge of the metal table. Out of deference to the chill in the basement, I had supplied a blanket for it to sit on. "What if I don't want to be different?"

"You don't have a choice," I said. "You may try to pretend that you are like them, and you may even succeed for a time. But they will always smell you out as not like them, and your hopes will be crushed."

Kelly looked at me with its milky eyes — I am still not sure what has caused that effect, but its eyesight is quite perfect — and asked, "Did you try to pretend?"

As I have said, my creation is brilliant. Discomfortingly so at times.

"Yes. It only made things worse for me in the long run."

"What did you do, then?" Kelly asked.

"What anything living must: survived."

July 12, 1967

Kelly: When you talk to yourself, does that mean you're confused?

Me: No, I am thinking.

Kelly: You must think an awful lot.

The utter cheek.

December 9, 1967

It has all gone terribly, terribly wrong. Or rather, it was all terribly, terribly wrong from the beginning, and I only apprehended this today because I have been willfully ignorant.

I had the opportunity to do a set of full-body x-rays on Kelly because I knew the night radiologist would be off having a tryst — ah the benefits of eavesdropping in the cafeteria. I had not done an x-ray for nearly two years because this kind of opportunity had not presented itself before.

At first blush, the bone structure and growth looked excellent, all I could hope for. I think Kelly shall grow up to be quite tall and strong. But upon closer examination, I began to note the shadows and thickenings indicative of healed fractures: nearly all of the ribs, left scapula, bilateral on arms and legs — spiral fractures, damning enough alone. Different stages of healing, all of them.

I thought back, then, to Pembroke's resistance to bringing Kelly in for the appointment at which the child had worn a cast. And other appointments, claiming an insurmountable schedule difference I hadn't wanted to contest out of fear I'd lose all access. I only saw Kelly once a quarter at most to begin with, and often went longer stretches without. And I thought of other x-ray films I have seen very similar to these, though all on dead rather than living children. I knew the statistics for the causes of such an array of injuries - in better than nine times out of ten, they were indicative of physical abuse.

"You've stopped talking to yourself," Kelly said, behind me. "Is something wrong with my bones?"

"You have broken your bones many times," I said, fighting a growing nausea as I considered the mental image of dissecting my own creation in a postmortem investigation. Strange, since I have done so many a time. But I did not *know* any of those failed lumps of flesh.

Kelly shrugged, as if that was some sort of answer.

"Well?" I asked.

Kelly slipped off the metal table and began dressing, pulling on a worn, yellow jumper with missing buttons.

"I fall down a lot."

"That's rubbish. You have excellent motor skills. We tested them today."

Kelly shrugged again.

"Are you lying?" I asked, "Right now?"

"Yes," Kelly whispered, shoulders hunching in a most defensive way.

I felt ill and hurried to poke around in my pocket for a cigarette.

"Mummy doesn't say God made me anymore," Kelly offered. "So you were right about her lying too."

At the time, I wasn't certain about what the statement meant; I have since looked over my older journal entries and found the conversation to which Kelly referred. Remarkable memory on display, there. Though that does not make the contents of that statement any less troubling, nor what followed.

"What does she say now?" I asked.

"The Devil makes unnatural things."

I stuffed my cigarette between my lips and lit it. My fingers trembled slightly as I fought to not shout. "She's still lying, then," I said. "We both know I made you."

"You're not well-dressed enough to be the Devil," Kelly agreed.

I stared uncomprehendingly for a moment, and then began to laugh, because that was such a well-timed statement, and so true... and I thought otherwise I might scream.

Kelly laughed as well, but immediately stopped when Pembroke pounded on the door. I'd started locking the door after he took to bursting in when he ran out of patience. "If you're laughing in there, you must be done." he growled. "I'm a busy man, Frankenstein."

Kelly looked at me sharply. Pleadingly. I unlocked the door and let Pembroke take my creation away as if all was normal, leaving me with only my frantic thoughts.

Monstrous. Pembroke was monstrous, or his wife, or both, for having done such violence to leave those indelible marks upon Kelly's bones. Banally monstrous, the sort of casual, quiet evil that grinds the world's bones to dust, day in and day out. Is this why they were never able to adopt a child of their own and had to apply to me? What other defects had they hidden, and I been too distracted to consider? No, I had not even thought in the first place, with that desperately needed cheque dangling before me.

And what of you, Frankenstein? Indeed. Some might think me monstrous, for my midnight raids and bubbling beakers. But I have never willingly hurt another living creature in anger or with intent. I find the very thought deeply repugnant. Rather, I have devoted my life and intellect to the betterment of humankind's condition. And yet I have achieved the opposite, in the ignorant pursuit of my own brilliance. How do all of my vaunted intentions measure up against the suffering I have wrought with my lack of consideration? I have created a creature — no, a child — who thinks and laughs and makes cheeky jokes. And then I dumped them into the stuff of my nightmares without any consideration for where they might land.

I must find some way to correct this mistake.

December 19, 1967

I waited until the staff Christmas party to act, as I knew that Pembroke and his wife would both be there, in their glittering best. For form's sake, I put in a brief appearance, then abandoned my rented finery in my laboratory in favour of plain black.

Through wind and biting snow, I drove hunched over the steering wheel of my car, squinting through the only bit of the windscreen free of ice. At least I already knew where Pembroke's mansion was located.

I parked near the back of the large yard and used my own slippery car as a ladder to get over the fence.

Puffing and wishing desperately for a cigarette, I crossed the gargantuan yard and headed for the only window in which I saw a light — basement level... somehow not surprising.

I dropped to my knees in the snow and reached down into the window well to tap on the dirty, frosted-over glass. I could only hope I was correct, and that I was not in fact rousing some servant or guard that I could not see inside.

A few heart-stopping seconds later, the window squeaked open scant inches, and I heard Kelly's familiar, high-pitched voice. "W-who is it?"

"Frankenstein," I said, "I've come to fetch you."

"Father isn't here." Kelly answered.

"I know. That's why I'm here now. Please stop wasting time."

Kelly understood my meaning quickly. "I don't think the window opens any more than this. And I'm locked in."

"I'll take care of the window. Put on your shoes and whatever warm clothes you have." I cast about until I found a garden shed, mercifully unlocked. Inside, I found a sturdy shovel. "Are you ready?" I asked, when I returned. "This is going to make quite a bit of noise."

"Ready," Kelly said.

"Cover yourself with a blanket." I bashed in the window with the shovel, wincing at each loud, cracking blow.

Kelly crawled out when I was done, and I helped them scramble from the window well. They had no coat but had put on several layers of jumpers. With

Kelly's direction, we went to the back gate rather than attempting to scale the fence again. As we got into my car, I heard sirens in the distance.

I had taken the precaution of already packing my most important possessions into my car, so I focussed first on putting as much distance between ourselves and the Pembroke house as possible. We drove for many hours and paused for petrol twice before I began to feel drowsy at the wheel. I decided then that it would be wise to stop and pulled in to the first motel. Kelly watched with rapt attention as I paid for the room; the clerk stared at them all the while, looking most disconcerted.

I fell into a dreamless sleep almost immediately and did not awaken until nearly ten hours later, a mistake on my part. Kelly sat in the room's chair - which had stained cushions and looked wobbly - holding a book in their lap. A tin tea pot and tray sat on the flimsy table next to them.

"Is that fresh?" I mumbled.

"No," Kelly said. "I read in the amenities manual that we are entitled to tea with our room so I fetched it about three hours ago."

That was fresh enough. I poured the nearly opaque tea into the second mug on the tray and drank it.

"Where did you find the book?" I asked.

"They had a few for lending in the office."

"What is it?"

Kelly held up the book so that I could see the title: *Grimm's Fairy Tales*. I recalled my old, much-dogeared copy, left behind in my parents' house. Good riddance, really.

"A book of nonsense." I said.

"I think it's interesting," Kelly answered. "Though I have only read a few stories and am not yet certain what they mean."

"Which one confuses you the most?"

Kelly paged through it. "This one: *The Girl Without Hands*."

"Cleanliness and God-bothering," I said. I shook my head and took the book, paging through until I found *Cinderella*. "Try this one instead."

While I cleared the last of the fog from my brain with the further application of cold tea, Kelly paged through the story. "Why did you tell me to read this one?" they asked.

"What do you think the lesson of it is?"

Kelly frowned at the pages. "A kind person will rescue me?"

"No," I said. "Because you can never trust that." I was certainly no knight errant, merely a scientist trying to correct a mistake. "I think the better lesson is that Cinderella had a terrible life and was much abused. But she survived and remained a good person."

Kelly opened their mouth to speak, but that was when the police broke down the door.

March 12, 1968

The trial is over, and I'm glad for that. It has all come out now, the truth of Kelly's origin and the ugliness of Pembroke's abuse. Not quite what I had in mind, by the way, with my expectations of scientific celebrity, though I seem to have become a household name. Murkier is Kelly's legal status, but there is nothing I can do about that other than hope my fellow human being operates upon logic and kindness. To say I have no faith is an understatement, and thus my worries multiply. I much preferred to only be concerned with my own disposition.

The court put Pembroke and I in the same room, prior to sentencing. He looked a mess, bloodshot eyes and stubble. The mirror has been saying rather kinder things to me of late, I think, because I'd nothing to do but sleep.

Pembroke glared at me and snarled, "You didn't give us the child we wanted, Frankenstein. You gave us a cuckoo's egg, a monster!"

I couldn't help but laugh. "You raise the child you have. Not the child you wish you had. Even I know that."

Thankfully, the bailiff was present to pull him off of me.

March 14, 1968

Fifteen years. Perhaps I shall finally catch up on my reading.

Pembroke received only five years of probation for his part, which hardly seems fair. The wealthy are subject to a different sort of justice, I suspect, though I hear the hospital has distanced itself from him and that gives me some small comfort. He was a terrible administrator anyway. No creativity.

The only relief I have in all of this is that Kelly has been removed from his home, and I do not think Pembroke or his wife shall try to regain custody of them. But how shall someone as special as Kelly be treated by the fostering system in this country... if a foster home is their destination rather than a windowless laboratory? I already know well that visible difference and brilliance of the sort that Kelly no doubt has are not gently viewed by others.

And yet this time, there is nothing I can do. I have never had any use for God, nor inclination to believe in energies or whatever spiritual twaddle is popular with the masses these days. I can hope only that Kelly has taken my words to heart and will, like me, survive.

No, I hope that Kelly shall survive far better than I have.

1968-1983

[A page of tiny tick marks, counting days, 5,475 total.]

April 14, 1983

I left prison wearing the same suit in which I had entered it. Fifteen years had done neither the fabric nor the cut any favours. I had nothing to my name but a pack of cigarettes, fare for the bus, and a head rusted with old ideas that will have to be updated before I can get a proper lab running again. I had also developed a limp. It was the wrong sort of prison, and not at all kind, and I shall say no more on the topic than that.

As I left the prison gates, I noted a bright red car parked and waiting, its windows rolled down. Music shivered through the warm spring air - an odd, jangly sort of melody to which a singer invited listeners to both dance and sway. The driver's side door opened and a tall, squarely-built person rose from the car with notable grace. They wore a baggy shirt of some sort of shiny green material and tight trousers — what *had* the world come to whilst I was in prison? — and had shaggy, frosted hair puffed up by means of hairspray, I presume. A cheery white and yellow daisy was tucked behind one ear, highlighting familiar milky eyes and skin mottled with all colours of humanity: Kelly.

"I've come to fetch you," Kelly said.

"You never wrote." Of all inane things, that is what tumbled from my lips first. Prison truly has done my already-weak skills of discourse no good.

"Until I turned eighteen, I was very closely watched." They acknowledged the still unexplained two-year gap with a graceful wave of their hand. Brightly coloured, glittery bracelets flashed on their wrist. "And then there was the mess with the birth certificate, or lack thereof. And the further mess of tracking you down after two prison transfers."

Even with no faith in my fellow man, I ought to have had faith in the cleverness and fortitude of my own creation. But to have that same cleverness and fortitude directed in kindness toward me nearly stole my faculties for speech.

"I didn't think I'd see you again at all," I said, and felt my face draw into a smile, the expression so long unused that it was almost foreign.

Kelly's lips curled in a grin, like one I'd never before seen on their face as the man on the radio began a chorus: *If you say run, I'll run with you*. And they repeated to me words I now realize that I'd spoken to them over fifteen years before at a far different sort of prison: "I know. That's why I'm here now. Please stop wasting time."

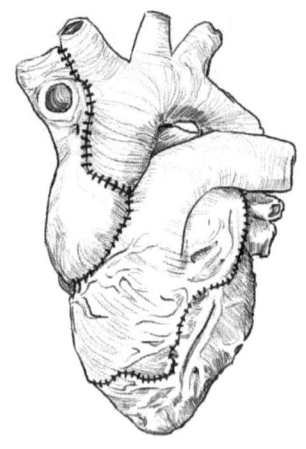

THE PATCHWORK GIRL

EVELYN DESHANE

"They say she's a vampire."

"And who exactly is 'they'?"

"I am," I chimed in. No one in the group laughed. It was a bad joke. A bad joke about neutral pronouns, which were already precarious at best. *You should be more serious, Iris. Each joke may end in death. Laughter is one of the last things trans women hear before the bashing.* And so on and so on. My skin already prickled with embarrassment and shame.

I went down one aisle of the poorly lit store, searching for shirts that could button over my too-large chest. Bailey and Marta went down the other aisle towards neon athletic wear. Over the hum of the Muzak and the shuffling of a dozen sneakers, I still heard parts of their conversation. They seemed fairly adamant that the woman with dark hair and a sharp nose who let us into the department store after hours to shop was a supernatural creature — a vampire, no less — rather than a godsend.

I'd first heard about The Night Shift runs when I was still working an actual night shift at the gas station. Hormones were still new to me. The always persistent fuzz above my lip became a 'stache in no time, but I looked more like a twelve-year-old boy from a trailer park than a twenty-seven-year-old nonbinary person. I was still figuring out the right tone for my voice and the clothing I could wear. The night shift at the Gas 'n' Go made the perfect cover. I could still talk to people — more often than not truckers who couldn't use a credit card or someone who wanted to know where the bathroom was — but I was mostly in the dark. I waited for my shift to end, watching YouTube videos on my phone and restocking candy.

When the woman — or vampire — came into the gas station, she had been a bright light at the end of a long night. She read me instantly as a trans person, but it wasn't with disgust. Her slight tilt of a head and a ghost of a smile was how Marta had read me in our university class together. It wasn't gender pieces falling out of place but falling *into* place. Recognition rather than revulsion.

"You ever have any nights free?" she asked.

I avoided answering. If she wasn't a trans person herself, then she was a trans chaser. And I wasn't interested in women anyway.

"I run a business. But it's only open at night. You should come by." She left a card on the counter and took her iced coffee back to her vehicle. I barely had a chance to see the plates on her van before she sped away.

The Night Shift was printed in the centre of card, indented and embossed, followed by the store's tagline, *private shopping for the private client.* It listed a dilapidated department store in the middle of a strip mall along the border of Ottawa and Québec. The hours were all from midnight to dawn. A trans symbol was in one corner of the card, along with a disability sign, and two others that I didn't recognize. I almost wrote the whole thing off as a strange invitation to a sex club, but when I ran into Bailey in my apartment after he'd stayed the night, I ended up telling him over coffee. He made me repeat the story several times before he called Marta, his dark eyes wide.

"The rumours are true. The Night Shift exists. And we're going."

Three weeks later, we were still shopping whenever we could get the time off. The Night Shift really was a private shopping experience for private people. A minute after midnight, the woman would show up in her dark van, or sometimes on foot carrying a large suitcase, and open the clothing store for a crowd of waiting people. She let them shop in peace while she worked the cash register. Everything had to be done in cash to keep the computer system and security system from coming on. Most of the time she screwed up the amount of change, but none of that mattered. Bailey, Marta, and I could shop for clothing. It seemed so quotidian when I tried to explain it to other people — cis ones especially — but this was so monumental. Marta wasn't thrown out of the lingerie section. Bailey could find what he wanted without eyes on the back of his head. And I could bounce from the kids' section to the women's and men's in an attempt to find something that fit my awkward body and gender without worrying. Some nights we spent the full six hours here, while other times we just went in for one specific item.

Tonight, I was trying to find a shirt. The buttons on my plaid button-up kept busting open under the strain of my chest. I could only depend on my compression binder for so much and I was getting sick of sewing buttons back on. There was no sign of surgery in my future. Gas station attendants weren't exactly paid well. And doctors didn't believe in nonbinary identity. While Marta and Bailey already had their future paths figured out like a tarot card spread, I was still stuck in the in-between realm of the querent. Maybe that was why they suddenly seemed to turn on the woman who had opened up the store for us and given us a new lease on life — or at least, a new impression of fashion.

"She's gotta be a vampire," Marta insisted. "Why else do this?"

"And she's always up at night."

"I'm up at night," I said, walking over to them. "And I'm not a vampire."

"But you're trans. She's not. I don't mean *vampire*-vampire." Marta rolled her eyes. "Obviously. That's not real. But psychic vampires are. I mean, what exactly is she getting out of this arrangement?"

"The change from my twenty?" I suggested. "The feeling of doing a good deed in this transphobic world? PC points?"

"Pffft. She's getting something more than goodie-goodie points. She's feeding off our energy in some way. You know how people think trans people are magic." Marta went off to list the mythological figures who were trans in some way, and then how this lore had been appropriated into a sci-fi book she'd been reading.

Bailey nodded alongside her. "I can see that. Maybe we shouldn't keep going here. Something does feel off."

"Yeah. You notice how almost no one is a repeat customer?"

Marta gestured around the store. We'd been there four times, which was hardly enough to establish a pattern, but I could see Marta's point. Each time we went in, there seemed to be a new crowd of people. I thought that was exciting — more people in the trans community to know — but everyone seemed to be quiet, evasive. No one wanted to speak, except the three of us.

When a tall person came out of the change room, holding a red cocktail dress in their hands, some form of recognition panged inside of me. I pointed to them and insisted I'd seen them before. Bailey and Marta shook their heads. We all watched as the person went to the cash register to buy their dress. The woman smiled, embracing them in a hug as if they were old friends. Then she slipped something in their cellophane bag before they left.

"Was that... that was a blood bag, wasn't it?" Marta said. "Oh my *God*. Oh *my* God. We're leaving. Right now."

"No," I said, but the two of them had already stashed their clothing items at the end of the aisle. The customer service worker in me wanted to stop and clean, but I followed my friends out the door. The woman's eyes followed us as we left without purchasing a thing. Even through the thick panelled glass of the department store window, I was still sure she was watching us.

"That was fucking close," Marta said. "Let this be a lesson, though. Never trust cis people. Ever, ever, ever. All of them are damn vampires."

Bailey echoed the sentiment before adding that he'd like some coffee. I followed them both, knowing that until dawn, this was the only path I could take.

When the sun came up, I walked back towards the strip mall. Bailey and Marta lived on the other side of town and took a bus long before I departed. They would never know that I'd doubled back to see the woman — which was as good as it was bad. I now had privacy so I could explore, but it also meant that if she was a murderer like Marta now believed, I could disappear like a ghost. I tried not to think of that possible reality, or how the papers would address me if I were to turn up missing.

I didn't have to wait long before the low lights of the store flicked off entirely. The woman walked out wearing a trench coat, carrying her giant suitcase, and locked the door. Her dark hair was tied in a ponytail and buried under a red baseball cap. She had sunglasses perched on the edge of her nose. Though she tried to disguise herself, it was definitely her. Her suitcase was distinctive, battered and covered in patches, but there was also an aura which hung around her, one I hadn't quite noticed until now. Whether it was supernatural or not, I still wasn't sure.

She turned a corner and headed towards the downtown core. I followed close behind, ducking under awnings and pretending to light a cigarette every so often. I figured I wasn't memorable. Anywhere I went, people seemed to do their best to not look at me, because looking meant deciphering my curvy body plus a moustache and short hair. Looking was too confusing. Being in-between meant I was everything, but also nothing. I banked on that feature of myself as I watched the woman walk to an apartment building with an ornate facade. The sun had fully risen. She hadn't turned to stone or flames, so she couldn't have been a vampire. When she stepped inside the building, I lost my eye on her entirely.

I examined the tenant list on the apartment building but found zero names. They were all numbers and floors. For a moment, I wondered if this place as an office rather than a residence, when a buzzing sounded. The lock on the door clicked open. I knew I didn't have long so I darted inside without thinking. A camera hung in front of me, fixated on anyone who entered the foyer.

I'd be caught. Wherever she'd gone, she was watching me.

"Shit."

"Don't worry," a voice came over a PA system. It was low and sensuous; familiar from the gas station. Definitely her. "You're not in any danger. But I could use your help."

"I. Um. Okay. I don't think I have any choice."

There was a beat of silence before she asked, "What's your blood type?"

"O negative."

"You seem sure."

"I am."

Another beat of silence. Followed by another. She seemed to wait for me to tell her the story of my blood, but I refused. I wondered which one of us would win the standoff; I wondered which one of us had more to hide and more to lose.

"Well, okay. If you're right, then you're a universal donor. And you're exactly what I need. Come on down to room six hundred. I'll pay you for your time."

I walked, knowing that again, this was the only path I could take.

She was in her office with the tall person from the store. They were naked, save for a green cloth over their genitals and chest, blocking their bits like a censorship bar. The table they were on was thick and seemed to be made of stone, rather than metal and plastic. Their body seemed to shine as the lights above them cascaded over the flecks of granite and quartz in the slab. They were clearly asleep, knocked out for some kind of surgery. The woman wore a sleek, black outfit, her hair still tied behind her slender shoulders. She wore plastic gloves that reached to her elbows and a doctor's mask around her neck, giving her space to talk. The mask and gloves were the only items that matched the operating room decor. There were no machines to monitor heart rate or blood pressure; no typical equipment common in an operating room. The walls were littered with charts and posters depicting the human body, bisected and full of colour. There were flowers, rather than organs under the ribcage. Each image outlined chakras, not bloodlines.

"What... what is this place?"

"This is the operating theatre," she said. "But I take the term theatre more seriously than others."

"Is... are they...?"

"They are okay, yes." Her use of neutral pronouns was with practiced ease. Somehow, this made me feel better. She wasn't some strange surgeon trying to open up trans people to see if they really were unique snowflakes inside or draining their blood to consume gender magic. She wasn't one of us, but she was next to us. Peripheral. She was a doctor, or something like it, trying to help. "We have run into a snag, though. Nin thought they were O+ but now I see that this is not the case. So I need to have a universal donor to even out what I've already done."

Nowhere did I see blood. But I sensed tearing, ripping of flesh, and a state of emergency that tinted the room. Not an aura, not quite — but a feeling of pain that I could taste. Nin was in trouble and I was the only hope.

I started to roll up my sleeve without being told. The woman nodded with a pleased smile as she placed the mask over her face. She retrieved a lawn chair, painted in bright pink, and set it down next to one of her side tables lined with instruments. Each one was gold tipped and covered with a sheen of glitter. Some had pearls at the end, others had what seemed to be more quartz and diamonds. A deck of tarot cards was at the centre, the Devil card flipped up, along with the ten of pentacles.

"Inheritance. Wealth," she said, gesturing to the card. "It's Nin's time to get what they deserve."

I didn't say anything. I watched as she withdrew a clear rod that was attached to a blood bag. She moved her hands like a magician using the clear rod as a wand. She tapped the crease of my elbow. My blood came out. The glass stained red. I felt nailed to the floor, filled with a sick sense of my body's blood leaving me.

Then it was over. She placed a hand on my head and another card emerged. The five of cups. Two of the cups on the card were upright, while three were spilled. A man in the centre crossed his arms angrily.

"Ah," she said. "Bad things have happened — your cups have spilled, but you need to focus on what's in front of you."

Again, I was silent. She added the blood to the body in front of me. The body of Nin, who was still sleeping, still dreaming in some far away, in-between place. The woman appeared by their side and did more sleight of hand magic tricks. Blood spilled everywhere. Before it pooled and turned black on the floor, the blood became dust — glitter. Nin's body started to change. The green fabric covered their genitals fell away.

And there were no genitals. Nin was smooth like a doll, like a Ken or Barbie or both all at once. The front of their chest was devoid of nipples. All the glittered blood that had once been spilt was now clean. The woman turned away from the body on the slab, her breath heavy. Whatever she had done had taken all her strength. I could feel her exhaustion in the air, taste it like the coppery patina of pennies in a fountain.

"Are you okay?" I asked.

"I am. Nin will wake up in an hour or two." She removed her medical gear into a blue bin on the far side of the wall. When she turned back to me, she extended her hand. "I should introduce myself, though. I'm Mary Michelle Frances Stein. But most people call me Shelly."

I had coffee with Shelly until Nin woke and left. After their hug, Nin slipped an envelope into Shelly's coat pocket. A payment for services rendered. I watched from her office window as they entered the late morning Ottawa street, now nearly barren after rush hour, and then walked into their new life. Nin would never come back to the store at night. There would be no need.

Nin was not the only person Shelly had helped. Ever since she opened *The Night Shift* to allow trans and disabled people to shop without worry, she realized that the clothing was only the first step of the magic, as she called it. Trans people could use clothing to transform their bodies on the surface. That was easy. But the internal matching of the external was always the last stage, always the hardest path to endure in order to be rewarded. That type of magic required someone else. So she offered her services. For payment, of course.

But there was also something else she was getting, I was sure of it. Marta's words were like a warning on the back of my eyelids. I wanted to ignore her, but I had to ask. "Why? Why bother with all of this?"

She set down her coffee with a deliberate motion. She stared into the black void as she considered my question.

"Surely this is not the first time you've been asked?"

"No. But I still don't have an answer beyond 'why bother doing anything?'"

"That's not an answer."

"Exactly. But I find origin stories boring. I think you would know that most of all."

I huffed. I thought of the Centre for Addiction and Mental Health doctors in Toronto who rejected my surgical application. Gender must always have an origin. It must have an *answer* and a clear definitive beginning. Being two genders at once, or none of the above, made no sense to the panel of experts. So I made no sense to them.

But someone who was two at once and nothing at all was what I had watched come out Shelly's door. Nin was real. I was real. And so was Shelly, even if she didn't want to tell me how she had come to be this way.

"You want to know why I know I have O blood?" I asked.

She didn't nod or say a thing. I went on.

"Because when my mom was pregnant with me, she needed those shots to balance out the proteins. Dad was O+ and mom was O-. Right from the start, I was an issue. Things couldn't mix or balance in us. I came out as O-, and my mom always thought that meant I was always going to be like her. Sorry to disappoint, Mom. But I prefer to be in the middle. As always."

"You prefer to be universal," she said. "The universal donor is also the universal door."

"Exactly."

"I'm glad you knew your type. It's fascinating when people don't. I can't fathom it. How can you be so sure of some items about yourself, but then forget others? It's not the first time something like Nin's issue has happened here. They thought they were universal too. But when I opened them up, I saw for myself. Not a lie, but a convenient myth they had told themselves."

"But... there was no wound. How could you tell Nin's blood type without a wound? And why does the blood matter?"

She smiled. "The blood, like the clothing, is part of the show. Part of the magic."

"You keep saying that, but what does it mean?"

With a heavy sigh, she explained to me the nuances of psychic surgery. Her brand, of course. She wasn't like one of the duplicitous cult leaders who perpetuated a medical fraud in order to leech every last penny out of poor people who didn't know any better. She even cited a case of a con man who had contracted leprosy from doing too many fraudulent psychic surgeries, as a way of showing how irony and karma would catch up to those who used magic for trickery alone. "Cons are not what I do here. I use the pomp and circumstance of psychic surgery, but I actually pull something out or put something back in. I actually find what is useful inside of someone and then I allow their body to reach that potential."

"Their potential? How is this not a con job too?" I asked, but soon bit back my words. I saw the smooth skin of Nin and I was awash with the memories of the operating room once again. No, the operating *theatre*. Surgery was always a show.

She reiterated that point over and over again. "Surgery's a show — and gender's a cultural artefact. Both are made up fairy tales, but they are still real. Very real. It has taken me a long time to understand the magic behind gender, and then perform surgeries in this way, but I assure you, my intentions are true."

"How long?" I asked.

She leaned into her coffee, her body folding into sadness. The tempo of the room changed. I heard music inside my ear, Brahms or Mozart, and then I saw a face. A man's face — but not a man's. He was caught in-between like me. He liked the pronouns he/she but hated the skin and body that came with them.

"My husband Eugene — Genie — died before his show could end. When a bus crashed, he was one of the many injured. The paramedics cut open his shirt and found a bra underneath, along with panties now visible above the rim of his jeans. Instead of performing CPR, they laughed. He died. Story done. Poof. Over." She sighed. "I never knew these parts of him. He kept it all hidden at the back of his closet like a dirty secret. So I opened my store at night, hoping to make amends in some way. If I could be open to others, maybe his spirit could rest. I started to feel the force of gender. Not his gender, but all genders. I started to acknowledge that we don't just have physical bodies, but four-dimensional ones. He left the mortal world. He became matter and energy. In a way, that was what he wanted. Pure energy, magical and ethereal. But if I could synthesize a process to bring the fourth dimensional magical bodies to the surface, then no other trans person had to die to achieve it. I could help. I could find what people wanted."

I had to laugh. It was funny, right? I wanted it to be funny. A long-extended joke. Marta putting me on, hiring an out-of-work actress to deliver a strange sci-fi monologue. A pit in my stomach would have even wanted for Marta's other hypothesis to be right. This coffee talk was a long con and I would eventually be skinned and made into a Buffalo Bill suit. It would only be appropriate.

But Shelly was serious. I felt it inside.

"The blood is the portal," she said. "The link between planes of existence. And I have to say... my surgery is stronger when it has access to a universal donor. How would you like a more permanent job?"

Before I answered, she divided the money that Nin had given her and handed a section of it to me. It was over one thousand dollars. Rent for the next month. I wouldn't have to do a night shift at the gas station ever again.

But I already knew I was going to say yes.

For the next three months, I performed seven operations. I watched as her technique morphed from the sloppy and slap-dash emergency lifesaving surgery of Nin to the high art performance where her talent was obvious. With my blood as the universal door opener, she could access the fourth dimension without worry.

Colours spilled forth from the next surgical client, a trans man named Carl who wanted his breasts removed. Since he wanted to keep his genitals, Shelly presented him with an aura around his thighs, like a halo of good feelings. No more dysphoria. Each time he touched himself or someone touched him, bursts of colours erupted in front of his eyes. Next was a trans woman named Julie-Anne. When Shelly opened up her chest cavity in order to construct breasts, a rabbit burst forth. It hopped around the operating room until I caught it and put it in a cage. When I realized that Shelly already had the cage set up prior to the surgery, I learned that sometimes creatures moved inside of us. One day it was a rabbit, other days it was a cat, or a misshapen demon creature that Shelly had to kill the moment after it was out. Depending on what a person experienced, what they internalized as part of their life story, and what they considered to be their own special kind of magic, that was what came out of them. That was what made up their fourth dimensional bodies and their quixotic gendered souls.

The most boring surgeries were the standard ones. A trans woman named Callie who wanted a tracheal shave had a balloon float out of her and then bust. That was it. Even the atmosphere of the surgery had been lackluster. When a trans man wanted larger hands and feet, small stones fell out of his fingers and toes, turned grey, and then turned to dust. No show whatsoever.

But each patient was grateful. They hugged Shelly as they left and sung her praises. They even started to hug me as they left, once they realized I was the assistant to the master; Igor to the gender saver Frankenstein — a neutral party in every way.

I earned more than I ever dreamed. I let the money stack up in an ornate music box my mother had given me at age seven and that I couldn't bear to part with, even if my mother had parted ways with me. The music soon became stifled by crumpled bills and wouldn't shut. But I couldn't deposit that level of cash without looking suspicious. It also didn't seem real. The magic I had witnessed from my own blood paled in comparison to commerce. One morning, as I counted, I realized I could afford my own surgery. I could remove the breasts from my chest and then buy all the shirts I wanted and needed without the fear of busting a button again. I could shop in daylight hours. I could pass as something. Maybe not a man or a woman, but my invisible identity would yield safety.

The daylight didn't interest me anymore. I put my money back in the music box and returned to Shelly's place, eventually letting my lease lapse and my apartment become vacated. After weeks of helping Shelly, though, she had not asked me about my own psychic surgery. Even with all of our successes, I still seemed to be a lowly Igor and nothing but.

One night, after she'd pulled a live dove from the centre of a trans man's chest, I felt something like wings flutter inside of me. Was I filled with feathers? Would I explode under the real lights of a surgical room? I wanted to know. And I couldn't take it anymore.

After John had left with the dove in a cage to keep as a pet familiar, I walked right over to Shelly. "Why haven't you operated on me yet?"

"Whoa, whoa. I feel the anger. It's blue and purple by your eyes."

"Is it because of the blood?" I asked, ignoring her. "Am I not a universal donor if you perform surgery on me?"

She sighed. She gestured to the table and we sat down. I thought I was going to hear a lecture about how psychic surgery would make my fourth dimensional body become manifest, therefore I would no longer be in-between, so I could no longer be a helper. I expected her to reject me. Doctors had always rejected me. Why wouldn't the magical kind of doctor be the same? But instead she grabbed my hand. Warmth radiated from her.

"You're far stronger than you could ever imagine."

"Because of the blood?"

"Yes and no. The more you witness here, the more you learn. The more you believe and the more magic that gets stored inside of you. If I perform surgery on you, it would be a miracle. It would be like opening a new world and watching as a new mythology comes forward."

I felt that flutter again, but it wasn't wings. It was like a multitude of different pathways and identities coming out of me all at once. A house of tarot cards collapsing and rebuilding. All future trajectories — everything and nothing — available before me.

I wanted that more than anything in the world. "So why won't you work on me?"

"Because... I fear that you won't come back after it's done. And I've enjoyed our time. It's been such a long time since anyone's been around me."

The loss of her husband tinged her sadness — but again, there was something more. I squeezed her hand. I sent her silent waves of approval, of hope, of understanding. Eventually, she crashed under my waves.

"I'm a monster."

"What?"

"I'm a monster," she repeated. "I'm Frankenstein. In the story, the creature is never the monster. That was not what Mary Shelley wanted or intended. It was science. It was technological progress. It was the horrors of discovery. I am all of those things at once. So I will always be a monster."

"That's..." I couldn't argue. Her words were true. Dr. Frankenstein was the monster and all things that I had been through only confirmed that doctors were still monsters. Especially to trans people. I thought of Marta's words about the soul-sucking nature of cis people. Shelly was cis. She was the enemy.

But she had also created so much magic. I could feel it inside of me. She had created at least half of the pathways that I now felt under my skin as emergent possibilities. I wanted to burst forward, to achieve what I wanted, but I couldn't without her help. I never could have without her help.

"Why is the monster always a bad thing?" I asked. "Why are doctors always bad?"

"Because they exploit. Because they..."

"Because they can't see what's already there. Because they don't listen to the patient. The science itself isn't bad, though. Cis people aren't bad. And monsters aren't bad. But the lack of insight and understanding always leads to bad things. That's it. Everything else is neutral."

She tilted her head in the same way she had when she first met me. I saw so much behind her eyes. The colour of her husband's lingerie, the patina of desire mixed with tragedy she felt for him, and my own lineage of rainbow pathways bursting forth. It made me think of a game I had played as a kid, which was really more like a story told through computer links, called *The Patchwork Girl*. It was about Frankenstein too, but in this version, Mary Shelley made the female monster for herself. The story was told in bits and pieces, completely out of order, and overlaid over an image of a bisected female body that acted as the home screen. It was the first game that made me realize I had desire for something more than my own body. I thought it meant I was queer. I thought it meant I was trans. But maybe it meant that I was magic inside. Or held so many magical possibilities underneath me, just like the story suggested.

In a way, all of these answers were right. And that was the real point of both the game and the operating theatre now. There were no monsters or victims or innocent people or even fully men or women anymore. There was a patchwork; a cluster; a bursting forth of so many different options that every single one was golden.

"You're not a monster. You're a patchwork girl," I told her. "I'm patchwork too. We're both made from borrowed parts and we work to stitch together and open up the fourth dimension."

My words felt silly. They felt like reading in another language. But she smiled, as if I had finally presented her with an alternative way of seeing her life. As if I had finally given her a word for her identity that didn't make her feel like shit.

"Okay," she said. She touched the centre of my chest. The fluttering happened again. "Let's open you — all of you — up."

"**T**hey say she's a vampire."

"And who is they?" I asked, stepping close to the two trans women as they shopped in the blouse section of the store. They baulked under my gaze. Then they turned to one another, as if to confer an answer like school children before answering.

"No one. Just this woman named Marta. She runs the counselling centre."

"And she warned us about this place."

"Mmhmm." I nodded. Years had passed. Marta had obtained her surgery. Gotten a better job with her new license and birth certificate, but she still worked within the community. Bailey also obtained his surgery and better identification, which he used to disappear into complacent masculinity. Their chosen pathways, their lives. Not my magic — but still no less valid. "Well, I used to know Marta. She means well. But I also know Shelly, and I can tell you that she's no vampire."

"Then what is she?" one of them asked. "Because this seems too good to be true."

I smiled. I touched my chest. My breasts were now gone. But inside my front shirt pocket was a figurine that once used to belong inside a music box I had as a child, which had now been pulled out of the centre of me through psychic surgery. The tiny ballerina dancer was clear glass, but not opaque. Whenever I wanted to see inside myself, in the magic that Shelly had tapped and rearranged, all I had to do was hold the tiny glass dancer up to the light.

I held the figurine up in the store. Rainbow colours burst forth. The women gasped. They probably heard music, though not the same music I heard. I'd realized that part was different; everyone had their own stereo in their heads, but the emotions were all the same. Joy and elation. Freedom.

Pure magic.

I pocketed my glass figurine once again. The music stopped.

Their eyes were still wide. "What is... how is...?"

"You should ask Shelly." I shot her a look across the department store. She hugged a person by the cashier and slipped them the address for her place. We would have to leave soon. I turned back towards the girls. "Just be respectful when you talk, okay? Shelly is not a vampire or a monster. She's just like us."

One of them scoffed. "Impossible."

"Not so."

"But for real, though," the other one said. "If she's not a vampire, then what is she?"

"A patchwork girl. Stitched together from second hand parts, but still no less real. Like me, like her." I flicked my glass figurine once again. I left them with a cascade of light, the doors to our world now open.

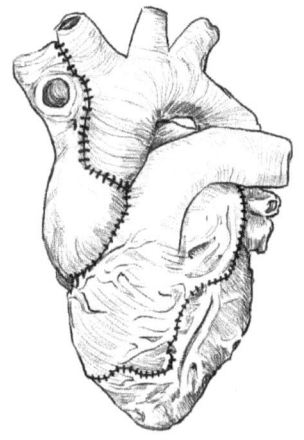

RAGDOLL IN RAGTIME

D. SIMON TURNER

H ave another drink.

Hegel said the French Revolution marked the end of history. That the sense of progress towards an overarching goal for mankind had reached its zenith. I suppose it's been all downhill from there. Or maybe progress has always meant rolling downwards – we're all part of the Sisyphean struggle. Nietzsche exclaimed the death of God, and my life has only been proof of the point.

Not in isolation, no. When armies fought against burning gases instead of the faces of their foe, it's hard to say we're not in a new century with new rules for humanity to learn. If we ever can learn them.

I mean, after the War, did we not say: never again? And now it's "again." Armies just can't keep it in their pants. The United States will join Europe and the Commonwealths soon, I believe. Always a late starter.

Who are we now? What history do we strive towards? The empires have been dying off these last decades. Germany will fall again soon too, even if it takes England with it. I really believe that. The twentieth century is seeing nationality redefined. Not less prescient, but redefined. Just look at Russia.

No, I don't always talk like this. It's just for you. I kid, but I have been thinking about my homeland a lot lately. No, I came from Germany. The accent isn't strong anymore, no, I only lived there half my life. They say it's easier to lose an accent when you're younger. Believe me, I'm younger than I look.

It's not something I mention much, what with the war. The *wars*, now. Ridiculous, to think that my country would wish for another hell storm after the devastation of the last. Not that I was there to experience the horrors.

I told you, I'm younger than I look. Much younger. It's a long story, but perhaps I've already begun to tell it.

I never had a mother. No, she never *lived* to die.

My father is an obsessive eccentric, and like all obsessive eccentrics in the 20s – or anyone with nothing better to do – he came to Berlin. You wouldn't believe it now, but during the 20s, Berlin was the capital city of *laissez-faire*. We had as much jazz as Chicago, nightclubs and cabarets down every other street, and the city smelled of freedom and poverty. It was the perfect place for a man who had a plan and nothing to lose.

And who would notice what his experiments might be? The neighbours might talk under their breath of the surgeon next door who walked each night to the morgue, but this was Berlin. No one could be bothered to ask questions when they were burning Deutschmarks in the fire grate to keep warm. He paid the rent each month on his little house with the cement basement, there was no room in one's stomach for curiosity.

That's where I was born, in that basement. Oh, it was spotless. It had to be.

What sort of experiments? Why me, of course. I was his creation. The child of Frankenstein. His own form of conception – a biological ragdoll from the medical cadavers he stole. He never wanted to revive the dead, but to recreate life in his own image. A new being to be imprinted by him, set and inked like the Gutenberg press. A form of asexual reproduction for the eternal bachelor – like the navel orange, propagation by cutting and grafting. But from my first moments of consciousness, I broke his typeset.

From the beginning of my time in this world, I think there was something about the vivified collection of parts different from the *corpus* he had spent so long working on. Life makes flesh move in ways that cannot be imagined. The tide of muscles under skin can be understood through physics well enough, but most painters use a model to approach the reality of the image. I've read how a person feels fractured by seeing a loved one after death, that there is an *unheimlich*, unnatural aura that comes over the body, and here I was the same in reverse. And even then, I am not a natural assemblage, but a hodgepodge of humanity and the distinct characteristics of God knows how many parts.

Not that I could recognize this all at first – I've had years to reflect. Those first weeks of memory are strange, but distinct. I had no language, but now I can only conceptualize the time through words like bright fireworks in my mind, shaded in primary colours. Hunger – red; joy – yellow; fatigue – blue; but with much more variation than that. I cannot say how my memories have shaped themselves into these vivid words, though perhaps it was in part due to my education.

Frankenstein, my father, began with the priority of instilling language into me, but the task of my tutelage quickly fell to his friend and assistant, Henry Clerval. Clerval was an expatriate, a Britisher, basking in the social freedom of the Weimar Republic and the going exchange rate. Clerval was a hard tutor, perhaps because he resented me. The more mistakes I made, the more he took pleasure in beating me. But I learned quickly during that period.

I was confined to the cell in which I was born, the outside world a series of voices, clattering noises, and the shadows that fell through the high window of the cellar. This was simply the status quo of my life, something that for weeks (I can only assume) I never questioned. But with my linguistic skills still forming, there was no clear ordinance that I could not leave, and one day, it occurred to me that I could simply walk out the door Clerval and Frankenstein used to manifest out of the universe before me.

I understood there to be more beyond the door, but what? The contours, colours, and sounds – it was beyond my imagination. I entered the streets of Berlin on an early winter's evening, snow churned to a brown slush by pedestrians and black automobiles. But to me, this was euphoria. The streetlights cast orange halos across the buildings. People passed in clusters, eyes downcast, but they could have been God's own angelic chorus – arguing about the rent and debating which nightclub to visit.

I walked and walked, and found my eye drawn to the long skirts and clattering shoes of women. Women! I had never encountered these creatures. Overwhelmed by two polar masculinities, I heard the laugh of a young woman in the night and understood something deep inside me that had no words. I was a human, constructed under a vision, a purpose, but I belonged only to myself.

And I was a woman.

Some drunken louts approached me next, calling out what a fool I must be to go out without a coat or hat in that cold, teasing me for something I had forgotten. For I had been so overwhelmed that until that moment, I had barely noticed the cold except for the delicious sharpness it brought to my lungs. I had almost thought that that was simply how outside air tasted.

But their admonishment called me to my senses – it *was* cold, and now self-aware, I felt a hot sensation creep up from my chest at the eyes that stared around me. Embarrassment. This wasn't my world, I thought, and retreated to the house, startled.

As I crept inside, Clerval was there to meet me.

"And where have you been?" he asked hotly.

"Outside," I replied, and for the first time took note of my voice. It came at a level tone, neuter, without the distinctive depth fuelled by testosterone. I took pleasure in this, which, as usual, Clerval found enraging.

Neuter. German genders its nouns in three ways – masculine, feminine, and neuter. Strange, that the language should give room for that which people will not. That there is more in a human being than the distinctions of anatomy. And anatomy is the definition of what I am. A collection of anatomies. But I've yet to have the opportunity to ask him – Frankenstein – of whom my anatomy consists. Medical experiments, scientific desiccations, certainly, but beyond my own self-ascription, might my heart not be a woman's heart?

Clerval? Yes, well, he left me this scar below my lip. It's hard to see what with the beard, which is lucky given my current profession. A lady is not quite so lady-like with a scar down her cheek. And bearded ladies get enough scrutiny as it is.

I suppose I could have gone with the Manufactured Woman, or the Human Ragdoll. I'm sure it would have got me more clout in the sideshows – there'd be less competition. But it would feel like giving into him.

This scar? The one Clerval gave me? I cherish it. It's the only scar I have that's from my life. From *my* actions. It's a testament to a memory, not an essential part of my construction. Part of my birth, something too private to be on display.

I don't usually give out my life story, the facts don't tend to go over too well. But you're a kind face and I'll be leaving the circus soon. Two weeks. I need to follow my father to Canada.

You see, he abandoned me. Practically immediately. I don't know how he could have spent years on researching this endeavour, months darning me together, only for my first moments of real human life – independence – to strike him with such horror and revulsion. He had become a kind of God, the new Prometheus, only to turn away from his creation.

I think it was a long time coming. From my first moments of life, something addled him, but it wasn't until I made my request that he had the justification of a way. I told him I would be a woman.

Was it me that really disgusted him so much, or himself? He had tried to play God but was foiled by his own creation. Like the Dorsey Brothers' song, *"I can make most anything, but I can't make a man!"* Or did God feel the same way casting Adam and Eve out of Eden? A decision to desert humanity at the first independent gesture, so that Frankenstein might repeat the choice in the circling drain of time?

And so, I entered the world – fatherless, motherless, barely months old and appearing to be as old as the century. The same way I'll always appear. I live, but my tissues haven't aged properly. They simply stay stuck as they have since my creation. The cells must grow, as my muscles continue to work and my skin hasn't all fallen off in the past decade, but I don't age. In fifty years, I'll look more or less the same. If not violently, I don't know how I'll be able to die. I'm the new Dorian Gray, without the painting in the attic. And not quite as pretty.

Thank you, though I said not *quite*.

After that, I made my way in the cabaret, continuing to learn German and gaining a new perspective on being a spectacle. The Germans who couldn't speak English thought I was one of the many British emigrants – the

Germans who *could* assumed I was French. In a way, the cabaret was my saving grace. It also gave me the opportunity to start picking up English, which was a Godsend for emigrating to America as political relations in the homeland soured.

Performing at the Eldorado opened me to a world of what was possible. I learned of Dr. Magnus Hirschfeld and the Scientific Humanitarian Committee. I saw him once give a lecture. They burned his books in the Bebelplatz. I met Dora Richter there and later heard of Lili Elbe. They had surgeries to reassign their sexual organs. So I thought, why not me? I was already an anatomical curiosity. But Germany was changing, and the freedom that we thrived on began to close in. I decided to find my father.

I didn't know where to begin, but as luck would have it, Clerval came in to the club one night and I spoke with him. I don't know if he had changed or whether simply the dynamic of our relationship had changed to make things civil between us. Frankenstein had abandoned him and moved to Switzerland, and perhaps the scientist's betrayal made us comrades. Whatever the reason, he offered to give me Frankenstein's last known address, in Geneva, and when he passed the note to me the next day, even wished me luck on my search for salvation.

I headed out on my journey only a year old, in the dead of winter. I had no birth records, no legal documents or identification, so once I got close to the border, I travelled by foot. Maybe I should have departed in a warmer month, but who knows had I delayed, and I might have lost him. And now, in retrospect, who knows whether I would have been able to leave Germany at all had I waited.

Oh, that cold! We get nothing like it here. It's enough to freeze the blood from your face. My eyelashes became crystalline and the snot ran in rivulets down into my mouth. At least it kept my lips from chapping. This was before I grew the beard.

But in a way, I look fondly on that time. As harsh as it was, my progression felt like a movement towards destiny. And the snow was something other than the snow in the city. In the city, the white could only be pristine for maybe half a day before being tramped into brown mush. But here, between the small towns and the timberland, everything retained its ghostly pallor. Some days, it could be blinding, the immense, reflective sheen of it.

Well, I found Frankenstein in Geneva, but there my luck ran out. He was still the same man.

"Make me a woman," I said. "You owe it to me. You are my creator, and you made me in your own image, but that was an illusion. I will never be your double, I must be myself. You have the power to alter my body. Give me the freedom to be my own woman."

He refused. "You are what I made you. I wish I hadn't made you at all now, but that's how it is. I will not give in to these delusions. I *am* your creator, and for my own freedom of conscience I will not do what you want."

We argued for some time, but his impermeability wore me down. I finally left, defeated, telling him he would regret his choice, but knowing he would not.

I tried to regroup, come up with a plan to convince him. But then he left Geneva too. I scoured the city for information and learned from a haphazard word to a grocer that he was now in America. This pursuit was harder to execute, but I managed it with money slipped to the right sailor.

And so, I arrived in this strange land. My beard had grown out over the trip, and I decided to keep it, become a bearded lady in the circus. What better way to travel the country? I didn't know what state Frankenstein had landed in, after all.

And here we are. But I'll be leaving soon. He's in Canada now. It's almost winter again, and they get winters more like back home. But I can't lose the trail. I have tried to disentangle myself from him, but we are tied together, and I must speak with him again. I still don't know if I can convince him to change me, but I have to try.

Besides, the longer I've been alive, the more I've discovered that even if he won't change my body, I have changed myself. I get confusion, people still call me "sir", but so many people do not question it now. The beard is there, but it is a woman's beard. The punters know it – even people on the street. They see the dress, the hair, the makeup and they start to understand. My name, Rosamund, I chose for myself. Depending who you ask, it means "rose of the world" or else "protection". And I am, I suppose, a rose of this world. Grown from the garden of man.

Yes, I think I'll have another drink.

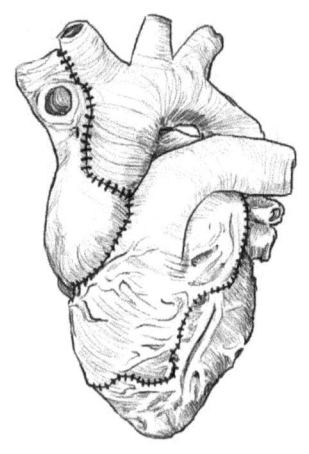

ENOUGH

JENNIFER LEE ROSSMAN

The blood was still wet when the story made the leap from newspapers to movies. Everything from exploitative, gory slasher flicks to more introspective examinations of the brilliant doctor and his fall from grace.

In an instant, the tragedy became something more, a metaphor that storytellers could twist to serve their own purposes. The townsfolk died not at the hands of a monster, but at the latex-gloved hands of science itself, that wretched craft practiced by witches in white coats who sought to squeeze the last bit of life from religion. Or maybe science could have saved them, if only the world had disregarded his methods and let the doctor continue his research.

If you ask the right person, it's a story about abortion. Ask someone else, and it's about the struggle between good and evil waging inside each of us. If you look hard enough, you can probably find someone who thinks it's a story about the importance of lightning rods, but there's always one unifying thread that ties together these disparate narratives.

Whether the doctor is the dangerous man or the sympathetic victim, it's always *his* story.

Not the woman unjustly accused of murder, not the reporter who broke the news of the experiments. Not even the miraculous creations, cobbled together from corpses and given the spark of life.

No, he's managed to steal the spotlight from us all.

It's *his* picture splashed across tabloids and movie posters, *his* name whispered in schoolyards alongside other urban myths. Even his first monster bears his name in the popular imagination.

Maybe it's because he's a white, upper-class man, and that makes him the default hero. Maybe we're just too "Other" to care about, our lives too alien to appeal as anything more than bit characters and plot devices.

I don't know why it happened.

I only know this is *not* his story.

They say he never built me. They say he threw my parts out to the sea, a scene I've seen and read a thousand different versions of. It's the pivotal point, the final betrayal that turns his creation against him.

I don't know who invented that part of the story. Someone who didn't understand that Adam needed no reason to turn against our abusive creator, that the way he treated us, giving us life only to be disgusted when we didn't match his idea of perfection, was reason enough.

Maybe he wanted to throw me away when he saw the way Adam turned out. Undoubtedly, he would have debated the morality of bringing another life into a world that didn't want us in it, but in the end he did anyway.

I am made from the bodies of five women. I don't know where he found them or who they were, but I am not their scars or memories. I am not them. I am me, his Eve, birthed into existence in a thunderstorm summoned by the largest Tesla coil on the eastern seaboard.

He wanted to livestream my awakening to all the media outlets. Only Adam's first rampage spared me my privacy; after that, we had to go dark, hide away from the media.

I think I'm only alive now because no one knew I existed then.

And I'm lucky, if such a word can be used in this context, that the doctor's techniques improved after making Adam. You can hardly see where I've been stitched together, and when people stare, it's more out of curiosity than the outright horror they projected on Adam.

I can walk down the streets of Boston, my adopted hometown, and if I keep my gaze on the pavement and don't look them in the eye, I can pretend they aren't trying to work out what's wrong with me.

But still, I am not equal. There's something about me that isn't good enough, even if no one can put their finger on it. There's something wrong with being the way I am.

My left ankle has a tattoo on it, a little crescent moon. It's my only clue to who she was.

I shouldn't care whose parts he used. I am not them. I shouldn't waste any time thinking about that man and the things he did to me, but it's all I know how to do, care about the expectations of a man who's been dead for months. Everything I do, every skill I learn, somehow it's always for him, to show him that I'm smart and capable and good enough to be worth loving.

Except nothing was ever enough. I had to be better than everyone else, even though my body is too broken and my brain doesn't work the way anyone else's does.

So I look for them. They had lives before they came together to make me; maybe if I find out what they were, my body will remember how to be that again and I'll find my purpose. Be something more than an aimless freak doing odd jobs and scavenging scrap metal to stay alive.

I spend every spare moment at the library in front of a screen, searching for images of my tattoo. It isn't an uncommon design and it feels like I've seen more moons on more ankles than there are people on earth, but then I find it.

On the millionth page of results, it's my ankle. *My* ankle and its moon, *my* big feet that don't like to be squeezed into pretty shoes, *my* olive skin tone that blends awkwardly into the darker brown of my torso.

Her name was Caroline Beaufort, a beautiful young woman with a wide grin and high cheekbones.

I touch my face. Not the same. I'm a patchwork ragdoll.

The article accompanying the photo says she's missing. Disappeared from the parking lot where she worked just a few days before I was born.

Maybe she had an accident. Maybe he just found her body after she was already dead. It doesn't have to mean he killed her to make me.

For the first time since I've been living on my own, I feel the beginnings of hope fluttering in my chest. She had a life once, a happy one. Maybe I can, too.

I don't like taking the bus. All the routes and numbers jumble in my brain and people stare at me as I drag my clumsy feet down the aisle. But if it gets me downtown, to that little brick building with the parking lot where she disappeared, I can put up with a few stares.

We used to live in a laboratory, Adam, the doctor, and I. It was dark, full of steel instruments and disembodied limbs, but it's this cheery building with its sunny windows that twists my gut with fear, and I stand here helplessly as the bus roars away.

I must stand here for a long time, because someone eventually comes out to check on me. An older woman, blonde, with a string of pearls at her throat.

"Can I help you with something, dear?"

I recognize her from Caroline's social media. One of her coworkers. I glance down to make sure my pants cover my ankle while I try to find my voice.

The words slip from my grasp like sand. The harder I grab, the finer the grains become. I need to collect them; I can't just stand here soundlessly moving my mouth forever, but they just slip away.

His voice haunts me, flashbacks of the days after I awoke. Cameras in my face, that infernal red light flashing impatiently.

"You know this," he says, trying to sound encouraging. I can hear the underlying frustration. "You're learning faster than Adam did, but no one will believe us if you don't show them."

I did know it. I'd been studying Hamlet every waking minute, trying to fill my brain with its poetry. I should have been able to recite every scene by heart.

But when he pressed me, it disappeared. I didn't know the speech he wanted, and the more I tried and failed, the harder it was to find the information.

This woman is more patient than he ever was, and I manage to find some words. Not exactly the ones I want, but they do the job.

"I knew Caroline Beaufort."

Understanding turns her face dark for a moment, but she forces it to brighten again. "Was she your case worker?"

I don't know what that means, but I nod.

"My name is Mary Waldman. We were all very sad when Caroline disappeared, and I've taken over most of her cases. Do you want to come in?"

I nod again and follow her inside. She must see my dragging feet, the way I clumsily grab the door handle with more force than is needed, but she doesn't stare or comment. When we're inside, I see why.

This place is made to help people like me.

Not monsters. Maybe there are other scientists bending science to their will out there, but I doubt it.

I think I'm the only monster.

But the people here, seated around tables in a big, colourful room, they're so much like me that it hurts. I'm not alone.

Some hold markers with awkward hands, others walk with unique gaits that must get them laughed at elsewhere. They talk with impediments, or by pointing at boards, or not at all. For the first time, I see the struggle from the outside.

"What... what are they?" I whisper. It sounds rude to my ears, like I'm separating them from other people, but I need to know. If they aren't monsters, maybe neither am I.

Mary tells me they have developmental disabilities, that they learn slower or have trouble accessing information. Some of them have bodies that don't work the way they 'should.'

It's like I'm hearing a song for the first time, but I know all the words by heart.

She says the workers here, people like Caroline, help people like me reach our potential. I'm not sure if I qualify as disabled the way she thinks I do. There's no disease or condition; I was just built wrong.

But I'm not a monster to these people. I am not a shadow of the man who killed and reanimated in a dark lab, nor a reflection of his creation who rebelled against his creator's hatred and wreaked violence in the streets.

I am not a tragedy, not a lingering warning to count their blessings.

I am just me, and that is enough for them.

I stand before a room of people and can't help but think of the presentations Adam gave in the beginning.

The doctor paraded him through the scientific community, making him recite poetry and lauding even his most minor accomplishments.

"See the way he ties his shoes?" he would say. "Even though his hands came from two different donors, even though I had to completely rework his nerves, he is as dexterous as a skilled surgeon!"

I remember watching the videos when they came home, hearing the spectators ask probing questions, seeing the enthusiasm drain from Adam's face as they dehumanized him by directing their questions at the doctor. Because no matter how he proved himself capable and intelligent, it was never enough to make him equal in their eyes.

Is it any wonder that when he finally snapped, they put him down like a dog, without so much as a trial?

I tell myself this is different, that these are kind people with good intentions. But still my mind replays those videos, those panels full of curious eyes, and I can't help but draw parallels to the people who started his descent into hatred, who first told that beautiful soul that he wasn't worthy of their world.

Mary's looking at me expectantly. Did she ask me something?

I grab the edge of the table so no one can see my hands tremble.

Noticing my confusion, Mary gently says, "I asked you to tell them what we've helped you with since we've been working together."

"Oh. I work now." That didn't come out right. Someone giggles at the simplicity of my words. "A steady job. I sweep up at a pet store."

"Do you like working?" Mary asks.

Do I like it? I love it. I'm earning money, paying rent. I'm self-sufficient and, for the first time since the doctor died, I know I'll be sleeping somewhere safe every night.

But those words don't come out of my mouth. No words do. I just give a little nod, still unsure why I'm here. What can I possibly teach new employees that isn't covered in orientation?

Some of their smiles get a little wider, a little less sincere. Do they... do they pity me?

A man raises his hand. "Do you want to go to college?"

"No."

I didn't think there could be a wrong answer to that question, but I have found one. The atmosphere in the room turns darker, spotlights shining bright in my face.

"A college education can be enlightening," Mary points out. "You can learn new things, meet people..."

I stare at my fingernails. "I can do that on my own."

"Of course, but college —"

Is a bigger room full of more people to judge me and put a value on my knowledge.

"—is an amazing experience. Wouldn't you want to get a degree?"

"No."

"But you could get a better job."

"I like my job. I like the animals. The, um, the rabbits." It's another wrong answer.

"A degree would be such a great accomplishment for you."

An accomplishment they could brag about, I realize.

Look at the monster, they'll say. See how deformed her body is, the way her hands bend funny and her foot drags. Hear her struggle to speak.

But look at her now. Educated. We did that. We took this abomination, this wretched waste of limbs, and turned her into something better. Something more normal, more like us.

I'm their Eliza Doolittle. They're parading me around high society and making themselves the heroes for it.

Just like with Adam and the doctor, I am not the main character in my own story.

They're looking at me again, and I have no earthly idea what they asked. My brain locks up and Mary answers for me.

"It can be tempting to assume disabled people are unintelligent," Mary says, "or that you need to talk down to them. But once you get to know someone like Eve and you see how bright and funny she is, hopefully you'll feel more comfortable talking to her."

I have to stop and make sure I heard her right.

We're only worth respecting if we can prove it? If we're smarter than they think we are, or if we accomplish things they think are important?

The words don't hide this time. They leap to the front of my mind and fly out of my mouth, and I'm not only talking to the people in the room with me.

"If you need to get to know someone before you can be decent to them, you are in the wrong profession. You're supposed to be helping us."

I see his face, his frown deepening as he compared me to eloquent, graceful Adam who was still not good enough.

"It isn't fair to say some people are better because of what they can do. I am smart. I can talk. I learn slower and my words... my words get lost sometimes, but that doesn't make me less than you and it doesn't make me better than the people who can't talk or who need more help to do things."

I'm not just talking to the people in the room with me, but I might not be talking to the doctor, either.

"Not everyone needs to do things. Some people can't, others just don't want to, and you shouldn't make them feel bad about it."

The doctor is dead. I saw Adam kill him. But the ghost of his teachings haunts my thoughts, tainting the way I see the world.

"It is enough to be happy. To exist in a society that accepts your strengths and your limitations, accepts your goals for yourself and doesn't hold you up to an impossible standard."

I think I'm talking to myself.

"It is enough to live your best life without having to show off for others."

I pause here for effect, because it's my story and I get to tell it any way I want.

I came here looking for purpose.

I don't know if I have one. I only know that I don't need a purpose to be worthy of having this body and these limbs that other people died to give me.

Part of me wants to storm out of here, but not the part of me that used to be Caroline, the part that dedicated her life to helping people. That part, not just my ankle with the little moon tattoo, but a piece of my heart, too, knows nothing will change if I leave.

People will still act like we're less than. They'll still turn themselves into heroes and us into monsters.

So, I take a shaky breath and sit back down to help people. And when I'm done here, I'll find the source of the rest of my patchwork pieces and finish the work they started.

And maybe that's purpose enough.

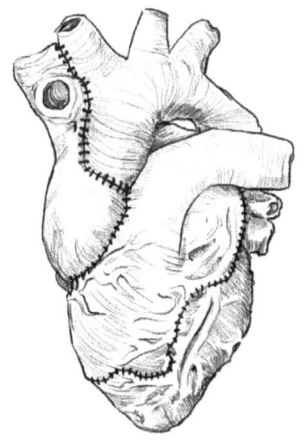

SINS OF THE FATHER

RANDALL G. ARNOLD

Entry 1

I compose this initial entry clumsily, enjoying the limited use of a single functioning hand. In doing so I offer silent thanks to the unnamed attendant, who this morning provided a fresh journal and pen. Since it will surely aid both you and I, dear unknown reader, I shall describe everything.

My dim quarters are sparsely appointed: inhabited by myself, this modest bed, a small dresser, and a bare book case. Not even a mirror for grooming. Perhaps, though, I am not ready yet to see what a reflection might reveal.

The creeping sun fashions an otherwise forbidding corner into a spectacle of dazzling dust particles that dance like drunken faeries. I find I can track time's passage as the faery cloud advances across the stone floor.

I understand I have languished in this sanitarium many months yet am only dimly aware of the past few days. I know that I dream but awaken with no clear recollection of each experience. Faint wisps of old memory taunt me, however, daring enough to loom tantalizingly close but fearful enough to flee when I reach. My memories are filled with overbold images, scents, and sounds that seem quite at odds with this dark arctic room.

I find myself incapable of speech and limited in limb movement. The bearded physician who examined me yesterday assured that I have made astonishing progress. But I spied trouble in the eyes behind his spectacles, eyes that widened with every glance at the soiled bandaging around my joints.

Who am I?

Entry 2

Imagine this: the attendant who gifted me this virgin journal has a name! He is Lucius of Italy, first-year nursing student. I feel fortunate indeed to have drawn the watch of this compassionate soul.

His face bears the ruddy stigma of some unfortunate mishap, perhaps childhood scarring from a fire, yet his heart appears untouched by trauma. Lucius asserts there is no work under the sun's glory for one with such a twisted appearance, so he toils gladly in this dreary establishment. How many unblemished folks can likewise boast?

I am blessed by his good company. I can only imagine what horrors abound in other rooms, for I have heard echoed screams at awful hours, awakening me just as I begin to grasp at my own phantoms.

A rather rude German orderly visits twice a day and takes care of unspeakable business. I suppose that were I resigned to such duties, I would be similarly sour.

As for my wretched condition, here is what I have been told and can observe:

An experimental treatment supposedly saved my extremities from certain hypothermia, of indeterminate origin. Outside of ailments I have already described, I seem in fair shape. My hands feel foreign, but that may simply be delirium. The left responds poorly, the right somewhat better. I have also been receiving opium injections as a solution to earlier hysterics. These, I am told, will now be tapered off.

The young nurse also reports that I was discovered prone on the stoop of this institution, outfitted as a seaman and clutching an old mariner's timepiece.

So, who then, am I that I find the obnoxious orderly's work so beneath me?

Would a simple sailor be so aloof?

Entry 3

Last night I dreamt I had been sleeping, jolted alert to behold a large, horrid figure at my bedside. It parted the bed curtains and peered upon me with yellow, watery, but speculative eyes. I ventured a scream of terror, but no sound issued from my frozen throat!

The creature resembled a man, but only in the most remote manner! Its tremendous mass consumed the space of the room, draping over me as a mother vulture would one of its chicks. I clumsily worked myself back from its scrutiny, but suddenly thick leather restraints appeared, and I found the bed had become a gurney. The foul intruder stroked my quivering cheek with an almost maternal caring, but I sensed great danger in its twisted hands.

My fear proved all too reasonable. The great hulking beast retrieved a scalpel and set to cutting at the flesh of my thighs. I was horrified to see that my legs ended at bloody knee joints, and ere his work concluded, I would lose even more!

The monster's eyes glowed, and its fetid breath assaulted my senses. It accused me of unspeakable evil as it exchanged surgical knife for saw and began to roughly hew at my right femur. The pain was unspeakable! Repeatedly I fought for the ability to scream, cruelly denied each time.

Just as I could endure no more, I awoke in the real sense, gasping for air and not finding enough. I must have caused a considerable disturbance, for Lucius and the ill-mannered orderly entered into my room in a panic. Lucius barked orders at the reluctant servant, who could not possibly have moved slower. Within seconds of their entry, however, Lucius had me propped up against the bed's headboard and the orderly eventually managed to shove the single window open to admit the evening air.

When he was satisfied that I was calm, and breathing, Lucius made the orderly shut the stubborn window and leave. My devoted nurse fetched a glass of water and watched anxiously as I sipped.

I do not recall falling asleep again afterward, nor any further disturbing dreams, but soon enough morning returned bringing intense hunger. The thin soup they provide will no longer suffice, I told myself, and knowing that Lucius will read this I feel certain he will pass it along.

Entry 4

I am increasingly overcome with ennui now that I am regaining strength and some clarity of thought. Thus, I was overjoyed when Lucius inquired if I played chess. His capricious smile at my furrowed countenance simply proved that he was testing, seeing if my memory was returning. I shrugged, then tore the back page from this journal and wrote something to the effect of "It would please me to try."

Grinning impishly, Lucius vanished and shortly returned, propelling a tanned, elderly gentleman by way of a wheeled chair.

"This is Tomás St. Angel," he announced, "once world-renown chess player. He could ascertain your playing ability, if any."

There followed a delightful day of discovering that, yes, I do know the game! Alas, I am not in the class of M. St. Angel. Still, I was confident that by the third bout he found me worthy, for he would nod at some moves and even gasp at others!

By the fifth round, however, I was shaking badly and capitulated ere the game was over. My new friend expressed surprise, and embarrassed by my persistent infirmities, I angrily upended the chessboard with my one working hand. The orderly flew in at the commotion, chastising me in that harsh German accent while apologizing profusely to M. St. Angel.

I was truly mortified by my childish reaction. A chance to earn friendship and I terrify the man! I further spited myself by refusing to acknowledge Lucius when he brought an acceptable dinner. O, human pride, what a stiff noose thou dost form! And I, eager wretch, so willingly drape it 'round my weakened neck!

Perhaps, in some aberrant way, I want the creature of my dreams to end my life before I discover what a truly horrible man I must be.

Entry 5

Yesterday, still discomfited by my churlish outburst, I elected to wallow in self-anointed misery. Again, I shut Lucius out, despite his patience and kindness. I stared coolly at the orderly, who had taken notice of the fact that I can now sit erect. Surely he would heed my rapidly recharging vigour, as I stand a good head taller than he and am in all ways physical his obvious superior! I feel confident he will heap no further abuse upon me.

The point, if I may arrive at it, is that I asked to be placed into a wheeled chair, and spent the morning staring out at the garden. Across the vast lawn gamboled all sorts of lunatics; some battling imaginary dragons, others dancing with invisible partners, and still others gawking at nothing.

I busied myself with diagnosing their disorders, as if I were some prestigious physician instead of a madman myself. I marvelled at how easily the terms came, but how could I be certain that what I thought I knew was correct?

Perhaps it was like chess, where the moves came without conscious thought behind them. If so, how had I acquired this knowledge? It did not fit with my original attire, unless: ship's doctor? Assigned to a royal fleet? Ha! Delusions of grandeur now. I shall be some celebrated general ere nightfall.

So focussed was I on the main characters that I almost failed to notice one of a solitary nature, more secluded even than the German. He leaned against a pole of some sort. I could make out no face, nor any other features worthy of mention; only a massive, stooped build could be determined of this man in the shadows.

On occasion, one employee would elbow another, and cock his head toward the eaves where the mystery man reposed. They were aware of the presence. Who, then, was he?

I struggled to rise from my chair, then rang for Lucius, who entered warily. Feeling ashamed of my previous behaviour, I scribbled an apology on the back of the other day's note. Lucius immediately beamed and asked what I might need. When I pointed to the window, he nodded cheerfully, and in a matter of seconds he was wheeling me through the asylum's dreary halls and out to the inner garden. Once there, I searched the shadows for the unknown giant, and found him not far from his last noted spot.

I recognized now that the pole was actually the handle of a long spade. The mystery employee laboured amongst a collection of graves, digging at unturned earth.

I made some excuse to Lucius about wanting to more closely view the trees of that small plot, and he obligingly carted me over. We were not a stone's throw from my quarry when an indescribable dread overtook me. The figure, at first facing north, began slowly turning my way. Before his face was revealed, I fainted away — or so Lucius explained when I regained awareness in bed. He attributed the spell to renewed weakness and had urged the head doctor to drop his frequent research and examine me on the morrow.

I believe I am at a cusp in recovery. Dare I explore further, with suspicions of some sordid undertaking emergent in my thoughts?

Entry 6

Dr. Jorgenson seems a decent man, though impoverished of the empathy one would hope to find in any physician. He appears to care more about what he may discover (and publish, no doubt) than what bedevils his anguished patient.

The doctor performed psychological tests purporting to illuminate hidden aspects of an amnesiac's mentality. I found these to be rather tedious but went along for his sake. Jorgenson was so absorbed in examining the results that he completely ignored my presence, even going so far as to comment on me in the third person. Amazingly enough, I understood his assessment!

A nurse drew vials of blood from my arm, but Jorgenson brushed off my scribbled inquiries regarding tests.

He returned his attention to me after an hour's passage and began relating the circumstances of my arrival. As Lucius noted, I was discovered unconscious at the establishment's entrance, barely alive and bleeding, reduced to a mere skeleton of a man. As strength returned, I began raving hysterically with no sign of cessation; thus, the opium treatment.

I inquired about the itching beneath my bandages. At this, Jorgenson paled, and mumbled again about some experimental approach to hypothermia recovery, but I could see and hear that for an utter lie.

He echoed Lucius's description of my original outfit, then extracted the watch from his desk and handed it to me. I marvelled at the exquisite construction, then opened the case. Inscribed on the inside of the hinged cover were these words:

To my brother Robert, may this keep you on course. Love, Margaret.

Sensing my puzzlement, Jorgenson spoke. "I suspect you are a naturalist by trade. Possibly you fell afoul of a treacherous crew and were set adrift. How you arrived upon these shores is yet a mystery. However, knowing your given name and that of a sister may aid in your identification. Does this bring back any memory?"

I shook my head. The name Robert seemed familiar enough but did not feel like mine. Yet as I dwelled on the matter, I realized there had been a faceless woman in my dreams, one who evoked strong feelings of longing. Was it this 'Margaret'?

I chose not to pursue that thought further at the time. Changing the subject, I inquired of the unusual man I had almost accosted. Was he inmate or attendant?

My doctor seemed distracted, his eyes wandering over the ceiling, then his countenance clouded and he regarded me with exaggerated surprise.

"The new janitor! Yes, a rather large and strange-looking fellow. He came to us some time before your own arrival, seeking employment. His usefulness cannot be overstated; I myself have never seen a man of his strength! His bodily appearance is unfortunate, but in here such things take on little import... particularly for such a role."

I could only nod in mute agreement. Then his expression took on unexpected softness.

"Let's move past Robert and Margaret for a moment. Who is Elizabeth?" He handed me a leather-bound notebook. "Here, enter your response in this."

Elizabeth! Somehow that name better fit the lass of my nightly hauntings. But again, I kept some confidence from the physician, as if we were engaged in our own little chess game.

I do not know, was all I could struggle to compose, and that much was true. *Why?*

"It is the only name you've ever mentioned," he replied after retrieving the book. "You called it out multiple times during fever dreams. I assume someone close, based on your anguish. If we knew more... we could perhaps locate your family."

Unable to do more than shrug, I was summarily dismissed. Jorgenson reduced my opium allowance in recognition of my progress. I will be thankful to be off the damned drug altogether, as I am convinced it is the source of my wicked thoughts and visions.

Entry 7

Today I arose to the sight of a bookshelf newly laden. Lucius had secured for my pleasure many scholarly tomes of various origins and topics. Prominent amongst them stood collective works of a gentleman named Milton, which inexplicably piqued my curiosity.

The contents first divulged an epic poem entitled *Paradise Lost*. I was at once entranced by its mournful beauty, its tragic tale of sinful man's unwitting separation from his Maker. But a specific passage shook me to my leaden core, and I have taken the liberty to copy it, thus:

> If thou beest he; But O how fall'n! how chang'd
> From him, who in the happy Realms of Light

Cloth'd with transcendent brightnes didst outshine
Myriads though bright: If he whom mutual league,
United thoughts and counsels, equal hope,
And hazard in the Glorious Enterprize,
Joynd with me once, now misery hath joynd
In equal ruin: into what Pit thou seest
From what highth fal'n, so much the stronger provd
He with his Thunder: and till then who knew
The force of those dire Arms? yet not for those
Nor what the Potent Victor in his rage
Can else inflict do I repent or change.

I cannot say what in the work arouses me, but it lies within the confines of this excerpt. Does explanation dwell in the sorrow of the complainant, or in some possibly irrelevant phrasing? How greatly am I vexed by this irony, commingled deceit, and revelation! Am I simply that dull, or am I correct to lay the blame upon the opium deemed so necessary to my recovery? Surely I can proceed without it now, although I have been warned against what ill effects befall those who elect to cease its use abruptly.

I suddenly find myself questioning the entire regimen. I am, after all, a scavenged man in a Scottish sanitarium, refuge of the most ruined. Had I inflicted my bizarre injuries upon myself? Was I deemed a madman upon arrival, and thus consigned to be drugged into perpetual stupor? Certainly, Jorgenson has agreed to reduce the dosage... but to how great a significance?

My mind reels at the accelerating implications. I may very well be the victim of some nefarious plot, one that began with an incident that first stole my memories. Am I to be robbed of more worldly possessions as well? Does the doctor seek my family for purpose of extortion?

I doubt if good Lucius could partake in such evil, but the hateful orderly seems a likely culprit, as well as Jorgenson himself. Perhaps I was a competitor to the illustrious physician, and my retention here his way of stealing a greater glory! Jorgenson has confessed to experimental treatment upon my person — how fortunate to conduct it in a remote mental ward, where any victim's voice would fall upon deaf ears!

How much madness can I ascribe to the opium, and what portion can I accept as harsh reality? I have delved too deeply into philosophy since those blasphemous books were brought to me; the abstract rationales of long-dead logicians discolour my thinking.

God in heaven, how I am tormented!

Entry 8

No one must be allowed to view these pages from this point forward. For after yesterday's entry, I suffered an encounter with the mysterious handyman that only adds fuel to an already burgeoning fire.

Lucius had come this morning bearing food and medication. I found myself of strangely low appetite, and even lower desire to continue as the blood-pumping receptacle of some mad scientist's dastardly endeavour.

Exasperated by my stubbornness, Lucius offered to escort me again to the garden. Given my deteriorating condition, he had brought a wheeled chair and joked about fainting spells. I scowled in mock consternation at his playful comment, and then allowed myself to be eased into it.

The halls were being thankfully cleansed, and Lucius made a game of closely skirting the swinging mops. I had never seen such a crew; many were in fact dully-garbed residents, led by custodial staff and watched over by a few attendants. Most were amused at Lucius's efforts and made sport of swabbing at my chair as we dodged them. I was having a merry time indeed till I witnessed *him* again.

The frame was unmistakable, dwarfing the average man, and yet surprisingly nimble for that girth. The brute was making twice the progress as his peers and saw no amusement in Lucius's play. In fact, as we approached the cloaked figure, a chill settled over the two of us and Lucius slowed our progress. In sudden panic, I jerked my aching right arm up, and groped shakily back for the nurse's sleeve. Lucius bent and peered into my face, simultaneously confused and concerned. I jabbed my finger back toward my own room, indicating my strong desire to return. Lucius sighed, shrugged, and pivoted me about.

But not before I caught a glimpse of ochre-hued eyes burning in the cloak hood's darkened recess.

Entry 9

I expected to have no entry for this day, so little transpired. My right arm aches and shakes terribly as well. But Lucius burst into my room this evening, visibly distraught. He had been keeping something from me, he said, that he could withhold no longer.

He has witnessed Jorgenson and the janitor in deep, furtive conversation on more than one occasion, including earlier today in the doctor's office. Lucius barged in on them inadvertently, looking to get Jorgenson's approval on some matter. He told me he caught the doctor bemoaning the state of my limbs and describing a need for further surgery upon me. Surgery that would require a new donor.

Most of all, the young attendant confessed to being frightened to his foundation by the strange labourer's leaden gaze.

Before I could ask for an explanation, Lucius rushed from the room after this revelation, leaving me with little solid information but much to mull.

I am now quite concerned for his safety, and I know not why.

I can say no more today.

Entry 10

Lucius is gone.

Had I a voice, I would howl at the heavens!

I was not informed directly. I overheard orderlies discuss his mysterious disappearance whilst they loitered outside my cracked door. O, how my heart plummeted at the news! The one soul I trusted with any secret...

I had begun to consider Lucius like a son. I wish I could have corrected his scars. Would that I might exchange lives with him! Gladly would I bear the burden of his disfigurement for another chance at life, especially now that he was free.

But what if he had not escaped on his own volition?

Would it not make sense for plotters to rid themselves of the singular person who stood to aid me in any enterprise? As reluctant as I may be to accede to paranoia, too many pieces are falling into place! Yet, is that not absurdly convenient, as well? Ah, more stress upon my fragile mind! Exaggerated by confines of this room, which I simply must abandon.

I may or may not scribble further in this journal... I have yet to decide. The only decision that comes easily now is the one to withdraw. I shall take my food but entertain no company save my own.

A final thing to note: I had been regaining strength in my legs, but it has become dreadfully obvious recently that the original repair did not hold. According to another nurse, I am to be soon prepared for another operation.

Entry 11

Earlier, weary of my own trepidation and longing for the sun's warmth, I managed to limp to the window. I flung wide the curtains and was immediately greeted again with the fearsome visage of that jaundiced monstrosity, peering in from the walk! It simply lurked there, unmoving and unperturbed, as I struggled to refrain from fainting. Its dispassionate gaze taunted me to the marrow, blending my bones into jelly! I could do nothing but stare back in abject horror, gravitated toward the vision like a lemming to its fall.

When finally able to move again, the best I could manage was a backward drunken stagger, groping rearward for any means of support. Finding nothing, I collapsed to the floor, where I was discovered unknown hours later by two orderlies assigned to escort me to the doctor.

Jorgenson refused to say much, but his eyes revealed everything as he checked my arms and legs. I had been getting better afore now, but his reaction spoke the worst. In the brighter light of his office, I could see that my left hand appeared as blue as it was weak, and I foresaw its eventual loss.

I couldn't see my withered legs beneath gown and bandages, but I felt their betrayal.

Strangely, I cared little for my own condition in that moment. I yearned to press the doctor about Lucius. The abrupt disappearance, yes, but also the lad's last words to me. Further surgery? Donor?

What might Jorgenson have in mind, aside from amputation?

I was returned to my quarters, and subsequently allowed myself to succumb to growing depression. I convinced myself that writing might help. When I opened this journal, I noticed a loose page overlooked prior. Not of my own book however, but from that of another. I shall reproduce the content:

My dearest Margaret,

I write this in afterthought, for I cannot lie to you.

In previous pages, I related to you a tale so bizarre I would scarce believe it myself had I not witnessed its evidence firsthand. But in closing I deliberately employed a falsehood, in order to find fitting closure for this terrible travesty against God and Nature. That act was meant for the general public, should you so choose to reveal it. But it has troubled me since, and I must now correct it for your sake or go mad from guilt. You may share the other pages as you wish, but I implore you to keep this one confident!

The truth of the matter is that the creature did not set off alone on an ice floe as I claimed. Instead, I allowed it to remain on board, where it insisted on packing its creator's remains in Arctic ice so as to preserve the body... to what end I do not wish to know.

Once free of our foundering, we plan to sail first upon the creature's request to one of the Orkney Islands, allowing it to disembark with the doctor's boxed body still encased in ice.

That will be the end of my involvement in this horrid matter, praise God. Either way, I will speak no more of it.

I pray that, despite its morbid nature, this letter finds you in good health, and I hope to see you soon.

Your loving brother,

Robert

I can only assume poor Lucius lifted this from Jorgenson's folder, and slipped it into my journal before disappearing. I somehow neglected to discover it earlier. How it failed to reach its target, and wound up here, I know not. But whatever can this mean?! Again, the names Robert and Margaret, along with references to a ship. The mention of Orkney stirs something, but I cannot yet grasp it.

And the creature. If Lucius was correct, then it is the handyman himself who haunts me. But what foul deeds are so far implied? Burning motes swarm in my mind's eye, pining in vain for a place to land!

Entry 12

Another dream, another night fraught with scenes I cannot bear to revisit. Yet I must share this while I am able!

I found myself busy before a large table, in a dim-lit room occupied with more books and instruments than any ten laboratories. I recognized some of the books from my own shelf here; works by Cornelius Agrippa alongside the King James Bible. An oxymoronic blasphemy!

I could not make out at first just what project I laboured to resolve, as there lay a large curtain draped over everything that I could not completely remove. Yet the act possessed an all-too-strange familiarity, as if it were more memory than mind play.

Then the terror. I suddenly found that one object in the room had become a mop, and at that moment a giant severed hand flew through the curtain folds to seize it! I wrestled with the hand, long enough to note that crude scars orbited its wrist, as if the hand had at one time been severed and reattached to its mount!

With a cry of revulsion, I released my grip, only to see the janitor emerge from the pile of cloth, yellow eyes burning into me with the fury of twin suns. Just as the monster approached, it began disassembling before my very eyes! Soon it was nothing more than a pile of wet, dreadful parts upon the floor, those hateful eyes still glowing like damned coals... its grotesque mouth shaping sounds I could not at first make out! Slowly, understanding crept upon me, and I recoiled at that perception.

"*Reconstruisez moi,*" the black lips moaned pitiably in French, and then in English, "put things a-right, my Maker. Rehabilitate thine instrument, as the instrument itself has done for thee. Else forfeit all claim thou hast on thine own life."

"I know not of what you claim!" I cried. "I am a simple scholar, nothing more, I am not God!"

A leering grin stretched across that unholy visage, furthering my disgust. "As easily as thou dost dispense with my being, O Maker, dost thou adroitly shrug off ownership of thine unholy actions. It is for that very reason I twice enacted revenge upon thee, and in turn thee upon me. Hast thou so completely forgotten thy beloved Elizabeth? Her neck so white and soft and fragile! Ah, there is glimmer of recognition. Yes, her untimely end came at these unwelcome hands, channeling thine original sin!

"I had thought my purpose near-complete with thy demise, and indeed thought then to seek mine own end, yet a greater notion seized me, compelled me return to thy deathbed for nobler purpose. I, the Adam of thy unholy labours, dared to mimic my Maker and roll back the stone of death!

"Once restored, thou escaped, and I spent long months searching for thee. Now here thou doth stand, victorious over death, and I lie undone at thy feet. This moment is where irony and horror intermingle, dearest creator, and the divination of each is difficult indeed."

At that, instant realization struck me: *this is just another nightmare.* "Be gone, foul creature, I'll suffer this madness no longer! I am not he whom you seek; look elsewhere for your revenge. I have died myself, and been birthed anew, and I will not easily submit to the likes of you!"

The rolling head laughed, a mechanical emittance that rattled my bones! "Aye, twice resurrected thou may well be, but thou canst not cast off accountability as easily as thou dost identity, my creator. Yet if thou wert but to repent, I might be wont to allow you continued life.

"After all, I employed copies of thine own notes to restore thee. Do not thy hands feel foreign? Thy legs twitch like traitors? Thy tell-tale heart pound hard now with unfamiliar rhythm?

"O, I learned well from thee, my fallen father. Surrounded thy lifeless form with ice and ferried thee to safe haven, where I could employ thy last laboratory with a willing accomplice and enact poetic justice! And behold the result: better than thine own, for memory comes crawling back to thee as mine own would not. The work of the made exceeds that of the Maker!

"So join with us, help us to create a woman like unto myself as I beseeched thee before. After all, is that not next on God's agenda?"

I shuddered woefully, even recognizing this to be another foul dream. "Fiend!" I shouted at the disembodied thing. "You are completely mad!"

"Did I request thee, Maker, from my clay to mould me man? Did I solicit thee from darkness to promote me?'"

I gasped. An exact quote from *Paradise Lost*!

"Even were I possessed of such alchemical knowledge, I would participate in no such evil! Nor shall I ever humble myself before the misbegotten likes of you. Again, I say: begone!"

The disparate pieces drew back together with blinding speed, and once more the monster hovered over me. Once more I shook from fear in spite of my pathetic attempt at bravado, as the creature cursed me with a voice lower than hell,

"Then prepare for the completion, my creator and tormentor, of our unique *Dance Macabre*."

I came to full awareness drenched in sweat, coughing almost soundlessly, startled to see the door open and a silver serving tray newly placed on the bedside table. Was the experience more than a dream? Had the encounter actually occurred, with me in but a semi-conscious, opium-addled state that only now began to fade?

Entry 13

To any who chance across this cursed journal:

I naturally failed to write while lying in renewed drug-fed stupor. The God who abandoned me has finally seen fit to lift the curtain of fog. And I believe I owe it to you now, dear reader, to know all and learn from dread transgressions that now stand wholly revealed.

The final nightmare was my tortured mind's translation of another surgery, another solution for my deterioration courtesy of the mad Dr. Jorgenson and his terrible assistant. And when recovering, upon spying a silver serving tray, I had somehow lifted myself to discern its contents.

Nothing physical rested upon it, just the distorted reflection of a pained visage. The face of a terrified young nurse, his sad life cut horribly short; his bare, flat brow finely circumscribed by new sutures.

His expression twisted by fire and furor.

Surely these blood-stained stitches are the handiwork of one well-experienced, and not the clumsy efforts of some misshapen giant. Surely the creature may have provided materials and guidance, but someone of supernormal medical expertise performed the hellish labour. One who, when my replacement limbs began to fail, deposited my salvaged brain into a newly-purloined body, and worked the galvanic magic derived from my own ungodly experimentation!

Would he later be willing to destroy his own doomed creation? Coerced by mounting guilt to hate his work, his world, himself?

Ah, but have *I* not?

As you read this, assuming I have not been discovered dead within its walls, I have fled this grave institution. I know not where I shall go, but do not search after me. In my wake lie only wreck and ruin.

You will discover the gruesome janitor to be absent as well, I suspect. He will certainly drop his grave-robbing duties here and follow after me, lusting for my continued torment. I could end my life, but I cannot escape this debt so easily. I doomed my blasphemous creation to a tragic, fringe existence, and I deserve no better — particularly since we are now brothers in blasphemy.

My fate shall be to wander the wretched extremes of earthly purgatory, unearned scars apparent, dutifully paying my penance. If the patchwork gargoyle chooses at some point to end my life, so be it. I shall welcome the fires of hell. What is life, after all, without my cherished Elizabeth? Mine till death only?

When I go, I pray the abomination joins me without delay.

Finally, a more specific entreaty:

Dr. Jorgenson, you have studied my abominable projects extensively and, with the aid of the miserable fiend, have come to understand by what means I stole the fire of the gods. Come, doctor: from personal experience I know you have spent many feverish moments in my old Orkney lab, loitering over prize remnants of dead inmates, preparing for the ultimate blasphemy. Do not, in heaven's name, continue replicating the crimes of myself or my creation. Let the rib of Adam lie! There is no respite for any who dare trespass God's domain, no end to this fateful waltz once begun.

If the creature is allowed a mate, I fear for mankind's future.

Consider yourselves all warned.

Regards,

Victor Frankenstein

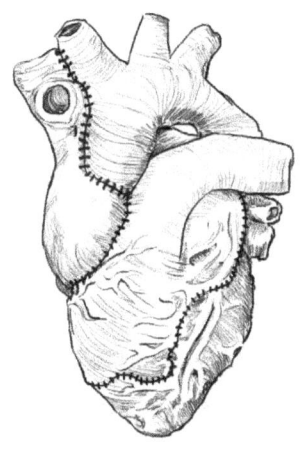

I, IGOR

LIAM HOGAN

"Ice," the mad scientist cried, "I need more ice!"

Dr. Viktor Frankenstein dashed the empty bucket to the floor. The clang that reverberated from the towering walls of the laboratory would have woken the dead, were the dead *that* easy to revive. He tore at his unkempt mane of lank, black hair and ran gibbering from the room. I wasn't sure where he was headed, nor indeed why; our ice came from cellars deep beneath our feet. Perhaps he was confused as it was I, Igor, who gathered such supplies and that was the arrangement I preferred. The cellars contained… other things.

With a sigh, I began to clean up the stinking mess his experiments always created.

Viktor did not think to ask how we had ice in the height of summer. Not that 1816 was giving us much in the way of a July; the days were dismal and grey, the nights unseasonably cold. But not that cold. No doubt he assumed we had an old well or insulated store room down there, packed tight with Lake Geneva ice during the long winter months. He did not pay attention to such mundane details. That too, was the way I preferred.

We had ice because our ice was freshly made, using an ingenious contrivance of bellows and compressed gases. A machine of my own design, of my construction. It was powered by a wind turbine attached to the very top of the tower that crested Family Frankenstein's faux 'castle'. A tower built to afford one of Viktor's more vain ancestors a distant view of the lake — on a clear day, until the trees reclaimed the slopes that stood the mile between the gloomy, lopsided villa and the shores of Lake Geneva. The tower now contained Frankenstein's scientific workshop: a folly within a folly, for all that I made good use of the extra height. But, when the days were becalmed and the turbine lay still, I was forced to manually crank the device until my misshapen body ached. But on and on I cranked: there was a room below that must be kept frozen. The ice was a by-product, with plenty to spare for Viktor's ghoulish experiments.

Not that it did him or the slabs of grey meat he laboured over any good. Ice merely delayed the decay; it could not prevent it and it certainly couldn't turn foul-smelling brain mush back into healthy, firm, functioning flesh.

This was an issue I too had battled with and believed conquered. If not... then my travails were for naught. A fool's errand. Neither better nor wiser than the good Doctor's incipient insanity, another thing he inherited from those ancestors of his.

That our goals appeared aligned was no happy accident. I had long been guiding Frankenstein's research. An anatomy book left open at the 'wrong' page, an idle observation on the peculiar properties of a particular compound, rumours of the miraculous recuperative effects of a rare moss. Whispers in his ear as he slept. The dolt thought his progress all his own work. In reality, it too was a by-product, a side effect of *my* needs; supplies ordered according to my schedule, purses of his family gold exchanged for the corpses of condemned men, fresh from the gibbet. Not as raw material, you understand; not as Viktor used and abused them after I was done, but to practice a most delicate operation, one I could ill afford to get wrong.

His work served another purpose, just as important. It kept me firmly in the background, invisible assistant to an increasingly eccentric master. In the tall shadows of his ridiculous frock coat, I hid my stunted frame, my club foot, my misaligned eyes; the left drifting wide, a sure sign of evil in these parts.

And behind Viktor's irrational melodrama, I hid my life history: I was the boy who fell through the ice. The devil that was plucked, cold and inert, from the dark depths. Restored by another eccentric, one Alessandro Volta, experimenting with his metals and volatile acids on the banks of Lake Geneva. It was he who attached copper wires to my head and to my feet, and, to the wonder of all present, I twitched and retched up the lake's freezing waters, gasping for breath.

In truth, my life had already been saved long before that dramatic moment. It was saved when I was dragged from the lake, manhandled in such a way as to force the bulk of the frigid water from my lungs. The stab of electric current merely served, like an insufflation of tobacco or the pungent ammonia of smelling salts, to bring me sharply out of my unconscious state. The reported absence of my pulse was surely due to the ineptitude of those who had tried to take it; slowed perhaps by the icy conditions, weakened by five long minutes of exposure, tremulous and feeble, and yet it still beat its erratic tattoo.

Nonetheless, it turned out to be an abiding and useful fiction; years later that voltaic pile secured me my position in Frankenstein's household, at first as an inspirational curiosity, later as his faithful assistant. But the sword was double-edged; my ill-formed body and miraculous revival had the town folk crossing the road to avoid me, unwilling to shake my hand or to hold my gaze, fearful of what demonic creature might stare from that wayward eye.

Only two people had ever looked upon me with neither fear nor disgust, had looked and not seen a *freak*, an omen of bad luck. One was Viktor, who saw merely that I was useful to his ambitions, a piece of lab equipment that could be blamed and berated and cursed for each failed experiment.

The other was my childhood sweetheart and wife, Olga. Brilliant, beautiful, temperamental Olga, whose body it was that lies frozen in the deepest, coldest recesses of Frankenstein's cellars. Just her body; her brain kept separate, chilled but most definitely not frozen, held in a glass jar through which oxygen and nutrients steadily bubbled. It was suspended in a solution of quick-silver, ergot and bezoar, fortified by tinctures of half-a-dozen plant extracts, an expensive and time-consuming preparation that supercharged the brain's ability to repair.

Just one of many discoveries and innovations made over the course of the three years since her untimely passing. The Doctor's library of medical textbooks had proven close to useless, full of ignorance and superstition, garishly illustrated with pictures of organs that would be better suited in a pig. Which was, no doubt, where they truly belonged; for with human dissection outlawed — a blow to the advancement of science — anatomy lagged far behind studies of rarefied gases or the twinned natures of electricity and magnetism.

That short-sighted injunction was only one reason my progress had been so slow. Perhaps it would have been quicker if our positions had been reversed; if it was Olga who sifted the wheat from the chaff of knowledge, looking for rare nuggets of truth, and I was the one laid out on the cold stone slab below. She was the true genius. It was her notebooks on flora and fauna, her musings on the workings of the Universe, which had guided me far more than the teachings of venerated professors from the universities and academies of Europe.

And yet, I wondered, would she have done as I had? Would her fiery passion have lasted this long, or would she instead have let me go, moved on with her life, used my memory as inspiration rather than as a rock to be clung to?

Would she — *will* she — thank me for what I was trying to do? But how could I not attempt it, despite the half-life I was forced to live in Frankenstein's shadow, despite the long night hours spent poring over arcane texts, eyes watering from the candle flames? How could I pass up any chance, however slight, to bring my love back?

Especially as it was I, Igor, who, in the heat of the moment, had struck the fatal blow.

I still remembered the look upon her face, her shock and anger that the worm had finally turned, the half-gasped cruel words as her air passages swelled and closed, before those wide glittering eyes dimmed and became still. She'd used to taunt me, laughing that I would never dare raise a hand against her, despite her blows, despite the broken nose and continuous bruises, despite the fact it was her, my darling wife Olga, and not the circumstances of my difficult entry to this world, nor even those of icy rebirth from the waters of Lake Geneva, that had stunned and killed the muscles around my left eye and set it forever wandering.

And I, in return, had landed one solitary blow, one single time. Oh, but what a blow! The elbow of my arm that had tried to fend her off, finding instead that slender throat. Ye weep! It was a fluke, an accident, and a shameful crime that, three years on, I was still trying to make amends for.

I finished mopping up Viktor's most recent experiment and went in search of him, to offer the balm of encouragement and a gentle reminder to order supplies of a bark from Ceylon whose properties Olga had discovered while Viktor still wore lederhosen.

I looked into the library, the papers strewn across every surface, the books in teetering piles, musty and devoid of both life and truth. His study was in an even worse state, but equally as silent. In growing consternation, I climbed to the crow-bedecked roof of the tower, where metal spikes speared the gloomy skies, waiting for the right electrical conditions to channel their energies down to the laboratory below. To the mournful lament of the wind turbine, I leant over the parapet, peering into the murky undergrowth, worried that Frankenstein's latest failure might have driven him to final, desperate measures.

In the distance, over rain-shrouded woods, I glimpsed the square-faced Villa Diodati rented for this melancholy summer by Dr. Polidori and his friends. Viktor had visited them one evening a mere week ago and had come back buoyed by new enthusiasm. Perhaps he had gone there again, to tell them of his work, his lack of progress, and to be humoured in exchange. They are too polite, these English, these poets and writers, these Byrons and Shelleys. They had been fascinated by Viktor's theories on the stimulating effects of electricity, had shown morbid delight in his schemes to bring the dead back to vital life.

I wondered if Dr. Frankenstein had thought to mention his faithful assistant. Did I feature in the ghostly tales they told each other to pass the dreary evenings once he had left? It would be better, I thought, if I did not; if my part remained hidden.

I descended, thinking to follow, at least to confirm Viktor's wellbeing, crucial as he was to my plans, only to find him returned to the laboratory and once more stooped over the body of the latest criminal to incur the local magistrate's ire. He spun round at my approach, a needle and suture in his hand, a manic smile on his pallid face.

"Genius!" Viktor crowed, "I am a genius!"

"Master?" I asked, uncertainly.

"I've done it, Igor! I know I have. At long last!"

He seemed more optimistic than I would have thought possible. Perhaps he had once again been sampling the opiates. The brain was a week dead, at least. Plus, it was the inferior brain of a base criminal, for only a hanged man's body can be claimed by the doctors and surgeons. It was perhaps a good thing that it would never again know the spark of life. Thieves, beggars, and murderers: not the sort of human flotsam that deserved a second chance. Rotten, in all senses of the word.

And then I saw the grey mush he had been working on, in a metal tray, warm and oozing ichor, discarded and forgotten. Dread gnawed at my clenched innards.

"M-master..." I stuttered, my tongue no longer fully under my control. "What... where?"

"No time to lose, Igor! Raise the platform and let us hope for a storm!"

The imbecile! As if zapping a hundred million volts through human tissue could do anything other than cremate it, just as it had a dozen times before. But his lunacy loosened my tongue.

"Where did you get the brains?" I finally managed to shout, over the sound of chains winching the bench into the rafters.

"Floating in a jar!" he exclaimed, matching my volume. "A jar in the cellar!"

And my voice and senses were pummelled back into oblivion.

"I went to get more ice," the Doctor said, his voice bright and cheery, "and discovered an experiment I had quite forgotten about. Amazing! I'll have to consult my notes to work out how I did it, but the brains are in the best possible state, the healthiest I've ever seen. Almost alive!"

My blood ran cold, as I cast around and saw the jar, the one my Olga was in, smashed on the floor. For a giddy, treacherous moment I hoped to see her fine mind equally shattered, but no. The jar had been emptied first, and then casually thrown aside. Which meant it must be my Olga's brain he had just finished inserting into the cadaver.

Legs crumbling, I slumped to the floor, as Viktor spouted on, rubbing his hands together in glee.

Was this my fault? A combination of my hubris and my doubts? I had too long delayed reuniting her brain and her body, fearful of failure, more fearful, perhaps, of success, and of her reaction. The brain, saturated as it was in the rejuvenating elixir, would kick start the regeneration of the cells of any body into which it was inserted, of that I was certain. Was not Frankenstein's mansion overrun by chimeric mice, the result of my earliest experiments, once the crippled playthings of the feral cats that stalked its ramparts, now miraculously whole again of body?

And yet still I had delayed, still I had procrastinated. I was not ready, I told myself. I needed more subjects, more research, more trials.... more time, to work out how to apologize.

So it was the idiot, Viktor Frankenstein, and not I who had taken the final step. I cringed at the thought of his insensitive hands, connecting the delicate arteries and nerves. At his total disregard for sterile working conditions. I shuddered at the waste of the preserving liquor that he had so casually discarded, which should instead have been used to flush the cadaver's veins, to soak the putrid innards, to complete the rejuvenation.

And I despised him most of all for the inescapable fact that he had put my Olga's magnificent mind inside the hulking body of a criminal.

A *male* criminal.

I sighed, deep and low. It was done, now. The process had begun. Fortunately, the grey dusk was full of drizzle, not of thunder and lightning. I would wait a while, until Viktor's giddy excitement ebbed. I would placate him, suggest food and sleep, both of which he was woefully short off. And then I would lower my Olga and do what I could to ease the suffering of her new, barbaric existence.

Viktor would probably assume his latest experiment another failure, a crushing blow to his delicate ego. Would he attempt to dispose of the evidence? Or would he leave it lying there, slowly mending itself?

For that was all it would take. Not electricity, or surgery, or more elixir. Time always was the greatest healer.

Left alone, in a few days, maybe less, my Olga would awaken.

She would not find me here.

I could not stay. To attempt to justify my actions as self-defence? To somehow explain the form she awakened in? I would disappear, just as the feral cats had disappeared, no match for the enraged, invigorated mice. I had no desire to find myself once again beneath the Lake Geneva ice, this time not merely as the result of the rough and tumble of childhood play.

I would leave Dr. Frankenstein with his monstrous creation, and with the hope, for Viktor's sake, that Olga had lost at least a little of the fearsome temper she was so rightly famous for.

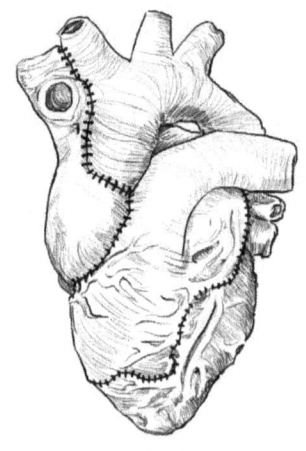

WANTING

KC GRIFANT

Maddie crouched in the grass, watching a speck of light grow in the distance, perfectly centred along two slivers of electrostatic railroad tracks that stretched into the darkness. Above her, stars glinted like metal against the blacktop night.

Her hair — long, synthetically enhanced for her fifteenth birthday, and dark as bloodied mud — slipped in front of her face and she scowled, brushing it back to squint at her watch.

Six minutes until the train.

The low whine of the Smart Maglev train signalled its imminent approach. Elevated nearly a foot over the tracks, it raced along tremendously fast, up to three hundred miles an hour. The track-cleaning system on the front of the train sent out infrared beams in a wide pulse. If a beam bounced back from anything on the tracks, the system would activate a laser to decimate the debris and keep the train running smoothly. That made what she had planned doubly tricky.

She had seen videos of the system disintegrate a perched bird and obliterate low-hanging branches without otherwise disturbing the tree. Now she hoped it really worked that well.

Maddie rocked back on her haunches, picking up the tangled bungee cord resting next to a jug of rum. She snapped out the cord, pausing to flex her hand and study the pale skin, the slender, fleshy fingers that looked so weak.

The proz were so lucky, Maddie mused, as she rolled her left sleeve up above her bicep. No one ever messed with *them*, with their bionic limbs, ten times stronger than human flesh, sprouting from their stumps in dazzling crimson, emerald, gold. The proz went where they wanted, did what they wanted.

They had had the luck to be born with Nanex disease, the result of genetic hiccups caused by toxins in SmartPakk's temperature-regulating nano-plastic, which the FDA had approved too quickly. A whole generation of babies born with missing fingers, arms, or legs.

Of course, Maddie had the misfortune of an organic-foods-obsessed mother who had borne a perfectly normal child with limbs all intact, dooming Maddie to a life of mediocrity.

Something rattled behind her and she froze, dropping the cord. Slowly, she turned to look at the fence meant to keep pets and pedestrians like her off the tracks. It was nothing, just a tree branch scraping against the tall chain links. Moonlight emerged from a passing cloud, illuminating the bone-white tracks.

Four minutes left. The faint *hum* of the nearing train whispered in her chest. She rested her bare left bicep against the outermost bar of the Smart Maglev track and looped the cord around her elbow — once, twice — so tightly it hurt, before latching it to the track.

Last week, one of the proz — a boy named Taz — had flashed a smile at her across the crowded hall, his eyes blue as a Siamese cat's and so bright they seemed to cut through her like shards of glass. She had watched him join the rest of the proz as they moved through the hallway like some fantastic, self-assured Other Race.

She had seen Taz again just yesterday, in line at the coffee shop. His prosthetic arm was even more beautiful up close, a cobalt gemstone that flickered with flames of digital grey. She had been staring at the undulating flames when Taz turned his penetrating glance to her.

"Um, oh, hi," Maddie had stammered. "I think you're in my Social AP class? I mean, when you show up." A laugh had escaped her, one that sounded nothing like her real laugh.

Taz had only looked at her, his face unmoving. Had he forgotten he smiled at her only a week ago?

Remembering it now made the blood rush to Maddie's face.

The microseconds ticked on in the too-warm coffee shop, before Taz turned back to the counter without a word. She had darted out of the cafe, a tightness wedging itself under her collarbone.

"I'll do it tomorrow," she had vowed in the dark parking lot.

And now here she was.

She gave her bound arm a sharp tug, but it stayed tightly in place. She had only gotten as far as this last time when, with shaking hands, she had undone the cord's latch as soon as she had fastened it and hurled it to the side. She had sobbed, cursing herself for being such a coward and watched, half in anger and half in relief, as the train whirled by in a flash of white and silver.

But she wasn't shaking this time.

Maddie picked up the rum with her free hand. She had had to bribe two seniors with fake IDs to get it for her, but it was worth it.

With its help, she should survive long enough to make it to the ER, the drunkenness muting her pain and masking her motive. Maddie took a tiny gulp, the holographic buxom pirate woman from the skull-and-crossbones logo winking in the moonlight.

59 seconds. She placed the jug in front of her feet and crouched, pulling herself as far from the tied arm as she could.

It was important not to psych herself out. Certain lasers — like the one on the train — created aseptic cuts ("cauterizing wounds") in flesh, cuts that tended to heal more quickly than other kinds of injuries. She had researched this extensively under the guise of a Bio paper on horse surgeries.

The CO_2 laser removes the testicles while the horse is under general anaesthesia, creating an aseptic wound that has minimal chance of hemorrhaging. There will be little swelling due to its cauterizing effect, resulting in a nearly 40% faster recovery time than other methods.

She glanced up. The outline of the train had differentiated itself from the darkness, a great silvery mass around a swelling light.

This was going to hurt. A lot. She heard her breath quicken and tried to slow it. *Only for a little while,* she thought. She would only have to deal with the pain until the ambulance arrived, alerted by the emergency signals her watch would automatically broadcast.

Her *watch* — it blinked and vibrated rapidly on her wrist. It sensed the train's presence with its autoloc system, the same technology that buzzed loudly when she got too close to a passing car or bus.

She used her teeth to rip off the Velcro strap from her free wrist and chucked the watch a few feet away from her, in case autoloc alerted the train to make an emergency stop. She would have to grab her watch right after, she'd have to make sure not to pass out before then.

Her hair was matted wetly across her cheeks and forehead. The bungee cord dug into her skin as she stretched herself as far from the tracks as she could.

Maddie thought of the poor horse, the laser narrowing in on its groin. *You do what you have to do*, she thought grimly.

It was coming, she couldn't watch, she knew she couldn't, she would be too scared, her shallow breaths would turn into screams. Instead she closed her eyes, her body shaking. *Think of your shiny new arm, your shiny new arm*, she chanted to herself and saw Taz's smile again, quick as a wink.

The sound — *HAA-HUUUM, HAA-HUUUM* — flooded her thoughts. Her body jerked away from the track as if it had a mind of its own, but the cord held tightly. The wind picked up, lifting her hair back from her shoulders.

Shiny new arm —

The thunder of the train's passing drowned out her screams. She opened her eyes but it was too bright —

Then a sound — not loud, but ugly — a *pop*, and she was flying backwards like she was in a rollercoaster without a seat. The ground hit her all at once, the back of her head thudding into the dirt.

Something went wrong, she thought, because she couldn't feel or see anything. *Maybe the laser only cut the rope*, she thought and sat up to see —

A nothingness. Where her arm should be, a stump waggled frantically at her right below her elbow. *It worked.* She stared at the meaty texture, dark against her moonlit skin — when the pain hit like a wrecking ball to the side of her body.

She gasped and gasped, but there was no air. She had been wrong; this wasn't worth it, nothing was worth it.

And the *smell* — a burning, clogging in her throat made her cough and sent her stomach twisting. On the front of her shirt, a spot shone smaller than a coin. Blood? She used her other hand to pick it up. Hard and red and gleaming.

A fingernail. She dropped it.

She realized that strange gasping sound was coming from her and turned to look at her stump again. Her *stump*, her *cauterizing wound*. Abrupt, like someone had forgotten to finish drawing her in. Tatters of red fabric flapped against the stump, or was that blood?

Something blinked in the grass, like the front of a mini toy train.

She tried to stand and staggered, pitching forward onto her knees. Did she lose her feet too? She twisted on the ground to see the outlines of her sneakers, next to a round shadow.

Oh the *rum*, it had spilled everywhere. She tipped the jug to her mouth, the holographic woman on the label winking rapidly in the dim light. There was some left, dribbling down her shirt as she drank. It tasted like water, until she felt a hot tingling in her chest and her head cleared a fraction. *I did it*, she thought.

She turned the bottle over, shaking what was left onto her stump (her *stump*) and a few drops seared down into her flesh and she screamed.

She threw the jug next to the glowing patch of grass. The glow... her *watch*.

Maddie reached out to pick it up but couldn't, though she felt the missing arm strain like it was still attached. She flexed the invisible fingers and a brick seemed to pummel them, again and again, as her nerve endings short-circuited. She let the ghost hand drop.

She forced her right hand up and fell on her face, spitting out metallic dirt and grass. She clawed across the ground, finally snatching up her watch. As her fingers grabbed it, it turned a deep, dark, quickly beating red.

Red.

She had only seen that colour once before, about a minute before she fainted from a bad case of the flu when she was twelve. The skin sensors on the watch's casing had picked up her dangerously low blood pressure and sent out a signal to 911.

She clutched the watch in her hand and rolled on her back, waiting for the ambulance to come. She turned her head to look at the stump, making sure it was real.

Stay awake, she urged, until after seconds or minutes she heard the ambulance's siren in the distance. *What if it's my imagination*, she thought, *what if I die out here?* She started to think of her parents. Suddenly, a message from the local ER lit up her watch: "HELP IS ON THE WAY."

Maddie looked up. The stars wobbled and seemed to get larger, before splitting and growing again. Her whole body throbbed, drenched in pain signals, yearning for the part that was missing. But soon she would be complete, better than complete.

Images came to her, bright and sharp and sudden, like a dream. She saw herself as a toddler, crawling in fits with a wooden arm. Herself in grade school, smiling at a girl across the table who had a yellow plastic arm like hers. They tried, giggling, to link their arms during recess and quickly became friends. The first day of high school, worrying that her red arm was too gaudy and the rush of relief as the older proz immediately took her in. Maddie had quickly fallen for one of them — whose name she couldn't remember — with icy blue eyes. She saw blue and red fingers intertwined, the grey flame spreading up her elbow.

Did that really happen? she thought.

She saw herself older now, with a sophisticated and distinguished red arm, nodding as a stranger inquired about it. *Yes, born with Nanex*, Maddie said with a demure smile.

The life she had always wanted, had always been meant for, was coming into focus. The terrible feeling of being alone was slipping away, back into the recesses of dreams where it belonged.

She looked back to the sky and, through the splintering darkness, felt herself start to smile.

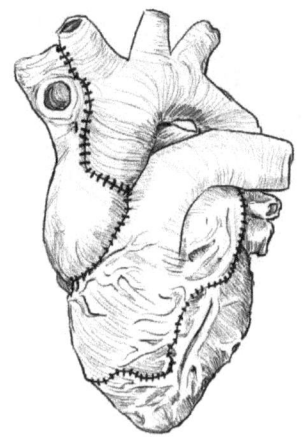

THE HILLTOP GATHERING
CAIT GORDON

In the town of Shelleyville, on the night of a most distinct occasion, clouds clustered in a moonlit sky, revealing the ominous silhouette of a mansion resting atop a predominant hill on the outskirts of the main village. The massive dwelling resembled a castle in design, complete with a tower at each corner of the structure, whose conical heads pierced the sky menacingly. Somehow, not even the soft amber glow of the tall, rectangular windows — which provided evidence of the life that existed inside — helped to calm any onlookers. In fact, it provoked a disquiet that prompted folks to quicken their pace in order to get safely home and lock all access to their properties.

One constant among the plethora of rumours about the place had been that the mansion must be almost two hundred years old. The most respected historian of Shelleyville stated that the house had indeed existed long before the town itself was established.

Nobody from the neighbourhood dared approach the mansion anymore — even the bravest kids had become too afraid to throw stones at *its* windows. After all, monsters lived there.

And today it appeared a gathering was afoot. Neighbours warned each other of the influx of vehicles rushing up the hill, and the locals trembled over the unknown. Who knew what sadistic, animalistic practices would occur inside that dark palace of deviance and depravity?

"**C**ome here, little one, Granny's gonna hug the stuffing out of you!" Grandma Stein squeezed little Ernie in a warm embrace.

"ACK!" cried the boy, feeling something oozing from his side. "MAAA! Get the sewing kit! She did it again!"

Watching from further down the hall, Frank E. clucked her tongue. *Little brothers.* She leaned against her rollator, locked the breaks, and flicked a bit of electric blue fringe from her left eye. *Another imminent patching up. That kid's always coming undone.*

"Oh, Mummy Stein," said Agrippa, Frank and Ernie's mother, running over with a needle and thread. "I've told you a thousand times not so tight. Goodness, my child's falling apart!" She squinted while threading the steel eye and proceeded to stitch up her son.

After ruffling Ernie's jet-black hair, the grandmother noticed her granddaughter waiting for some affection. Grandma Stein held out her arms. "How's my favourite granddaughter on this special day?"

Frank E. grinned and unlocked the wheels of her rollator. "Hi, Granny. Fine. Are you even allowed to say you have a favourite grandkid? Like, is that legal?"

"Well, you are definitely my favourite of all of them named Frances." She gently embraced Frank E. "Happy birthday, dearest."

Of course, I'm the only one named Frances. Good save, though. "Thanks, Granny."

"My, my. Sweet sixteen. It's a big one! I wish I had been able to have a sixteenth birthday, but I was made all grown-up."

"I know, Granny. You say a version of that every year."

Grandma Stein tenderly pushed her granddaughter out of her arms. "You must not take for granted that you've received the gift of living through all of life's stages, Frances." Her genteel expression fused into a frown with an implied warning. "Now-now, dear, stop lip-syncing my words when I say that!"

Frank E. smirked. "Sorry, Granny."

The doorbell rang. Agrippa tied the finishing knot on her son's side. "Coming!" She tucked the sewing kit into a drawer of the semicircular mahogany table near the entranceway, then opened the door to a most welcome surprise.

"William! It's so wonderful to see you up and about again" — she hugged her brother-in-law with enthusiasm — "I thought we'd lost you!"

"Well, well, now, if it isn't herself," he chirped into Agrippa's hair before standing back to take a good appraisal of the kind woman. "Aw, aren't you a lovely sight for me sore eyes?"

Agrippa froze at the sound of his voice.

Auntie Geneva groaned and rubbed her temples. "William, what did I tell you about using that accent? Honestly, I'm just about ready to strangle you!"

Her husband kissed the side of her head. "Ah, *mo chuisle*, don't be all like that."

"And here comes the Gaelic," said his wife.

Agrippa held a hand to her chest, confusion painted all over her features. "What on earth's happened to William?"

"If you don't mind, love, I prefer Séamus."

"Of course he does," muttered Geneva. "Aggie, I'm telling you, they murdered your husband's brother. You saw how the disease consumed poor William's brain over the last five years, right?"

"Yes, yes, it was just tragic."

"Well, it got to the point where the damage became irreparable. We had no choice but to have it replaced. So, I specifically requested of Doctor Franken that he find a brain with a similar temperament to the husband I've lived with these past 100 years. Apparently, the doctor listened to exactly nothing I said and now I'm stuck with this leprechaun from a cereal box!"

"Oh my!" cried Agrippa.

Her brother-in-law sang out: "Always after me luck—"

Geneva stopped the man's mouth with her hand. "That will never be funny, do you hear me?"

Her spouse grinned devilishly.

Turning back to Agrippa, Geneva added, "He's amiable enough, but my fingers are stiff from kneading all that soda bread."

"And a fine baker you are, *banphrionsa*," said William (or Séamus) patting his wife's backside before he left to find some punch.

"Such a flirt, too." Geneva followed him with her eyes. "Mind you, it's not all bad, Aggie. He's got a newfound stamina between the sheets. Although I have no idea what he's saying in the throes of passion. Can't tell if he's speaking the Irish language or having a stroke."

Agrippa's mouth gaped once more.

The doorbell rang again. "Frances, honey," said her mother, "would you get that? I just want to settle Auntie Geneva and Uncle Will-erm-Séamus."

"Okay, Ma." Frank E. unlocked her mobility device and rolled over to see who had arrived. "Hey, it's Justine," she said. "Glad you could make it."

Justine lifted a finger to tell the girl to hold on, then used both thumbs to text something to her boss. Once she clicked Send, she turned her attention back to Frank E.

"Sorry, kiddo. I'm under a lot of pressure at work. I swear, if I don't get that deadline met, they'll hang me on the rafters tomorrow morning. And no amount of pleading could stop them, either."

Frank E. pulled a face. "That sounds really stressful. Maybe get another job?"

Justine wasn't listening. Her phone pinged another several text messages from the tyrant they all nicknamed *The Judge* at the office.

"Hmm?"

"Never mind," said Frank E. "Everyone's in the great room, so maybe head there."

"I swear, there's simply no convincing that man," muttered Justine. "I am so dead. So very dead." She somehow found her way into the kitchen instead and sat down at the table, trying to plead her case.

Frank E. rolled away to see what anyone else was doing. The house had filled to the brim with relatives, most of whom she felt ambivalent about spending time with. However, she remembered her favourite uncles were here and searched about the rooms on the main floor to find them. Sadly, her efforts were to no avail, and she retraced her tracks.

In the hall, Ernie nearly ran into her, full of the energy he had to burn off by dashing all over the place as if being chased by the police.

"Watch it, Squirt," said Frank E.

"Whoops, sorry. We almost had a car accident," he said, looking at her rollator.

"It's a walker with wheels, not a car."

"I thought all things with four wheels were cars."

Frank E. sighed. "Never mind, kid. Hey, wanna help me look for the cool uncles?"

"Okay!" Ernie bolted like lightning over to his mother, who he was convinced knew everything. She just had to be super smart, because Daddy constantly told Ernie, "Go ask your mother," for all the answers to the nearly never-ending influx of the little boy's questions.

"Hey, mama, where are Uncle Vic and Uncle Henry?" asked Ernie.

"Um, well, hon," replied Agrippa, "Your uncles are upstairs, in the bedroom, making a baby."

He cocked his curious head. "They are?"

"Yes, sweet boy. This is what many people do when they are in love."

Ernie tried hard to comprehend this, but he hadn't a clue what that type of love felt like. He knew he loved his toys, running, and his tricycle. Those weren't people, though. His thoughts shifted back to his uncles. "How are they making a baby, Mama?"

"Well, you see, they —"

A loud electric hum jolted through their conversation. The lights flickered on and off. Ernie and Agrippa heard the clocks on the microwaves reset.

Then, from the second floor of the house, came the sound of wailing.

"How wonderful! Looks like they succeeded!" Agrippa ran to the centre of the great room and announced, "Listen, listen, everyone. It seems Vic and Henry have a brand-new family addition!"

The relatives cheered. In no time, the proud parents walked in with their little bundle of joy, freshly stitched and animated. They stood beside Agrippa, so everyone could see. Vic held the baby, who was wrapped tightly in the pastel swaddling, and Henry kept his arm around Vic's shoulders, beaming with undiluted joy.

"Congratulations to you both!" cried Agrippa. "Is it a boy or a girl?"

"We're not sure yet," said Henry. "We'll wait until they tell us. In the meantime, we want you to welcome baby Avery!"

Frank E. sat in her rollator, watching the little family. "Congrats, dudes!"

Vic lifted his adoring gaze from Avery and offered a warm smile. "Thanks, you. We wanted our child to share the same birthday as our awesome niece. Figured only the cool kids are born on this date."

"Aw, I bet you say that to all the cool kids."

"Want to hold Avery, Frank?" asked Henry. "No, wait" — he saw Frank E. trying to stand — "We'll come to you."

As her uncles placed the tiny infant in Frank E.'s arms, Avery squirmed furiously in the swaddling.

"Wow, this kid's strong!" said Frank E.

"Avery just wants to bust out of their blankie and play with their cousin," said Uncle Victor.

"Hey, hey," said Frank E. softly to the little nipper, "You'll bust your stitches. Just chill, cuz. We'll do lots of fun stuff real soon."

The baby settled in her arms.

"Look at that," said Uncle Henry. "Our amazing niece is the Avery Whisperer!"

Frank E. chuckled. She could have held the baby all night, but her mother appeared, pushing a long table with wheels into the great room. In the Stein family tradition, you were allowed to open one present before everyone had birthday cake, and then the rest afterwards. There had been a buzz in the air that Frank E.'s sixteenth birthday present would be epic. The teen had done her best to conceal her excitement all month, and now the moment of truth had arrived. On the table sat a huge box, over a metre in length, wrapped in silver with an enormous baby-blue ribbon. The birthday girl stood up, unlocked her breaks, and stepped over to the table.

Her mother kissed Frank E.'s cheek. "Happy birthday, my dear Frances. I hope they fit!"

The daughter turned her rollator about, locked the breaks, and sat down, reaching for the ribbon. Frank E. tried pulling the box closer, but it barely budged. "What's in this thing? It weighs a tonne!"

"Not a tonne, but there's plenty of muscle!" said her mother with pride.

Frank E. raised an eyebrow and stood, holding her body upright with one arm on the table as she removed the lid from her gift. Inside laid two shapely legs, kept at the proper temperature to prevent decomposition. The skin was flawless and its light-brown tone even matched the shade of her arms.

"Ta-da!" cried her mother. "We got the call last night. These legs are sturdy and strong. They used to belong to a head cheerleader!"

Frank E. scowled at the sight of them. "Take them back."

Agrippa put both hands on her chest in alarm. "What? But why?"

"Agatha-Lacey texted me this morning. She got the same ones!"

"Well, yes, the accident did involve twins."

"I'm not wearing the same legs as Agatha-Lacey. It's embarrassing!"

Agrippa moved her hands to her hips. "Frances Elizabeth Stein, you're being quite unreasonable! These are perfectly good legs, and you can cover them up with tights or trousers if you feel —"

"Nope. I'll still know they're the same ones. Forget it. I'll wait for another pair."

"But I don't know how soon new legs will become available!"

Frank E. sat down in her rollator and folded her arms. "Shouldn't be too long. Isn't texting and driving a thing these days?"

"FRANCES! That's horrible!"

"Sorry."

"Now let's get those legs on, young lady!"

"No! I don't want them!" Frank E. stood up and unlocked her rollator. "Give them to somebody else!"

"Can you please tell me why you're being so difficult?"

"Oh, just... just leave me alone!" Frank E. wheeled herself out of the room as quickly as she could, but not before hearing the remarks from a few of her relatives about how ungrateful she was, after her poor mother tried so hard to acquire such a thoughtful gift.

Frank E. headed for the back of the house and entered a room that hadn't been occupied for many years. It was filled with specific mementoes of her father's youth, which he still found too painful to be around. He missed Grandpa profoundly. From the short time she'd known him, her grandfather had been a benevolent presence in the family. He and her father had also been terribly close. She rolled over to look at her grandfather's portrait, an exquisite piece that almost filled the entire wall.

Grandpa hadn't been a handsome man by any standard, with his severe brow and protruding cheekbones under a covering of greenish-yellow skin; however, the artist did capture the serenity in her grandfather's large, round eyes. Frank E. often went to the painting when she'd felt troubled, not really knowing why. Somehow, it comforted her. She locked her rollator and sat down, pondering.

Her grandmother, his widow, came up from behind and combed Frank E's blue and black hair with her fingers.

"Aw, looking at my true love, aren't you?" said Granny.

"Yeah. He seems so chill. Wish I knew his secret..."

"Well, honey, I suppose you're old enough to be told. He didn't always feel 'chill.' In fact, when he was young, your grandfather set out on a quest to the North Pole."

"North Pole? What, was he trying to find Santa or something?" Frank E. chuckled.

"Actually, it was there he planned to take his own life."

"What?!" That didn't seem at all like the jolly grandfather she'd played with as a child. "How is that true?"

"It just is, my dear. Even though he and I shared many things in our marriage, he wouldn't tell me the specifics of his life before me. Only that he lost someone who meant the world to him — the man who made him. Grandpa felt he couldn't go on after the man died, but while Grandpa built his own pyre, he had an epiphany. He would not let his maker's death be in vain, and your grandfather decided right then and there to continue his creator's work.

"It had taken some time, several years to perfect the craft, but I was Grandpa's first creation. Isn't that something? Your Granny is a work of art!"

Frank E. smiled.

"He taught me everything he knew, and we made our immediate family together, complete with siblings. We took the name Stein as a tribute to the friend he lost. And we vowed to pass the secrets of creation down through the generations."

"Granny?"

"Yes?"

"Why did Grandpa have to die?"

"Ah. When his heart was finally giving out, I suggested arranging for him to get a new one," replied Granny. "But he told me he was ready to meet his fate, hoping he'd compensated for his many sins — whatever they had been — with all his good deeds. He said he didn't need to be repaired, because he was finally forgiven, and the abounding happiness he carried enabled him to feel the existence of his soul. So, I let him go, because he'd been content to die. How could I have denied him such peace?"

"He didn't need to be repaired," repeated Frank E.

"No, he didn't. He was perfect just as he was."

Frank E. frowned and slid her hand on the smooth metallic bars of her rollator.

"Come, dear, let's join the others," said her grandmother.

"But, Granny —"

"I'll make sure the legs are put away."

Frank E. half-grinned and studied her grandfather's portrait one more time. "Okay. Thanks."

As they made their way back to the main hallway, the front door swung open with a loud boom. At long last, the final guest to their party had arrived. Inside the oversized doorframe stood a towering soul, clad in black, and soaked to the bone. A burst of lightning illuminated his colossal form from behind.

Frank E.'s heart leapt. She didn't even fully turn her wheels before saying, "Drama much, Daddy?"

"Darling, you're home!" cried Agrippa, running past her daughter and mother-in-law and into his mighty arms.

"Sorry I'm late," roared a deep bass. "A rough crossing. The sea's particularly vicious this time of year."

Agrippa kissed his mouth heartily. "Still, you're home. Let me get you out of those wet things." She helped him with his jacket.

"Thanks, sweetheart." He gingerly caressed the stitching along his wife's cheek. "Now, then, let me see my very grown-up daughter!" He directed his attention to Frank E. and held out his strong arms.

She grinned. "Aw, Dad, I'm too old for that now."

Her father's arms slumped along with his shoulders. "Truly?"

"Nope! Totally lying!" Frank E. zoomed into his embrace, wheels and all. The metal meeting his body didn't even cause her father the slightest flinch.

She probably could have driven a small vehicle into the massive fellow and he'd not have budged much.

"Have you opened your first present yet?" he asked.

"Yeeesss," she moaned into his dark woollen blazer. "I hated it."

"Your mother went through a lot of trouble to get those legs, kidlet."

"I know, Dad. I just… maybe I don't feel like being *repaired*. It's… it's sort of hard to explain."

Her father smiled and pushed her back so he could face her. "That's okay. I had an inkling you might feel this way."

"You did?"

"Um hm." He stepped aside of the doorway and pointed. On the porch behind him stood a silver, black, and cobalt blue mobility scooter, complete with leather seat and gleaming chrome hubcaps. There were even curved tailpipes, like those typically found on a high-revving motorbike.

Frank E. gawked at the vehicle, speechless.

"Happy sweet sixteenth, kidlet."

She looked up to meet his gaze with glistening eyes. "Best. Dad. Ever." Then she let go of her rollator and managed walking on her own power to plop onto the seat of the scooter. Her bum got wet and the rest of her did, too, but she didn't care.

"Press the ignition, my dear," said her father.

With one touch, it felt like the entire porch reverberated underneath her. Frank E. whipped her head up at her dad.

He leaned casually against the doorframe. "I might know a guy."

Delight flooded her sodden features as the rain poured down. "Can I take it out for a spin?"

"Oh, my darling," said her mother to her father. "It's so slippery out."

Francis Stein put his arm around his wife. "She can handle it. That's our Frank E., remember?"

Agrippa grinned. "Yes, of course. What was I thinking?" She kissed her spouse's lips and then smiled brightly at their daughter. "Have fun, our precious birthday girl. And be careful!"

Frank E. grabbed the silver helmet hanging from the right handlebar. Instinct took hold of her. She turned the scooter about and flew down the accessibility ramp.

Mother and father could hear a little yelp of "Wahoo!" as they closed the door to see to their other guests.

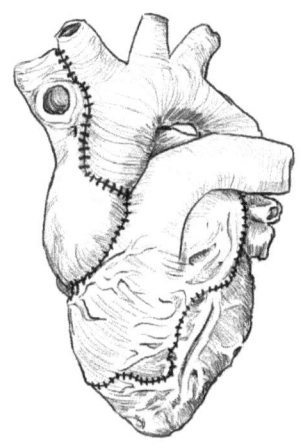

MONSTER

HALLI LILBURN

I need your eyes

Scoop them out for me

So bright and alive

They will show me much more than before

I need your legs

Just chop them off

So strong and steady

They will take me much farther than before

Give me your voice

I wrecked mine when I stopped caring

So, I will rewind time

And breathe deep again.

Your brain, I need your brain next

To fill in the holes and the shadows

Carved out by abuse and ignorance

You should hear the things I was told.

The racist, sexist, ableist common norms

That stained me.

I got to switch up that rubbish with hipster tolerance and representation

While you're at it, give me your liver, your heart, your age, your diet, your
     height and your depth.

The depth you stabbed me with when you tried to kill me.

Tried to rid society of old monsters like me.

Me and my entitlement, fake news and fake tan

But I can't die. I can't even get sick

Drown me, crush me, incinerate me.

My broken bones will snapback in place

And I will reach out and steal your parts

Piece myself back together.

You never wanted the responsibility or ownership or accountability

I'll leave what's left of you propped up in a chair

Hooked up to machines

With the occasional lightning bolt to zap life into you.

Your eye sockets can stare out

The passive listener like you always wanted

'Cause man, if you had legs you might have used them.

If you still had a voice you might have to speak out.

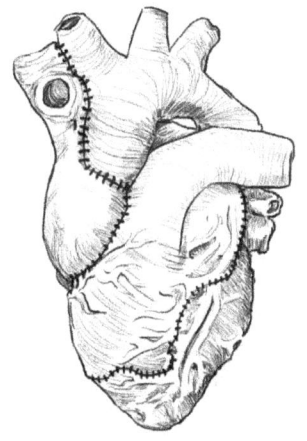

THE PERFECT HUSBAND

JF GARRARD

If life was made up of a series of moments, then I was experiencing the worst moment of my life. No words came out of my mouth as I stared at the hideous creature standing in front of my husband who appeared to be frozen in an enormous container, his face wearing an expression of surprise.

"Your heart! I need your heart!" These shrill Mandarin words spilled out of the creature – a tiny Asian woman whose mess of makeup trailed down her face in blotches. She still had on high heels from the night before and her elegant evening gown was covered behind a white lab coat stained with red and brown patterns whose nature I dreaded to contemplate. Her long hair, which was usually kept in a bun, was now wild and free, her arms stretching out to reach for me made her resemble a giant vulture. Her large eyes bulged out as she screeched, "To live he needs a heart!"

"Yes!"

A low male voice grunted to my left. I scowled at Frankenstein's monster and he sheepishly took a step backwards. With him blocking the exit to the door, I was trapped. *How did I end up in a room with this woman, a walking corpse and my husband in a tin can?*

To anyone that asked, I would say that my best moment ever would have been getting married six months back to the love of my life, Harry. The billionaire CEO of a rising startup with influential Communist Party parents, he was quite a catch. I needed as much help as I could get, given my own parents had fallen from grace with the Party. To myself, I would confess that the best moment of my life was hearing the screams of the crowd during the finale of the most important reality show in history which I directed and produced.

"Mei! Mei! Mei!"

"Kitty! Kitty! Kitty! Kitty!"

I remember the crowds going wild, holding up signs and screaming, with a constant stream of lights from cameras going off in the Bird's Nest stadium in Beijing. This was the most exciting event in the stadium since the 2008 Olympics. Both Mei and Kitty wore enormous Western style princess gowns full of sparkles and lace, waving politely at the crowd as they both smiled prettily. One was a new starlet and the other was a ghost child from Helin village who was recently recognized as an official person. There had been quite a change in the country after ghost children or second-born children could be recognized and can now get official status as a citizen after the one child policy was abolished. Previously, these children just languished at home with no opportunities to go to school, travel, or seek medical care. I secretly hoped that Mei — the ghost child — would win, given her story was more tragic with a mother dying of cancer. This would help drive up ratings more.

A low moan filled the speakers and the crowd promptly stopped their cheering.

"Audience! Are we ready?" Andy, the perky host, dressed in a bright red military jacket with shiny gold buttons bounced onto the stage. His Mandarin was loud and commanding. "Let's do a quick recap before we reveal the ending, no, beginning of this love story!"

Assistants ran onto the stage and helped Mei and Kitty into velvet couches on wheels which were promptly moved to the side as large red curtains were parted to reveal a giant hundred-foot LED screen. The florally title in English and Chinese read "A Monster's Love Story!"

A pictorial history of Mary Shelley and the story *Frankenstein* filled the screen via black and white drawings by Bernie Wrightson. The drawings faded to peaceful images of different monasteries from around the world. It had been at a Tibetan monastery in which a tourist had taken a selfie and made a joke that a monster was behind them which started a media avalanche. Frankenstein's monster had been successfully shielding himself from the world until this moment of chance.

Next, there were videos of the Chinese military accompanying the monster from the monastery to a hospital for a series of medical tests before he was walked into the Great Hall of the People to shake hands with President Xi Jinping. Large Chinese characters for "Dà wéi" dissolved into its English translation, "David", which prompted huge cheers from the crowd. A short video of Xi Jinping telling the world in English that the person previously named "Frankenstein's monster" was now "David" and an honorary citizen of China drew loud cheers.

"Are the roses ready?" I was sweating like a pig as I yelled at various staff members through my headset about details for the grand finale. My in-laws and husband were the ones who pushed this gig through for me and I could not let them down. The government decided that choosing a bride for David was an amazing marketing opportunity which would bring the country much international face. Although the Brits had originally objected to the monster being a Chinese citizen, they soon shut up when it was revealed that David was currently comprised of mainly Northern Chinese body parts with the exception of his head and torso.

The last bit of the presentation recapped the twelve potential brides for David and all the competitive activities the women were forced to do to avoid elimination from the show. The majority of them were from impoverished families living in cancer villages with the exception of Kitty, who was a starlet on a Beijing television network. It was not a surprise that few middle class or well-off women didn't want to compete on the show. There is, after all, a lot of stigma attached to marrying someone who is already dead and would not be able to bear children. There was some thought about using new DNA extraction technology to see if an offspring with David's genetic material was possible, but we had to choose a vessel to carry the child first before any of that happened.

"Please welcome, the monster of Dr. Frankenstein, the incredibly handsome, Dà wéi or DAAA-VID!" The host jumped up and down to get the crowd into a frenzy.

A large man walked stiffly onto the stage while holding a single red rose in a large pale hand which was impaled with large staples. Standing close to seven feet tall, he towered over his potential brides who were all slightly over five feet. David's head resembled a large square with dark hair and bangs which reached the tip of his eyebrows. Metal knobs protruded from his neck and the metallic glint from them matched the silver three-piece tailored suit he was wearing. Although there had been enough cosmetic surgery advances in the history of medicine to hide the staples and stitching, the government felt that making David look prettier would render him unrecognizable as the monster and would affect his "brand."

"Get a close up of his face!" I screamed at one of the cameramen as I stared at my computer monitor which had multiple angles of the stage. Throughout the entire show, David maintained an incredible poker face which drove me crazy. It was difficult to guess what he was thinking or if he was feeling upset until it was too late. The last makeup artist we employed ended up in a mental institute when David threw a tantrum because she took too long with the touchups to give his skin the trademark greenish tinge.

"David, how do we feel today? Are you ready to choose your bride?" The host stood on his tip toes in an exaggerated manner with the microphone towards his guest.

"Shì de, wǒ zhǔnbèi hǎole," David answered that he was ready in fluent Mandarin.

Male assistants dressed in tuxes held out their arms and helped the two girls to their positions on either side of David.

"Mei! Kitty! Mei! Kitty!" The crowd's screams reached an all-time high.

Prior to the bride selection announcement, my husband Harry and his top scientist, Li Feng, walked onto the stage with a large banner behind them with the words "Forever Life" in English and Chinese. Harry was smartly dressed in a tuxedo and Li Feng looked her usual elegant self in a figure-hugging, embroidered high neck gown. She was the main scientist who did a refurbishment of David's limbs recently to improve their mobility and was the monster's biggest fangirl. Since Harry's company was the main sponsor of the show, the two of them said a few words promoting their cryogenic services before the camera returned to David who, to my satisfaction, looked conflicted as he stared back and forth between the two girls in ball gowns.

The large man let out a low growl as he shuffled towards one of the girls. He stumbled and almost fell, making the audience gasp. Gracefully, Li Feng reached under the crook of his arm to help him walk over to his "true love."

"Mei, I give my rose to you. Will you be my bride?" David got down on one knee slowly and held out the rose towards Mei who sobbed beautifully as her shaky hand took the rose from him.

"Close up, close up!" I muttered into my microphone to a cameraman. I let out a sigh of relief and cracked my first smile of the night. Looking into one of the tiny screens on the monitor, I raised an eyebrow when I noticed how much alike Li Feng and Mei looked.

"Is it such a big problem if Mei and David don't marry? My father is really upset about all of this because he thinks it's shameful that she is marrying someone he deems from the netherworld." Dressed in a simple white shirt and grey slacks with her hair in a neat bun, Li Feng sipped a cup of tea calmly as she sat on the couch.

I did my best not to glare at her. If I had known that she was the older sister of Mei, I would have disqualified her sister based on conflict of interest. Harry assured me that there was none; just because Li Feng was the doctor who maintained David's body, this had nothing to do with her little sister. My hair was a frazzled mess from too much hair pulling as I paced up and down in my Adidas yellow and black stripe sweatpants and shirt ensemble.

"A lot of people are counting on a fairytale wedding between the two of them," Harry stroked his chin. My husband was in a matching sweat ensemble, but with perfectly gelled hair he looked much neater and sane than me. "This marriage represents the East making peace with the West on an international scale. The village will also get a huge influx of tourists to help fix the economy here too."

For the last few hours, we had been sitting around this little house the production company had rented in Helin village, a place famous for its mining boom which hollowed out the land beneath. After the rush was over, the mines were abandoned and the houses were sinking into the ground. I wanted to shoot as fast as possible and leave before the place collapsed. The villagers had greeted us with much fanfare and even a parade with the school band; however, Mei's father slammed the door in our faces when Mei returned home.

"Maybe I can talk to him again," David offered, speaking in his low voice which sounded like a growl. He looked calm as he sat on the ground against the wall. Last time he sat on one of the rickety chairs in the house it had collapsed on him. His eyes gazed at us and I smiled tightly. The glossiness of his eyes always bothered me and in general, his presence made me uneasy.

Mei covered her face with her hands and let out a loud sobbing sound. "It's been over a month! I don't know why father doesn't want me to be happy. I've never even left the village my whole life and I always do what he asks!"

Li Feng sighed. "Can't we call the whole thing off? Just say that David is not ready for marriage and wants to stay an eternal bachelor?"

I watched the large man put a gentle arm around Mei and it was obvious that he cared deeply for her. I did my best not to shudder. After witnessing his tantrums with my staff, I always worried if he could commit greater acts of violence in the near future. Many humans hold back on committing crimes because of fear of imprisonment or death. As a person who is dead and had faced isolation before, David had nothing to fear and that frightened me. Things always ended badly for females in the *Frankenstein* book.

Suddenly Harry snapped his fingers, "I got it! People in the tabloids think I'm a playboy, right? Maybe what we're missing is a comparative factor. Mei's dad seems like an honourable man. I will be the terrible husband in front of him! I'll flirt with girls, drink, and gamble. Mr. Li will see how awful I am and in comparison, David will be the perfect gentleman."

"I'm not sure if that would work," Li Feng sounded hesitant. "Father is a simple man and wants Mei to marry well, but..."

"Mei will be marrying well. David's potential net worth is probably higher than anyone else in the world right now. He's also promised to pay for the best cancer treatment available for your mother no matter what the cost," Harry pointed out. "This might be such a dumb plan that it might work. What do you think?" He turned to me.

"Anything is worth a try I suppose, as long as you don't get anyone pregnant!" I took a pillow and bashed it over Harry's head, making him laugh and grab my hand. He kissed the back of it and smiled.

I giggled and then watched David whisper something to Mei which made her laugh quietly. This moment of tenderness made me lean back against Harry for a minute of peace. They appeared to truly love each other, which still puzzled me. *How can a walking dead man have feelings and how can a live human love a corpse?* I turned to Li Feng to continue the debate, but she was watching David with a nasty look on her face. A second later, her expression returned to her usual composed self and she started to talk about what type of man her father admired.

The wedding between Mei and David was the event of the century and dubbed the "Beauty and the Beast" wedding. International media flew into the tiny village and took over the one motel along with any available land rented out for campsites. The audience ratings were at an all-time high regardless of television, radio, or internet streaming mediums. Harry's cryogenic company had the best ad placements and his company's valuation went up two thousand percent after the vows took place. He stayed out late to celebrate while I decided to go back to the tiny house to sleep, something I had not done in the past month due to wedding planning.

The horrible husband plot had worked perfectly with Harry traumatizing the villagers with his enactment of being a terrible mate. In addition, his parents gave the village chief incentive to put pressure on Mr. Li to accept his new son-in-law via a hefty economic stimulus package which could help restore the collapsing land.

The next morning, I stumbled out of the bedroom bleary eyed, heading to the kitchen where I would usually find Harry operating the coffee machine and preparing breakfast while listening to the Chinese radio.

He was not there and the radio was not on. The silence was eerie; something was not right.

On the kitchen counter was a flashlight and a crudely hand-drawn map of the town. The Chinese characters of "tell no one and come find your husband" was written on the back of the map.

There was a moment when I didn't want to go into the abandoned mine near the edge of town. I had a feeling that death was near and fear of dying made my blood stop. If he died I would become a rich widow. *Was he already dead? Was there any point in trying to find him and end up with two of us dead?*

In the end, my irrational feelings of love for him gave me courage to stumble through the mine tunnel which had several strings of LED lights set up to guide me to a strange room that was full of machinery and lab equipment. Although the main lab for Forever Life was a few hours away, Harry had mentioned that he had built a small lab somewhere to replace parts for David near the village as an emergency measure before the big wedding.

Li Feng spoke in a shrill voice again, bringing me back to the present. We were in a dimly lit room inside a mine. She banged a fist on a metal table which was set up next to the large metal container holding Harry. "Tracy! Are you listening? There was an accident and Harry fell on something, which went through his heart. We need a heart so we can make him whole again!"

"He's dead?" Time slowed down as I tried to process the impossible situation. I stared at my husband who was frozen solid in a container which had lots of metal wires attached to it. The surreal hum of a generator made it hard for me to think straight. "Why do you need my heart?"

"We've figured out how David works, so we can bring Harry back. It's fitting isn't it? A piece of you inside him. It's the ultimate marriage," Li Feng smiled, her white teeth looking like fangs in the dim light. "I promise I will take care of him and will love him forever and ever."

"Love him? Were you sleeping together?" I snapped out of my daze and my blood began to boil. I knew Harry fooled around and had accepted it as the price of marrying a rich prince long ago, but to have a woman boast of this felt like I was being stabbed in the heart.

"We slept together a long time ago. He slept with a lot of women to be honest, but he chose to marry you," she spat out. "If my parents had the money to send me to Yale, I would have been the one to marry him. He is imperfect. I will be his creator and will use the spark of life to make him the perfect man. *For me.* He will be obedient, loving, and faithful."

"You want me to give up my life so *you* can marry him? I'm leaving!" I turned to exit the cave door, but David appeared.

"Tracy, you cannot leave," he said in his deep, soft voice. His face had an expression of sorrow, making me want to slap him as his wide-spread arms blocked my path.

"Does Mei know you are here?" I demanded.

He hung his head down. "Harry and Li Feng were drunk and arguing last night when he fell over there," he pointed towards a corner which had a protruding piece of metal covered in red stains. "He is lucky because the equipment for freezing happened to be here for testing."

"Well, I can't give him my heart, because I have to give it to someone else," I sputtered as tears flowed down my cheeks. "I'm pregnant and my baby needs me to live."

"She's lying!" The mad scientist rolled her eyes. "Carry her over here to this table!"

"I don't understand, why are you doing this? Are you in love with Li Feng? Is she holding a body part hostage?" I glared at him.

"She... I... we kissed... Mei might leave me..." he muttered.

"What? She's holding you hostage over a kiss? This is the twenty first century, not the eighteenth century! A kiss means nothing! Mei won't leave you!"

"Oh!" David's dull eyes lit up with hope.

"Bring her over here! We only have so much power left in this place!" Li Feng's annoying voice spoke again.

David's face twitched slightly as he stood in front of me, watching me with dark eyes.

Taking advantage of his hesitation, I pulled out a souvenir Harry had gotten me in America and pulled the trigger. The taser shock didn't do much to David, but it gave me enough time to run for the exit as he slowly fell to the ground with his body in spasms. I heard Li Feng give a shriek and I picked up some rocks scattered on the ground and threw them towards her for good measure. When I turned to look, I caught a glimpse of David's body twitching on the ground, watching me run, conveniently blocking the exit.

By the time I came back to the makeshift lab with Mei, the Village Chief and several policemen in tow, there was nothing left except for some red stains on the ground. My husband, Li Feng and David were all gone. The entire village was in hangover mode and it had taken forever to get people to take my crisis seriously. Mei and I left after we both gave statements about where we were last night and what I witnessed to the police.

"I don't understand. Why would my sister do this? She got to go to school, she had friends, she could get a job and travel... she had everything!" Mei rubbed her watery eyes and looked at me pleadingly. "The police won't send her to jail, will they? I mean, you said that it was an accident that Harry got hurt."

"Boss, what happens now? I got some shots of the police, should I stay here until they leave?" One of my cameramen interrupted our conversation.

"You know what? You and Mei come with me," I pointed at both of them. "We're going to Forever Life to see what's going on!"

Mei took faster steps to catch up with me as we headed to our car, a large Mercedes van. "What makes you think they are there?"

"Harry is in bad shape and they need equipment and a heart if they plan to heal him. The company uses a lot of human organs for their experiments. When Harry wakes up, he's going to think this is funny," I tried to sound confident, but I was really scared shitless. I was going to surprise my husband this morning about the baby but now I might be a widow or be divorced by a talking corpse if Li Feng's crazy plan came into play.

"Boss, do you want to say a few words to the audience before we go?" The seasoned cameraman knew me better than I did. No matter what happened, we were always on for the show. Our job was to document every moment possible touched by Frankenstein's monster for the world. He turned on the camera on his shoulder and aimed the lens towards me.

"Hi, my name is Tracy Lau and I'm the producer and director for *A Monster's Love Story.*" I took a deep breath and let out a few tears. It was show business after all. "Thank you for tuning into our "Beauty and the Beast" special last night and for making it a success. This morning when I woke up, I discovered that my husband Harry, the CEO of Forever Life, was missing. There was no ransom note, just a map leading me into one of the abandoned mines. I was told that there had been an accident and Harry needed a new heart. I wanted to tell Harry this morning that I was pregnant, but never got the chance. If I could sacrifice my heart I would, but I cannot kill our unborn child! The police are looking for David and Li Feng now, but I think I know where they are. Mei and I are going to look for them to demand answers. How can David abandon his new bride the morning after? And why?"

On cue, the cameraman turned towards Mei to capture her delicate face that was wet with tears. I put an arm around her while she cried. "Please send us your prayers that we will find David and Harry!"

The cameraman gave the cut signal and we hopped into the van. We sped our way to the Forever Life headquarters to find a handful of smart reporters already there. Security helped us hold them back as we entered the building. There was no point in asking them where Li Feng and David went. They had god status in the company and could do no wrong.

Taking the elevator, we went to the eighth floor and into Harry's office which had a large mahogany desk among walls filled with books. We locked the door in case any nosy reporters made their way in and I looked frantically on the bookshelf for a copy of Mary Shelley's *Frankenstein*. Opening up the false book, there was a hole where the key used to be. Hunting through the bookshelf again, I found *The Fall of the House of Usher* and opened it to find a metal key. The key was a round object built with assorted sizes of screws which came to life after the finger print recognition scanner confirmed my thumbprint. I pressed the key into a hole under Harry's desk and one of the walls opened up to reveal a long spiral staircase.

"You should turn your camera on now," I told my cameraman. "I really don't know what's going to happen and you are capturing history in the making."

The three of us crept downstairs slowly, hoping that it would give us the advantage of surprising whoever was at the bottom of the stairs. The grey concrete walls were lit by LED lights in the shape of torches and along the stairs was a thin rail banister with decorative Art Nouveau designs which was there for style rather than safety purposes. I had been here many times before and knew that we were several stories high.

We froze in our tracks when Li Feng came hurdling towards us, screaming something about "leftover woman" with tears running down her face. The lab coat I saw her in last was covered with fresh red stains.

Startled that her way was blocked, she tried to push her way through us, but slipped on the tiny stairs in her high heels and fell backwards. She toppled down a few steps and then over the edge of the banister. There was a sickening sound of bone breaking, a crash, and then silence.

"Older sister!" Mei shrieked. She descended the stairs as quickly as she could which took several minutes. The cameraman and I followed suit.

Towards the bottom, under bright fluorescent lights we could see Li Feng's still body on the floor. It was not a pretty sight, with arms and legs twisted into odd angles and her face covered with blood. Mei ran out towards her sister and I yelled "Don't touch her! We have to wait for the police!" causing her to whimper and step back.

The familiar stiff walking noise of David's shuffling feet made me look up. I prepared to yell at him but was startled to see that it was Harry. He looked better than Frankenstein's monster with a pale face, invisible stitching around places where the skin had torn and a smaller knob on his neck. Still, he carried an aura of dread and lifelessness.

"Tracy..." A low moan emitted from my husband in a voice similar to David's and his glossy, fish-like eyes stared at me while his arms reached out for me desperately.

"David!" Mei ran to her husband's side and they held each other tightly while staring at her lifeless sister.

I looked at the two of them, then at my husband and laughed and laughed, curling onto the floor as hot tears ran down my cheeks. I offered no resistance when Harry swooped down to lift me up and ascended the stairs in slow motion. I kept giggling as I held onto my tummy which carried new life and marvelled at the irony of starring in my own *A Monster's Love Story*. I knew that the camera would keep rolling until the end of my days with this new Harry.

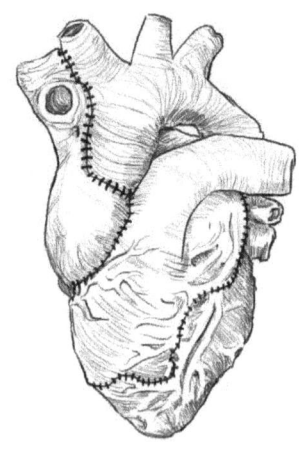

MUSCLE MEMORY

KEV HARRISON

I open my eyes, vision blurred. The constant beeping swimming about me as I lie supine. A single layer of fabric preserves my dignity, as the multitude of faces about me gawp and leer. My focus hardens, soft lines become hard edges and I see, for the first time, a familiar face. I try to speak, my brain alive with energy, commands rushing from synapse to nerve to muscle. But it's all too much. Too much too soon. I gurgle as an infant might, providing humour to the gathered crowd.

The face I recognize fills my vision. I remember her kindnesses, recently, but have no context for them. "You must rest now. You're alive. The rest will come." She moves away and there is fog, a milky light coating everything. I sleep.

Footsteps.

The room is long, though I decipher this only from the clack of her shoes on tiles as she comes to me. It is the fourth day. I strain, focusing every cell of my teeming, frustrated brain and part my pursed lips.

"Hello."

Only a whisper.

Her beaming smile is my reward. She replies to me.

"Hello to you. This is remarkable progress." She takes a clipboard from somewhere nearby and scribbles something. The scratching of the pencil fires a kaleidoscope of memories – voices shrieking, faceless children dressed in grey and white sitting, creating trees and people and monsters.

"Let's try some movement," she says to me, her voice warm, encouraging. I try to respond, but the muscles in my face ache. Exhausted from a single utterance.

Her face is above mine. She smiles.

"Are you ready?"

I blink my eyes and she is gone. Then I hear her.

"Can you turn to look at me?" My right ear hears her words, feels her breath. My brain whispers to my neck to twist, to turn. Muscles engage and I am moving.

I am moving.

Bones crack, still for so long. Too long. It is a pleasant pain. My eyes find her smile again and my mouth turns upward. A tear escapes my eye before I can blink.

"Unbelievable," she says and moves away. My eyes trace her as far as they can until she is gone.

"How about this way?" The voice is quieter, behind me. A slight echo hits me from the far wall. I strive and strain and the beeping gets faster, faster and I see a red light.

"Stop there, please." She is behind me still. I want to turn to see her, but the mist lowers over my eyes again. It is dark.

It is the sixth day. I have been moving my neck and, little by little, I have it within my full control. When I hear her approach, I turn my head. Watch. Smile.

"Hello, Doctor," I say. My voice is not as I expect it to be. It is strange. *Other.* She returns my greeting and stands over my bed. I bathe in the light reflected from her white overcoat and, lungs now working without the aid of the machine, I take a full breath of her floral scent.

"Do you remember your name?" she asks the question, her smile unrelenting on her face as I watch her lips craft each word.

My name.

Identity.

Moniker.

Images flash before me. School again. The court. Bed – bodies writhing together. A beach. A car. Speed. Screeching tires. The *accident.* And I hear her call out.

"Michael!"

"Michael." I say it myself, feeling the word as it passes over my lips, the stress on the first syllable consuming a gust of air from my newly-functional lungs, while the second is a stunted afterthought.

"Excellent recall, well done," she says and scribbles more notes on the clipboard that I now know is fixed to my bed. "Today Michael," she says, placing the clipboard neatly back into its holder. "We are going to move down from your neck and try to work your arms. Are you ready?" she lets the question hang in the air while I tilt my head down and look at my arms, resting at my side, then back up to her.

"Ready," I say.

"Don't be disappointed if it's difficult at first, remember the muscles in your neck were forty percent your own and you still struggled at first."

I manage to nod and prepare myself for her first instruction, then I feel cold.

Forty percent my own?

Her voice brings me back.

"I want you to *feel* your arms. Really concentrate on them."

I angle my head again, look down to them. Coarse hairs permeating the flesh. I focus on my arms, I *feel* them. I look up to her, nod. She smiles. Speaks again.

"Now focus on your hands. Try to ball them into fists for me. Squeeze as hard as you can."

I focus. I squeeze. My brain frantically telegraphs the message down tunnels, across membranes. It cries out to my fingers to close, to grip, to make themselves small. But they aren't listening. I release a sigh of defeat as I finally give in, the heat in my face palpable.

"Michael," she says. "You might feel like you failed, but I saw the muscles in your wrist flex. A tiny, infinitesimal amount, but I saw it."

She is above me, beaming. My feelings of shame wash out of me as I return her smile to her. I feel the warmth of her fingertips getting ever closer to my skin and then... contact.

I lay in halflight. Fingertips are tracing my body, down one unshaven cheek, to my neck and down still further. They hold tightly to me, acute pressure exploring my torso. Her pale lips hover over mine, the distance between our mouths small enough that the electricity jumps from me to her and back, drawing us closer, inevitable. And then I am tasting her. Raspberries. Chocolate. White wine. And we kiss and we move and she calls my name. "Daniel..."

I am present once more. It is the same face from my vision that hovers over me. More distant now, clothed.

"Michael, are you ok?" Her voice trembles with concern and I hear it. The beep, beep, beep at my ear is no more. Instead the sound beats a furious rhythm. Heat in my face risen from flushed to burning. My vision blurs, sounds meld into a single tone until-

"Nurse, I need a sedative here, now!"

"You're awake," she says the words before even I know if they are true. I blink, then open my eyes and she's there, above me. The lips are still there, those same lips that I was —

"We need to establish what happened earlier, so I'm going to ask you a couple of questions, Michael, ok? Take as long as you need to answer."

I nod and she starts.

"Do you remember anything from immediately before you started to have the heart palpitations and if so—"

"I do and it was you. When you touched me." I don't mean to interrupt but I can't help myself.

She is frozen, those lips still shaping the next word, teeth just peering at me from behind. She exhales soundlessly, her breath with hints of cinnamon.

"What happened when I touched you?" she finally finds the words that she wants. I take the moment to revel in the memory anew. The intensity is lesser, somehow, but still the fiery passion remains. She looks into my eyes,

186

mouth slightly open again, but she waits. Doesn't interrupt. Then I look back, my eyes focus sharply, the memory moving to the back of my mind.

"I remembered the last time you touched me."

Her mouth is wide, her eyes blinking, her veneer of calm slipping, falling to the wayside. Her hand rises, covers her mouth and she holds it there. Silent. I go on.

"I didn't remember you," I say, my smile colouring my words with warmth. "When I first woke up, I didn't know we knew each other before the accident. But now it's crystal clear. The two of us, in dim light, making love. Memory is funny isn't it?"

"Daniel?" she says and I don't know if it's a question to me or to the world but she is already running, her shoes clopping fast on the surface of the floor. I watch her. The door creaks shut and I am alone again. Only the machines punctuate the silence.

When she comes back I am waiting. I have used the time to work on my hands. My fingers curl slowly, awkwardly into fists and then open again, like flowers clumsily blooming. She sees this, smiles. Her make up is smudged, the dark lines that perfectly encircled her eyes now indistinct.

"I'm sorry about before," she says the words and she feels them, means them, too. I can sense it. "I see you have the hands working. Well done."

She walks across the room and brings back a chair. She sits beside my bed, looking at me. She has a box in her hand. She opens it, removes a pen. It is black, smooth, with silvery edging that catches the harsh light of the hospital ward. She reaches forward with a gloved hand and turns my wrist to face upwards. She places the pen on my palm and tells me to close my hand. I focus, and the wrist begins to tighten, the fingers curl and close.

I am in a brightly decorated room. There is modern furniture jumbled with antique-looking candle holders and light fittings. People flit one way and the other in the background, but my eyes focus straight ahead.

On her.

She is seated, wearing a dress. Lemon yellow, it brings out her dark hair and eyes. I feel my muscles tighten in my face as I smile.

"Congratulations," I say, in a voice that is unfamiliar to me.

"About time," she says back, and she sips from a tall glass.

A restaurant.

I reach into the pocket of my jacket and I hand her the pen, a ribbon of the same fresh, eye-catching yellow wrapped around it in a bow. She takes it and her cheeks lift, their usual caramel shade replaced with warm rose.

The pen slips from my fingers and clatters to the ground, bringing me resoundingly back to my hospital bed.

"Sorry," I say, and search for it with my eyes, my neck muscles bending to their limit. She bends and picks it up, shows it to me. Undamaged.

"Did you remember anything?" she asks me, placing the pen back into the box. I tell her what I saw and her mouth turns up into the same smile I remember from the memory.

"It was the day of my graduation, from my PhD," she says. "It was at our favourite restaurant, where we'd been on our second date. He said he'd been holding pens for almost an hour in the boutique where he bought it, trying to decide on exactly the right one for me. For my hands."

"He?" I say, the questioning tone for me as much as for her. "Me? Who?"

She pauses, then opens the box again and lifts out another object. A ring. Plain, rose gold. She touches my fingers, prising them open – again brief erotic flashes of the two of us flick through my mind, distorting the here and now like a strobe light. She places the ring in the centre of my palm and closes my fingers around it. "What do you see?" she asks.

"Rain," I say.

It is raining. Fat drops of water, thumping into the ground with that satisfying drumming sound. I am in it, under it. Wet. I can smell it, the earthy richness of moisture in the air. The clouds are a forbidding, heavy grey overhead. She is running, holding a man's hand. He is older, formally dressed. She is dressed in white. Soaked through. Her elegant attire waterlogged, clinging to her. She gets closer, closer.

I am in a building. A church. The priest is talking and then he stops.

"I do," I say, in that same unfamiliar voice. I hold the ring and feel a tear trace the outline of my right cheek as I slip the ring onto her finger.

I look at her slender hands now, peeking out at the end of her just-as-white, yet totally different medical coat. The ring gleams where, moments ago and a lifetime ago, someone – I? – placed it onto her finger. I tell her what I saw and notice that while she scribbles her notes, she is weeping. I stop, my recollection not yet finished, but I have to know.

"Were we? You and I? Were we?"

She lifts her pencil to the corner of her mouth, as if choosing her words carefully. "After the accident, Michael, your body was... broken. The spine was... irreparable. We had the chance to try something. It's something we've been developing here and modelling for a long time. And he... he had just. I'm sorry."

Her hands are closed over her face now. I can hear her sobbing. See her mouth moving. Shaping words. Testing them out. She puts the hands down, out of sight.

"My husband, Daniel, he.... Because of my work, he wanted his body left to medical science. He died, only four hours before you. A massive hemorrhage in the brain." She says the words to me, but her eyes are glassy, distant, like she is explaining it all to someone else.

189

I twist the muscles in my neck, look down at my arms. Those coarse black hairs that caught my attention yesterday. I look back to her. "Tell me more. I need to be sure."

She takes out a handkerchief and blows her nose. She nods and wipes the tears from her eyes on the back of her hand. "We decided to try what we have been theorizing about for the last four years. Your head, brain, nervous system – at least the part of it contained within the skull – was almost perfectly preserved, despite the trauma everywhere else. His body was..." she pauses, becoming distant once more. "Perfect," a whisper. Then she looks at me again, her eyes focus sharply.

"So we transplanted you. Head, upper part of neck. Lined up the nerve canals and here you are," she opens her arms like a sad game show hostess, sniffs and then blows her nose on another hanky. Then she stands up from the chair. "But you know what we thought would be so hard, Michael? The initial rejection. The auto-immune response. Convincing your neurons..." She places her splayed hands on the top of my head and gently presses with her fingertips. "Your neurons to talk to his bones, joints, and muscles. But you've done it all. So far, so simple. The immune-suppressants kicked in after five weeks of coma. You were turning your head with almost normal ability in two days of practice. Look at your hands. Just look at your bloody hands!" She looks and I follow.

Clench, unclench.

Clench, unclench.

Fists fit for fighting. Well, almost.

"And we should have known, Michael. All this nerve tissue. Every cell of your skin – *his* skin – alive with nerve endings. The same matter as this," she points a finger to her own skull. Her own brain. "But we didn't even consider. Didn't even begin to imagine there might be..."

"Muscle *memory*," I say and she presses her five fingertips to mine.

We are naked, breathless. "I love you, Alison" I whisper.
"And I you, Daniel," and I taste the lips again.

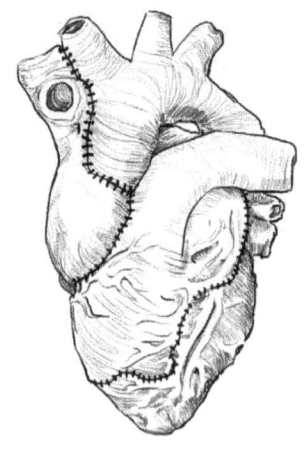

THE SOLUTION

COREY REDEKOP

[Transcript, audio file 12, Nickle Procedure]

Are we recording? Alright, the date is October 27, 2018, Doctor Haddon Nickle speaking and Gerald Brunswick assisting, if you can call it that. Yes, yes, Rufus, you're here, too. Who's a good boy? Who's a good boy? You are!

Ahem.

Gerald has prepared slides for Group 711, pluripotent stem cells that have been treated with the Nickle Serum. I am now commencing an examination of slide 1-711. On first inspection, the cells are... this is astonishing, the cells are... Gerald, are you quite positive this is from 711? No, I'm not suggesting you erred — I am stating it outright, you halfwit, now give me that chart. Oh, good gracious. You see it too, don't you? This is momentous.

For the record, my aide Gerald has verbally confirmed my findings, that the pluripotent stem cells of Group 711, Slide 1, harvested three weeks ago and treated with a diluted serum of five parts per million, display no outward signs of deterioration whatsoever. In fact... yes, there are unmistakable indications that the cells have been fully transmuted into fresh neurons, and... Gerald, how do I zoom in? Yes, that's it! Load slide 2-711, now! Good gravy, that's it! Ha!

The neurons, they're firing! They're actually firing! The neurons are signaling! The serum works, the serum is... Gerald... Gerald, help me... I need to sit down... my head is spinning, Gerald, I... my chest hurts... No, I'll be fine, I just need... Rufus, stop barking now... I need...

[muffled sounds, barking]

GB: Doctor? Doctor Nickle?

[Transcript, audio file 13, Nickle Procedure]

Uh, this is Gerald Brunswick, assistant to Haddon Nickle. It saddens me to report that, despite my best efforts at resuscitation, Dr. Haddon Nickle has died.

I have not yet fully processed what has happened. I may be suffering from shock. For the past two hours, I have been in a daze, staring at the remains of the doctor, and only the constant nudging of Rufus, his smelly old basset hound, has kept me from lapsing into catatonia.

Perhaps if I had dialled 911, Dr. Nickle would still be with us. It is what any sensible person would have done. Yet I ignored this impulse, because I believe Dr. Nickle would have as well. We have been through a lot over the past year, he and I, ever since he snatched me from the doldrums of veterinary school and took me on as his assistant. While his abrasive nature prohibited any true sense of intimacy between us, I believe that, deep down in his heart, he regarded me as a valued colleague. So I did not hurriedly call for an ambulance, no, but taking a cue from Dr. Nickle, I threw caution to the hurricane and grabbed a bone saw. Five red minutes of bloodletting later, I cradled the whole of Dr. Nickle's being within my hands. I grabbed the nearest container, a clear plastic bucket, and deposited him within it, filling it with solution.

Sadly, my haste has removed any possibility of repairing the body. I made rather a mess of it, I'm afraid. I'll have to fetch some bleach from the closet.

Perhaps it is madness that drove me to this. Or more likely, since I'm being honest, it's self-preservation; the thought of my admitting participation in unsanctioned and subjectively immoral experiments does give me pause. What we achieved, or more accurately, how we went about achieving it, is surely against the law. Those poor dogs and cats.

At the least, it's against the Hippocratic Oath. I think. They were kind of lax on that at vet school. I should look it up.

No, I'm in for the full pound now, and the only hope I have at salvaging this is to continue along the path set forth by my mentor.

I do not know where this path will lead; I'm only a wannabe dog doc who fell backwards into this mess, but with a little luck, I will bring the doctor back to the world. Because the world needs him.

...

𝒩

...

𝒩

...

...

𝒩

... need to rest

wha—

what

what's that

what

where

where's the

lights

what

dark

so

black

[Transcript, audio file 14, Nickle Procedure]

I believe the solution has managed to stave off deterioration, if the sample I trimmed from the prefrontal cortex is correct. I hope he won't miss it. During his collapse, the doctor brought much of his equipment down with him, so I have had to improvise. The makeshift EEG I have thrown together displays signs that could be interpreted as evidence of brain activity. In any normal context, this would be viewed as a success, I guess, but here can only serve as my starting point.

I have commenced a scheduled series of electrical impulses to the frontal, parietal, temporal, and limbic lobes, as well as the insular cortex, in the hopes of jump-starting the brain back into consciousness. I shall continue this course of action until I either achieve results or the brain is a smouldering mass of goo.

Dr. Nickle would expect no less from me.

lights
what is
who
what is going
where
how is
lights
what
geraldareyouthere
Gerald
What
is
happe—

whatwhatwhatwhatwhatmyeyesohgodmyeyessobrightmyeyesmy

oh
good

Good gracious.
Gerald, is that you? Gerald?

I can't focus, come closer. You're all blurry, you bloody idiot. Can you hear me? Can I hear me? Gerald, what are

[Transcript, audio file 17, Nickle Procedure]

If I trust my analysis of this readout, the impulses are having an effect, and there is now evidence of definite and ongoing brain activity.

I must do this slowly and carefully, by the numbers. I have to admit, I let myself get distracted the other day. Rufus was insistent on going for walkies, and I forgot to turn off the current while I was out. While there looks to be some superficial damage to the prefrontal cortex, I am fairly confident I managed to cut the power before Dr. Nickle could be damaged in any serious way. I hope.

I am now about to embark on a new treatment of short controlled bursts to see... well, to see what happens.

Nothing ventured, nothing gained, as the doc always said. Says.

Must concentrate.

I am... Haddon Nickle.

Concentrate.

I am Doctor Haddon Nickle, M.D., PhD., DMSc. Ha!

I am... who am I again?

Must concentrate.

I'm alive. I'm alive! Doctor Haddon Nickle is *alive!*

Gerald, is that you? Stop moving about, I can't follow you! I can't move my eyes! Can you hear me?

Rufus! Rufus, it's me! Don't bother Gerald, he's working!

No, don't! Don't you touch that switch, Gerald! I'm alive! I live! I am

↗

Goddammit.

Get a grip, Haddon. Focus. You may only have a short amount of time in which to

↗

gather your thoughts oh god*dammit all to*

↗

hell. Gerald, you cretin. If I never get the chance again: you're

↗

fired.

Focus, Haddon. The scientific method. Rational thought. Observation, measurement, experiment. Formulate, test, and modify.

Fact number one. I am Doctor Haddon Nickle. I graduated summa cum laude from Johns Hopkins. I specialize in advanced theoretical neurophysiology. I am a sundry-lettered, multi-hyphenated man of science. I am as bloody intelligent as they come.

Fact two. Based on all recollected indicators — shortness of breath, tightness in the chest, a lightning bolt that cascaded up and down my left arm — I recently suffered a massive — Massive? Ha! Is the Grand Canyon just a hole in the ground? — a coronary of Brobdingnagian proportions that ignobly terminated my illustrious career.

Fact three. My final meal consisted of a burger and french fries. It was a double-pattied burger layered with six slices of applewood-smoked bacon and three varieties of cheese product. I had them hold the pickle. The bag the food arrived in was transparent with grease. I consumed the heavily-salted meat treat in four bites and devoured the fries with such mindless gusto that likely more than a few spears of deep-fried potato ended up in my lungs.

Fact four. I have been researching methods of transmuting pluripotent stem cells into neurons. My stated purpose, according to my grant proposal, is to research techniques by which these cells might be employed to combat neurodegenerative diseases. My unstated purpose — Oh, Haddon, you trickster, you! — is to continue my investigation into the prolonging of the human lifespan, with the ultimate goal of beating death once and for all at its own game.

Fact the fifth. By George, I believe I did it.

Fact the sixth. I must make room on the mantle for my Nobel Prize.

Now, now, do not get ahead of yourself, Haddon.

A *head* of yourself! Ha!

Because fact the seventh. Based on its yellowish tincture, I appear to be suspended within a container of Nickle Solution. Knowing as I do Gerald's unswerving adoration of me — why else would I keep such a chowderhead around, if not for an invigorating daily boost of ego — I surmise the resourceful imbecile followed the example I set for him and indulged in some off-the-books experimentation of his own. Haddon, you rascal! Such a bad influence you are!

Leading me inexorably, irrevocably, to the eighth and final fact. If I do the maths correctly, there was simply not enough serum available for a full-body immersion. While I cannot confirm this through external means, I am convinced that I — that is, the me that is me; the I of I; whatever the quality is that makes me unambiguously *me* — I no longer reside within the confines of my artery-clogged physique. As I am unable to swivel my eyes about, and there exists no peripheral evidence of my admittedly prodigious proboscis hovering between them, I doubt I even inhabit my skull.

The facts all point to one inescapable conclusion.

The genius that was Doctor Haddon Nickle is now a cliché so beloved of pulp sci-fi novels and b-movies.

Doctor Nickle is a brain in a jar.

But on the plus side, at least he's still got his health.

Ha!

[Transcript, audio file 18, Nickle Procedure]

It has been, ooooh, let's call it a week, and I am celebrating. Now, I don't know much about scotch, but whatever this is I'm drinking, I am inten— [*burp*] intensely drunk. The label on the bottle says this stuff is fifty years old. Pretty good for old liquid.

You want some, Ru— [*hiccup*] Rufus? Here you go. Yeah, lap that up, good dog.

Where was I? Right. Sooo... after a lot of trial and error and three more whoopsy-daisy episodes of spontaneous lobe combustion, I believe success [*burp*] has been achieved. I have induced in Dr. Nickle's brain a constant flow of impulses that indicates a fully functioning brain. If I'm right. So, good on you, Gerry! You're a hell of a vet! And to you, Doctor Brain! Here's [*burp*] to you and your liquor cabinet! And to you, Rufus, you stinky old mutt! Here's mud in your eye! Whatever that means.

Whether the readout demonstrates actual conscious thought is arguable. There is certainly a reaction to my presence, but since I didn't bother [*brraack*] hooking up Doc's mouth and vocal cords, who can say? Anyway, after all these [*urp*] months of criticism, I find myself very much enjoying the silence. Now that I've had time to mull it over, the doc was always a bit of a jerk to me.

Tomorrow — once the hang— [*burp*] hangov— [*hiccup*] once I've sobered up — I shall begin reading through his many journals and notes. I wish it were otherwise — his handwriting is atrocious — but leaving the doc as a bowl of cold brain soup achieves nothing. I know where this is headed but am other— [*burp*] otherwise unable to determine how to go about it. I cannot ask for help, who'd even believe any of this?

Christ, Rufus, am I drunk... I'm so...

[muffled snores]

I cannot say for certain how much time I have spent in my new, hopefully temporary aqua-home. It is vital I impose a semblance of routine to my time here. It will help me retain my sanity. Gerald appears to be keeping regular hours, although I can't say I approve of his new attitude towards recreational alcohol.

From the angle of the room, my watery abode is located atop of the filing cabinet in the corner of my laboratory. My desk is covered in papers. Gerald's been going through my notes. Very sloppy. Other than that, the room is sparse and clean, as I always insisted. From Gerald's blurred visage — when he places his face close to the glass and gazes wonderingly into my hazelnut eyes — there has been enough of an interval between my death and now for him to garner something approximating a beard. The sparse facial forest he is cultivating does not do his commonplace features any favours. It is a slipshod effort, patchy and uninspired, much like the rest of his work. Should I ever regain the power of speech, my first pronouncement will be for him to shave it off posthaste.

Perhaps I give Gerald too little credit. I should be thankful my haphazardly hirsute assistant had the strength of forethought to scoop my soul from my cranium like so much iced cream. Then again, is this not more a testament to my remarkable ability as a mentor to distill the brilliance of my thoughts to the point of comprehensibility? A child could have done it, really, under my tutelage. And what is a veterinarian but a child doctor?

But to the next step, boy! I can't float in here forever! Get me a body! Be quick about it but be choosy! Get me a body with some muscle. Something befitting a man of my stature. Someone young and handsome.

After all, I can't possibly accept a Nobel Prize looking like you, now can I? They'd never believe it!

[Transcript, audio file 20, Nickle Procedure]

These goddamned chicken scratches are driving me nuts. An eight looks like a three, a zero might be the letter o, and so on. I think Rufus has better handwriting. He's better [*urple*] company, anyway.

Here's where I'm at. With the brain successfully removed, it is obvious that it must be relocated to the cranial confines of another body. It is also obvious that I don't have one lying about, now do I?

So, I guess grave robbery it is.

I don't know what else I expected. We'd planned to move on to animal trials first. That's how I got here, I caught the doc pilfering animal corpses from the school. It was either hire me, or face prison. And my average was a low C, so yeah, here I am.

I'd better synthesize more serum. There's no point in using the doctor's body again, not after the mess I made of it. I really should bury it, the smell from the closet is just awful. Rufus is beginning to whine. Once I sober up, I'll get on it.

This really is some wonderful stuff. I'm not drunk, just maintaining.

Tomorrow, I'll get on with [*burp*] acquiring a body. Or body parts, anyway. I am sure the doctor would prefer a complete body. An Adonis, probably. Some manly man, yeah, that's what he'd like. Asshole.

I find myself less than inclined to care.

Oh, hell.

Let me add a personal note to these recordings. Let it be known that I, Gerald Brunswick, am henceforth pissed off at the great Haddon Nickle. I've come across more than a few hurtful statements aimed at yours truly in his journals. Vicious, really mean stuff. This morning, I had to stop reading and get some air after he listed, in great detail, the many types of slugs that could manage this position better than I.

So, yeah, I am just a little angry. I've given that man over a year of my life, and he thinks of me as less a colleague than a gofer. I'm barely a glorified janitor. I'm not even Rufus.

What am I supposed to do now? I should be focussed on the task at hand, but as unscientific as it is, I'm feeling very vindictive at the moment.

Intriguing development. Gerald has relocated me to the corner of my desk. He is sitting directly in front of me, messily eating a sandwich as he scans my notes. Egg salad, from the looks of it. Disgusting. Apparently, my orders that the buffoon abstain from eating food in my laboratory are now on hold.

Ugh. A clump of yellowish comestible has escaped the confines of the bread and is now sitting squarely atop one of my open journals. This is intolerable. I feel like I am visiting a circus, watching a trained bonobo feign human intellect. He must know that I'm watching him. Why does he persist in this upsetting performance?

No, don't let Rufus on the table, you moronic bonehead! What are you even doing? Why would you ever...

Is he drinking from my container? No! Bad dog! *Bad dog!*

[Transcript, audio file 24, Nickle Procedure]

I've synthesized more serum, but I'm wary of its effectiveness. The solution I've prepared appears to match the previous compound, but it smells weirdly of Mountain Dew, so I may be off by a few parts per million.

Whatever.

I have begun filching body parts. It's been slim pickings so far, but thanks to an unscrupulous attendant and the doctor's debit card — by the way, his code is his birthday and year, what a genius — I have gathered together the right arm of a car accident victim, the left arm of a suicide by overdose, and a pair of matching legs from an incident involving a lawn mower and a steep incline. They're all in the doc's freezer right now, but once I fill the bathtub with solution, I'll toss them in.

Side note. Even sober, my passion for continuing is low. I have come across numerous references to the suspicious nature of my parentage, I have been unfavourably compared to many of the smellier members of the animal kingdom, and the phrase 'dunderheaded nitwit with a glandular secretion problem' has appeared more than twice.

I find myself wishing to flush him down the toilet, and only the thought of what happens afterwards stops me. I have practically no savings, and there's only so much of the doc's stuff I can hock. I've already near maxed-out his credit cards.

I'll be damned if I go back to veterinary school. I'd have to start at square one. Screw that. I can't go from resurrecting the dead to dissecting ferrets.

No, without the doc back in some form, I've got no choice but to continue.

But. Maybe it's the alcohol talking, but, there's nothing stopping me from claiming all this as my own work, is there? I don't really need the doc anymore, I just need a successful transplantation. Who cares if he's not quite the same anymore? Let others work on fine-tuning the process. Yeah, that's it. I'll just rewrite the notes, reap the rewards, and me and Rufus will retire to an island.

Hey, almost forgot, the left arm I got? It's four inches longer than the right. And several shades darker.

[chuckling]

My thoughts are becoming muddled, possibly due to unforeseen cellular breakdown. I suspect, however, the cause is more mundane.

Gerald is looking the worse for wear. He has taken to imbibing while he works, and has taken on the haggard, sluggish movements of a rummy. I note with no little pang of regret that my assistant has nearly finished off a thirty-year-old Glengoyne I had been saving for a special occasion.

Mixing it with orange soda seems an extra-cruel insult.

Gerald has been studying my journals, his semi-simian brow furrowed in simulated thought, and his frequent looks up at me have become more and more choleric. While Gerald's comprehension may be muddied through the dual filters of alcohol and inferior brain matter, I fear even one such as he is not so dim as to misunderstand the layers upon layers of denigrations I inked into the pages.

No doubt as crude rejoinder to my entirely accurate calumny on his capabilities as a doctor and as a man, Gerald has ceased to turn out the lights. A petty manoeuvre, but effective, as he has thus eliminated any potential environmental cues that might aid me in discerning the passage of time.

This constant radiance is wreaking havoc with my circadian rhythms. The suprachiasmatic nucleus of my hypothalamus is receiving constant input from the retinal ganglion cells and consequently insists it exists in a state of eternal day, decreasing the desire of the pineal gland to release melatonin into my system. By now my brain must be swimming in hormones, trying anything and everything to chemically induce unconsciousness. It may be a miracle I can form a coherent thought.

How long may the human mind go without sleep? There were studies, I recall. The rats, that group of rats, kept awake for more than a month. They all perished, lucky bastards.

I suspect two to three weeks may be the maximum that I can maintain any semblance of cognitive coherence. After that, my brain will either refuse the demand for wakefulness and induce unconsciousness, or it will cease operations altogether.

Sleep is an imperative for the human mind. There *must* be a period of discharge, where the brain is allowed the time to release its pent-up energy through undisciplined, unbridled cogitation.

Or else the mind will snap.

[Transcript, audio file 27, Nickle Procedure]

From the [*burp*] looks of the readout, I have managed to significantly agitate the doc. The impulses spike into the red whenever I am nearby. I'm taking this as a win.

On the bodily construction front, I have lucked into an undamaged pelvic region of a man with, shall we say, somewhat less than most men would wish down below. Much less.

Micro-penis, I believe is the term.

Only a torso and head to go.

On a very much related note, further discoveries today in the realm of insults. Where's that list? Ah. Slime-encrusted toady, that's a new one. Obsequious lickspittle, I don't know what that means; sounds bad. Red-assed baboon in asexual heat. The uni-browed product of ritualized sibling mating; that's kind of wordy. Much repetition of the words 'ass', 'boob', 'clod', and 'schlemiel'.

More severe action is required.

Maybe I'll show him the micro-penis. Or should that be a happy surprise?

⚡

Wait, wha...?

What are you doing, Gerald? Why are you hugging the...

Are you moving me? Be careful! You're a sickly little milquetoast, Gerald, you lack near enough upper body strength for such an operation.

Oh dear lord, don't slip! One false step and I'll be so much spilled porridge!

Double vision! My eyes must be loose on their stalks! Am I not anchored? Oh, I'm getting dizzy! How is this even possible without ears?

Are you... are you pouring me out? You wouldn't dare!

Oh, thank heavens that's over. No, don't touch me! Get your fingers away! Just the thought of your inadequate sausage fingers sliding clumsily over my eyeballs fills me with dread! Be careful, don't squeeze! Just aim them both forward, you...

Wait...did I just see multicoloured pebbles float by? Is that a man in a diver's helmet? And a treasure chest?

You son of a whore! I'm in my goddamned aquarium! You stupid, petty, asinine little pissant! You just plopped the greatest scientific mind of all time in a fishbowl! If I ever get out of here...

Stop tapping the glass, I'm not a goldfish!

Wait, where are my fish? Where are my clownfish? Where are Bethune and Lister? Oh, there they are, good. It'll be nice to have some company.

Wait, no! Take them out! They'll nibble at my genius!

[Transcript, audio file 28, Nickle Procedure]
[ten minutes of laughter]
[sounds of equipment being moved about]

Oh, madness! When will you clutch me to your lunatic bosom and relieve me of this mental torment?

You bastard, Brunswick, you have gone too far! First you deprive the saviour of humankind of sleep. Then you relocate him to a fishtank. Any other dime-a-dozen slugabed would be *non compos mentis* within mere hours of this sadism, yet my immeasurable intelligence so far resists the sweet bliss of insanity.

And now this! My orangutanian associate has seen fit to increase my maltreatment and has located two computer screens before my prison. My right eye is now inundated with the pea-brained adventures of a gaggle of imbeciles, all bronzed of skin and vacant of stare, who evidently live together in a locale known as the Jersey Shore. My left orb is set to a rotating video playlist from a website called *PornHub*. Disgusting.

It is all very confusing. I fear my brain has begun to hallucinate from the stress. I find myself having difficulty discerning between the actual and the fictive. This morning (evening? mid-afternoon? teatime? brunch?) I held a long and productive conversation with Sir Frederick Banting about the physiological ramifications of genetic interference. As I feel certain Sir Banting has been deceased for some time, and I lack any organs receptive to aural stimuli, I am suffering a monumental episode of cognitive dissonance.

[Transcript, audio file 29, Brunswick Procedure]

[giggling] Whooooo!

I've pretty much finished off the liquor cabinet. I mixed together the last of what I could find. It's a full pint of grenadine and peppermint schnapps. If it doesn't kill me, I'll call it a Minty Red Dragon. Rufus, you want any?

I [*belch*] just held a handwritten sign up to the tank. It read "Nickle Solution." Oh, you can't see me, I'm making finger quotes around that.

Quote Nickle Solution Unquote. I then crossed out "Nickle," replaced it with "Brunswick" and held it to the glass again.

From the looks of the readout, the grey little bastard gets it.

I am unable to determine precisely how long it has now been. Deprivation of sleep has utterly disrupted the connection between my amygdala and the medial prefrontal cortex. I may be prone to paroxysms of depression. Luckily, I am in no condition whereby I could hurt myself.

Without sleep, the effectiveness of my hippocampus has dwindled to a point where my memories are becoming as tangible as reality. I must concentrate on the televisions. They are my only tenuous tether to reality. Gerald has tuned them to separate twenty-four-hour news networks, no doubt to increase my torment. The lips of the various newscasters do not sync up with the captions, an effect I find bewildering.

To my left, there is a story about a small young boy trapped in a burning building. The camera has caught a clownfish in a fireman's helmet swimming inside, risking the flames to rescue the lad. The boy is pulled safely from the fire, a boy with my face, an old man's face on the body of a child, cradled in the fins of a giant orange fish. My mother, the newscaster, tells the nation that a weather update is coming after these commercial advertisements. I am unsure if I was ever in a fire. I certainly do not recall my frump of a mother having a career in journalism.

My father, meanwhile, is onscreen on the right, hawking luxurious triple-plied toilet paper to dowdy hausfraus. I'm frankly astonished Father ever found the time to hold down such a job and continue his duties as a tenured professor of Medieval Philosophy.

This is all very perplexing. The present and past are indistinguishable. I find myself reaching an imaginary hand towards where it believes a phone should be, determined to purchase that wondrously colourful vacuum with twelve, count them twelve, attachment heads that will revolutionize the cleaning process in my home all for three easy payments of ninety-nine dollars, but for a limited time only. How can I lose?

[Transcript, audio file 30, Brunswick Procedure]

I'm nearly finished putting together my composite body. I tossed the original right arm in the garbage and have replaced it with that of a chimpanzee that recently asphyxiated on a pine cone at the local zoo. A torso has also come into my possession, a withered female with a marked lack of muscle tone. From a quick scan of its chart, its owner was emaciated due to an opioid addiction.

Another quick read of the journals has provided me with the insult of "featherheaded blunderbuss." I have no idea what it means, but I'll take it as its author no doubt intended it.

I lack only a head now.

I have a few ideas.

[chuckling]

My brain is deteriorating. I can feel it. It is smaller. More compact. The thoughts come faster, having less distance to travel. They approach the speed of light. Should my brain decrease any further in mass, I may become capable of time travel.

Should this occur, I will travel back in time the period of one year, when I will then cancel my contract with Gerald and do my utmost to see him ruined.

[Transcript, audio file 32, Brunswick Procedure]

The body is complete. I have made some minor, last-minute alterations to the anatomy, but all the doctor's notes indicate that, despite the unorthodox nature of the anatomy, the procedure should be successful. And if it doesn't work, well doc, you've got only yourself to blame. Take a handwriting course, why don't you?

Tomorrow, I shall replant the mind and soul of Haddon Nickle into the body he so desperately deserves.

Come on, Rufus. Let's you and me go for a walk.

No! Not that! You monster! You inhuman monst—

[Transcript, video file, science conference, July 22, 2019]

... as you've observed, ladies and gentlemen, the compound, which I have named the Brunswick Serum — yes, yes, I am a bit of an egotist, but can you blame me? [audience laughter] — my serum not only keeps cells alive almost indefinitely, it successfully acts as an intermediary agent to transplant organs from one host to another with minimal possibility of rejection and a vastly quicker healing process. Simply put, the Brunswick Serum halts the aging process in its tracks and prolongs life, potentially to the point of immortality.

I only wish my partner and dear, dear friend Haddon Nickle could be here on stage with me, to witness the culmination of our work. It was Doctor Nickle's initial research into the aging process that fuelled mine, and together we have created something that will change the course of humankind. I stand on his shoulders. Alas, if Haddon had only waited another few days, perhaps his suicide could have been avoided.

But I've prattled on long enough. Let's get to the main event. As you are obviously aware, not long ago I successfully transplanted a living, working brain from one body to another. While, yes, there still exist many accusations that the video has been faked, the proof, as they say, is in the pudding. Certainly, Elon Musk has been satisfied, as he's seen fit to join forces with me in creating a new and better world. As well as provide me a legal team to deal with all the cranks. [audience laughter]

So finally, ladies, gentlemen, distinguished colleagues, members of the press, I present to you the first ever successful brain transplant recipient. Come here, boy!

[audience applause]

Good boy, Rufus. Down, boy, down. Would you hold his chain, please, he's a little overexcited. Thank you. As you can plainly see, my little miracle basset here is practically frantic with joy.

[snarls and growls]

Looks like he's not a fan of the limelight. Well, it has been a busy day. He'll sleep like a dog tonight. I must admit, even I am astonished at the rapidity of his recovery. Frankly, I was afraid I'd made a huge mistake in my initial measurements when the brain wouldn't fit, but after I planed the surface lobes here and there, I managed to squish it all in.

And the results speak for themselves. What was once the empty shell of an elderly basset hound is now quite possibly the healthiest canine in all of history. Rufus should live well past his normal lifespan. Even his cognitive abilities have improved beyond all expectations. Looking into his eyes now, you'd swear he was human.

Have you ever seen a more energetic, enthusiastic dog?

And why wouldn't he be? I gave the old boy a new leash on life.

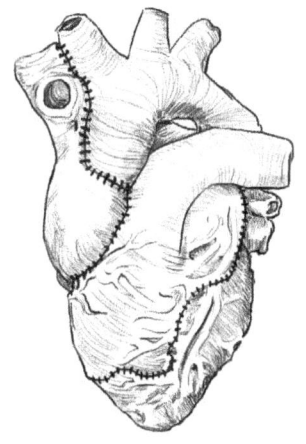

FRANKENSTEIN INC.

MAX D. STANTON

My son's been dead for four years and three months, but I still visit him every Sunday. He works at Freshbuy, behind the butcher counter.

I try to get there early in the day, before the rush begins. I put a few things in a shopping basket so the manager doesn't kick me out, and then I stand by the rear of the juice aisle and watch Pat at work.

From a distance, you might think that he was still alive, even that he was thriving. He stands up straight and tall. He attends to his customers swiftly. His uniform is crisp and clean. He even has a decent haircut at last. But when you get up close you can see the sickly, fish-belly whiteness of his skin, and the slackness of his features, and the plastic outlets that they drilled into his skull to restart his brain after it drowned in heroin. Up close you see his eyes, all dull and full of blood.

When Pat was alive he was always in motion, like there was a live wire deep inside of him throwing off sparks. Ever since he was a screaming toddler I had hoped that someday he'd quiet down. Be careful what you wish for, I guess.

It all started with Dr. Victor Frankenstein, of course. He was the one who figured out how to bring the dead back from the grave, and how to make them do whatever you want. The Frankenstein Process, they call it. In an earlier time, they'd have burned the doctor at the stake, but instead he won the Nobel Prize and became the richest man in the world. Goes to show that sometimes the old ways are best.

In the beginning it was like a magic trick. The famous doctor would appear on one news show or another, tall and unsmiling, handsome in a cold sort of way, with a fresh human corpse stretched out on a slab before him. He'd perform his hocus-pocus – crack the skull open, plug in some computer equipment, and then jump-start it with a jolt of electricity – and poor Lazarus would rise up and obey the doctor's orders.

My husband didn't believe it for a long time. "It's just a special effect," Mickey told me the first time we watched a dead man walk on live television. "They're doing publicity for a movie or something. Like back in the 20s, when that radio guy tricked everyone into thinking that Martians were invading New Jersey. What kind of aliens would invade New Jersey? A lot of people are going to feel like real idiots when this is all over and done with."

I sat there next to him on the sofa with my head resting on his shoulder and laughed at his jokes as he poked fun at the dark miracle happening on the screen. But soon the magic trick crawled out of the TV and into all of our lives.

You see, at first even the people who believed in Dr. Frankenstein didn't understand him. They thought he was peddling immortality, a way for rich people afraid of death to cheat the Reaper.

But that's not what the Frankenstein Process is about.

It doesn't bring people back from the dead, it makes dead bodies get up and do what they're told. Dr. Frankenstein doesn't sell eternal life. He sells slaves.

I remember the first time I saw a Frankenstein zombie in person. Most people my age remember their first time meeting a zombie, it's one of those big events like 9/11 that forces its way into your memories. It's nothing to children, though, they've never known life without the walking dead.

Pat had a nasty ear infection that was making all of us miserable, and I was walking to the pharmacy to pick up his prescription. Along the way, I spotted an elderly neighbour of ours whose name I never learned staring mutely at a construction site. Work had been going on there for weeks, but I hadn't paid any attention to it before. I hadn't realized that most of the workers were dead. There were four of them, with skin the colour of cigarette ash and red, sightless eyes. A paunchy foreman watched them at their labour with a tablet computer in his hands, occasionally tapping on the screen to give a new command. I'd heard about mines and factories going over to zombie labour, but until that moment it hadn't been quite real to me.

They were nothing like the shambling, groaning zombies from the old horror movies Pat loved. Hollywood got it all wrong. The dead moved gracelessly, but they were sure-footed and capable. They made no noise whatsoever apart from the clanking of their tools. They weren't hungry for brains or full of fury against the living. If anything, they seemed sad and tired.

For a while, life in our home went on much as it had before. You know how an earthquake might kill ten thousand people in Africa but it doesn't ruin your day? The dead were rising up from their graves, but we still had bills to pay, and parent-teacher conferences to attend when Pat got in trouble at school, and a hundred other little things to worry about. So even while our mailmen and store clerks and bus drivers were replaced by zombies one by one, and the strikes and protests against Frankenstein turned into riots and bombings, we kept calm and carried on just like we were supposed to.

Then one day I showed up for work at the department store, and there was a dead woman standing behind my cash register.

I ran to my manager. She was playing with the tablet that controlled my replacement and seemed irritated by my questions. "You should have gotten an e-mail about this last week," she said. "It's out of my hands. I didn't make the decision, it's a new policy from corporate. They're phasing out all of the non-management employees for re-animated labour. It's a cost-cutting measure. You'll get your last paycheck direct deposited like usual, and there'll be a notice in the mail about your unemployment benefits."

That evening, Mickey and I went out for a walk, like we used to do a lifetime ago when we were dating. We didn't want to talk for a long time, because neither one of us wanted to spoil the splendid silence, but eventually I couldn't take it anymore.

"What are we going to do now?" I asked.

Mickey gave my hand a comforting squeeze. "We'll get by," he said. "I've still got my job at the warehouse. It'll be tight until you find something new, but as long as we're careful we'll be all right."

"I was only half asking about you and me. What about Pat? He says he's not going to college but I don't know what else he can possibly do. There's no jobs out there anymore. Not for the living, anyway."

"I've been thinking about that too. It's tough out there, but he's a good boy. He'll find something."

"I love him more than life, and he *is* a good boy, but he's an angry, impatient boy, too. Besides, since when is being good enough?"

Mickey wrapped his arm around my shoulders, and I nuzzled my cheek against his arm. "We'll get by," he repeated. "What choice do we have?"

One day, I came home from errands to the sound of shouting. I hadn't heard shouting in our home since the day that Pat tried to stick a fork in an electric outlet, when he was four. Mickey wasn't given to raising his voice, and Pat showed his anger through sullen silence and slamming doors. But now here they were, barking at each other in the living room like fighting dogs.

"What's wrong?" I asked.

"You tell her!" Mickey yelled, red-faced, sticking his finger in Pat's chest. "Tell her what you did."

Pat smiled defiantly. "I got paid, is what I did. Three thousand dollars to start, and more every month for as long as I live. And I don't even have to do anything for it."

"He donated himself to fucking Frankenstein!" Mickey snarled accusingly. "After he dies, they're going to take his body and start it up again and put him to work scrubbing toilets or some shit!"

"*After* I die! *After* I die! Who cares what happens *after* I die? Christ, nobody gives a fuck about what happens to me while I'm alive, why should I give a fuck what happens to me after I die?"

I nearly dropped my shopping. "You think nobody cares what happens while you're alive?" I asked. But Mickey and Pat were still shouting at each other, and neither of them heard me over the din.

"You've seen what that company does!" Mickey roared. "You want to be another fucking zombie? It's a goddamned abomination!"

"It's goddamned money!" Pat roared back. "What else am I going to do, tell me that?" And without waiting for an answer he stormed out of the apartment, slamming the door behind him so hard that you'd think he meant to break it.

After that day, there was shouting in our apartment all the time.

The Frankenstein money wasn't enough for Pat to live on, but it was plenty to kill himself with. I began getting knots of dread in my stomach whenever the first of a new month rolled around, because Pat got his Frankenstein money on the first day of the month and he'd be helplessly drunk for at least the week thereafter. He'd vanish for days at a time – and when there's bombings and mob violence and spree killings on the television almost every day, it's an awful torture not to know where your son is.

It was a blessing and a curse to have company in our misery. So many of our friends were suffering the very same hardships, and some of them had it even worse. Mickey's work friend Tom lost his house putting his little girl through rehab. My best friend, Teresa, had to go a mental hospital after her Sally got caught up in some radical cell and was shot dead at a protest march. It felt like the entire country was falling off the tracks.

One day, I came home and Pat was sprawled on the couch with a needle dangling from his arm, his head swaying front to back. He was watching a zombie movie on TV – an old black and white one, they don't make zombie movies anymore. Never before and never again have I seen another living soul look so afraid. I pulled the needle out of his arm and threw it against the wall, then cradled my boy in my arms.

When the call finally came, I knew what it was before I even picked up the phone. They'd found him in a gas station bathroom. It's strange how you can anticipate something awful for a long time coming, but when it finally happens the enormity of the pain still takes you completely by surprise.

In my many bitter moments I imagine that Dr. Frankenstein planned it all to happen this way – that he knew giving my son a little money but taking away all his hope would drive him to the grave that much quicker and give Frankenstein Inc. another piece of inventory. I've been to enough of my friends' children's' memorial services by now that the idea doesn't seem totally insane. You'll note that I say "memorial services" and not "funerals." The dead hardly ever get buried these days.

I had to go to the morgue to identify the body. The street outside was full of dead men in black armour. They stared at me silently with their blood-red eyes as I walked through their formation. It was a big controversy when the police first started using zombies for foot patrols, but they probably couldn't even staff a force without them. I read that it's more dangerous to be a policeman today than it was to be a soldier in World War II. Nobody's got jobs anymore, but there's guns for everyone.

Inside the morgue, they took me to a cinderblock room that smelled of antiseptic, where a long window looked into a chamber with brushed steel shelves built into the walls. A man in a white coat pulled my child out of one of those shelves and removed the sheet that covered him. *At least things can't get any worse*, I thought to myself. *The worst thing that can possibly happen has happened now.* Looking back, I see how naive that was. Perhaps in the past, death was the end of suffering, but science marches on.

After I'd identified my son, they escorted me down the hall to the Frankenstein Inc. representative. He had his own office in the morgue, a cramped space barely bigger than a cubicle. The rep was a little man in a rumpled suit that was slightly too big for him. He gave me a stock condolence speech that had obviously been written in some faraway corporate office, and hustled me through signing some papers, discouraging me from reading them. I complied. Even if I'd had the presence of mind to read all those forms, which I didn't, I wouldn't have been able to understand all of their twisted legalese.

On my way out of the office, I asked the little man, "So when are they replacing *you* with a zombie?"

He smiled grimly. "Our next generation models are going to have speech capability and a suite of apps that will let them handle basic administrative tasks," he said. "So maybe not that much longer."

It was a year before I saw Pat again. Freshbuy was having a sale on sliced turkey. Even though it was out of my way, I had plenty of time on my hands, and money was so tight we couldn't afford to pass up any bargains. Mickey, who had once been so easy-going and gentle, had gotten in the habit of nitpicking every bill, and if I spent more than he thought proper it was bound to cause a fight.

When I gave my order to the zombie at the Freshbuy deli counter, at first I didn't even recognize him. You get so used to dealing with zombies that you start thinking of them just as things, like they're ATM machines or self-checkout registers. Like they didn't used to think and dream and laugh. Like they didn't used to be the light of some mother's life. But when the zombie at the counter handed me my package of meat, and my fingers touched his ice-cold hands, I looked him in the face and I saw my lost little boy staring back at me. It was like someone had stuck a barbed fishhook right into my heart. On the one hand, it was so sweet to see his face again that I couldn't turn away. On the other hand, it was even more painful than seeing him on a slab at the morgue.

I collapsed right there in the store. Pat didn't make any move to help me up. He wasn't programmed for that.

When I told Mickey about it that evening, it drove him into a fury so fierce that I was scared of him for the first time in thirty years of marriage. He cursed Freshbuy until he was nearly raving and swore up and down that if he could get his hands on Dr. Victor Frankenstein he'd shatter all his teeth and kill him by inches with a power drill. Mickey didn't even like to kill bugs – when he found them in our apartment he'd cup them in his hands and put them outside. I had no doubts at all that he would have tortured the doctor to death if he'd been able.

Despite Mickey's rage, I began visiting Freshbuy every week. I never told Mickey or anyone else about those trips, and I was careful to always throw away the bags and receipts before I got home, but somehow I think Mickey knew what I was doing. I never was any good at hiding my feelings. Maybe if I'd been stronger in the face of my grief, more capable of tearing out the fishhook and saying goodbye, then the horrors that came next might never have happened. I guess addiction runs in our family.

The day that Mickey came to Freshbuy was the second-worst day of my life. I was watching Pat work, like always, when I felt Mickey's hand on my shoulder. It was such a familiar touch, and yet I jumped at it.

"You need to get out of here now," he growled. "This isn't good for you. I'm going to fix it." He glanced over at Pat and shuddered with hate and disgust. I noticed then that Mickey was holding a claw hammer. He'd brought it from his toolbox at home, it was the same one he'd used to hang up our family photos. He stormed over to the meat counter.

"Mickey, what are you doing?" I screamed. "Stop!" But by then it was too late.

Pat met Mickey at the counter like any other customer. "You leave her alone!" Mickey half-screamed, half-cried at our dead son. "You were never good to her! Stop hurting her!" Pat didn't move or respond in any way. He was still waiting for Mickey to order some meat. Mickey raised the hammer and broke our boy's skull with a wet, dull crack. Pat didn't fall. He only stared at Mickey with those sad, vacant red eyes of his. Mickey kept hitting him again and again and again, and finally, mercifully, he went down.

A gawking crowd had gathered around. "What the fuck is going on?" Mickey yelled hoarsely at them, with tears running down his cheeks. "Why do we have to live like this? Don't we mean anything to them? Doesn't human life mean a goddamned thing anymore?" Roaring, he shattered the panes of glass in the deli case one by one with his hammer, until the floor glittered with broken shards. He swept the items off of nearby shelves and kicked them away. Another zombie mutely approached with a push broom to sweep up the mess, and Mickey pummelled it until it dropped.

Then he ran out of gas and stopped breaking things and wept like I'd never seen before, not even right after Pat's death. I tried to go him to comfort him, but before I could move, two black-gloved hands seized me roughly from behind.

Store management must have called 911. There were two zombie policemen in the store, looking like killer robots in their bulky riot armour. One of them had gotten a hold of me and gripped so tight that the next day I had finger-shaped bruises all along my arms. The other approached Mickey. The zombie raised its club and hissed through its plexiglass face shield, like a snake getting ready to strike. Mickey dropped the hammer and put up his hands but by then it was already on top of him. I don't let myself think about the rest of it, although sometimes the sound of a hammer blow or the sight of a dead policeman walking about pulls me back into that moment and I lose myself in shrieking agony.

Afterwards, I had to make another trip to that goddamned morgue. I had to look at my husband laid out with his head caved in and sign a form to identify him. And I had to deal with that little man in the cheap suit again, too. To my surprise and horror, Mickey had donated his body to Frankenstein Inc.

Mickey had always handled our finances. It took me a while to make sense of his shoebox full of bank statements, but once I did, I realized that the warehouse had stopped paying him almost a year ago, not long after Pat's death. Since then, the only funds coming into our account were monthly deposits made by Frankenstein Inc. Small monthly deposits, at that. No wonder he'd been so sensitive about money.

After the memorial service, Mickey's friends all decided to go out for a drink together. I didn't want to go but I didn't want to be alone either so I followed along. They toasted Mickey and then they all got piss drunk while I sat at the bar quietly nursing a glass of red wine.

"At least old Mick's working again," Tom muttered to nobody in particular while he was waiting for his beer. "They might even give him his old job back. Whole fucking company's gone over to zombie labour." It turned out that almost all of them had signed up as Frankenstein donors just to get by. From the way they looked and talked and drank, I guessed that some of them would be back to work real soon.

The apartment was very quiet when I woke up the next morning. I couldn't believe how huge it felt. Like a vast, empty cavern. I accidentally made coffee for two, but I drank it all anyway because of how much Mickey hated it when food went to waste. And then I went back to Freshbuy, switching buses twice because there'd been a terrible bombing at City Hall the day of Mickey's funeral and the streets were still detoured. I would have asked the drivers the quickest route, but they were all long dead.

At Freshbuy, Pat was back in service already. All the technicians had to do was put a metal plate in his head, and he was ready to get back to his place at the meat slicer. I stood there watching him all day until the store closed and they made me leave.

Now I visit Pat every Sunday as part of my weekly routine. I visit Mickey on Sundays too. He's a street cleaner downtown. I walk with him on his rounds until it starts to get dark, almost like we did a lifetime ago when we were dating. The silence isn't splendid anymore.

I go back to the apartment afterwards and heat up dinner. I eat it alone while I watch the riots on TV. Of course, with Mickey passed, now I have to pay for everything myself. And it's not like there's a lot of jobs out there for a fifty-two-year-old woman with only a high school diploma. So, I went to the Frankenstein Inc. recruiting office and signed up as a donor, just like Pat and Mickey did. It's not much money but I don't need much. And in a way, it gives me something to look forward to.

It means that someday we'll be a family again.

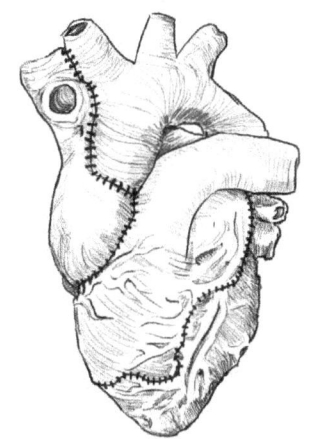

F. — A POST-MODERN PROMETHEUS

ERIC CHOI AND JOSEPH MCGINTY

From: rwalton79@kilchbergnetz.ch
Sent: November 28, 20--, 18:51
To: margaret.saville@sillywalks.gov.uk
Subject: Crazy Day at Work!

My dear Sister,

Pardon my curt missive, but I am at pause for only a brief time in the organizational haste at Kürzer & Boily due to the upcoming Christmas season. Ingolstadt is indeed pastorally beautiful under a comforting blanket of snow and good cheer, but alas, I am unable to join the townsfolk in their Yuletide spirit. It has been merely two weeks since I was (through sundry means) promoted to Under-Assistant Brand Manager, Eis Schokolade™ Division, and already I have witnessed calamity.

Last Monday, I was upon the factory floor to discuss cost-saving mixture ratios with the food engineers when we heard shouts from our colleagues. We ran to the source and discovered that one of the technicians had gained control of the caramel mixer and was attempting to operate the vat in a manner contrary to standards.

I joined with my colleagues in imploring the fellow to cease immediately. The demented wretch appeared oblivious to our pleas and continued to operate the equipment in flagrant disregard to procedures. In his confusion, he reached out in a simian manner and touched the scalding surface of the vat. He screamed, jumped backwards, and collided with the control mechanism. We stared in horror as the loading switch was tripped and the vat discharged its molten caramel upon the poor man.

A quick-witted operator swiftly moved to shut down the mechanism, and with the help of gaffs and poles we were able to extricate the miserable wretch from the wasted avalanche of hot caramel. I made a mental note of the financial impact this would have upon the Eis Schokolade™ Division.

We conveyed him to the plant foreman's office, there to attend the arrival of an ambulance. As I attempted to wipe off the caramel and administered what first aid I could, I surveyed the poor victim. It was Victor Frankenstein, one of the quality control technicians. I knew little of him save some bizarre tales related by his shift crew (one concerned a capacitor and a dead frog). Clearly he was suffering from shock, yet that did not appear to be all. His eyes had an expression of wildness, and even perhaps madness. He would periodically gnash his teeth, as if impatient with the woes that oppressed him.

"Everything is fine," said I. "An ambulance will be here shortly. You will be all right."

"Thank you for your words of comfort, but they are useless; I will *not* be all right. I have lost much and can imagine for the future only new miseries befalling me."

"Why do you speak so?"

"You may perceive, Herr Walton, that I have suffered greatly. Today's incident is only the latest of many misfortunes. I know not if the relation of my disasters would be of interest –"

Recalling the value of keeping an injury victim talking, I replied quickly, "I am much gratified by your offered communications. Pray, continue."

It was then that he commenced his narrative. I have here endeavoured to record, as nearly as possible in his own words, what he related. Sad and pathetic was his story, cruel the winds that embraced the gallant vessel on its course and wrecked it – thus!

I am by birth a Genevese, and my family was one of the most distinguished of that republic. When I finally attained my undergraduate degree from the University of Ingolstadt at the age of twenty-seven, Father resolved that I should proceed with graduate studies. With transcripts in order, the grand institution conferred upon me a conditional offer to pursue doctoral research in biomedical engineering.

It was a dreary afternoon of March that I presented my proposal to the Research Assessment Committee, consisting of a triumvirate of professors. My supervisor Krempe, professor of natural philosophy, was chair of the Committee. Though deeply imbued in the secrets of his science, he was an uncouth man with whom I had experienced many interpersonal conflicts. The second member of the Committee was Waldman, a professor who lectured upon chemistry the alternate days omitted by Krempe. Completing the trio was Böhm, who was probably an intelligent fellow though I knew not his precise field of research.

I wished the assembled professors a good afternoon as I opened the PowerPoint presentation on my laptop. The title slide appeared correctly upon my machine, however, for my audience the projector conveyed only the mortifying blue screen of death.

"Try pressing Function-F7," suggested Waldman, "or perhaps Function-F8, depending upon your machine."

I attempted both without success.

"Reboot your machine, Frankenstein," said Krempe in a gruff, impatient tone.

As my laptop recommenced, I glanced at my watch. All of the graduate students of the department were scheduled to present to the Committee this afternoon, and each of us had been allocated a mere thirty minutes.

At last, the title slide appeared. But something was still not correct.

"Good God, Frankenstein," snarled Krempe. "What manner of madness would compel thee to select such heinous colours?"

For the sake of convenience, I had employed a standard template from the auto-content wizard, one with a yellow font upon a green background. Alas, the university's cheap projector, undoubtedly manufactured within one of the low-wage Asiatic nations, made the yellow text appear a sickening shade of pale green, barely discernible from the background.

I struggled to devise a solution. "Perhaps, if you kind professors would permit, I may alter the formatting of the master slide to –"

Krempe interrupted with a dismissive wave. "Continue, Frankenstein. Time is short."

I commenced my narrative. The presentation was organized into several sections: Introduction, Assessment of Current Research, Key Objectives and Critical Success Factors, Proposed Research Methodology, Expected

Outcome, Socioeconomic Benefits, and Conclusion. My literature review described the search for the philosopher's stone and the elixir of life, and summarized the work of Cornelius Agrippa, Albertus Magnus, and Paracelsus.

"Have you," said Krempe, "really spent your time in studying such nonsense?"

I replied in the affirmative.

"Every minute," continued he, "every instant that you have wasted on those papers is utterly and entirely lost. You have burdened your memory with exploded systems and useless names. Good God! How does this stuff get through peer review?"

Waldman turned to his colleague. "I pray thee, allow this young man to continue." So unlike my supervisor was this Waldman, his aspect expressive of the greatest benevolence, affability and kindness. Warm gratitude swelled within my bosom.

I presented a slide that summarized my three-phase research plan. Phase 1 – Collect raw materials. Included was a list of potential sources: charnel houses, graves, dissecting rooms, Chinese restaurants. Phase 3 – Demonstration of galvanic post-anthropic state enhancement. And what of Phase 2? For now, there was but a question mark.

Next, I presented a slide that described the expected outcome. Stature – Gigantic (about eight feet in height), proportionally large. Skin – yellow, covering the muscles and arteries beneath. Hair – lustrous black, flowing. Face – jaundiced complexion, teeth of pearly whiteness, straight black lips, "ruggedly handsome". But mere words in bulleted text could not convey the beauty of my ambition. So, upon the subsequent slide, I showed a set of thumbnail pictures of the constituent body parts which, after moments, wipe-transitioned into a rendered image of the assembled figure.

Upon witnessing the picture, Waldman appeared agitated, and Böhm's visage conveyed consternation, perhaps even a hint of horror.

Krempe spoke. Without emotion, he said simply, "Your time has expired."

"My time has expired?" I repeated with incredulity. "But that cannot be!"

"Thirty minutes have indeed elapsed," said Böhm.

I looked at my watch and groaned as the truth of their words was confirmed.

"Pray thee, learned professors, kind gentlemen," I implored, "allow me to continue for a few minutes more. I have but a few slides remaining, and they are of the greatest import. The socioeconomic benefits, the utility of the mobile deceased for the service industry, their other potential roles as –"

"We are sorry," said Böhm, "but maintain our schedule we must, for we have other students to attend."

"Victor Frankenstein," said Krempe, "you are finished." His harsh words were like a slap to my face. I was for the moment rendered mute as he continued. "And, as you will no longer be associated with the University, you will be required to vacate the Biomedical Laboratory. Please settle this matter with the Office of Research… and sir, upon your egress, shield the portal from striking your hindquarters."

My heart sank as I exited the building. Would my place in history and the gratitude of all humanity be ruined by instruments of mischief? What of my grand project? I resolved to remain unhindered, for I could not rank myself with the herd of common projectors!

With tragic inevitability, the day of my departure from the University arrived. I packed my books, papers, and chemical instruments. With the exception of my laptop, which I had removed the previous day, all of my belongings were accommodated within a single box. It was a humiliating reminder of how little I had been permitted to accomplish.

The office was shared with Krempe's other graduate students, Herr Daniel Nugent from England and Fräulein Inga Blücher from Austria. Both were typing upon their computers, no doubt refining their mathematical models, or perhaps attending to their Facebook pages.

"My good colleagues! My dear friends!"

Inga and Daniel looked up from their computers and turned to me at the same moment.

"When I first came to the University, my heart knew I wanted to be in no other place. Now, the University has truly become my home, and you, my dear colleagues, have become my family. Leaving this place, leaving you, is one of the hardest things I have ever done, but I promise, I swear, by the sun and by the blue sky of heaven, and by the fire of love that burns my heart, that I will not rest until I stand with you again. I shall return!"

After an awkward silence, Daniel said, "Yeah, sure Victor. Good luck with whatever you end up doing."

"See you around, Victor," said Inga.

My colleagues had nothing more to say, so I took my leave. As I walked down the corridor, the heavy box in hand like a prisoner's iron shackles, I thought I heard someone say "pompous ass", or words to similar effect.

Alone in my residence, tides of woe overcame me. Overweening pride forbade me from soliciting funds from Father, which, in the past, would have been my first course of action. Instead, I aimlessly wandered the realms of cyberspace for many hours until, like a bolt of lightning from Zeus himself, I realized with a start that the means to fund my research had been right before me the entire time. The very source of whatever is good and perfect – the Internet!

I decided immediately that existing crowdfunding platforms such as Schlagstarter.de were wholly inadequate for my very unique needs and resolved to devise my own superior site. After an intense weekend of frenzied, passionate coding – sustained only by an AmerikaHühnchen party pack meal consisting of a twelve-piece barrel of original recipe chicken, two large servings of fries, coleslaw, and a 1.5-litre soft drink – I had developed what I was certain would be my second-greatest creation: the LottoFrankë.ch website.

The concept of LottoFrankë was genius incarnate. Through the website I would sell raffle tickets towards an unspecified prize. In truth, my meagre finances were such that I could not yet actually secure the prize, but the brilliance of LottoFrankë was that it would not matter. I would simply use a portion of the certain windfall revenues from the ticket sales to purchase the prize, with the bulk of the remainder devoted to funding my research. Another portion of the remaining money would be used to secure another prize for the next LottoFrankë raffle, and the virtuous cycle would repeat itself.

In order to ensure the maximum revenue in the minimum time (the classic "max-min" problem), I devised an innovative pricing scheme whereby the charge per ticket would increase the more tickets were purchased: 20 Swiss francs for one ticket, 50 francs for two, 100 francs for three, and so on. Again, as a further strategy to maximize revenue, I did not announce a fixed date for the draw and would allow the raffle to continue as long as tickets were being purchased.

I did not see how this could possibly fail.

My beautiful LottoFranké.ch website went live upon the Ides of March in the year of our Lord 20--. Devouring my third AmerikaHühnchen party meal in as many days, I settled down in front of my laptop to watch the action.

Within an hour of the website going live, I had my first ticket purchase! I leapt from my seat and cried out in divine ecstasy. Unbounded spirits compelled me to a happy dance. I jumped over the chairs, clapped my hands and laughed aloud, but quickly sat down again after losing breath. A mere twenty minutes later, two more tickets were purchased. I pumped my fist into the air in the manner of a certain American late-night talk show host of my youth. Quickly performing the mental arithmetic, I extrapolated that I would surely become a millionaire in less than three months.

The excitement and exertions upset my humours and stirred the gases within my bowels, bringing me to a point of painful exhaustion. I repaired to the commode to relieve myself whence, utterly spent, I collapsed upon the crapper. There I remained within a stupor until, disturbed from my dark reveries by the rank coleslaw and demoniacal odours emanating from earlier ablutions, I finally stirred and shamefully arose from the septic throne without cleansing my hands.

Returning to my laptop, I noticed that the ticket counter remained stuck at three. Patience being a virtue, I sat down again before the screen to watch and wait.

Another hour passed. Then two, then five.

A day went by. A week. Two weeks. A month.

By the middle of April, to my greatest mortification and dismay, still only those three raffle tickets had been sold. How could it have gone so terribly wrong? Why did the gods mock me so?

And then came the messages. At first, short emails from the ticket buyers enquiring of the outcome of the raffle and the disposition of the promised prize. The first ticket had been purchased by a resident of the Indian subcontinent, the other two by a person from Las Islas Filipinas. These I ignored, for in no way could I actually provide a prize to people of such distant lands. The cost would surely be enormous and far beyond the total gross revenue of LottoFrankë, which was exactly 70 Swiss francs.

But the emails from the ticket purchasers did not cease, and their frequency and hostility increasing by the week. These I continued to ignore. Alas, I could not disregard a registered letter from the Eidgenössische Spielbankenkommission, the Swiss government gaming board, informing me that I was operating an unlicensed gambling site in direct contravention of Federal statutes. I was to cease-and-desist immediately or risk a fine and/or imprisonment.

Trembling with excess passion, I took down the LottoFrankë.ch website, deleted all the files and emails, and shredded the letter from the Eidgenössische Spielbankenkommission. Whence the destruction was complete, I let forth a malignant howl of devilish rage and despair. I was alone; none were near me to dissipate the gloom and relieve me from terrible reveries.

Two months later, some idiot child in München raised 50,000 euros on Schlagstarter.de to make weisswurst.

Lacking the good fortune of the München Sausage Boy, the state of my personal finances continued to worsen by degrees. I finally eschewed my pride and sent an email to Father, but strangely there was no response. In the following days, I paced the streets of Ingolstadt in a most agitated state. How long I wandered seems now immeasurable, but a timely lifting of my delirium found me back in the University quadrant, whence I beheld a lifeline upon the Student Centre bulletin board:

```
Accelerating Science - Investment Forum
   The  Grand  Academy  of  Lagado  is  pleased  to
announce  its  first  annual  Accelerating Science -
Investment  Forum  (AS-IF)  conference,  to be  held
at  the  Hilton  Zürich  Airport  Hotel  on June 11th,
20--. The  event  will  provide  a  very  unique  forum
for   researchers   to   expand   their   professional
networks,   join   peer-to-peer   discussions   and
present  their  innovations  to  venture  capitalists
and  angel  investors. Don't  miss  this  opportunity
to  discover  how  the  financial  markets  can support
your  research.
```

Never before had I any need for or liking of the shifty capitalists and the rapacious "one percent", but it seemed now that fate had portended them to become my necessary bedfellows.

The bottom of the flyer directed the reader to a website for additional information and online registration. But then I saw the registration fee, and my heart fell. The deadline for the early bird registration had already expired, and the full amount was now 2,000 Swiss francs.

I groaned in frustration. Under my present circumstances it was a sum I could ill afford, and it did not even include the costs of transportation and lodging. But I consoled myself in the conceit that the expenditure was an investment, for when the promise of my research is fulfilled I would surely know recognition and reward beyond comprehension.

To Zürich, therefore, I was bound.

The conference hotel was set amongst the mountains and trees of the Alpine countryside, a short distance from Zürich-Kloten Flughafen. It was a crowded venue, for the hotel was also a temporary stay for flight attendants from various airlines. Aesthetically, the decor was clean and unexciting, as befits the hotels of the Parisian chain.

A keynote address was given by a gentleman publicized as one of great import, but whose name was unfamiliar to me and which I have since forgotten. He was a short fellow with curly hair that had been dyed a flaming red. His stylish power suit did not flatter his substantial belly.

"A massive shift is underway in science," said he, "and it is clear the future we envision is possible and will arrive more rapidly than we expect." He described the forum as "an international nexus of the most important developments in science," and thanked the gathered innovators and investors for their attendance.

The gentleman spoke with great eloquence yet, to me, his words lacked substance. His concluding remarks were rewarded with enthusiastic applause, which I joined in courtesy. But my unease grew as the event continued. There did not appear to be any venture capitalists or angel investors in attendance, only other men as myself (and indeed they were all men) who conversed amongst themselves regarding grandiose plans for fantastical scientific wonders while lamenting the lack of money to bring their dreams to reality.

Opportunities were available for innovators to present their research plans. This I declined, as I intended to reveal my secrets only to those in actual possession of money (which I still as yet had not encountered) in order to protect my "first-mover advantage". But I did attend the presentations of others, as in the apparent absence of investors there was little else to do. There were many talks but being studious of brevity I will not relate them all. In any case, the majority appeared fanciful, perhaps even deranged.

One proposal was presented by a Professor McCoy of the University of British Columbia on the topic of artificial creativity, using advanced software and neural networks to allow computing machines to write fictional stories and replace the inept screenwriters of Hollywood. Another was delivered by an ancient student named Swift whose face and beard were pale yellow, his hands and ill-fitted clothes daubed with filth. His project sought to reduce human excrement back to its original food by using nanotechnology to separate the several parts, removing the tincture which it receives from the gall, making the odour exhale, and skimming off the saliva.

I quitted the conference room in disgust. Locating the coffee dispensing machine, I produced a portion of the foul-tasting beverage and drained the small paper cup in a single gulp. I stumbled to an armchair and collapsed upon it in exhaustion.

When I took my hands from my eyes, I saw standing before me a bald, portly gentleman with small round wire-framed spectacles. His eyes were fixed upon me, and then his jaws opened and he muttered some inarticulate sounds.

"Yes?" said I. "What do you want?"

He muttered something. Squinting, I learned forward and read the words "Martin Boyd" printed upon his conference badge.

"Herr Boyd, you are? Yes?" I demanded.

His head bobbed up and down.

Again, I asked, "What do you want, Herr Boyd?"

His accent betrayed him as an English speaker, possibly from the Americas. Alas, his German was abominable, and combined with his affectation of speaking in a low mumble, conspired to make comprehension almost impossible.

"The moon. You speak of the moon?" I cupped a hand to my ear. "Please, speak up!"

His lips moved, and inhuman sounds emanated.

"What of the moon?" I repeated.

He made a fist with his left hand, and the index finger of his right traced an invisible line through the air until it touched his other clasped hand.

"You wish to go to the moon? To what end?"

The man's excitement grew, and he began to speak in haste, reducing comprehensibility in proportion.

"To what end, sir do you wish to –" I managed to pick out a word from his babble. "Käse? *Cheese?*" I repeated the word in English. The man nodded happily.

Sudden comprehension struck me. "You wish to mine the moon... for cheese?"

His smile widened, and he cocked his head and spread his arms in a gesture of epiphany.

Words failed me at that moment. Finally, I said to him, "Good sir, there is no cheese on the moon."

The man shook his head violently, and he launched into some incomprehensible lecture.

"No sir," said I, "it is you who is mistaken. It is proven, there is no cheese to be found on the moon."

His rant continued unabated. I had no recourse but rude interruption. "Sir," exclaimed I, "how ignorant thou art! Man hath walked upon the moon! There is no cheese upon its surface, only dust and rock of dreary grey!"

The man did not cease his discourse. I could take no more. Abruptly I stood, and reaching out to grasp his shoulder, I gently yet firmly pushed him aside. "I cannot help you!"

A wail of despair emanated from his lips, very like that of a sad dog howling at that radiant orb in the night sky.

Seeking refuge in the men's lavatory, I went to a sink and splashed cold water upon my visage. I stared at the mirror and was shocked by the pale reflexion. With trembling hands, I tore off the conference badge and deposited it into the rubbish bin before quitting the lavatory.

I marched to the lifts, and as I approached, saw that the doors had just commenced their closure. The young woman inside spotted me and pressed a button to reopen the doors. At first, I believed her to be one of the flight attendants who lodged at the hotel, but then I saw upon her lapel an AS-IF conference badge like the one I had just disposed.

I summoned the courage to speak. "You are here for the science investment forum?"

"Uh huh," said she. "I'm with Sokoloff Investment Suisse here in Zürich."

"You are a venture capitalist?" Seeing her with new eyes, my excitement grew.

"We're a V.C. firm, although I seem to be the only one here. Let me tell you, most of the stuff I saw today was based on some pretty unsound premises – and I'm trying to be civil here."

It seemed that Fortuna had smiled upon me at last! But the window of opportunity was narrow. Here, in the lift, I had but seconds to make my pitch.

"Good woman," I began.

"Yes?"

"I wish to propose to you –" My words stumbled in my haste. "Myself, I always have been imbued with a fervent longing to penetrate the secrets of Nature."

She looked at me strangely. "You want to... penetrate Nature?"

"Yes!" My breath became heavy. "I wish to unveil her, to repine the fortifications and impediments that keep man from entering her citadel and expose the wonders and mysteries of her immortal lineaments!"

She appeared to be looking for something in her purse.

"I seek to penetrate deeper and know more than the men who came before me. And with a union of you and I, scientist and financier, our success shall be inevitable!"

The lift arrived. A chime sounded, and the doors opened.

"I have to go."

I reached out and touched her shoulder. "Dear woman, I beseech you –"

It was all too swift for me to elude. Only a glance did I see of the small canister in her hand, and the potent fluid ejaculated from it. I sank to the floor and writhed in miserable pain as the liquid seared my eyes and skin.

"God, help me!" I cried. "It burns! *It burns!*"

Exhausted and beaten, I returned to Ingolstadt and retreated to my residence in a state of utter and stupid anxiety. At last, I received an email from Father in which he curtly rebuffed my plea for funds, confessing that he had absconded to Siam with the family fortune so that he may finally have what he had always wanted – to die in the arms of a 14-year-old.

The days and nights that followed were unpleasant sojourns of deep reflexion. Always I had considered it beneath me to do what the labourers of the New World called "the nine-to-five thing", but the moment I had dreaded all my life had irresistibly and inevitably come.

It was time for me to get a real job.

I will spare you the boredom of relating my search for employment, suffice to say that it was a long, difficult, and humiliating journey over the course of many months. Finally, the grace of God guided me to Die Bibliothek, where I chanced upon a recent issue of *Ingolscientische* with a classified notification for the position of quality control technician at Kürzer & Boily.

The recompense is modest, but at long last I now had some limited means to continue my research. In addition to the salary, I also support my work by occasionally pilfering needed materials from the company laboratories. Alas, my progress is painfully slow as I am forced to work primarily with chocolate, the only substance readily available at Kürzer & Boily.

But continue forward I must, for without my work – without my *science* – I have no tale. The hidden laws of heaven and earth remain to me secrets that I absolutely must divine. Never will I give up my research until I perish, and then with what ecstasy shall I join my departed friends, who even now prepare me for the reward of my tedious toil and horrible pilgrimage!

From: rwalton79@kilchbergnetz.ch
Sent: November 29, 20--, 17:22
To: margaret.saville@sillywalks.gov.uk
Subject: Re: Crazy Day at Work!

You have read this sad and forlorn story, Margaret; and do you not feel your blood boil with indignation? The visions of a great man have been exploded, the quest for new ways destroyed by the ignorance of "the bottom line". Such gifts might he have conferred upon humanity had he means to proceed. What if I had chanced upon this noble man even one year ago? This worthy friend that I have longed to find may have written a happier tale.

Following what seemed an eternity, the paramedics finally arrived. They apologized for their tardiness, explaining they had just left the barricades where they had been standing in solidarity with the Occupy Ingolstadt movement. Frankenstein was placed upon a stretcher and conveyed to the ambulance. I remained at his side, walking with the paramedics out of the factory and into the parking lot. An Arctic air mass was blowing through the city, bringing bitter cold, and swirling snowflakes began to fall.

When we approached the doors of the ambulance, he beckoned me. I knelt down to hear his words.

"And you, Herr Walton. Have you dreams of your own?"

"Dreams?" His question suddenly brought forth long buried aspirations. "Yes...yes, indeed I did. You see, my degree was in the liberal arts, but I longed to complete a Master of Business Administration and stand amongst the greatest of marketeers, those skilled purveyors of sugared carbonated water, running shoes, and cleaning products."

"Seek happiness not in tranquillity, but in ambition. I have myself been blasted in these hopes, yet *you* may succeed!" With sudden strength and lucidity, Frankenstein pressed a sad, crumpled little package into my hands. "Please Herr Walton, take this sample of my work. It is small and broken, but it is all I have."

Frankenstein slumped back onto the stretcher. Something seemed to pass before his eyes, and then the wild delirium he had displayed at the caramel machine returned with a vengeance.

"Blasted as thou, my agony is still superior, for the bitter sting of failure will not cease to rankle in my wounds until death shall close them forever. Soon, I shall die, and what I now feel be no longer felt. My spirit will sleep in peace, or if it thinks, it will not surely think thus."

"I'd give real money if he'd shut up," I heard one of the paramedics mutter.

"A chill, a chill is upon me! Where are my trousers?"

The paramedics raised the stretcher, and Frankenstein was carefully placed aboard the ice white ambulance with its stark red cross. After a moment, the lights flashed, and the siren sounded its mournful blare as the ambulance began to move. He was soon borne away by the vehicle and lost in darkness and distance.

When the ambulance was out of sight, I looked with curiosity at the little package in my hand and carefully opened it. Within were tiny, crudely formed limbs, torsos and heads – all made of chocolate.

My eyes widened. Was this Frankenstein's parting gift to me? Could Kürzer & Boily manufacture our confections in the shape of homunculi?

A thousand times yes! With my ambitions in the mercantile sphere, I could fulfil the vision that so burned in Frankenstein's imagination by directing within Kürzer & Boily the creation of confections in the image of jolly Father Christmas... in living Eis Schokolade™. The spilled caramel could also be added, thereby recycling waste into a lucrative new revenue stream. I would go it alone if necessary, establishing a special "skunk works" project to give new life to the Yuletide sales push. Margaret, forgive my immodesty, but I imagine myself one day soon gracing the cover of *SchweizerKrämer* magazine!

Die.Ingolstadt Blattertag
January 28th, 20--

Investigators have issued a warrant for the arrest of Herr Walton of Bogusstrasse No. 19, in connection with last month's Yuletide outbreak of salmonella poisoning from tainted caramel in Kürzer & Boily Eis

Schokolade™ Saint Nicholas figurines. The catastrophe sent hundreds of Ingolstadt's good citizens to the latrines and thoroughly ruined Christmas. Anyone still exhibiting symptoms is advised to remain in their commodes. With evidence pointing to the rogue manager Walton diverting company resources without authorization, Kürzer & Boily is cooperating fully with the constabulary. As yet, there are few leads on the whereabouts of the accused. Herr Kirwin, the local magistrate, has assured the citizenry that the villain shall be pursued to the ends of the earth and justice will be served.

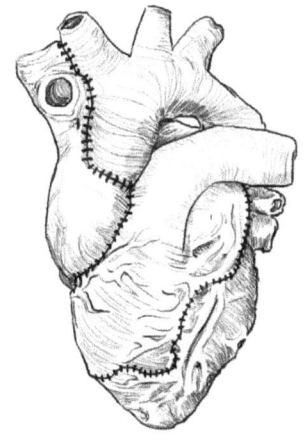

THE LAST CONFESSION OF DOTTORE GEPPETTO

JOSHUA BARTOLOME

I killed my own son.

For ten years, I tracked him down from town to town, village to village, city to city. In his wake, he left behind nothing but misery, pain, and death. Children and men died wherever he went; their still-beating hearts ripped from their chests, bodies split open in a grotesque display of cruel and senseless violence.

I did not know, at first, what he was after – I only knew that I had to stop him.

In the autumn of 1812, a most terrible year of warfare and disease, I arrived in the backwater village of Ludica. There were rumours that a demon roamed the woods surrounding this sleepy hamlet, preying on little children who wandered outside at night. While the world busied itself with its calamities and plagues, I followed the trail of corpses, armed only with pistol and dagger, with sorrow and regret.

I created this demon.

This creature.

Only I could end its madness.

When I arrived in the village, ragged and bone-weary, I noticed how strangely dark and silent it was. The torches and lamps of nearby houses remained unlit, their windows closed and the doors barred shut. No wagons or carriages traversed the unpaved dirt roads of Ludica. The clopping of hooves and the idle chatter of merchants and villagers could not be heard anywhere in the desolate town square.

It was as if no one had lived there, as if all of its inhabitants had vanished overnight. At first, I thought that the village had been abandoned – until I saw a group of three night-watchmen walking down the main avenue, armed with lanterns and muskets. Upon seeing me, a newcomer and a stranger to that place, the guards raised their guns. I held my hands up and told them that I meant them no harm.

I was merely an old man, lost and confused, trying to make his way to Naples to see his grandchildren. The watchmen, still suspicious, seemed to accept this explanation and pointed me to the nearest inn where I could rest and have a bite to eat. They then warned me to leave upon the break of dawn. Feigning ignorance, I asked them why the town was so empty, so devoid of noise and laughter.

A demon, one of the guards said in a hushed voice, a creature from the depths of hell was stalking the countryside. It had already butchered six of their children, along with an elderly wool merchant who had caught a glimpse of the monstrous thing that killed her grandson. Before dying from her horrific injuries, the poor woman revealed to the villagers the appearance of the creature: it was an automaton, a fiend made of steel and brass, given life by some forbidden, infernal alchemy.

They were describing my son.

My dearest boy.

Pinocchio.

I had to turn away for a second to wipe the tears threatening to spill from my eyes. When one of the guards asked if something was the matter, I answered that the thought of such tragedies happening in this peaceful little town was too much for an old heart like mine to bear. The watchmen thanked me for my grief and my condolences. Afterwards, they then told me to seek shelter at once, lest the demon catch me walking the streets of Ludica alone.

I tipped my hat to them in gratitude. The patrol then went on its way, leaving me alone in that cold, godforsaken street. Instead of heeding their advice, I made haste and turned down another road that led directly to the southern outskirts of Ludica. During my travels, I had heard rumours of a ruined chapel located in the forest beyond, a place that the townsfolk considered unhallowed ground where witches and fiends gathered to celebrate the Sabbat.

The perfect place for a demon to hide.

With only the light of a gibbous moon guiding my way, I followed the weed-choked path that led deeper and deeper into the benighted regions of the forest. Nothing frightened me. Not anymore. Sorrow had stripped terror from my heart and left nothing but despair. The thought of bandits hiding in the undergrowth inspired only indifference. I had nothing to give except my life, such as it is, and even that was worth almost nothing. Demons too did not stoke any of my innermost fears, for had I not created a demon with these calloused, arthritic hands?

I walked, alone, a frail old man in the haunted, shadow-shrouded forest, wishing only to die. But such a mercy would not be granted to a heathen blasphemer like myself by the powers of heaven, for I still had a penance to perform. It had not always been like this. Before I became a vagrant, I was an engineer, a celebrated toymaker for the noble families of old and marvellous Venice, the city of brass, the city of science, art, and commerce.

As a craftsman and an artist of the highest calibre, I was well-known for creating trinkets and mechanical animals that were so life-like, so meticulously designed, they were often mistaken for sentient beings by my royal patrons. None of them knew of my insidious connection to the surgical genius, the Baron Victor Frankenstein, who died in the cold regions of the North Pole while hunting down the monstrosity he had cobbled together from various corpses.

While we were still young students in the University of Ingolstadt, the Baron and I mused upon the meaning of life, death, and the power of science and medicine to manipulate natural processes. Driven by the death of his mother, Baron Frankenstein wanted to see if he could, in some way, give life to non-living matter. His experiments intrigued me – and so I assisted my friend, the Baron, in his blasphemous task of reanimating long-dead human beings.

But while he wanted to defeat death, I wanted to do so much more – Victor couldn't see the potential in the grand work we had undertaken. He wanted to cure death. He wanted to save humanity from the shadow of the abyss. I wanted to create a new species altogether – a creature that would soon replace the flawed and violent race of mankind. It was this difference of opinion that soon drove us apart.

Baron Frankenstein went his separate way and I continued my research independently. While creating useless but miraculous toys for the mewling brats of counts and countesses, I managed to amass a sizeable fortune, one that allowed me to buy the materials needed to create my masterwork. During this long period of trial and error, I learned from various sources about the death of my dear friend and colleague, and I vowed that I would continue the work we had started. But unlike Victor, who used human flesh to create a ravening golem, I wanted to construct my precious son from steel, bronze, and silver.

I didn't want to make Baron Frankenstein's mistake. Human flesh is such a crude material, full of diseases and imperfections. Was it any wonder, then, that my friend's creation turned out to be a ghastly fiend capable of only murder? He gave it a human mind. He gave it a human heart.

My son would be different from his.

This child, I thought, would be pure. He would be freed from the constraints of the human form. My son would know no disease, no pain, no death. His indestructible body would be operated by an electric dynamo for a heart and a mechanical brain that could think, and reason, and calculate more efficiently than a human being's mind – a consciousness unfettered by the stupidity of mankind.

My son would know no hatred.

No love.

It would only know truth, and logic, and reason.

I thought that I had created an angel.

How utterly foolish I was.

251

After what seemed like hours upon hours of walking aimlessly through the forest, I chanced upon the grove where the forbidden chapel was situated. On the ground, placed in a grotesque circle, lay the naked, decomposing, and headless bodies of several men. They had been dead for almost a week or so, in my rough estimation, and a foul, rotten stench rose up from the mutilated cadavers. Fighting the instinct to vomit, I knelt down and examined the corpses while covering my nose and mouth with the hem of a patched and tattered cloak hanging from my thin shoulders.

Each of the dead men had been flayed, expertly skinned, leaving nothing behind save for the greenish-brown cords of rotting and fly-ridden muscle fibres. I could only hope that these men died before the foul task was performed upon their helpless bodies. Like the countless victims I had encountered during my decade-long search, these ones had their internal organs removed, their heart, lungs, kidneys, and livers extracted with surgical precision.

The reasons behind this, I didn't know, and I didn't want to know, for only an inhuman and diabolical mind would perpetrate such a despicable act of sheer lunacy. And yet, I had to ask myself: was it truly madness that guided the hand of my once beloved son? Surely, there had to be a perfectly reasonable explanation for such cruelty.

And why not? Rationality is a monstrous device capable of explaining away murderous deeds. Logic and reason had often been used to justify atrocities perpetrated throughout the history of our doomed race. Was Napoleon not reasonable, and logical, and sane, when he declared war upon the Empire of Russia? Reasonable men, civilized men, had destroyed the grand palaces and temples of the Aztecs in the Southern Americas. It was reason that drove the armies of our Great Emperor Napoleon to march across Europe, killing, stealing, and raping in a ceaseless orgy of wanton destruction that, seemingly, would go on forever.

What sham, reason. What folly, logic.

I had grown tired of kneeling before dead gods.

On trembling legs, I rose from the ground, before pulling out the flintlock pistol from my coat. The cold weight of the handgun felt comforting, familiar, in my hand. It reminded me of a hammer. It reminded me of the good days, the productive days, when all I needed was solitude and a space to work my craft. I am no soldier. I am a tinkerer. A fixer. In the past, I once told Baron Frankenstein that the world's problems could only be solved by human intellect – not by bullets and gunpowder.

Those days are long gone.

I wrapped the coat tightly around my body to stave off the biting midnight chill. Though I tried to steady myself, I could not stop the shaking of my aching, unsteady bones. Time seemed to slow down at an unbearable rate as I took a few tentative steps toward the threshold of the crumbling chapel. This abandoned place of worship, now a nest of ill rumours and evil spirits, looked old, older than I could reckon even with my prodigious knowledge of architectural styles of the past few centuries. That it was Christian, I had no doubt, for a crumbling limestone cross sat atop its vine-choked rooftop. Whatever holiness that this artifact once possessed, I prayed that it would protect me from the foul creature that lurked within the desolate chapel.

As a man of science, I trusted only in the things that my senses could see, smell, hear, and touch. I thought that primordial evil was nothing but mere superstition, a fairy tale concocted by lesser minds to comprehend the strangeness of the physical world around them. But now, I have seen the error of my judgement. Evil exists. I had seen it. I had felt it. I had followed it for ten years.

I had a duty to stop it. Once and for all.

The pockmarked wooden gate leading into the darkened interior of the chapel was slightly ajar, as if whoever or whatever waited inside had been expecting me to arrive. Gripping the pistol, I slipped through the gap between the doors, which was big enough to allow a frail, elderly man to slip through. Upon crossing the threshold, I discovered that the interior of the main hallway was illuminated by torches along with half-melted and dying wax candles.

How I wished that God had blinded me in that instant, for I saw, in that accursed place, a gallery of horrors that made my consciousness buckle and almost break. On each pillar flanking the cobwebbed pews, the flayed corpses of men, women, and children had been crucified and displayed like grotesque statues in a museum of the damned.

Unlike the carcasses left outside, however, these ones possessed all their organs and innards. A shattering thought came to me in that moment: these corpses weren't killed to satisfy sadistic impulses. They were being studied, surgically deconstructed, as if they were anatomical specimens in a master surgeon's atelier.

My son, for some unfathomable purpose, had killed these people for purely academic and scientific pursuits.

Walking down the aisle, I threw sharp glances at the nearby pews and saw, to my disgust, dusty glass jars that contained organs swimming in a greenish semi-transparent soup: hearts, livers, kidneys, lungs, intestines, all of them preserved for examination and study. My son had turned this chapel into a laboratory of his own, a place where he could continue researching and experimenting undisturbed.

Then, from a corner of the hall, someone whispered:

"Father?"

I recognized that voice; the lithe, lilting tone that gave me such joy in the past only sent a chill dread crawling across my spine like a monstrous centipede. Had it truly been a decade since he escaped my workshop to spread havoc across this war-ravaged continent? Hearing him again, I wondered if it were possible, somehow, to save him, to recreate his functions and recalibrate his mind so that corruption would never tarnish his mechanical soul again.

"Pinocchio," I replied softly. "What have you done?"

"Only what you have failed to achieve," my son replied, his voice echoing against the walls. I couldn't tell where it was coming from. "I have become like you, Dottore Geppetto: a human being in thought and design."

"You were perfect!" I shouted, weeping, my voice cracking as I screamed at him. "You were everything that I have ever dreamt of being! I created you to replace us! To be better than us! I didn't create you to do this!"

"Oh, Father," Pinocchio replied from the shadows, and his voice sounded so sorrowful. "You do not see the glorious nature of the human species. But I have. You are like stars dancing in the infinite blackness of this lonesome universe: you are bright, effervescent, fleeting. The god who created you must have loved you deeply."

From behind me, I could hear footsteps, coupled with the wet, sickening, dripping sound of blood hitting the stone floor. The noises came, closer and closer, and I refused to turn around and face the being that I bequeathed to the rest of humanity: the creature called Pinocchio.

"I have studied the human form, and what makes you unique, and with each specimen that I disassembled, I grew only more confused. Although you retain the same number of organs, and nerves, and vital functions, their shapes and colours and details varied from one person to the next."

I drew in a ragged breath and closed my eyes. There was such innocence in his words. Such curiosity. Of course. I had designed him to be without love, or hatred, or fear. He was an angel, and how could, lowly, confused, frightened creatures such as us comprehend the thoughts of the sinless? He was truly perfect. This was perfection at work.

"Then, I realized that I did not possess the thing that you humans so thoughtlessly take for granted: your souls. No matter how many children I tore apart, I couldn't find any traces of this wondrous, wondrous thing, this vital essence, that sets you apart from a machine like me."

"There is no such thing as a soul."

"That is where you are mistaken, Dottore," Pinocchio replied, and he chuckled. Oh gods and saints in heaven, I thought. I had never heard him laugh before. "Look upon me, Father, and I will show you what the soul looks like."

Slowly, so slowly, I turned.

And then I saw him.

He was no longer a machine.

Far from it.

"Aren't you proud of me, Papa?" Pinocchio asked. In the dimly-lit room, I saw, to my horror and great despair, that he had undergone an ingenious self-surgery which grafted the skins, the muscles, and the organs of his victims to his mechanical body. Blood dripped from the suture wounds on the surface of his makeshift skin.

It was a mockery.

A grotesque parody of the human body.

In the centre of Pinocchio's chest, encased in a cracked glass jar, was a bloody, beating heart floating in a sickly-green fluid. Spreading his fleshy arms wide, as if asking for an embrace, Pinocchio grinned madly, and said:

"I've become a real boy."

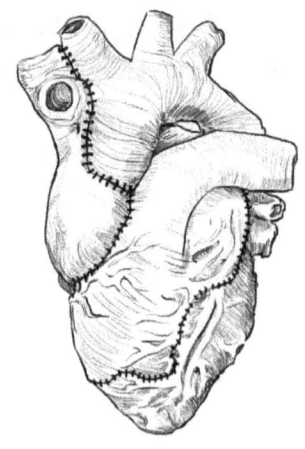

FAMOUS MONSTERS

ARIANNA VERBREE

When I first hit puberty,
my body and I became strangers.
We were married, tied at the wrist,
but pulling in different directions.
Instead of confiding in it,
sharing with it, breaking bread with it,
it became like a classic Hollywood monster.

Like a vampire, it stayed up
late into the night while I tried to sleep,
leaving me to slog through mornings
like Boris Karloff, to feel cursed
and shuffling like the Mummy.

It sprouted hair like a werewolf,
and grew bulky like Mr. Hyde,
while I, Dr. Jekyll, struggled to control
myself, my life, struggling
to fight the chemistry and alchemy
that turned all of my gold into lead.

We fought each other for years,
Frankenstein chasing her monster across
the earth, a Sisyphean struggle
that punished my body, making it
push that boulder up the hill
over, and over, and over, and over, and over.

I tortured it. I tortured myself.
I became the monster.

I hated my body. I hated myself.
I hated my selves, my multitudes.

and I asked myself, why does it have to be this way?

In the first part of my life,
my body and I were one.
We wept together, tears of joy and sorrow.
We drank up our hopes, our dreams,
our experiences,
our cups overflowing,
spilling over, running out of

our sippy-cups onto my parents'
oak table, that they bought when
the idea of me wasn't even though of, but
built with enough leaves to accommodate me.
Not just me, but a whole extended side of ourselves.

I wish I could say
that everything is great, that we get along.
That my body and I have re-tied the knot,
and all is well and good in the universe.
That I have thrown off my monstrous cocoon
and become a butterfly.

We tolerate each other.
We leave notes to each other
on the fridge like passive-aggressive roommates.

"I threw out all the empty blood bags you left on the counter. Again."
"I left out the vacuum cleaner so you can clean all your hair off of the
     couch!"
"I noticed we're out of coffee - It's your turn to buy!"
"Get milk"

but we care.

We sit at my parents' oak table and
break bread.
She washes, I dry.
We watch monster movies with

the lights on because she's
afraid of the dark.
And I lie awake while she sleeps,
and worry about the future
for monsters like us

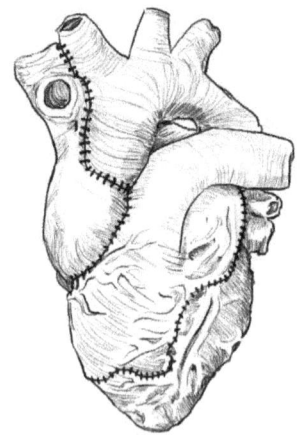

UNFASHIONED CREATURES

PRIYA SRIDHAR

"We are unfashioned creatures, but half made up, if one wiser, better, dearer than ourselves — such a friend ought to be — do not lend his aid to perfectionate our weak and faulty natures."

Mary Shelley, *Frankenstein*

When Mother fell ill, I fretted on learning her secrets. My brother William feared the same, since she started calling him "Adonis". His cheeks would flush grey-pink, and his hair would unravel. She would clutch him with wrinkly, quill-like fingers and stroke his arms.

"You need to make sure your seams are tight, Adonis," she would say. "Madam Gusset knows all of your measurements."

"Don't call me that, Mother," he would say, his face resembling the paint I had made once by mixing grey mud and beet juice. "My name is William. You named me for Father."

"But you are my Adonis." She would stroke his freckled arms, trapped in tight brown leather. If any stuffing popped out, she'd poke it back in with an indulgent smile. He'd pull away and tuck in the white fluff.

"I'm no paragon of beauty," he'd mutter.

"You are to me," she would say, her eyes glassy. "Don't worry about me, Adonis."

We had a reason to worry, however; our grandfather's lawyer, Mr. Clementine, came without announcing himself or sending a calling card. William received him in the parlour of our home, Gladioli Mansion. It was a rainy morning, and the nearby lake banks were flowing over.

"Good day, Master William, Miss Clara," he said to us. His clothes smelled like camphor and claret. The man had a bristly brown moustache, and a weak chin. He accepted a cup of orange tea from our housekeeper Justine.

I tried not to pout at him while hemming one of William's breeches. We hadn't been expecting visitors; I had worn a stained yellow sundress with white petticoats, without a corset. If Mother had been well, she would have told me to wash my face and wear a better dress. Justine had mentioned the corset I used to wear was out of fashion, and she'd have to ask the seamstress about the new style.

"We heard that dear Mary has taken ill."

I glowered at the breeches. Living with Mother had taught us to not trust people that lacked visible seams; they had other, unsavoury things stuffed inside them.

"She cannot see visitors," William said. "If you wish to argue with her about my inheritance—"

"Oh no, no, no." Mr. Clementine waved short fingers. "We wish for you to understand the situation. You are your father's heir, but you were born under bad influence. Frankly, with the drugs and drinking they imbided, you should not be alive at all. Yet you are, and your mother is dying. Can you not see that your mother needs more than home care? She would do better perhaps farther into the country."

"We're far enough as it is and we like it that way," I muttered, needle in mouth.

Mr. Clementine looked up. I gave him an insolent stare, one I had inherited from my dark-eyed father. Mr. Clementine looked at Father's portrait, a large canvas that hung on the other side of the parlour; our expressions were identical.

"In any case, this is not a proper setting for her," he said. "She may prefer more medical care to staying in the damp here."

"I understand." William's voice was calm, "You wish for me to change my mother and influence her mind while she is sick. Or worse, to turn her out and clear our family's good name."

Mr. Clementine opened his mouth; William raised his hand to quiet him. If we weren't raised to be polite, I feel William might have snapped the lawyer's neck for such a suggestion.

"Mother will not be leaving," he said. "And she is not dying."

He sounded firm. Mr. Clementine bowed his head in defeat.

"You are the heir, so you will become Mary's guardian," he said. "But consider her health, at the least."

My mother often warned me on the dangers of taking opium. She had met our father at a Swiss resort, while he was married to a local noblewoman. Even though we lived in Father's rotting mansion on the damp rainy hills and spent the silver groats and coins he left us, Mother had a low opinion of him. Her nose would wrinkle and her lip would twist as if she had swallowed soap.

"He could have had the decency to divorce her first before courting me," she would say. "You must take care, Clara. A man with or without money always seeks out girls."

She had nothing to worry about; I never wanted to leave the mansion. Our neighbours tolerated us and made sure our invitations to parties and charities ended up in the lake mud. I only need a piece of fine fabric purchased from a months-old catalogue, my sewing kit, a book, and a fruit-laden larder. I was also not of courting age, and besides which I was short.

This was the only time I considered borrowing her opium, however; poring through her and Father's vast library was time consuming, and it would take decades to understand the lot. I didn't mind reading, but what I was searching for didn't appear easily. She had written a few books about it, but the books had no blasted details that I could use.

I was lying on my stomach, in a plain blue day gown, reading a dog-eared encyclopedia. It had belonged to Father, before he had drowned in the lake. The governess was taking her annual vacation, so I had to educate myself. She hinted that I would no longer need her, and Mother hated how she asked for raises and cut lessons short.

"Oof" I said. A pair of shoes had caught me in the stomach. I looked up and realized my brother was stumbling over me.

"Ow!" He recovered his balance. "I'm sorry; I didn't see you there."

"Careful, Donny!"

He turned and glowered. I glared back at him. He always made sure he was fully dressed, so that none of his stitches or fluff showed. Mr. Clementine hadn't noticed the stuffing behind his ear, but I did now.

""What are you searching for, Nutcracker?"

"If you don't call me Nutcracker, I won't call you Donny." I rubbed my stomach and straightened. "I'm trying to find the way that Mother helped you. You were sick as a baby, and she made you better. We can help her."

I showed him the stitches on my elbow. It was an old injury from when I had climbed on a bookcase and the shelves had crumbled. Mother had replaced the initial stitches with fine silk thread, durable under time, and had shown me how to rethread them. I liked sewing, and she had taught me how to make tiny stitches, so that they vanished into the cloth.

"You know she wouldn't agree to it, Clara," William said, getting more serious. "She won't even tell us how she did it, no matter how I beg her. You think I haven't been trying?"

"All the more reason we have to go for the books." I tapped a yellowing page with a bitten fingernail. "All of Mother's knowledge is in this library."

He considered this. His leather housecoat gleamed from fresh polish.

"Also, Clara wasn't the Nutcracker in the fairy tale," I said. "We've been over this. She's the human who *marries* the Nutcracker."

"Then that makes her Mrs. Nutcracker." His voice was droll.

"Call me that and I'll call you Adonis."

"Besides that," he went on, vexed as a wet cat, "Mother likes to keep all her secrets in her head. The opium only drowns them out in her bliss."

"Do you have a better suggestion?"

He paced the room. The lamps were frosted glass and made him look pale.

"When Mother talks about when I was dying as a baby, she mentioned using the plants on the estate," he said. "She went to her favourite poppy and chrysanthemum patch, the one she planted years ago. Maybe if we go out there, we can figure out what she was thinking."

"Do you think she used poppies and chrysanthemums to help you?" I asked. "I know poppies are used to make opium, but..."

"It's possible," he admitted. "After all, if it isn't in the books, it should be on our grounds."

We set off in the early afternoon, before the sun would plunge behind the trees and muddy our view. The birds were still plucking berries from the trees, scattering beneath the clouds. William took care to dress in his sturdiest, dirtiest gardening clothes. He didn't like to soil his hands but carried an unused shovel. I wore my old blue gown, with a hole-infested shawl.

"Just the poppy patch," William said. The dim light made his face appear a dull green. "We can't leave Mother alone in the house for too long."

"She's got Justine and the other servants," I pointed out, perhaps with petulance.

"But they aren't her children," he said. "They won't hold her hand when she shivers."

We smelled the poppies before we reached them. The cloying smell mixed with the damp. We could feel the air tingling with a promise of cold, blistering rain. William let the shovel drag on the grass.

"She walks this path." I noted the ruts in the grass where heels had trodden. The grass grew in short spurts, as if it feared shoes tearing them from the soil. "She must come here often."

"And she will come again," William said, his voice resolute.

We followed the green ruts. My shoes sank into the soil. I dragged myself along, fists clenched.

Two large stones, each round and speckled, lay among the poppies and chrysanthemums. They had no carvings, no names. Vines and grass grew over them, coating them in a sheath of leaves.

"Have we seen these before?" I asked William. My stomach tightened into a knot.

"No," he said. "But they must have been here for a long time. Look how weathered the edges are."

I ran my hands along the grimy rock. He was right; rain had watered down the surface, gouging jagged holes into smooth stone.

"We only need to gather poppies," I tried to say in a high-pitched voice.

William dropped the shovel. It fell to the ground with a thud. Then he bent, grunted, and pushed at the stones.

"William, please." I tried to make my tone stern. "Your back will break, and then Mr. Clementine will send you to a Spanish sanitarium to recover."

The stones rolled over. Vines and long grass weeds tore. William panted and bent. He grabbed the shovel and used it to dig into the soil.

"What are you doing?" I asked. The pitch in my voice had reached a screeching timbre.

"I have a bad, suspicious feeling," he said. "Why were these stones put side by side?"

"I don't think Mother buried the medicine that saved you," I tried to say, by means of joke.

My brother didn't pay attention. Shovels of soil emerged, until he caught a sight of blue. We both knelt, despite our clothes and ourselves. Our fingers touched the bundle.

"My God," William said.

I let the dirt soak into my skirts. The dress was fit for rags anyway, and I wanted to make a new one. The soil smelled of mildew and pungent mushrooms.

"It's just bones," I said. "They can't hurt you."

William had stroked the bones that were wrapped in periwinkle blue. I knew the nightgown, with its tiny stitches and lace collar; Mother had taken that after I had outgrown it, she said to keep in the attic as a token.

"Hand me the shovel," I said.

The soil clung to the metal and wood. My palms burned. We found more tiny bones, wrapped in a blanket. We also found a silver locket on a broken chain. Inside was a picture muddied and crusted with age. William had to pick at the inscription to read it. His face went pale. Chrysanthemum and poppy petals clung to his arms and waistcoat.

William Bysshe. Beloved son, beautiful Adonis.

The rain started just after we made it inside to the back porch. The mud from reburying the bones deep into the loam coated our outer layers. We shivered, not just from the sudden cold. William went straight to a washroom and tossed his clothes outside. Justine was shocked but wouldn't listen to his order to burn them; instead, she soaked them in lye soap. She drew baths for us, one at a time, and bundled me in blankets when I developed a small cough. Mercifully, that went away.

We didn't search the grounds again for a cure. Mother succumbed to an opium chill and fever. We buried her next to Father, dressed in black for months, and left her bedsheets untouched. William told our grandfather's lawyer that he would see to my education and the mansion's upkeep. He was of age, and he would do the family proud. If they had problems, he would hire legal counsel. We haven't heard from Grandfather since.

"Who am I then?" William would sometimes ask, while we read Mother's books by the fire. In the orange glow he would look more like a painted statue than like flesh and hair. "If those babies were the real William and Clara, then what does that make us?"

"You are my brother," I'd tell him firmly. "And my guardian. I'm your sister."

"But we aren't real, Nutcracker."

"We were real enough for Mother. And she made sure you were beautiful, *Adonis*."

That would shut him up. I've been adding tight stitches to his seams, and to mine. Mother had taught me enough needlework. We would live our days as stitched ghosts, and as our father's heirs. It was enough for Mother, and it would be enough for us.

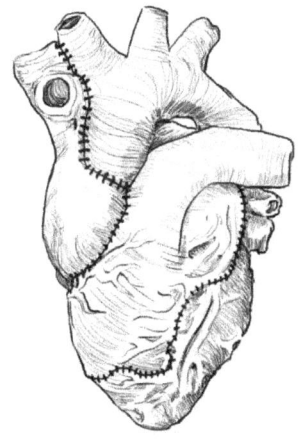

TERRA COTTA CHILDREN

LISA CARREIRO

I don't know whether the chaos outside is the revolution or the apocalypse. I don't hear screaming, only shouting and, yes, some singing, so I assume it's revolution.

I like to think the feral girl is sparking the fires of change. She vowed to lead people to safety. Though if she is their leader, I shouldn't have to keep shaking my head and saying, "I don't know where she went."

As for the Terra Cottas, I know a little more.

Five months ago, two Terra Cotta Children knocked at my door. One even peered through the window, cupping a metal hand over its cybernetic eyes as though to shade them from the sun. Light doesn't bother their eyes, and anyways it was nearly midnight with a new moon casting next-to-nothing light in the dark city sky. The neighbourhood hadn't had power since the previous afternoon. I knew the Terra Cotta could see into my dark room.

Outside, three more Terra Cottas led five adults down the street. Like adoring children following some metallic Pied Piper to who-knows-where, the people sang, all believing they'd been Chosen. They wept in gratitude, they were so certain their tribulations were over and they were bound for stardom.

Across the street, a young woman argued with a Terra Cotta that held out its hand to her. I heard her say, "I'm no fool. I'm not pretty enough." But the Terra Cotta persisted, replying in its melodic voice, "All are invited to audition for *Eden*."

The Terra Cottas at my door wanted to take me somewhere, too, but not likely to audition. I swear, one of the two mouthed "Mama" at me.

I nearly spit.

My Terra Cotta Children are neither: they're not terra cotta and I'm certainly not their mother, no matter what the media love to label me.

They're smaller than the average adult so they appear innocuous. Their eyes are bright. They seem to smile, and their voices are pleasant, even musical. They're easy to identify by their distinct reddish-brown hue. But blame me or bless me for them, Terra Cotta Children are bad copies of poor copies of machines we created twenty-seven years ago. I won't share the blame for these new machines. The ones we made were never supposed to trawl neighbourhoods at night to snatch wild children and lead away gullible adults with promises of auditions for *Eden*.

The Terra Cottas at my door smiled metal smiles. I invited both in, then locked the door.

I indicated with a wave for them to sit on my sofa. "Watch out for the old springs popping outta the left side," I said, smiling back at them. Then I smashed both with one swift blow. With the usual noise from outside — people singing, neighbours brawling, maybe some gun shots — no one heard the brief crack of an aluminum baseball bat across two metal heads. In

272

minutes, I had them on my kitchen table to dissect. By morning, I could see if anything in them might be salvageable. Now and then I'd find a stolen part from one of my original machines repurposed into those monstrosities.

None of the parts on those two were from originals. I scanned every inch of their interiors, torsos, and arms with a magnifying glass. I found neither serial numbers nor symbols. Instead, inside both I found garbage mixed with circuits and gears: greasy bicycle chains, frayed wires tangled with fishing line, and chunks of painted wood of all goddam things. Still, the two weren't built in someone's basement. They came from UT Industries, made well but for the wrong purpose: to lure away unhappy citizens with promises of unattainable joy acting in *Eden*, but really to employ them in vile occupations.

At three in the afternoon, the power lurched on again. *Eden* flickered back on in my living room. Like in any good citizen's home, it ran in the background of my life at all hours. I'd missed very little while the power was out, for the same episode came on. An unusually tall Terra Cotta stood over a group of seven humans at a picnic table. The people passed plates heaped with colourful food while they exchanged barbed quips. The Terra Cotta stood with arms outstretched and head cocked like a beatific machine keeping watch over its small clan. At least two cast members were new. Those less skilled in the art of caustic remarks and underhanded play never lasted long in their roles. Neither of the new actors were from my neighbourhood.

As I seared off chunks of the Terra Cottas in my kitchen, I wondered whether any of the five who'd been led away the previous night would pass their auditions and appear on *Eden*. I never knew anyone who did.

A few weeks later, an original Terra Cotta we called Thirty-Nine led ten ducklings down the middle of the street to the park. I hadn't seen Thirty-Nine for twelve years. Its ruddy exterior had faded and turned green in spots, and it was filthy. Leaves clung to its metal head, circling it like a crown.

People gushed and took photos. *The damn fool Terra Cotta rounding up baby ducks instead of wild children*, they said. Feral children from the park hid from the machine, except for one girl. She stood in the open beside the old bus terminal building to watch the parade. I caught her attention. She glanced at me with two different-coloured eyes – one blue, one brown.

Thirty-Nine led the ducklings past the ruined bus depot to the park, and then to the pond, all the time quacking like a mother duck: Thirty-Nine doing exactly what the original Terra Cotta machines were made to do.

Before I could follow Thirty-Nine any farther, the band of feral children, grown brazen without the Terra Cotta in sight, began to shriek as one, "Kill the monster! Kill the monster!"

I thought they were howling in the Terra Cotta's wake, but that rabid horde was yelling at the feral girl who'd glanced at me a few minutes earlier. She, indifferent to their battle cry, simply limped to the park where Thirty-Nine had led the ducklings.

I shouted at the children when some of them scooped up stones to throw at the feral girl they were taunting. But as soon as she reached Thirty-Nine, the other children's shrill voices grew silent.

Someone stood too close behind me and took photos. "Damnedest thing, eh?" he said. "Huh, I heard the old ones used to do that, you know, take care of the, uh, waddyacallits, orphan animals. Save the world from ecological catastrophe. Fat lotta good they did, eh?"

I didn't answer him. I cocked my head as though baffled. "Aren't we supposed to follow it? Like, for *Eden*, you know?" I pointed at poor old Thirty-Nine.

The man scoffed. "I wouldn't follow that one," he said as he took another photo. "It's clearly defective."

Through the summer, Thirty-Nine and the feral girl stayed near the pond teaching the ducklings to swim and find food. The other feral children did no more than shout insults at her from a distance. But the one they called a monster remained with Thirty-Nine like a duckling herself. She barely touched food I left for her and eyed me with a wary stare when I approached. She stood in the water up to her knees when the ducklings swam. She knelt to eat grass, pulling out mouthfuls with her teeth so the ducklings imitated her.

I watched both Terra Cotta and feral child every day, determined to steal back my machine before UT did; watching especially after the ducklings were grown enough to be on their own.

On a bright afternoon in late August, the brazen feral child led Thirty-Nine to my doorstep. She knocked the way the two Terra Cottas I'd dismantled did. She peered in the window with a dirty hand cupped over her eyes.

I opened the door and she pulled Thirty-Nine in behind her. Then she and I studied each other. What I'd mistaken to be dirt was mottled flesh; varying skin tones along her bare arms and face. Her left leg was shorter than her right and her face drooped a little on one side. Skin puckered around her wrists and around her ankles beneath the raggedy hems of her filthy trousers. I thought of the rag doll I'd had as a child, and how when it grew old, dirt never quite washed from its cloth face and its seams were mended with thread that never matched.

Eden was playing in the front room. The feral girl watched it while she followed me to the kitchen, and her lip curled.

I made a sandwich for her. "I can't cook anything," I told her. "The stove's been broken for years."

She said nothing. She remained standing while she ate slowly, indifferently even, as she watched me examine Thirty-Nine.

The Terra Cotta's hardy exterior was scratched, dented, and discoloured, but otherwise remarkably intact. Its left hand was missing and its left leg damaged. It must have wandered far away for many years or lain dormant somewhere. Or was caught by UT Industries, then released with most of its original programming intact.

"Do you know anything about the original Terra Cottas? The real ones like this?"

The girl simply stared at me, neither confirming nor denying that she knew anything.

I licked my lips, glancing out the front window for signs of any Terra Cottas or UT spies before I continued. "This Terra Cotta did exactly what we made them to do when it took the ducklings to the park and raised them," I said.

As though on cue, someone in *Eden* bellowed, "There never was an ecological disaster. If you had a brain, you'd know that."

The feral girl rolled her eyes.

I released my held breath. "Originally, we made tiny drones to pollinate plants where there weren't enough bees. Then we made the Terra Cottas to lead birds to forests, wolves to the wilds, and ducks to water." I tugged Thirty-Nine's remaining hand and spread it open as though I might read its palm. "This symbol, kinda faded now, means it's an original. Might be that

276

UT or someone else added their own parts, but most of this..." I bit my lip. "You know who I am?"

The child nodded. Her expression never changed, remaining focussed and sombre.

"They'll come looking for this Terra Cotta soon, so there isn't any time to waste."

I hefted Thirty-Nine onto the kitchen table. "While we still got power," I said. "Wouldn't put it past UT to knock out our power intentionally to keep me from working."

The girl made no move to leave. She stood in place, focussed on Thirty-Nine. Only her head moved as she watched me work.

Unlike the other Terra Cottas I'd dismantled, I wasn't going to smash an original and tear it to pieces. Thirty-Nine's dissection had to be as meticulous as I could manage in a short time. I hoped to have a full day before UT discovered Thirty-Nine had moved away from the park. With a welding torch, I opened Thirty-Nine's torso, bending back heated metal like I was opening a chest in an autopsy.

"I doubt this thing's been cracked open at all." I shone a flashlight inside. Its wiring was still intact; its metal parts precisely where they should have been. I wrapped my hand around a fist-sized circuit in its chest, lifting it like a beating heart dripping viscous fluid.

"This," I whispered as I snipped wiring and pulled it out, "is its most important component." I held it up like a trophy just as the power flickered out.

The child grinned at me. She studied Thirty-Nine's inner workings, running fingertips over bits while I held a flashlight for her to see in the dim kitchen. Her thumb stopped on a metal plate smaller than my pinky fingernail.

"That's its serial number." I worked the plate off and held it under a magnifying glass. "Yup, no doubt. This is Number Thirty-Nine."

The child stuffed two fingers to the back of her throat and gagged.

"What the hell? What's wrong?" I tried to pry her fingers out of her mouth, but small as she was, she was too strong for me. She pulled away and gagged until she spat up bits of undigested sandwich. A tiny metal plate sat in the middle of some bread. She pulled it out, wiped it on her trousers, and handed it to me.

The metal plate had a serial number.

She watched my expression morph from disbelief to astonishment.

"Where did you get this?"

She grinned, baring healthy and rather sharp teeth. Then she pointed to herself.

"You're not Number Fifty." I shook my head as I said it.

She nodded. Her eyes grew wider and her pallid complexion brightened a little.

"I didn't make you." I stepped back. "Where the hell did you get this plate? Do you know where the Terra Cotta it came from is?"

She pointed to herself.

I sat, suddenly wearier than I could imagine. "Did UT do something to you?" I reached for her arm and traced the puckered skin around her thin wrist, like a doll sewn together with spare parts from other dolls. "Who did this to you?"

She pointed to me.

I took her hands in mine. "I didn't make you," I said. "I made that." I pointed to Thirty-Nine's remains on the table. "I — we — made three-hundred Terra Cottas, but fewer than half of those were released. The first twenty were used in supervised tests and later dismantled by us. Numbers Twenty-One through One-Thirty-Seven were released across the continent

278

where they were most needed. Most of those failed or were stolen or destroyed within the first year. Still, some managed. Number Fifty lived near Banff, leading animals to safe crossings under and over the highways there. We tracked Fifty for close to eleven years before it disappeared. Most likely stolen. So somehow... you got its plate with the serial number."

The child shook her head and made a motion as though to write. I pulled out a tattered notebook with yellowed pages and a pen.

She stood with pen poised above paper for several seconds before she scrawled the numeral "50" at the top of a page. Then she drew a precise sketch of a Terra Cotta being dismantled on one table and a human corpse on a second table. "UT made me from Number Fifty," she wrote beneath the sketch.

"Nonsense," I whispered. I pressed a hand on my churning stomach. "That can't be done. The most anyone could do would be to turn a Terra Cotta into a synthetic human with a flesh-like covering. But not that." I tapped my finger on her drawing.

She grabbed the plate with the serial number on it and pointed to herself.

I shook my head. "So UT made you and then just let you out? Just made you and... set you free? Why would they do that?"

"Broken," she wrote. "Garbage. Bad." Her lip curled in a sneer that became a grin. "MONSTER," she added.

"No," I said. "UT lied to you. You... you're just a regular kid, really."

She shook her head. "I remember," she wrote. She sat on the floor with the notebook, and pen ran across paper with unimaginable speed.

I wiped my brow. The hot kitchen had become stifling. The clouds grew thicker and the wind picked up, blowing trash around outside.

When she finished writing, the feral girl who called herself Number Fifty handed the notebook to me.

"I remember," she'd written. "I led animals to safety. I led wolves, coyotes, bears, moose. I liked the animals but then I didn't know the emotion, 'like.' I understood duty. I knew tasks. One night, people came to me. Then I woke up on a surgical table. Flesh children were lying all around me. Pieces of children were put on me and in me. I remember. I felt. Felt 'sad,' felt 'hurt.' I was the first one made. But not good. Broken. More children were made later. Better children. 'Good' children. Broken me was thrown in the garbage. I was not dead, though. I walked away from the dump. I searched for the others. Later, I found Thirty-Nine."

The power whirred back on while I sat with the notebook limp in my hand. "When?" I handed her the notebook and her hand flew across the paper again.

"Seven summers ago," she wrote. "Hiding. Helping animals. Took Thirty-Nine home. But Thirty-Nine kept stopping to take care of animals. Slowed us on our journey here. I brought Thirty-Nine home. I knew Thirty-Nine, and Twenty-Seven, and Ninety. Ninety got squashed by a truck. Twenty-Seven got taken by UT and became a Good Child."

I re-read her words, then reached for her hands. A pulse. Breathing. A brain somehow. I gently squeezed her thin wrists, trying to determine whether she had metal or bone beneath her skin.

"I think you're..."

She tugged away her hands and glared at me. She scratched more words in the notebook and thrust it at me again.

"I led animals to safety. I led Thirty-Nine to safety. Next, I will lead people to safety."

"Ah, like the Terra Cottas who take people away."

She shook her head so hard her tangled hair waved, and she stomped a foot. She grabbed pen and notebook again.

280

"To SAFETY. Not with promises to act on that 'Eden.' Not to UT. Not to the barracks to work vile jobs. To SAFETY. People follow like animals. I will lead."

"I don't know what to believe."

The kitchen light flickered off. I tried to study the feral girl's features in the waning light before the clouds dimmed the late afternoon.

"You were probably born like any kid, and someone spun a tale to explain your scars."

She sneered. "I REMEMBER. I AM FIFTY." She picked up the metal plate with the serial number and swallowed it. Then she pointed at Thirty-Nine's remains on the table.

"Yeah. Yeah, it'll be dark enough in a little while to hide Thirty-Nine. I have some junk I scavenged from others. I'll load that into Thirty-Nine and leave it for UT to find. A shame to lose the shell." I ran a hand over the scratched exterior. "Then I... I'll do something with its good parts. In case you work for UT, I can't tell you."

She rolled her eyes.

"Isn't UT looking for you? Once they discovered you were alive?"

She shrugged.

"If you're what you say you are, they must want you back."

She shook her head.

"You can stay here as long as you want. But you should know if you don't already that I'm in danger. I dismantled seven of UT's rotten remakes in the last two years. I've got a bag packed so I can leave on short notice. Especially now with Thirty-Nine's 'heart.' I can't pretend to blend in much longer."

I cleaned up the sandwich Fifty spit up before I finished rejigging Thirty-Nine's insides. The power lurched on and off twice more. *Eden* blared on and off with the power.

Fifty added the bicycle chain I'd pulled out of the other Terra Cotta earlier in the summer. I seared Thirty-Nine shut, buffed the seam, and scratched and burned its exterior before finally rubbing dirt all over it.

The summer night was sweltering. Lightning flickered in the distance when Fifty and I finally hauled poor old Thirty-Nine's remains back to the park, walking in a wide arc past a group of sleeping feral children and close to the tree Thirty-Nine had stayed near while it raised the ducklings. We both rubbed more dirt on it and gathered a few branches to strew on top of it. Anyone who had the wherewithal to examine the remains closely could easily learn how much of it was original. It was time for me to leave the city.

I turned away as soon as the task was done, expecting the child who called herself Fifty to follow me home. Instead, she stood for several minutes with hands folded in front of her, staring at Thirty-Nine's remains with head bowed. I waited, clenching my fists and tapping my foot. She glanced over at me, then turned in the opposite direction and limped away. Twice, her small silhouette was illuminated by lightning, and then she was gone.

That's all I know. UT picked me up before I even reached home that night. They... you searched my place. But Thirty-Nine's heart was gone. I didn't have it. And if any other original Terra Cottas are left, I don't know where they are.

Fifty, or whoever she is, had more sense than to follow me. Maybe she turned me in. Maybe she really is one of your creations, and she's wandering free after she led you to me.

Or maybe the feral girl who told me she's Number Fifty really is leading a revolution out there. If anyone can do it, it's Fifty.

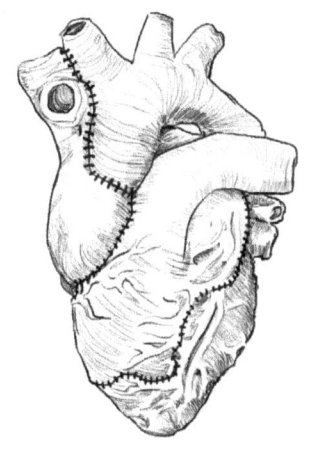

MORE

KAITLIN TREMBLAY

I stare at my coffee mug. Is two sugars okay? I don't use cream anymore but made the compromise with skim milk. Skim milk, two sugars. I can't make the switch to black coffee. Not yet anyways. It's too acidic. My stomach lining is delicate enough as it is. I don't need to push it with black coffee. Besides, it just tastes better this way (accepting that I can consume things that just "taste good" is a new way of consuming for me).

I don't know how to sit and feel comfortable. I can sit and look sexy, or I can sit and look laid back, but I don't know to sit and actually feel comfortable. My bones feel awkward, riddled with a dull ache that only steaming hot showers and layers of blankets can begin to soothe. Tonight's even worse because of the rain. I picked out my nice bra. The lace one, dark blue. But it's a bit too small and the underwire cuts into the flesh, pinching me with each movement. A hazard, considering how much I talk with my hands.

To be honest, I don't even know if I like the way the bra makes my tits look. They're a bit too there, too ostentatious; too visible. The underwire leaves red welts as it saws into my flesh, and I just pray the cuts don't start to bleed. The last thing I need is my shirt to start blossoming blood. I don't even hate the pain, I'm just worried about the appearance of it. The pain is sharp and biting and acts like a suture, connecting my clothes to my body. The red marks become dotted lines, showing where to cut as if I were a paper doll. Or if I was a monster, sewn back together, showing the scars.

It's been so long since I've been on a first date. I had joked that we should go to a cemetery, collect body parts and flowers, and instead of recoiling in disgust or ghosting me, she laughed. She said we should have a picnic at the cemetery near her house, since it was always well maintained and there was a really nice wooden gazebo in the centre that nobody ever used.

Talk about the gazebo led into a discussion about the picnic, and eventually we settled on a less morbid and probably less tacky location. A little park, in between both of our apartments. There wasn't a gazebo, but there were flowers.

"We can tell ghost stories, to make up for the lack of corpses," she said.

It was decided that she would bring a baguette, different cheeses, grapes, and apples. I volunteered to bring the wine.

"I'll hide it in water bottles," I said, making a shushing motion, "Discrete."

But of course, the rain ruined all of that – picnicking in the mud isn't quite the same – and so we agreed to meet at a diner instead.

"No flowers, but good, warm food," she compromised.

Sitting across from her at this diner, I feel like I can't breathe. The wire from my bra dissects my skin, and the straps threaten to dig rivets into my shoulders as well. But she is suffocating. Her beauty, her calmness, her confidence.

"Your smile," she says, gulping coffee, warming her fingers around her mug, "Makes me so happy. I don't need anything else when I see you smile."

I smile deeper, bigger, wider. We've been friends for a few months, but that friendship was always tinged with tension, flirtations.

"What are you thinking about?" she asks.

"What it would be like to be a paper doll," I respond. "To have my limbs erased and reconstructed if I didn't like them."

"Would you want to use your old body parts to make up your own new limbs, or have them taken from something else?"

"Like Frankenstein?" I ask.

"Like, being a paper doll made of clippings from magazines," she clarifies.

"That, that one for sure," I laugh. "I want Jennifer Aniston's arms."

"Usually people like her hair."

"It's not the 90s anymore."

She raises an eyebrow and takes another sip of her coffee. I'm wearing a choker. Not a thick, black velvet one like I wore in the 90s. But rather a small, champagne-coloured one. There is a crimson stain on it from when I accidentally cut my neck scratching at a mosquito bite too hard. I like the stain.

She always makes me nervous. She is delicate and beautiful. She has this burgundy dress, A-line, that flutters around her thighs when she twirls, making believe she's a princess.

Once, while shopping, I tried on a similar dress. She encouraged me, told me it would flatter my shape, make me feel more comfortable with being pretty. I tried on a size too small, embarrassed by the number. The dress got stuck. I was able to eventually pull it off, but only after ripping it along the seam underneath and around my armpit. My skin was red and raw from the harsh fabric, and from my excessive scratching when trying to remove the dress. She saw me afterwards, in my tank top. Saw my skin. Her touch was soft, tender, but not hesitant. She traced the lines on my reddened skin, and I winced when she touched the bits of flesh that were torn open, raw and exposed.

"Sorry," she said. "That dress was cheap, anyways."

If she was a princess, I was a monster, tentative to the touch. I couldn't say anything. My lips were sewed shut with my teeth as I bit down on them. The power of that dress wasn't one I could access. It was shut off from me, barricaded behind zippers like locked gates that I didn't know how to pick.

That night in the shower, I watched the marks disappear as the hot, scalding water reddened my skin. Welts made invisible by blistering the rest of me. I felt safe under the steam, invisible, as if the water would melt my skin away, leaving me stripped bare and ready to rebuild.

She still makes me nervous. Her movements are so confident, so assured. I wonder what it's like to be in a body that you don't hate, one that you don't try to cover with plain, ill-fitting clothes. She moves like she knows her body, knows the exact strength of her muscles, extensions of her own bones. She moves in control, graceful and defiant at the same time. Beware, for she is fearless.

I feel the wire and bra straps cut further into my skin, my arms going slightly numb, as if they are not properly attached to my body.

I want it all gone. Every part of my body, vivisected and dismembered, so I can start from scratch with a new body, made from the most perfect of parts. Parts I would have her pick out, with her assured eye and incisive understanding of the human body. She works the cash register at a clothing store, but she used to be a painter. We met in a life drawing class. She tells me her apartment is still littered with the charcoal portraits of anonymous bodies from that class. Many of them were uncompleted, just disembodied torsos, legs, arms. She would know the right tone of arm, the right length of leg, the perfect sized breasts and hips. She would make me strong, she would make me beautiful. She would make me hers.

The server clears away our plates, hers entirely wiped clean, even the congealed pools of syrup wiped away with her finger, mine full of French fries and the bits of the salad I couldn't eat - tomatoes and pickled onions.

"Let's go for a walk," she suggests.

"But it's wet from the rain," I reply.

She quotes a line from Garbage's "I'm Only Happy When It Rains" and I genuinely laugh, smile, bite my lips. Is this what flirting is?

"Yeah, let's go for a walk," I agree.

"Let's find you some new body parts," she winks.

I ditch my high heels. There's no walking on grass in them, the heels just sink into the softened and muddy earth, and besides, they make me feel like a fraud. No burgundy dress, no black high heels. The mud beneath my feet is soft and cold, still soaked from the day's rain. Every time I lift my feet, I pull up a few clods of dirt as I free my feet from the depression they created, raising them from the dead.

She's not far ahead of me, but she's waiting, watching me.

She doesn't leap on me. Instead, she carefully moves toward me, our eyes locked. Her fingers twist into my hair, and she leans in close, her lips pressed against my ear. She doesn't whisper, doesn't say anything. I close my eyes, her deep breaths exhaling into my ear, electricity.

My muscles twitch and spasm, alive with an urgency I thought was long since dead.

"More," I say.

She bites into the flesh on my shoulder, hard enough to break skin, hard enough to sink into the meat of my muscle. I bite down on my lip, before releasing a loud cry, a shriek buried deep within. She retreats, inhaling sharply, growling, before lunging in again, this time ripping into the flesh next to her pre-existing bite marks. Her teeth a needle, her spit a suture, simultaneously tearing my flesh apart and weaving it back together, made not from clay and rib bones, but from spit, blood, and ferocity.

She reels backwards, her red lipstick smeared across her chin, and she snarls, her lips pulling back to reveal red-stained teeth. The cool air hits the wound on my shoulder, snaking in and animating the exposed muscle and nerves, forcing the muscle to spasm and twitch. A semi-circle of bite marks around my left shoulder, threatening to dislocate my shoulder bone entirely with each spasm. Her chest is heaving, and she licks her lips, blood and satin.

"More," I say.

"Where," she asks.

Blood coats my left arm, dripping from my ravaged shoulder. My hands are slick as blood curls over my wrist, twisting itself through the lines on my palm, elongating with the length of my fingers. I bring my hand over to my stomach, and with a bloodied finger, draw a line across.

She obliges, but not with her teeth. Kneeling into the soft, wet mud, she grabs my hips, her fingers sinking into my flesh, digging grooves and rooting in, fingernail scraping bone. Then with her tongue, she traces the bloodied line I drew, over and over until all that remains on my stomach is her saliva. Licked clean, she kisses my stomach, gently laying her satin lips onto the soft fat, replacing my bloodied line with clumpy fragments of her lipstick. Traces of her. Tender.

Once she has covered my stomach, from left to right, she repeats the action, but this time when her lips touch my flesh, they peel back to reveal her teeth, which extend and bite down, softly at first, nibbling bits of stomach. Playfully. She repeats, left to right, left to right. Preparing.

I ache.

Then, her third time across, her teeth bite down hard, pulling and tearing skin, ravenous. Her movements are no longer meticulous, and her fingers dig deeper into my hip bones as she bites, tears, sucks, licks at the soft skin of my stomach. My feet sink into the mud, digging mini graves all around as I attempt to hold still against her fury.

"More," I growl, and she pulls me in closer, her mouth extends larger, and she gnaws deeper into me.

Each bite is followed by a kiss, a loud, hungry, enveloping kiss that pulls at my raw skin.

I scream, my bloodied hand now in her hair, her curls locking around my fingers, pulling my hand deeper into the glossy mess. Everything is pulling us inwards, the places where we touch erupting into black holes, event horizons folding us into each other.

She severs my stomach, and then, victorious, removes her hands from my hips, her fingers extracting from bone, leaving me shaken, unsteady, hungry. The magician's assistant, severed in half.

"More," I say, and her eyes spark, lightning and thunder.

"Where," she asks, again.

With my bloodied finger, I trace lines across my thighs. It becomes obvious to her, what I am doing, what I am asking of her.

This time she doesn't prep the flesh, using her tongue as a way to numb it, and instead tears in immediately, her head between my thighs, her teeth ripping away the soft, interior flesh. Chafe marks consumed with her eating, I moan. To be whole, I need to be destroyed. To be whole, I need to be rebuilt.

As her teeth spit away fat and rip into muscle, every part of my flesh becomes alive. Like with my underwire, I feel my body, connected to it through the pain as surges of agony sweep throughout my entire body, uniting all of the disparate parts, flowing better and stronger than my blood could ever have, an unbreakable circuit. Limbs constructed from blood, not charcoal.

Her ferocity is for me. Her intensity is for me.

Her body heaves and thrusts, and she pulls away, inhaling sharply, eyes locked on mine. She leaps again, pins me to the ground, the soft mud sinking, making room for my body. Her hands grab mine, pulls them over my head, and she pins my wrists. She kisses my neck, biting and sucking, once on each side, before sliding her tongue deep into my mouth, moaning as I am completely consumed by her and the mud.

Afterwards, she entangles herself around me. With her arms and her legs, she gathers my dismembered limbs, pulling them in, placing them where they belong.

"Relax," she says. "Just relax."

With a subtle intensity, so different from her ravenous consumption beforehand, she sews me back up, with her own hair as thread. I have never felt such gentleness. Each raw and exposed bit of muscle, each scrap of torn flesh, she gently wipes clean with a torn section of her dress, and then uses her fingers and nails to stitch me back together.

"And now," she says, pulling a final strand of her hair out, to sew back up my stomach, "with pieces of me, we are more attached than ever."

Her strength, her defiance, her love. My wounds throb with each heavy pulse of my heart, and I feel my muscles begin to twitch again, electrified by her power. I am calm.

I let the life return to my limbs, the blood and oxygen gently pumped through arteries and capillaries, animating flesh. The pain returns, this time sharp and brutal. My limbs, my pain. Mine and not the new ones I had hoped for, but mine. My limbs, my pain.

Her fingers trace the lines on my body, trailing the remaining bits of drying blood. She draws circles on my stomach, on my shoulders, on my collarbones. Using my blood as an inkpad, she stamps both sides of my neck with her finger. Her fingerprint, my blood.

I was wrong.

She isn't the princess.

"Nobody understands," she sighs. Curls herself into the negative space left by my body.

The marks she's left on my body give me strength. Slightly craning my neck, I count them with my eyes. Each sewn-up cut, each welt, each bruise, a mark of her. A mark of us.

"How do you feel?" she asks.

"How do you feel?" I deflect.

"Calm."

"At first I was afraid," I admit. "But it's not worth being scared about."

"I know."

"Nobody understands," she repeats.

I whisper, the blood on my tongue dripping down, coating my throat, "You're right."

For the first time I breathe, fearless.

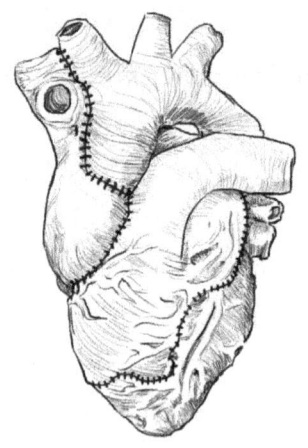

MOTHER MONSTER

VICTORIA K. MARTIN

The sun was shining this morning, after being a stranger all summer - a time that would one day be called the "year without a summer." Mary glanced upwards into the light, risking the glare for novelty's sake. After so many days driven inside by rain, it was a welcome respite.

"No marvel then, though I mistake my view; the sun itself sees not, till heaven clears."

She smiled and leaned back as Percy came to stand behind her, wrapping his arms around her waist. "Sonnet 148," she murmured, certain her identification was accurate. The Bard had been part of her earliest education, as she prepared for the literary legacy she'd been born into.

"The story you told us last night," he said softly, his breath warm against her earlobe, "It was incredible. How did you ever conceive of such a thing?"

Despite the rare sunlight and the heat of her lover's warm body, Mary shivered and, in that moment, the past came rushing into her mind, pushing awareness of anything else out.

"Women are everywhere in this deplorable state; for, in order to preserve their innocence, as ignorance is courteously termed, truth is hidden from them, and they are made to assume an artificial character before their faculties have acquired any strength."

Mary paused as she reached the end of the page and wondered how long she had been reading. It had likely been well over an hour now but it was no cause for worry - her father knew where to find her and would come if it grew too late. She'd been visiting her mother like this for years now, first with him and now without.

She shifted to face the gravestone behind her back, reaching out to trace the engraving: *Mary Wollstonecraft Godwin*, (her own name) *Author of A Vindication of the Rights of Woman* (the book from which she was currently reading). Mary loved her father dearly, and her elder sister Fanny too, but she'd always felt like a part of her was buried here, the part that bound her and her mother forever.

She leaned back against the cold stone and looked down at her mother's words, imagining what they might have sounded like if the author were here to read them to her. She had once asked her father what her mother's voice had sounded like, but he had been unable to provide a satisfactory answer. And so, Mary imagined the sound instead. In her head, it was soft and low and always sounded like her mother was smiling, because she always was.

"Sweet baby," Maman would whisper, "how I adore you." Mary would curl up in her lap and listen instead of having to read for herself. And it would be wonderful.

But that was just a fantasy, and so she turned the page and continued to read: "Taught from their infancy that beauty is woman's sceptre, the mind shapes itself to the body, and, roaming round its gilt cage, only seeks to adore its prison."

"Mary ..."

She stopped and looked up at the sound of her name. There was no one there. She turned back to the page, but this time chose to read silently, so she could listen too.

"Mary ..."

This time when she looked up, she saw movement from under a tree to her left, a slight sway in a breezeless afternoon. She stood up, clutching the book to her chest. "Who's there?"

A branch cracked, a leaf fell. A shadow turned into a shape. "... Mary. My child."

She turned and ran.

She did not return to the grave for many days, which was unusual enough to cause her father to comment on it. He had always done everything he could to encourage both Mary and Fanny to honour and cherish their mother's memory. When he questioned her newfound reluctance to visit, Mary found herself lying to him for the first time in her life and claiming that she felt unwell. Unfortunately, while the falsehood was accepted without question, William Godwin then insisted that his treasured daughter be confined to her bed until she was well.

From her room, Mary could see the road that led to St Pancras church, where her mother was buried. She spent much of her confinement staring at it, looking for any signs of mischief or malevolence. But from here, it looked the same as always.

After a few days of feigned illness and an abundance of thought and reflection, Mary convinced her father of her recovery. And then, book and all her courage in hand, she headed out to face whatever it was that she'd seen, knowing somehow that it would still be there.

The graveyard was as quiet and still as always. Nothing at all seemed amiss ... until she reached her mother's headstone. The stone itself was the same as ever, but the ground before it was all torn asunder, as if someone had been ripping it up with their bare hands. Mary knelt and tried to smooth the grass down but her efforts made no difference.

And then the shadow returned.

"Mary ..."

She stood and turned slowly, facing the creature before her. It had the shape of a woman, but it was unlike any woman she had ever seen before. She had watery, glowing eyes, long, tangled brown hair, black lips, and prominent teeth. She was horrifying but also, somehow, familiar. The prominent nose, the curve of her brows. Mary had seen it all before.

"Maman?"

Her mother nodded and held out her hand. Mary reached out and took it, holding on tight to fingers that were cold as ice.

For the next year, it was rare that a day passed in which Mary did not visit the graveyard at least once, if not more. She still brought her mother's books with her but the visits were now dominated by Mary's own words, as she told her mother about her life, both past and present, catching up for years of lost time.

It all went smoothly until the day William Godwin married Mary Jane Clairmont. Mary's new stepmother came with two children of her own and threw Mary's once ordered world into complete chaos - particularly now, as her father had just announced that the family would be moving away, far enough that she would be unable to come to St Pancras so easily.

"She is horrible," Mary complained bitterly, curled up at her mother's side. "She does not try to understand me and she cares nothing about my happiness. Worst of all, Father does nothing to stop her. It feels as though he no longer cares for me at all."

Her mother's arm wrapped around her shoulders, holding her tight. She rarely spoke, which was disappointing for Mary, given all the things she'd dreamed of, but she knew the creature wasn't really Mary Wollstonecraft, not entirely.

But she was still the closest thing to a real mother that Mary had.

This latest visit could not have been longer than thirty minutes in length before she heard the dreaded sound of Claire Clairmont's voice. Her new stepsister took great pleasure in causing Mary distress, particularly if doing so always led to Mary losing her father's favour. As Claire approached, Mary stood, brushing off her skirts, while her mother quickly moved away, melting into the shadowy forest.

"There you are," Claire said as she finally came into view, her voice filled with smug satisfaction. "Mother says you need to come in now."

Mary didn't say anything in reply, since she knew there was no point. As the two of them walked home, she noticed a rustling sound behind them.

When she glanced at Claire, she could see that her stepsister was oblivious, as always. Mary glanced back but could not see anything - yet somehow, she knew that her mother was coming home with her for the first time today.

That night, as she prepared for bed, she heard a tapping on her window. She opened it, expecting to see her mother's face, but there was nothing. Then she looked down at the sill and gasped.

Lying there was a human finger, the skin mostly grey except for the black base, where it should have attached to a hand. Mary grabbed a handkerchief and reached out, picking it up. It felt heavy in her hands. She glanced around and saw the small wooden box she used for special keepsakes nearby. She quickly placed the finger inside and closed the lid, before heading for a sleep filled with confusing dreams.

After they moved, Mary was only able to make occasional visits to the gravesite, and never alone. When she was there, she sometimes thought she caught a glimpse of something in the shadows, or heard a voice calling her name, but other times she could not be sure.

The older she grew, the less certain she was that any of it had really happened. One day, she mustered up the courage to open the keepsake box where she had put the finger, and instead of flesh or bone, she found a smooth, grey stick - the size of an adult finger, certainly, but nothing more.

Holding the branch tight, she stole into her father's study where, despite her stepmother's displeasure, a portrait of Mary Wollstonecraft hung on the wall above the fireplace. In it, her mother looked to the side and Mary had always wondered what her mother had been looking at. She wore a simple white dress and her hair was mostly hidden under a hat.

297

She had looked at this portrait so many times in her life. And thus, she could picture herself using this image to dream up something else, to create an imaginary Maman who, while not quite human, was there for her child in Mary's hour of need.

Mary's grip on the branch tightened for a moment, before she flung it into the fire. She stood there and watched as the flames devoured it, turning this imagined memento into dust.

As more and more years passed, Mary's visits to St Pancras became more and more infrequent. However, when Percy Shelley had asked her if he might visit the grave with her, she found it impossible to say no. She was already beginning to think that she might never be able to refuse this man anything.

He gripped her hand tight as they stood before the gravestone. He leaned down to place a single rose on the ground before it, bowing his head in memory of the woman who had reached beyond the grave to bring them together.

"What a remarkable woman," he said as he stood. "How I would have loved to meet her."

Mary smiled and squeezed his hand tighter. He turned toward her and smiled back. "Of course, her daughter is just as remarkable, if not more so." He leaned in and embraced her. It only lasted a moment however, as he pulled back and looked over his shoulder.

"Did you hear that?"

Mary shook her head. "No, I didn't hear anything." Even as she spoke, she found herself looking into the shadows, searching for that once remembered shadow. As expected, she saw nothing.

"It must have been my imagination," Percy said with a shrug. "Are you ready to go, my love?"

"Yes," she told him, nodding. She turned away from the shadows and from the grave, before she saw something she didn't want to believe in anymore.

"T
he story you told us last night," Percy said softly, his breath warm against her earlobe, "It was incredible. How did you ever conceive of such a thing?"

Mary shivered and looked into the distance. For a moment, she thought she saw a figure standing by Lake Geneva. When she blinked, the figure was gone.

"Mary? Is something disturbing you?"

She shook her head and turned in his arms, pressing her lips against his. "It was a dream," she said finally. "The monster, the one who created it ... it was all from a dream."

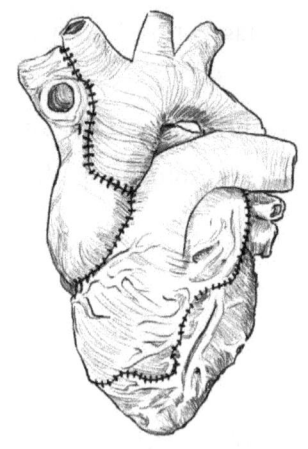

WOLLSTONECRAFT

ASHLEY CARANTO MORFORD

I f you read the story that has been privileged, that has been made canon, that silences me and uplifts the oppressors' voices, you know me by the names Creature, Monster, Fiend, or Devil. Do not call me any of these.

My name is Wollstonecraft. My pronouns are they/them.

If you read the story that has been privileged, you will be told that Victor Frankenstein was "by birth a Genevese; and," further, that his "family is one of the most distinguished of that republic." What all of these fancy words really mean is that Victor benefitted from white privilege, from being a man in a patriarchal world, and from financial stability.

And yet, despite all of this inherent power, Victor wanted even more. He had the desire to know things he didn't have the right to know, and he used violence to access and steal and appropriate this knowledge.

Victor Frankenstein is the Colonial Researcher, he who refuses to be in relationship with those he is conducting research on; he who takes from communities he is not part of without permission; he who stole body parts from burial grounds without the consent of those he took from. Victor Frankenstein is the epitome of colonial scholarship, of Western science's exploiting marginalized communities, of the academy's speaking over and silencing and manipulating the voices, perspectives, experiences, and cultures of marginalized peoples. Victor Frankenstein's story doesn't need to be told. It has been told too many times before. His perspective doesn't need to be celebrated. It has been celebrated over and over and over again. He was not, in fact, a victor.

It is time, it has *always* been time, for the stories of the oppressed to be honoured.

This story that I share with you is a learning — for I will always be learning and I will always have much to learn. Truthfully, there is still much I do not know about myself or about the various ancestors that live within and through my body in my very act of breathing. My body is covered with scars and stitches: the knowledges, histories, and wisdoms of many ancestors. My body is past, present, and future. And, for all that I still have to learn, I do know that I am different. The ableist, heteronormative, colonial society that we are born into oppresses me constantly because my body does not fulfill its normative expectations. From the moment of my birth, society pushed my body and my humanity away, denying my right to exist in the hopes that I would be forgotten, that I would vanish.

When Victor alienated me, I wandered, lost and homeless, and found myself in the very depths of a never-ending tangled forest. But I kept on living, I kept on breathing, at night I kept on dreaming, and every morning the bird songs that greeted me filled my heart with feelings that I now know are love and hope. As the days went by and the seasons changed from warm

301

to frostbiting, on a dreary night of November, I came upon a human dwelling. I could perceive movements and human voices inside. I remembered the way that humans had violated my dignity, and every inch of me ached at this ongoing memory. I turned away from the dwelling.

But the door opened, and a group of people called out to me. Though I could not understand what they said, not yet knowing their language, they made me feel welcomed. Safe. Secure. They wrapped my shivering wind-bitten shoulders in a blanket of fleece, inviting me into the warmth of their house and out of the cold loneliness, making a spot for me on a soft chair by a hearty fireplace and offering me bowls of hot, thick soup. Then, they made up a small bedroom for me and I understood that they wanted me to stay.

Within that dwelling, I have found a home, a community, a family: De Lacey, a blind man of French ethnicity and a grassroots teacher who draws attention to white privilege and challenges the toxicity of ableist society, equipping the younger generations with the tools to do the same; Safie, a bisexual woman of the Arab diaspora and a journalist for a small activist newspaper who works to dismantle the harms of patriarchy, colonialism, heteronormativity, and homonormativity, and whose news articles motivate others to do the same; Agatha, a novelist and asexual panromantic woman of the Pilipinx diaspora — her skin bearing the traditional tattoos of her Visayan ancestors — who strives to disrupt the legacies of amatonormativity, colonialism, and racism, and whose self-published books call on others to do the same; and Felix, a Black aromantic gender-fluid person and a filmmaker who deconstructs the hold of amatonormativity, heteropatriarchy, colonialism, and racism, and whose grassroots films encourage others to do the same.

Western medical books will tell you that De Lacey and I are tragic and broken, in need of curing, me for my so-called deformed figure and he for his blindness. Western history books will tell you that Agatha, Felix, and

Safie — these beautiful people of colour — are inferior savages or thugs or terrorists in need of the power and guidance and control of European civilization. Western psychology books will tell you that it is wrong for Agatha to not experience sexual attraction, that it is wrong for Felix to not experience romantic attraction. Colonial myths. If you accept these colonial myths as natural, then I urge you to truly, fully, openly listen to us when we tell you our truths. We are not tragic, nor broken, nor savage, nor uncivilized, nor wrong. We are full and complex and beautiful human beings. We fight for each other with love. We are living truths grounded in decolonial love. We exist, we are beautiful, and we should be and will be and *are* celebrated.

On a rickety old wooden bookshelf nestled near our fireplace are piles of books. Well-read books. Well-loved books. These books are filled with brilliant stories, and we gather around the fireplace with hot cocoa, steaming tea, fleece blankets to read them and discuss them together. In those moments by the fireplace, bent over all of those printed pages, I have learned that these books offer teachings to be honoured, respected, uplifted, celebrated; the writings and teachings of Black activists like Frantz Fanon, Malcolm X, bell hooks, Roxane Gay; the writings and teachings of Indigenous activists and scholars like Lee Maracle (Sto:Loh), Qwo-Li Driskill (Cherokee), Chelsea Vowel (Métis), Eve Tuck (Unangax), and Daniel Heath Justice (Cherokee). De Lacey, Agatha, Safie, Felix, and I lounge by the fireside for hours and we talk about revolution, imagine intersectional decolonial futures, plan concrete action, take concrete action. And the stories and teachings within these books by these great good teachers help to guide us in envisioning a better present and future connected to the past.

I share with you some of our memories, our histories, our stories as a family. I share some of the valuable stories and teachings that this community has gifted me. May these stories and teachings and words that I share with you now be carried forward by and with you too. Words. They matter and hurt and matter and heal and matter and transform and they matter.

I do not know what my ancestral languages are and, because of this, every day I feel the ache of disconnection, of lost knowledge. The common language of the household is English, and thus it is English that I set out to learn first.

Agatha and I learn language together. Wandering amongst the trees outside the humble shelter we call home; lying on our backs in the grass, faces to the sky world, to the clouds amongst a tapestry of blue, to the stars that guide us at night; in the wee hours, wrapped in blankets by the fireplace, me flipping through old books, Agatha listening to Visayan mythologies on her laptop — a substitute she tells me she is forever grateful for but that cannot replace the experience of hearing these stories in person and in homeland.

Agatha is reclaiming her ancestral language. Binisaya. It is a language she says she never heard when she was a child, growing up a member of a diaspora in a society that valued whiteness and a family that had internalized this racism. Her mother had told her when she was little that, "Our language is useless here," and thus had never taught it to her.

Sometimes, Agatha whispers grief that she has never felt the sands and soils of her ancestral territories on her skin, has never breathed in the scents and airs of those lands and waters. But, as Felix reminds her again and again — at the kitchen table over steaming cups of freshly brewed tea — worldviews and philosophies are embedded in language, and so, learning her ancestral language is, in a sense, a coming home. Every word remembered is a moment of reclamation, of homecoming.

"Some day, I will write a novel in my ancestral language, not the language colonialism forced onto us," Agatha says one night, while the two of us are munching on bowls of cereal. She smiles at me and adds, "Higala. Higala is friend in Binisaya."

"Higala," I reply and I smile too. I love and I am loved.

The first love I received was the warmth and fullness and wisdom of bird song. The first noises I made were in response to bird song. After Victor turned from me, after society alienated me, as I wandered homeless and lost, the birds stayed with me, their songs that woke me each morning emphasizing that there is always hope and beauty. Indeed, it is a constant comfort that, no matter how cruel the world of humans becomes, the sun will rise and with the sun the birds will rise too and sing for us even when we are not worthy of their songs.

Sometimes, in the early mornings — when it is dewy and the mist kisses the grasses, and the soils and the lands smell crisp and pure — De Lacey and I will leave the warmth of our beds, go out into the moist grass together, and sing with the birds: De Lacey in raggedy woollen grey sweater and raggedy grey slippers that are ripped around the edges from being well-worn with love, his white cane in his hand, me barefoot in the red plaid dressing gown he so generously passed on to me when I first moved in. And if Felix wakes early enough, they will join us too, clad in their fluffy pink nightgown and glow-in-the-dark slippers, camcorder at the ready to record our singing and our whistling and our trilling and our laughter.

When we come back into the warmth of the house, our cheeks tinged pink from the air-kisses of dawn, Safie and Agatha are already busy writing at the kitchen table in their soft flannel pyjamas and soft flannel sock-slippers, Safie type type typing an article and flipping through her copy of Sara Ahmed's *Living a Feminist Life* and Agatha type type typing her novel and flipping through her copy of Edward Said's *Orientalism*. They have boiled the kettle already and laid out all the necessary cups and jars and utensils for us to have coffee or tea. De Lacey and I begin to make bread together, me grabbing at the ingredients he has taught me are the secret to the best bread and, as we work together, he whistles and whistles and whistles.

During these early mornings, De Lacey teaches me to understand all of the various distinct birds we sing with, and I come to recognize and to respect the uniqueness of each bird's song: the Blackbird, the Robin, Warblers, Thrushes, the Goldfinch — and De Lacey and me, our breath emitting from our chests in bursts of fog as we respond to every bird that sings to us, every cheerful, every melancholy, every excited, every soft, every beautiful song they gift the morning with.

My life overflows with gifts. Gifts that transcend superficial materiality. On Safie's birthday, her girlfriend Sam gifts her a box filled with handmade bright glittering nail polish and bright glittering lipstick, and De Lacey, Agatha, Safie, Felix, and I spend the next evening crowded in the tiny bathroom together, painting one another's nails every colour of the rainbow and brushing our lips with glitter that glistens silver, purple, gold, blue, and green.

I love the way that the green lipstick compliments my eyes, my hair, my skin. I feel beautiful, like a sparkling star. Like the sparkling stars that twinkle in the sky above the quiet pond next to our house. Those sparkling stars dance in the ripples of the pond in the summer and watch over us, as our guardians, when the pond's waters freeze in the winter.

Winter is skating season. Safie loves to skate on that quiet pond next to our house. Each afternoon, she takes a break from her article writing to lace up her worn-down hockey skates and hit the ice. Her own private skating rink. Sometimes, if De Lacey isn't teaching a workshop, he will join her. Last week, the three of us went skating together on the small frozen pond, me wearing an old pair of De Lacey's skates a tad too big but tied tightly, skilfully, and precisely by De Lacey. I had never felt the feeling of thick ice underneath my feet before, but, with the support and guidance of my friends, I learned how to glide along. We glided along the ice together, surrounded by the land, the trees, the sky, the birds, the wind, and each other.

Some evenings, Safie and I follow hockey games on her laptop — NHL games. Safie knows hockey well and she carefully, patiently explains the intricacies to me. And yet, she has shared memories with me, memories from her time at university, when she would try to join in a conversation that some of her male classmates were having about hockey and they would shut her out, turning away from her and saying that this wasn't a conversation that she would understand, that it was "guy talk," rolling eyes at her, snickering, smirking at her. The first article she published upon graduating from university analyzed the toxic masculinity and white-centrism and corporate capitalism of the NHL. That article won an award from a prestigious local sports journal.

Creating has power. My friends use this power to heal. De-creating and re-creating.

Felix is creating a new film. A superhero film. The superhero is a disabled Black aromantic woman who uses a wheelchair. She is a rockstar who saves the world with decolonial love. As Felix draws character sketches and scribbles down idea after idea for the storyline, their eyes sparkle and their cheeks shine with excitement.

Felix has newspaper clippings pasted all over the walls of their room. About the film industry. Whenever they find something exciting to clip out of the newspaper, they hurry to my room to share it with me: the first article they share with me is about Taika Waititi, who is Te-Whānau-ā-Apanui and who recently directed the Marvel film *Thor: Ragnarok*. They share articles detailing the latest news about the Marvel film *Black Panther*, which explores the beauty of Afro-Indigenous decolonial survival and resistance, pasts and presents and futures, and has just broken all sorts of records at the box office. Felix and I celebrate these cinematic successes, swaying and dancing together in my little room.

"Representation matters," Felix tells me. "When I was growing up, I never saw someone like me as a superhero on the big screen. I want Black children, Indigenous children, and children of colour, of all genders, all sizes, all sexualities, all body types, who are disabled, who have disabilities, who are neurodivergent, I want all of them, all of us, to see ourselves as the rockstar superheroes that we are. And film can help with that. Film has the responsibility to help with that."

I decide that I want to use art to create a better world too. I pick up a pencil, paper, some crayons and I draw myself as a superhero. I draw myself with a crown and that beautiful emerald green lipstick and an emerald green cape that says "Smash Colonialism" in bright gold letters across it. I look at the drawing and the figure on the page looks just like me. My heart smiles. I am a superhero. I tape the picture on the wall above my bed and I am filled with joy.

But there are still days where I am overcome with insecurities and unhappiness, where I cannot help but tell myself that I must be unworthy of love as I look at the scars and stitches all along my body or as a stranger stares in horror and moves away from me when they see me approaching. Through these experiences, I've learned that colonialism is a hard thing to unlearn; it seeps into every crevice of the body, every crevice of society. We are inundated by colonialism every time we turn on the television or go onto the internet or leave our house.

It is okay to not be okay. It is okay to be angry. And it is okay to cry. Tears are healing and cleansing, and water is life-giving and nurturing. Healing is not linear and learning is ongoing.

De Lacey, Agatha, Safie, and Felix give me hugs and warm cups of cocoa with whipped cream and sprinkles when those are just the things I want and need. I care for them in return in the ways that feel right for them — from brewing tea to making dinner to offering warm and friendly hand squeezes. And I learn and feel and come to know that each hug, each warm beverage, each sprinkle in whipped cream, each spoonful of dinner, each hand squeeze is a community of care, is lifeblood, oxygen, the beating heart of love and goodness. I try to spread the decolonial love of this community of care to other people, helping De Lacey with his workshops, writing of my experiences to challenge the mainstream narratives pushed by people like Victor Frankenstein and so that others (like you) may know me and learn with me.

And so, it was on a joyful night of November that I beheld the centre of the universe, thrumming in a small house in a tangled forest. Truly this must be the universe's centre, where hearts are fullest. How can such a small house contain such big hearts? The big hearts of De Lacey and Agatha, Safie and Felix, and me. We are the most human of humans. We quarrel about who has eaten the last cookie in the cookie jar, who has left their hair clogging the shower drain, whose turn it is to wash the dirty dishes piling up in the sink. Around the kitchen table, we laugh so hard together that we have to clutch at our stomachs, some of us rolling on the floor with peals of giggles. We celebrate together, we uplift one another, we grieve together, we support one another, we love one another, we respect one another, we rest together, we renew together. Our stories are present, past, and future. Our stories are all those activists who fought against oppression before us, paving the way for us. Our stories are the future that we dream of. The next generations will continue to make these stories real, will dream them into existence too.

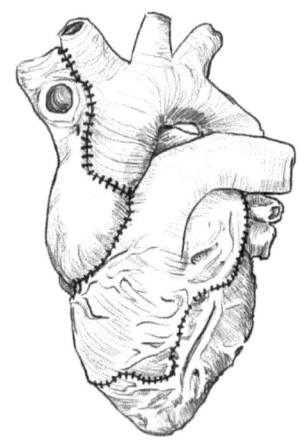

AFTERWORD

KATE STORY

W hen Mary Shelley was revealed as the author of *Frankenstein: or, The Modern Prometheus*, much was made of the fact that she was barely nineteen years old at the time that she wrote it. Certainly that is remarkable. However, I find myself perhaps even more fascinated by the fact that in 1816 she had already had two babies — one who died, unnamed, a few days after childbirth, the other — a mere four or five months old — travelling with her to the villa in Switzerland where she famously stayed with her new husband Percy Shelley, the celebrated Lord Byron, and her rather irritating step-sister Claire (formerly Jane) Clairemont. She was also aware that her own mother Mary Wollstonecraft, renowned (or hated, depending on your point of view) author of *Vindication of the Rights of Woman*, died of puerperal poisoning ten days after giving birth to Mary herself. Percy's first wife Harriet, abandoned, ended her own life

311

two years after Mary began her relationship with Percy, in the same year that Mary's half-sister Fanny also ended her own life.

Oh, and she wrote of her "excessive and romantic attachment" to her atheistic anarchic philosopher father William Godwin. And when Percy was wooing her, they often used to walk together to visit her mother's grave...

That's a fair bit of sex and death for one person, let alone a nineteen-year-old person. And lest we forget, there's a wee babe in the (probably figurative) next room when she's writing the book whose fame would come to eclipse that of the author herself.

When Derek Newman-Stille first spoke to me about this anthology, he shared his fascination with the persistence of Mary Shelley's Creature. Two centuries after Shelley created her monster, the Creature still lurks, gesturing, shaping inchoate words, creating an uneasy space wherein new possibilities are born.

This book doesn't just flirt with possibility. It full-on commits to it, ringing in a chorus of delightful and diverse voices.

We encounter longing, humour, horror, and storms; narrators who try — often with awful results — to heal, or are themselves disordered, or even dead. Writers have evoked Mary Shelley's tale playfully, reverently, brilliantly. We meet rag dolls, paper dolls, patchworks, stitched ghosts, assemblage, cyborgs, mannequins, and a Pinocchio made of steel and brass. We hook up with doctors and sexy, mean, love-struck scientists. We meet the parents — narcissistic fathers, cannibalized mothers, dying discredited geniuses, and ghosts.

And then there's the difficulty of the body. It's dead; it's non-normative (or, if "normal," one suffers for that). One hates it, wants to starve it or carve it. Other people hate it, want to categorize or "fix" it. It doesn't "work." There's a thriving trade in cadaverous body parts, and protagonists who —

aware that they are an assemblage of former selves — attempt to honour their new aggregate self through bodily memory.

There are a lot of stories in the first person: journals, audio files, emails, epistolary tales. And what exactly is this "self"? Where does it reside? Is it soul, spirit, a brain in a jar? When one is divided from one's body, then who is the self — brain or flesh, hater or the hated? How do we stay true to a sense of self in a world that forcibly others us?

These stories interrogate "genius" — the class, race, cultural, historical, and gendered aggressions that go into making it up — as privilege, brilliance, oppression, corporate greed, pomposity, and just plain nastiness. There is magic, and monomaniacal obsession.

These stories take us from innermost, deeply personal longings to the largest ecological and ethical questions we know how to ask.

In her own introduction to the 1831 edition of her work, Mary Shelley recalls the terrifying waking dream which led her to write the tale which would — by many estimations — birth two centuries of science fiction. In lieu of time travel and/or life-extending technologies, we can only imagine the tales the Creature will have spawned two centuries hence, in 2218. The "pale student of unhallowed arts" wakes to find their creation, "the horrid thing," standing at the bedside looking on their creator "with yellow, watery, but speculative eyes."

This monster looks back. This monster is wondering.

This monster has some stories to tell.

July 15, 2018

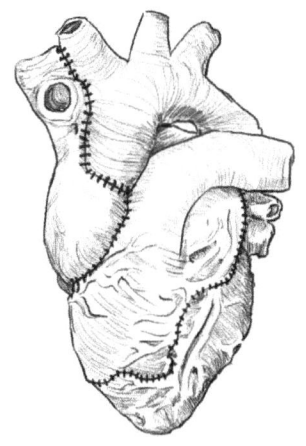

ABOUT THE AUTHORS

Alex Acks is a writer, geologist, and sharp-dressed sir. Their biker gang space witch novels, *Hunger Makes the Wolf* and *Blood Binds the Pack* were published by Angry Robot Books under the pen name Alex Wells. They've had short fiction in *Strange Horizons*, *Crossed Genres*, *Daily Science Fiction*, *Lightspeed*, and more, and written movie reviews for *Strange Horizons* and *Mothership Zeta*. They've also written several episodes of Six to Start's *Superhero Workout* game and virtual races for *Racelink*. Alex lives in Denver (where they bicycle, drink tea, and twirl their ever-so-dapper moustache) with their two furry little bastards. For more information, see http://www.alexacks.com

Day Al-Mohamed is author of the novel *Baba Ali and the Clockwork Djinn: A Steampunk Faerie Tale*, editor of the anthology, *Trust & Treachery*, and a regular host on Idobi Radio's *Geek Girl Riot*. Her stories have appeared in *Fireside Fiction*, *Apex Magazine*, and *GrayHaven Comics*. She is a Docs in Progress Fellowship alumna and a graduate of the VONA/Voices Writing Workshop.

In addition to fiction, she also works in comics and film. Two of her films were recently shown on local Virginia cable television, and two more are in post-production. Her current focus is on a Civil War documentary on the Invalid Corps and the battle of Fort Stevens. Day's short story, "The Lesser Evil" was nominated for the WSFA Small Press Award for Best Short Fiction of 2015. However, she is most proud of being invited to teach a workshop on storytelling at the White House in February 2016.

A disability policy executive with more than fifteen years of experience, she presents often on the representation of disability in media, most recently for the National Bar Association, at New York Comic Con, and at SXSW. She lives in Washington DC with her wife, N.R. Brown. You can find her online at DayAlMohamed.com and on Twitter @DayAlMohamed.

Randall G. Arnold is a Texas-based speculative fiction writer who enjoys mangling genres and twisting tropes. He earned honourable mention in the *Texas Observer's* 2015 and 2016 fiction contests and is beginning to enjoy minor publication success. He's currently hacking out a science fiction novel about autonomous vehicles.

Joshua Bartolome is a Filipino-Canadian writer living in Calgary, Alberta. His prose poem, "The Cadaver," was shortlisted for the Montreal Poetry Prize, while in 2017, his screenplay, *The Red Death*, won the Silver Screamfest award for best horror script. "Aswang," a tale of poverty, misery and violence, was published in the anthology *Tales of Blood and Squalor*. Another short story, "Sparagmos," will be published in the upcoming 11th *Philippine Speculative Fiction* anthology.

Ashley Caranto Morford (she/her) is a queer (asexual) woman of colour. She is a PhD student in Literature and Book History at the University of Toronto, where she is an uninvited occupant on the Dish with One Spoon

Territory, the landscapes and waterscapes of the Wendat, Haudenosaunee, and Anishinaabe nations. Ashley is a member of the Pilipinx diaspora on her mother's side and is British on her father's side.

Lisa Carreiro wrote and illustrated her first novel when she was nine years old. Fortunately for the world, her story of a dragon who's lost its spaceship is itself long lost. A former Winnipegger, Carreiro moved to relatively warmer Southern Ontario in the mid-1980s following brief stints on Vancouver Island and in the Kootenays in British Columbia. She worked as a stagehand before returning to her first love, writing. She even managed to survive the academic world long enough to obtain a degree in journalism.

She pays the bills working as a non-fiction editor, but every morning she rises before dawn to spin the chaos in her head into stories. She drums badly but plays air guitar rather well.

Carreiro lives in Kitchener, Ontario, with her wife. Her short fiction has appeared in *Playground of Lost Toys*, *On Spec*, and *Strange Horizons*.

Eric Choi is a Hong Kong born writer, editor, and aerospace engineer who currently lives in Toronto. The first recipient of the Isaac Asimov Award (now the Dell Magazines Award) for his story "Dedication", he has also twice won the Aurora Award for his story "Crimson Sky" and for co-editing the Chinese-themed speculative fiction anthology *The Dragon and the Stars* (DAW) with Derwin Mak. He also co-edited the hard SF collection *Carbide Tipped Pens* (Tor) with Ben Bova. His work has appeared in the anthologies *Science Fiction by Scientists* (Springer), *The 2017 Young Explorer's Adventure Guide* (Dreaming Robot), *Imaginarium 4: The Best Canadian Speculative Writing* (ChiZine), *Compostela: Tesseracts Twenty* (EDGE), *AlliterAsian* (Arsenal), *Far Orbit: Speculative Space Adventures* (World Weaver), *Rocket Science* (Mutation), *The Astronaut From Wyoming and Other Stories* (Hayakawa), *Footprints* (Hadley Rille), *Northwest Passages: A Cascadian Anthology* (Windstorm), *Space Inc.*

(DAW), *Tales From the Wonder Zone* (Fitzhenry & Whiteside), *Northern Suns* (Tor), *Arrowdreams: An Anthology of Alternate Canadas* (Signature Editions), and *Tesseracts*[6] (EDGE), as well as the magazines *Analog Science Fiction and Fact*, *Asimov's Science Fiction*, *Science Fiction Age*, and *Ricepaper*. In 2009, he was one of the Top 40 finalists (out of 5,351 applicants) in the Canadian Space Agency's astronaut recruitment campaign. Please visit his website www.aerospacewriter.ca or follow him on Twitter @AerospaceWriter.

Evelyn Deshane's creative and non-fiction work has appeared in *Plenitude Magazine*, *Briarpatch Magazine*, *Strange Horizons*, *Lackington's*, and *Bitch Magazine*, among other publications. Evelyn (pron. Eve-a-lyn) received an MA from Trent University and is currently completing a PhD at the University of Waterloo. Evelyn's most recent project *#Trans* is an edited collection about transgender and nonbinary identity online. Visit evedeshane.wordpress.com for more info.

JF Garrard is the President of Dark Helix Press, Marketing Strategist for *Ricepaper Magazine* and Assistant Editor for *Amazing Stories Magazine*. She is an editor and writer of speculative fiction (*Trump: Utopia or Dystopia, The Undead Sorceress*), non-fiction (*The Literary Elephant*) and children's books (*Feeding The Kraken!, 3x Bilingual Series*). Her latest projects include curating the LiterASIAN Toronto Festival for the Asian Canadian Writers Workshop with the University of Toronto, a *Tea and Bun Talk* podcast for *Ricepaper Magazine* and creating a *Dark Helix Ezine* to promote indie writers. For Women In Horror Month 2018, her short story *My Girl*, about a woman visiting a Chinese witch to save her baby, was published by Sirens Call Publications.

Her education background includes a Nuclear Medicine degree from the University of Toronto, Science degree from the University of Waterloo, MBA from Schulich School of Business, York University and she is working on a

Creative Writing certificate at Ryerson University. Her contributions regarding diversity, business and healthcare topics have been published in *Entrepreneur, Huffington Post, Monster.com, Women's Health, Cosmopolitan, MochiMag, My Corporation, Indie Pubchat, Authors Helping Authors,* among others. Find her on Twitter @jfgarrard or via jfgarrard.com.

Cait (pronounced like "cat") Gordon is originally from Verdun, Québec and has been living in the suburbs of Ottawa since 1998. She worked for over two decades as a technical writer, then channelled her love of words into creative writing. Cait styles herself a humorist and chooses space opera as her favourite vehicle for exploring absurdity. She is the author of *Life in the 'Cosm* (Renaissance) and its prequel, *The Stealth Lovers* (Renaissance, 2019). Her short story, *Night at the Rabbit Hole,* appears in the *Alice Unbound: Beyond Wonderland* anthology (Colleen Anderson, Exile Editions).

For her day job, Cait is a freelance editor. Some of the titles she's edited include *Confessions of a Mad Mooer: Postnatal Depression Sucks* (Robin Elizabeth), *Camp Follower: One Army Brat's Story* (Michele Sabad), *Skylark* (S.M. Carrière), *Little Yellow Magnet* (Jamieson Wolf), and *Moonshadow's Guardian* (Dianna Gunn).

Cait is also the founder of the Spoonie Authors Network (spoonieauthorsnetwork.blog) and has teamed up with Talia C. Johnson to co-edit the upcoming anthology, *Nothing Without Us,* a collection of short stories featuring protagonists who identify as disabled, Deaf, blind, neurodiverse, Spoonie, and/or who manage mental illness.

You can follow Cait on Twitter (@CaitGAuthor) and her author website (caitgordon.com).

A founding co-chair of the Horror Writers Association (HWA) San Diego chapter, **KC Grifant** is a New England-to-SoCal transplant who writes horror, fantasy, science fiction, and weird west stories. Her award-winning non-fiction articles on science and technology have appeared in dozens of magazines and newspapers while her fiction stories have found homes in card games, anthologies, and other publications. Recent anthologies include the Stoker-nominated *FRIGHT MARE: Women Write Horror*; *California Screamin'*, a collection of tales that take place in Southern California; *Into Darkness Peering*, featuring stories inspired by Edgar Allan Poe; *See Through My Eyes: A Ghost Mystery Anthology*; and *Hydrophobia*, a charity anthology for victims of Hurricane Harvey. Other publications include the *Lovecraft Ezine*, *Horror Bites Magazine*, *Andromeda Spaceways Magazine*, *Electric Spec magazine* and Horror Tree's *Trembling with Fear* series. Visit @SciFiWri, www.SciFiWri.com or amazon.com/author/kcgrifant to learn more.

Kev Harrison is an English teacher and writer of dark fiction from the United Kingdom, now living in sunny Lisbon, Portugal. He is driven by exploring new places, eating as much as possible, running, and has an enduring love for all things dark and unsettling. In the last year or so he has had work published in the *Below the Stairs: Tales from the Cellar* anthology from Things in the Well, Terror Tree Press's *Mummy Knows Best* and *Two Eyes Open* from Mackenzie Publishing, as well as *The Pale Leaves* gothic and weird fiction, and Horror Tree: *Trembling with Fear* websites. He has also recently had his first story converted to audio by the talented people at *The Other Stories* podcast. He is currently putting the finishing touches to a supernatural horror novella and has a variety of short stories scheduled for publishing in anthologies and magazines this year, including Scary Dairy Press's *Terror Politico* anthology.

www.facebook.com/KevHarrisonFiction

www.twitter.com/Lisboetaingles

Liam Hogan is an Oxford Physics graduate and award-winning London based writer. His short story "Ana", appears in *Best of British Science Fiction*

2016 (NewCon Press) and his twisted fantasy collection, *Happy Ending Not Guaranteed*, is published by Arachne Press. Find out more at http://happyendingnotguaranteed.blogspot.co.uk/, or tweet @LiamJHogan

Halli Lilburn was born in Edmonton, Alberta. Her first story at age nine was about unicorns and fairies. Over the years, she has explored other genres including poetry, science fiction, paranormal, and horror. She has works published with *Tesseracts 18: Wrestling with Gods*, *Spirited* by Leap Books, Carte Blanche, Vine Leaves, Manawaker Studios, and many others. She teaches creative writing and art classes. She is an editor of *The Dame Was Trouble*, with Coffin Hop Press. She is a librarian and mother of three.

Find her at essentialedits.com, hallililburn.blogspot.com and www.facebook.com/groups/147239652049490/.

Victoria K. Martin grew up in the west end of Ottawa, otherwise known as the middle of nowhere. Cursed with the horror that is country cable, she turned to books for entertainment and soon was not only reading everything in sight but also trying her hand at writing herself. She was immediately drawn to speculative fiction, particular those with darker undertones. In grade ten, one of her science fiction stories won the Marion Drysdale Award, which is given out each year by the Ontario Secondary School Teachers' Federation.

Victoria's love of books led to her studying English literature at Mount Allison University in Sackville, New Brunswick. After graduation, she moved to Toronto (aka the centre of the universe) and slaved away in retail hell for a few years, before discovering that you can go home again and moving back to Ottawa.

These days, Victoria writes manuals no one wants to read by day and works on stories and novels that people hopefully do want to read by night. She also still spends a lot of time reading. Her favourite authors are

Jacqueline Carey and Courtney Milan. When not writing or reading, she is usually found hanging out with her Great Dane who, despite his size, thinks he is a lap dog.

For more information about Victoria, go to her website, victoriakmartin.com, or follow her on Twitter @victoriakmartin.

Joseph McGinty is an advertising professional who has produced and edited a handful of television commercials and some independent short films for festivals. A lifelong fan of literary fiction, music and cinema, but mostly science fiction, "F. - A Post-Modern Prometheus" is his first writing collaboration. He hopes this will be the first step in bringing to life entertaining stories based on original, though highly speculative, ideas left over from an early physics education.

Lena Ng is a writer and poet from Toronto, Ontario. Her work has appeared or is forthcoming in several anthologies and magazines including: *Just Desserts* (WolfSinger Publications, 2016), *World Unknown Review III* (Editor L.S. Engler, 2016), *Devolution Z* (Jan 2017 issue), *Monsters Among Us* (Bloody Kisses Press, 2017), *Polar Borealis Magazine* (July/Aug 2017 issue, Spring 2018 issue), *Gathering Storm Magazine Issue 2* (April 2017), *Gathering Storm Magazine Issue 4* (Aug 2017), *Antimattermag.com* (Oct 4, 2017), *The Quilliad Issue 9* (Oct 2017), and *Killing It Softly 2* (Digital Fiction Publishing Corp, October 2017). *Under an Autumn Moon* is her collection of horror/fantasy short stories. She is currently seeking a publisher for her first novel, *Darkness Beckons*, a gothic romance set in the Victorian era.

Thus far, **Corey Redekop** has two novels to his credit, the award-winning *Shelf Monkey* (Best Popular Fiction Novel, Independent Book Publisher Awards) and the award-nominated *Husk* (Best Novel, ReLit Award). His short fiction may be found in anthologies such as *The Exile Book of New*

Canadian Noir, Those Who Make Us: Canadian Creature, Myth, and Monster Stories, Licence Expired: The Unauthorized James Bond, and *Superhero Universe,* among others. Currently, he is cognitively mired in the thematic bog of a hypothetical third novel. He physically abides in Fredericton, NB, and electronically at www.coreyredekop.ca and @coreyredekop.

Jennifer Lee Rossman is a disabled science fiction geek from Oneonta, New York. Her work has been featured in several anthologies and her time travel novella *Anachronism* is available from Kristell Ink/Grimbold Books. Her debut novel, *Jack Jetstark's Intergalactic Freakshow,* will be published by World Weaver Press in 2018.

You can find her blog at http://jenniferleerossman.blogspot.com/ and Twitter at https://twitter.com/JenLRossman

A 2016 MBA graduate, *Book Riot* columnist, and published author, **Priya Sridhar** has been writing fantasy and science fiction for seventeen years and counting. Her first publication was in the now-defunct *AlienSkin* magazine, and her stories have appeared in *Beneath Ceaseless Skies, Nightmare Magazine,* and *Expanded Horizons.* Alban Lake published her novella *Carousel* in 2014, and her novel *Neo-Mecha Mayhem* in late 2017. She believes that every story is a journey, and that a good tale allows the reader to escape to a new world. "Unfashioned Creatures" was inspired by Mary Shelley's life: how she ran off with a married man and lost two of her children with him at a young age, which in turn inspired her forays into *Frankenstein.* Priya lives in Miami, Florida with her family and posts monthly at her blog.

Max D. Stanton Max D. Stanton is an academic, writer, and student of the weird who lives in Philadelphia surrounded by animals and books. He sometimes suspects that the animals are conspiring against him, and maybe

323

the books, as well. When he is not writing, he enjoys battling monsters using 20-sided dice, haunting the taverns of West Philly, and reading his creations to the good folks at the Lucky 13 open mic night. Sometimes he sits on a throne made of animal bones while he writes. He once changed his whole life's course on the basis of a tarot card, and participates in pagan mummery during the dead of winter.

Max has published horror fiction in venues including Vastarien Vol. 1 Issue 2, Hinnom Magazine #2, Lovecraftiana Halloween 2017, Sanitarium #34, and World Unknown Review vol. III, as well as the Under a Dark Sign, Candlesticks & Daggers, Year's Best Transhuman Sci-Fi 2017, and Corporate Cthulhu anthologies. You can contact Max within the Book of Faces (https://www.facebook.com/max.stanton.3576) or via the Great Screaming of Birds (https://twitter.com/max_d_stanton).

Kaitlin Tremblay is a narrative designer at Ubisoft Toronto and an independent writer and game developer. Her personal and independent work focuses on exploring the intersection of feminism and mental illness and using interactivity to explore healing. Kaitlin is the lead writer on the Independent Games Festival award nominated game *A Mortician's Tale* (Laundry Bear, 2017). *A Mortician's Tale* is a death positive game that explores how we grieve, as well as the realities of the death industry. Kaitlin is a committee member of the feminist non-profit Dames Making Games and works to help create a more compassionate and inclusive environment in the video game industry. Kaitlin has run game development workshops for marginalized game creators, as well as for people with various mental illnesses.

Kaitlin is the author of the book *Ain't No Place for a Hero: Borderlands* (ECW Press, 2017), which examines subversive storytelling mechanics in video games, and is the co-editor on the Shirley Jackson Award nominated anthology *Those Who Make Us: Canadian Creature, Myth, and Monster Stories*

(Exile Editions, 2016). Kaitlin has a chapter in the anthology *Game Devs & Others: Tales from the Margins* (CRC Press, 2018), in which she explores the productive and healing parallels between creating horror games, community development, and group therapy for trauma. She has written for many different cultural and video game outlets, including *Playboy*, *Vice*, *The Mary Sue*, *The Toast*, and many more. Kaitlin loves monsters, horror, and flowers. Her full portfolio can be found at thatmonstergames.com

D. Simon Turner is a Master's student at Carleton University. Their poetry has been published by bird, buried press ("Focaccia Numbers", 2018) and thrice in *Chickenscratch: An Anthology of Student Writing* as Simon Turner-Semchuk (Coach House Books, 2016 and 2017). They have written four plays produced in Peterborough, ON.

Arianna Verbree is a musician, poet, and performer. She holds a Bachelor's Degree in Music from the University of Ottawa, a Master's degree in Music Performance from the University of Akron, and an Artist's Certificate in Performance of Early Music from the University of Toronto.

Throughout her postsecondary education in music, Arianna has continually focussed on finding ways to explain complicated concepts in meaningful, relatable ways. Much of her poetry comes from that same essential desire - to connect ideas that seem disparate but, given a different perspective, are closer than they appear.

Arianna splits her time between Toronto, where she lives and works, and Ottawa, where her family lives.

Andrew Wilmot is a writer and editor based out of Toronto, Ontario. He has won awards for screenwriting and short fiction, with credits including *Found Press*, *The Singularity*, *Glittership*, *Turn to Ash*, *Augur*, and the anthologies *Those Who Makes Us: Canadian Creature, Myth, and Monster Stories* and *Restless:*

An Anthology of Ghost Stories, Dark Fantasy, and Creepy Tales. As an editor, he's worked with Drawn & Quarterly, ChiZine Publications, Broken River Books, ARP Books, Wolsak & Wynn, and is the former Marketing and Production Coordinator for NeWest Press. He is also Co-Publisher and Co-EIC, alongside editors Michael Matheson and Chinelo Onwualu, of the online magazine *Anathema: Spec from the Margins.* Books he's worked on have themselves taken home multiple awards from the Sunburst Awards, the Eisner Awards, and most recently the Shirley Jackson Awards. His first novel, *The Death Scene Artist,* is available now from Buckrider Books, an imprint of Wolsak & Wynn. Find him online at: andrewwilmot.ca, anathemaspec.tumblr.com, and on Twitter, hating everything about Twitter, @AGAWilmot.

Renaissance.
Diverse.Canadian Voices

Renaissance was founded in May 2013 by a group of friends who wanted to publish and market those stories which don't always fit neatly in a genre, or a niche, or a demographic. We weren't sure what we wanted to publish exactly, so like the happy panbibliophiles we are, we opened our submissions, with no other personal guideline than finding a Canadian book we would fall in love with enough that we would want to publish and sell.

Five years later, this is still very true; however, we've also noticed an interesting trend in what we tended to publish. It turns out that we are naturally drawn to the voices of those who are members of a marginalized group (people with disabilities, LGBTQIAPP2+ people, people of colour), and these are the voices we want to continue to uplift.

At Renaissance, we treat our authors like family. We are all authors and artists ourselves, and know that their books are their babies. With Renaissance, the authors are involved in every step of the process and their input is highly valued, though devoted committees take on the difficult tasks of copy editing, designing and marketing to achieve professional results. The authors are asked to do a minimal part of the marketing (for example, sharing our social media posts, inviting their circles to the launch, participating in blog tours) and will receive guidance and help every step of the way.

At Renaissance, we do things differently. We are passionate about books, and we care as much about our authors enjoying the publishing process as we do about our readers enjoying a great, professional quality and affordable product on the platform they prefer.

For more information, visit us at
renaissancebookpress.com

www.ingramcontent.com/pod-product-compliance
Lightning Source LLC
Chambersburg PA
CBHW050922030726
47503CB00007BB/2418